Good Fortune

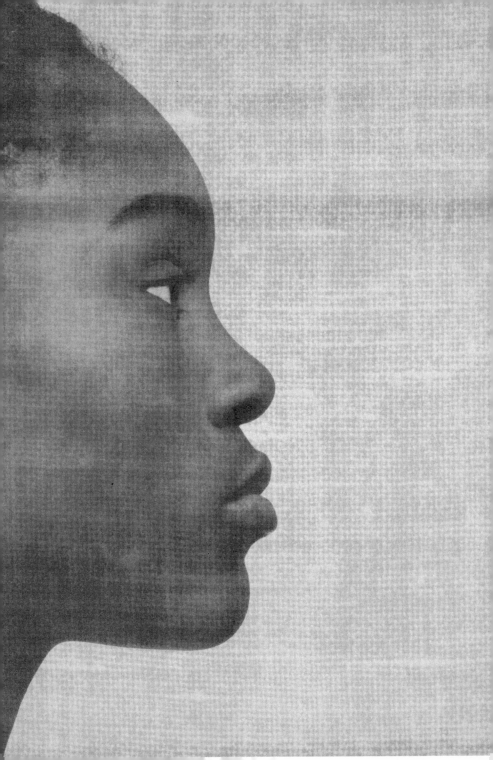

Good Fortune

Noni Carter

SIMON & SCHUSTER BFYR

NEW YORK LONDON TORONTO SYDNEY

SIMON & SCHUSTER BFYR

An imprint of Simon & Schuster Children's Publishing Division
1230 Avenue of the Americas, New York, New York 10020

This book is a work of fiction. Any references to historical events, real people, or real locales are used fictitiously. Other names, characters, places, and incidents are products of the author's imagination, and any resemblance to actual events or locales or persons, living or dead, is entirely coincidental.

For information about special discounts for bulk purchases, please contact
Simon & Schuster Special Sales at 1-866-506-1949 or business@simonandschuster.com.
The Simon & Schuster Speakers Bureau can bring authors to your live event.
For more information or to book an event, contact the Simon & Schuster
Speakers Bureau at 1-866-248-3049 or visit our website at www.simonspeakers.com.
Book design by Laurent Linn
The text for this book is set in Arrus BT.
Manufactured in the United States of America
2 4 6 8 10 9 7 5 3 1
Library of Congress Cataloging-in-Publication Data
Carter, Noni.
Good fortune / Noni Carter.—1st ed.
p. cm.
Summary: Brutally kidnapped from her African village and shipped to
America, a young girl struggles to come to terms with her new life as
a slave, gradually rising from working in the fields to the master's
house, secretly learning to read and write, until, risking
everything, she escapes to seek freedom in the North.
ISBN 978-1-4169-8480-1 (hardcover)
[1. Slavery—Fiction. 2. African Americans—Fiction. 3. Southern
States—History—1775–1865—Fiction. 4. Youths' writings.] I. Title.
PZ7.C2474Go 2010
[Fic]—dc22
2009036270
ISBN 978-1-4169-9863-1 (eBook)

FIRST EDITION

To Great-Great-Great-Great-Grandma Rose,
my ancestor; my angel

For more information about facts versus
fiction, visit the author's website at
www.nonicarter.com.

Recommended reading includes
The Norton Anthology of African American Literature,
edited by Henry Louis Gates Jr. and Nellie Y. McKay.

PROLOGUE

THE NIGHT WAS CALM AND PEACEFUL, ALMOST SEDUCING TO A child of four years. I watched as a strange light blanketed the sky, as if to package reality and toss it out, over the horizon. Then the night came alive; moonlight flickered; the trees swayed more wildly than the wind dared them to; the stars danced, clapping the earth like the feet of tribal people, black skin digging into ground. The night reveled in its boundless freedom, and allowed the calm to dip into a careless chaos. The night grew tense and swirled about me as I held the woman's neck loosely, my four-year-old arms resting on her soft shoulders. She stood tall, her movements both gentle and confident, and the trees about us beckoned towards her, jealous limbs reaching down to grab and claim for their own. Her teeth glistened, smile radiant, so outstanding that the moonlight itself found a need, in all of its magnificence, to try and steal its glow. To these I shot angry glances and held on even tighter. My mother was mine, and they needed to know it.

I turned my small head, searching for the eyes of Mathee, and found myself gazing into their brilliance. Bringing her lips to my forehead, she wrapped me in a kiss, and set me down on my feet, robbing her warm hand from the flesh of my own palm so I could dash away into the hut.

My small knees bent, and I dropped to the floor, sitting on hands, watching Mathee follow me inside. Her hips swayed daringly, and her smile remained set, making real without words the depths of her love only a child could understand. Objects stirred, suns and moons passed by as Mama knelt by me, but I took no notice; I was oblivious to it all.

There was nothing, there was no one but my mother and me.

The two of us breathed in unison, our smiling lips just a hair's-breadth apart, one palm pressed lightly up against another palm, a nose loosely brushing the tip of another nose, eyelids fluttering against each other's. She closed her long fingers around my small hand.

I've missed you, my child.

But, Mathee, I've been here.

You forget, my beautiful flower, you're dreaming.

No, Mama!

She disappeared from the hut, and I was suddenly standing outside, alone.

The stillness hung like a shadow in the air. It was the calm before the storm, before that stillness disappeared with abrupt suddenness and tumbled into turmoil. The clouds burst open, and the thunder put forth the loudest noise I had ever heard. A lightning bolt struck the ground and the sky breathed fire upon the roofs of the village huts. Frantic villagers poured out, screaming, panicked, and terrified, running every which way. Four-legged beasts galloped about, carrying on their backs monster-men who bore fire sticks in their arms that cracked louder than the storm above their heads and that left bodies lying dead on the African soil. Flames grabbed what they could, devouring the land, feasting swiftly and with greed.

Then I was back in the hut, as was Mama Mijiza, or Mathee as I called her. She sat looking tenderly over my shoulder. I turned and followed her eyes, her soft smile that bounded across the room toward a small boy who sat still and silent on a gray cloud. He was gazing at nothingness, large eyes watching everything with a calm, distracted patience, taking it all in.

I've missed you, he said to me.

But Sentwaki, I'm here.

You forget, Ayanna, you're dreaming.

No, brother!

The little boy leaped past me, his legs long and quick like his mother's, and disappeared into the confusion of the night.

With a furrowed brow, I turned to reach out for Mathee again, to brush my nose against hers, to feel the soft touch of her fingers against my own fingers as she counted out my four young years in a singsong voice. But instead I found myself staring into the face of a monster-man. His eyes were deep red, and his snarl brought screams to my lips. He opened his mouth, and from it, silver chains flowed like snakes, wrapping my body round and round. . . .

Mama Mijiza!

I called, but no one answered. I ran out, searching, climbing over houses, ascending to the tops of trees, flying above the waters, searching, searching, and searching some more for that face—soft cheeks, warm skin, light kiss.

3

My feet splashed against the mud, the African soil snatching at my ankles, trying hard to steal me back.

Where is she?

Here.

Sentwaki was back by my side, holding tight to Mathee's hand.

Mama Mijiza, what's going on?

Hush, my child!

There was fear in her, I could feel it, I could see the panic lining her forehead. She began running, moving with the rest of the villagers, her dark skin glistening in the rain, her hair smelling like home. I could hear my mother's heartbeat, the only sound that filled the air: *thump-thump, thump-thump, thump-thump—*

Crack!

The world around me shattered into a million pieces as her body came crashing to the ground. A trembling hand, dark liquid smeared on chest, on skin, Mama's blood staining the cloth I had ripped from her clothes.

Mathee, get up! Answer me, get up!

A shudder, a horrible scream, and then nothing left but scowling silence and a lone, faltering heartbeat: *thump-thump, thump-thump, thu—*

It stopped.

We stood, Sentwaki and I, saliva dripping from our mouths, bloody cloth grasped in my hand, staring at Mama who lay there silently, her eyes fully open, unblinking.

I followed the trail of blood with wide eyes, blood that reached up past my toes, grasping my ankles, binding my wrists, and reaching inside to snatch my heart. It blinded my vision and choked the breath from my lungs. But like water trapped in a circling current, my mind kept spinning back to the image of Mama's blood-smeared face and her unmoving eyes.

And again, the little boy sat on his gray cloud, gazing at nothingness, large eyes watching it all with a calm, distracted patience as the blood swallowed him, too.

Someone was screaming.

Mathee!

I realized it came from my own lips. Then my world went black.

Bound

by

the

Whip

CHAPTER

❧ 1 ❧

HIS HAND CAME DOWN UPON MY CHEEK HARD AND FAST. Stunned, I staggered backward.

"Look at all dis cotton you left behind, gal!" I looked up to see the overseer's hand nearing my face again. I flinched as he smacked me once more, sending me to my knees. I stared at the ground, seven years' worth of hard labor in the fields burning under my veil of obedience.

"Next time I find you skippin' ova cotton like it don't matta nothin' in the world to you, you gonna find yo'self beaten, gal, you understand me?"

"Yessuh," I answered.

"Now get up and pay attention, understand?"

"Yessuh," I said slowly, lifting my body from the ground.

Doing cotton for Masta was a lot of work. On his plantation in the western part of Tennessee there was the land preparation, the spring planting, the weeding and the plowing, and the harvesting near the end of August. Then, after it was picked, some folks would remove the small green seeds from the cotton in the ginnin' house. When we weren't working on the cotton, we tended to a small cornfield Masta also owned.

The year had come back around to the harvesting of the cotton. Picking was tough, especially when the frost would start biting the bolls. I preferred the hoeing or the planting, but for now, it was time to pick.

When I first started fieldwork, I admired the folks who could pull that cotton out of the bolls with a single hand, a single swipe, their eyes set somewhere else. Then they'd take that cotton and easily slip it into their sacks. Not a single branch would break in the process. The breaking of a cotton branch or the destroying of an entire plant in whatever manner was cause for punishment. The overseer would ride by and strike any slave who committed this crime with the whip that hung by his side.

The work didn't seem so bad during my first days out in the field; that is, until the days started stretching out longer and the work sent aches throughout my body. My young hands would clumsily snap a branch and struggle to pull the picked cotton out of the brown bolls and get it into my sack. At the end of the day, my hands would be bloody and calloused.

Even before the sun rose in the mornings, we were awakened to begin our workdays, sometimes having to line up in rows for a slave count before heading to the fields to pick. Our bodies were so accustomed to this work that sometimes I felt as if we were merely walking flesh, our minds still lost in sleep. The overseers would come by nearly every day to check our progress, warning us with a slap if we were too far behind. There were two of them, and they'd always find an excuse to drop three or four extra bags near our feet to fill up. They'd never forget if we happened to pick more one day than we did the last, and they'd be sure we picked a little more the next. We couldn't leave until the last bag strapped to our backs was filled with that cotton. Then, at the close of the day, we'd watch, grateful almost, as the sun set, giving us relief from its hot rays. I don't know why the sun chose to glare at us like it did, hours on end, bringing glistening sweat to our bodies as if we'd done something against it. Only long after sunset would we be granted leave.

On that day, with the overseer's hand imprint still burning in my flesh, I continued with my work. There was nothing else I could've done. I hated the fields that stretched as far as my mind would allow. It took me a long time to figure out how I could daydream, like I did when I was young, and work at the same time. The overseers thought they had snatched that mental freedom. But Aunt Mary, the mother figure that cared for me on that plantation, used to tell me that you could always find the greatest joy and freedom in your mind. Even so, it felt like a slap in the face to stand there, sometimes, staring at the never-ending rows of white cotton. With a quick reminder from a slave hand yanking at my dress, telling me to "bend down an' pick so I wouldn't get lashed," I would return my attention to the row of cotton that surrounded me. With anger spinning in my mind, I would think of how we were engulfed in the white man's world—nothing but a world of whiteness. If only we could get rid of all that cotton!

Later on, when the sun had set and the moon was high in the sky, I finally trudged home. My legs were heavy; my feet dragged behind me.

I walked past several silent houses in the slave quarters and only picked up my pace when I spotted a woman standing and waiting for me in the doorway of a small cabin. Mary's posture looked anxious, and I quickly embraced her as I reached the door, my cheek brushing up against her chin.

Mary spent most of her time as a house servant but helped out when needed in the spinning house, making clothing and other materials. I was very small when I first came to the plantation at the age of four, and Mary was the one who took me into her arms without a word. Mary said as soon as she saw me, she knew I was a child of hers, just not blood-related. From then on it went without saying that she would be the mother I had lost and that her son would be the brother who'd been sold—and so, lost to me—when I first came across the seas to this land. Daniel was two years older than I was and was born a year or so after Mary's first child, which she had lost. He had never been afraid of much, and that worried me a little bit. It didn't take much so-called wrongdoing around these parts for a defiant slave to end up limp and lifeless.

Mary ran a hand slowly across my short, black hair, which rounded my head and sat two or three inches high on my scalp. Then she pulled back and looked me over, her eyes running past my large, dark ones, past my eyelids batting with fatigue, past my shoulders slouched with a long day's worth of work, and on down to my dirt-caked feet.

"Look at you—got holes in them pants I just done sewn you, from workin' hard out there in them fields. And looka here, you growin' out of 'em already." She shook her head back and forth, but that gesture and the heaviness lurking behind her voice were negated by the kindness in her eyes.

"Seem you even darker today than you was jus' yestaday," Mary said quietly.

"That sun ain't got no mercy."

My skin was very dark: When I was younger, the children told me I looked like the nighttime. I preferred to remember images from my homeland, from the black land way across the seas, images of me rolling in the dark soil and rubbing its similar color into my skin. It was something that made me a bit different from others around the plantation. It was clear to Mary, and to many others, my native origins weren't from close by, and Mary said there weren't too many folks like me who came straight from their ancestral lands. It had changed she said, from the days of her youth.

It was early in the year 1821. I was young, just about fourteen years old, according to Mary, who had helped me keep track of my age. Like most other slaves, she didn't know hers. She told me once that when I first came here, it had taken quite a while to break past the resistance I had layered myself with. I wouldn't talk, I wouldn't look at anyone straight, and I could never sleep through a full night. Then one day, after a few weeks of the same, Mary found me crouched in the corner of the cabin, holding up four fingers and touching each one with a finger from my other hand. I repeated this over and over again. She figured that wherever I had come from, someone had taught me how to count the years I had been on this earth, and she decided to continue with that cycle. Mary knew children well, and I seemed to be around that age. She had walked over to me, silently, and touched her own fingers as she had seen me do. She then brought one of her fingers to the four I was holding up and then repeated the same. After a while, she had taken my hands in hers and brought my fingers to her lips, kissing each one by one. It was the first time we had bonded, and she kept that moment close to her heart by helping me keep up with my age.

It was nearing the end of September and, if we'd kept track right, I'd be turning fourteen when the first flower bloomed, signifying the beginning of springtime. Mary told me I was growing up slowly; she said I'd be as pretty as they get, and that made me smile a bit.

I wiped away the sweat on Mary's forehead that glistened in the moonlight, and gazed past her drained face into her eyes. She shook her head back and forth again.

"You sho' had a bad one last night, Sarah." I nodded solemnly, remembering Mary waking me that morning, silencing my muffled screams from distorted dreams. She'd wiped away the sweat I was drenched in and dried my streaming tears, which seemed to flow from a place deep inside that connected those broken dreams with a reality I couldn't remember well at all.

"You rememba it this time?"

I shook my head and sighed. "Only bits've it, Mary. Ain't no dif'rent from befo'."

"What 'bout them parts that got you cryin' like that?" Again, I shook my head, but with less assurance. My nightmares didn't come often, but when they did, I'd wake up, baffled, wondering why I couldn't remember the images that had flitted so quickly and disjointedly across my mind's eye. Most of them remained buried in a place inside of me, perhaps for the best. And yet in all the years I had been having those dreams after arriving on the plantation, some of the same images had returned to me again and again: a smiling face, a warm hand, large and staring eyes, the smile wiped away, empty, lifeless, and that word, that name, Bahati. . . .

"Well, it sho' didn't last long this time round. Maybe . . . maybe you ain't gonna have 'em anymore."

"Mary, you say that every time."

She sighed heavily and shook her head. "I knows I do, but . . ." She looked down at my hands and ran a soft finger over the dried-up blood.

"Well, anyhow, 'nough of that. I do got somethin' to say 'bout you workin' in them fields, tho'. Hate to see you out there durin' pickin' season. They should have you carin' fo' the livestock, or in the orchard or somethin'. I'ma pick up my nerve and ask Missus if'n you can work in the house like I do—fo' good." I smiled warmly as Mary rambled on as she always did. She led me through the doors and placed a bowl of cornmeal on my pallet.

I rinsed off my face, hands, and legs in the cold-water

bin on the floor before filling my hungry mouth with the little food that lay before me. To finish off my nightly rituals, I dived thankfully into bed—a small, itchy pallet large enough only for part of my body. My feet and ankles no longer fit.

"You know, Anna, I'm s'prised you wake up in the mornins high-spirited, countin' on the day bein' different, an' come back at night, sleep the minute you hit that pallet, just to wake up the next day with the same high spirits as every mornin'," Mary said as she gathered the half bucket of water to dump outside and then refill for Daniel.

"Ain't nothin' else I can do, Mary. I look fo'ward to the mornin' breeze, anyway," I said with a grin, my cheek pressed hard into my pallet. She shook her head, washed out my bowl, and blew out the lamp.

If I had fought to keep my eyes open for another five minutes or so, I would've seen Daniel drearily saunter in. Instead, I fell heavily into sleep.

CHAPTER

2

I AWOKE WITH A START. MARY WAS SHAKING ME SO HARD I felt dizzy.

"Sarah, chile, get up! Missus want you workin' in the house."

"Doin' what?" I asked with a wide yawn, wondering why Mary was trying to wake me before my usual morning hour.

"Jus' normal housework firs' part've the day, an' back in the fields fo' the rest," Daniel explained for her. He was always up earlier than the two of us, carving something out of wood. I lifted myself slowly from under the rags that served as my blanket and gazed at my brother.

"What you makin' *now*?" I asked him.

"Ov'rheard somebody say she wanted a box fo' all the scraps Mama sneak home sometime. Purty lil' gal wit thick black hair . . ." He stopped when he saw my wide grin.

"I ain't that lil' no mo', Daniel," I said as he tossed the small box into my waiting hands. Daniel stood and stretched, shaking off the squeeze I had just given him in thanks. And just as quickly as I woke, he had picked up his tools and was headed out the door, content with his gift giving.

The majority of the week, Daniel was assigned to do carpentry work, which he learned from Uncle Joe, whose time on Earth was almost spent. When Daniel was much younger, even before I came to the plantation, Ole Joe took a genuine interest in him. With Masta's permission, he trained Daniel to fix objects and create fine wagons and carriages that Masta rode in.

Mary came back in with the washing water and told me about what Missus had planned.

"She got you workin' with the younguns, cleanin', an' doin' whateva housework she ask you. Gotta get up earlier, too, not as early as me, but its all fo' the betta." I rubbed the sleep from my eyes, and after eating an ashcake and rinsing my tired limbs, I followed Mary out the door.

There were other tasks besides housework and fieldwork: livestock tending, corn cultivation, and carpentry. Housework had been Mary's responsibility, the job she had done for most of her life, and she wanted me to join her.

It was unfortunate that Missus marched into the kitchen when she did that first day. My attention had been grabbed by a small landscape painting hanging on the wall. Before she spoke a single word, she drew the stick she seemed to carry with her constantly and hit me heavily across my leg. Then she leaped back and stared with her beady eyes, waiting to see what I would do. It stung, but I stood as still and as tall as possible, dragged my startled eyes to her feet, and washed my face with a blankness Mary had taught me to compose myself with—that face of obedience.

"You the new one?" she snapped at me after seeing I posed no threat.

"Yes, ma'am."

"Slow as a dog. You clean in here, but don't stare like that. Nothing in those paintings have anything to do with you. Wash the kitchen floors, and break from the fields during the evening to serve us dinner. The rest of the morning you'll spend with the two little ones. I can't be with them every hour."

"Yes, ma'am," I said hurriedly as she leaned my way with the stick again.

"Well, get to it, then!" I hustled past her to fulfill my task.

After a week or so, Mary came home with a longer dress for me to wear in the house, a "fine gift" from Missus. This dress, two pairs of pants, and two blouses were all the clothes I had. I wondered how many house hands had held it before me. I did many tasks in the house, including sewing many things they couldn't get to in the spinning house, which meant that I could hide scraps of material to keep for myself for later use. I cleaned where she asked me to and stayed shy of the kitchen when I could, since I didn't have the skills to prepare the large meals Mary fixed for the family.

Oftentimes, I served the family and their frequent guests. The routine was not hard to learn. The first evening, I carried steaming bowls of corn, baked ham, greens, biscuits, and rice—all served for the normal evening meal. I prepared the table with trembling hands, my stomach blinding me with a sensation of hunger that surged so deep, it must have touched my soul. Following the order that Missus barked out at me to retreat to the corner, I envisioned the bowl of cold food with a small piece of hard, stale bread that was provided for the slaves for a day's worth of work and sweat. It wasn't fair—I couldn't understand it—and I wallowed in this feeling a little too heavily. I missed Missus's first call for me to clear the table and serve dessert. Not until everyone grew silent did I turn to see all the faces, flushed red with the heat of the room, turned toward me. Quick as lightning, I rushed to the table to do what I was told, hoping to miss the woman's backhand, which came flying across my face anyway. After the dessert had been set and I stood again in the corner, I felt misery rise suddenly in me, so ruthless that it caused tears to well up in my eyes. But I held them back, gulped down the fire in my throat, and commenced building a hard shell over my feelings.

The servants of the Big House seemed different from those in the fields. In the fields, all were equal, and punishments were given out according to the misdeeds. In the house, however, life seemed a stage of secrets and deceit. Those who felt it necessary vied for Missus's best attention while trying to stay true to the values of slave row. When a servant won the confidence of Missus, bitterness appeared in the others, and the desire to please grew stronger. I kept my distance from the chaos, as Mary seemed to do with ease.

Along with my other duties, I had the job of watching Missus's two little children, young Masta Bernard and young Missus Jane. The children were hard to cope with; around them, neither my thoughts nor my feelings seemed to be my own. When playtime rolled around, a younger slave hand named Nancy would join us to rock the newborn, and the two little ones would play the game of guessing what the two of us were feeling. Their ignorance angered me, but I learned quickly that in the Big House, an angry slave was a sold slave. The trick was concealment. Mary quietly taught me how to keep it all inside, behind my eyes, buried, because danger couldn't find its way that deep. Out in the fields, I had been taught to sing from my soul. Masta and the overseer swore we were as happy as little children. But it wasn't that way at all.

The two little ones had just started learning to read and write in a school that lasted no more than a few hours of the day. When at home, practicing, they had me act as the student, and they would teach me words and numbers as best they could. They told Missus they learned better like that, and she took to the idea well. Not once did it seem to cross her mind that I could actually use what they were saying and learn like her white children. I was too absentminded in her opinion. But I concentrated hard on those days, listening closely as they spoke and watching carefully as they copied down lessons, not being allowed to copy the words myself. Their game became my fervor and gave me a reason to wake with excitement in the mornings.

"There are twenty-six letters in the alphabet; the word *God* got three. Spell it!" It was a typical afternoon after the children returned from school. Young Masta Bernard stood over his younger sister and me, pointing his writing tool at us like he had seen the teacher do.

"I know!" young Missus Jane squealed. "G-o-d."

"Uh-huh. And you"—the writing tool came within an inch of my face—"what letter makes the 'puh' sound in *apple*?" I pursed my lips together and bent my eyebrows inward as if I were thinking really hard. I knew what it was, I knew exactly the letter, for I had practiced the alphabet backward and forward in my mind. But I couldn't show them how closely I was focusing and how quickly I caught on.

"Well, teacha, I . . . I don't rightly know that. . . ." Before all my words could escape my lips, young Masta Bernard had pulled out a flat piece of wood and smacked me on the knee. The little girl snickered.

"What that fo', young Masta Bernard?" I asked, a light frown on my puzzled brow.

"'Cause it was easy," responded the girl with a giggle. "E-s-y!"

That don't sound right. Must be two e's together make that eee sound, I suppose, I thought to myself.

"No, Jane!" the little boy scolded with his words, without a thought about striking her with anything. "It's e-a-s-y."

Oh! So e and a together make that eee sound too.

That was the routine for a day during the week that would end with their completion of writing assignments. Their harsh words and "punishments" made no difference to me. I had found a type of freedom I doubted many others like me had.

Where I lived, most Masters around didn't want or allow their slaves to read or write. We were made to believe that darker skin equated with a less intelligent person. I thought about this long and hard during hours in the fields, considering the consequences, and figured the two ideas didn't match. If we were so much less smart, why was it so bad for us to learn? Perhaps they were afraid slaves would turn out to be as smart as they were. I don't know how I figured that, but once it was in my mind, like everything else I held strongly to, there was no chasing that idea away. Just because we couldn't read their books didn't mean we couldn't use our minds. Besides, education came in different ways. And imagine—if that knowledge were mixed with book knowledge, we'd be able to fly our way back to Africa!

The consequences of learning to read were severe for slaves. Stories of a slave's tongue or fingers getting cut off haunted me from time to time. Surely I had a right to learn! I could hide, but was it really worth the risk? I didn't know. But these lessons served as an advantage to me, and I took that seriously. I would store in my head every word that slipped out of their "innocent" little mouths, to go over in my mind in the fields.

My secret churned in my heart. I was getting educated!

CHAPTER

3

"I KNOW WHAT HAPPENED TO MY PAPA, SARAH. BIN ASKIN' Mama fo' years—she wouldn't say nothin' 'bout it before. Jus' keep her mouth tight an' shut. Wouldn't nobody round here tell me, eitha," Daniel said to me. It was a late Sunday afternoon, and the two of us stood under a lone tree a ways from the field.

"How you find out 'bout it, then? An' why you jus' tellin' me now?" I asked. My brother had his back turned to me and was bent over a wooden board, busy with his hands. His white shirt stuck to his rough, copper-colored skin like bark to a tree. He was only an inch or two taller than I was, so it wasn't his height that declared his presence. Instead, it was his chiseled features on his otherwise round face which seemed to reflect emotions that raged like stormy seas within. And his eyes—soft, chestnut brown mirrors of a piece of heaven that couldn't be found on Earth—could level the meanest of souls or could pacify the sharpest tongue with only a look.

"One mornin', a few weeks back, I was up early, as always, jus' a mindin' my business. You was still sleepin'. Mama wake up, still sleepy-like, say she got somethin' to tell me, think I oughta know. Jus' start right into it, tell me the whole thing, an' didn't leave me no room to say nothin' 'bout it. She looked at me for a minute when she was done, then jus' walked on outta the cabin."

He spoke loudly enough for me to hear, even though he wasn't facing my direction. The story of Daniel's father had always been a mystery to me, though one I'd never thought too deeply about before. But that mystery must have stirred in Daniel's soul quite often. I was afraid to hear the story, afraid of hearing evidence of yet another injustice born from the world we lived in. Despite this, I listened.

"Sarah, his name was Isaac. Good man. Wasn't so tall but was a good worker, Mama said." Daniel set his tools down, turned toward me, and leaned against the tree.

"But she say he have a head on 'im jus' as dangerous as any wild creature you'd see. He worked hard, an' in all them hours he worked, Mama say things was a cookin' up in his mind that the strongest wind couldn't blow from it. When she had me, he told her he wa'n't gonna have no son've his livin' like he did." Daniel dropped down to a seated position.

"Mama tell him he ain't got no choice, but Papa say to her he was gonna run away, figure out the road pretty well, make them a home, then come back fo' us. Mama say she pleaded with him, told him all she could think of to get him to stay, but he had his mind set on goin'." I shifted uneasily in my place.

"Two days after he left, his dead body was the only

thing that came back. Nearly drowned in the river. Dogs found 'im half-dead on the bank, dragged 'im out jus' bitin' him up. He died in the mornin' from what Masta said was the cold eatin' him up on the inside, an' blood loss. Back on the plantation, Masta used him as an example—told the gathered slave row that none of 'em'd be spared if they tried the same."

Daniel's eyes clouded over before he dropped his head and let it hang low.

"What 'bout Mary?" I asked him softly.

"Don't rightly know. I asked her, but she walked out mumblin' 'bout Missus." I nodded.

"That wa'n't nothin' easy for her to tell you, Daniel."

"I know it wa'n't. But she knew I needed to hear it."

I sighed. "I'm . . . I'm sorry to hear 'bout your papa," I whispered to my brother. He looked up at me, and in his eyes I caught sight of a pride I had never seen before. And behind that was a special look, one of bonding, almost as if the telling of his story and him entrusting me with it bound us together even more strongly.

CHAPTER

❧ 4 ❧

THE SUN BEAT DOWN HEAVILY ON OUR BENT BACKS WHILE WE dragged our feet aimlessly through the fields, chained together by our submission, surrounded by nothing but white cotton.

The sun ripped at our skin, forming blisters with its harsh slaps. It shone so strongly that our eyes couldn't turn to the skies to ask heaven why, so we turned to the earth, dug holes with our fingers, and screamed into the dirt, mouths open, eating, begging, pleading . . .

Suffocate me, please.

Suddenly, everything changed. The chains of submission turned into heavy, real chains that dug into our wrists. We were surrounded by water—an ocean that had been so familiar to my young mind. I screamed at it: Why are you helping them drag me away like this?

But my words came up as bubbles, and I turned sad eyes away and fell back into place in line.

Why, nature, do you sit by quietly, watching these horrors transpire?

It responded with a resounding, indifferent silence.

And you, little boy, why do you throw up that way? Did you forget to eat your meal this morning? That's all right, there's no able-bodied person left in the village who will touch your food. So please keep moving forward. Don't you know if you stop this line, they'll pull you out and we'll never see you again?

And old woman, why are you wailing in such a way? Did you forget to provide for the sickly old man before they came and dragged you away? Please don't cry—his fate is surely not as devastating as your own. But please hush. Don't you know they like the silence? Don't you know they're headed this way with sticks and stones to strike you down?

I flew back and forth between the drooped shoulders, lowered eyelids, and dragging feet, listening to these people's heartbeats, hearing them tell of their stories through silence.

And then I was pushed back into line.

A monster-man came riding by, and urine ran between my legs from the fear that shot through me, and yet the line moved forward, feet dragging right through the puddles I made. Nobody noticed. Nobody cared. There was such a heaviness in step, a weariness of heart, the tension in my own chest spilled over in teardrops that would not stop running. But then my tears turned to screams that bounced off bodies and slapped me in the face.

Our feet dragged to a stop in front of a boat—a toy from the deepest dungeons of hell. Men, women, and children were shoved down, down, down, prodded, pushed, grabbed, tossed into the bowels of the ship.

What does this mean? Haven't we already walked through hell?

The monster-man laughed in my ear.

No, that was only hell's gateway, a pitiable forerunner of the journey that lies ahead.

We were swallowed by a darkness we could feel with all our senses. We could smell its nauseating stench, feel its fatal tug, taste its poisonous air, see its writhing ugliness, and touch its repulsive weight.

One body, two bodies—no, legs into chest! Yes, fold them like that. Good. Three bodies, four bodies—toss them to those waiting hands, and they'll be sure to stack them in as close together as possible. Good. Five bodies, six bodies—we need all the space we can get!

I screamed, dug, scratched, and fought my way back out. I threw myself out of the ship and onto the shore. There to greet me were waters murky with the redness of death. Bodies lay in the shallow waters staring up at me.

And there was Mathee's face, her soft skin bloated by the water's lust.

Another scream, then hands were yanking me back inside. . . .

The dreams started about a year after I arrived on the plantation. They'd come all of a sudden, images, events, and feelings from my past too raw and savage for my emotions to handle and for my conscious mind to hold on to. They came very frequently at first, and I always woke in early mornings screaming and sweating and bound to haunting feelings. This set concern in Mary's breast, but she had predicted that the dreams would go away after a few years. Although she was wrong, they had become less pronounced and far less frequent. I could go months without the memories or images playing with my sleeping mind, and I had learned, somehow, to turn the wild morning screams into nothing more than moans.

"You rememba it this time?" Mary asked me that day. I shook my head back and forth.

"Mary, why you gotta ask the same thing? My answer ain't gonna change," I said with a smile.

She sighed. "That ain't gonna change, Sarah—now watch it!" she scolded as water from the mop I held splashed onto me.

In addition to cooking for the household, Mary took care of Missus's most personal needs. If there was a special request, Missus would turn to Mary first, before all others, and bid her to carry out the task in whatever way Mary thought best. It was a strange bond where Missus still assumed her position of superiority but never had reason to enforce it. Mary was just a strong woman and seemed to attract at least that recognition, despite her "place" as a slave. Missus trusted Mary, perhaps because the two had spent the majority of their living years in the presence of each other.

I didn't see Mary as often as I had anticipated. My errands and work many times took me away from the kitchen. But there were some days when I'd be ordered to stand by Mary's side and help, or help her when she stitched. This day was one of those rare times when I could be alone with Mary in the kitchen. I took my sweet time scrubbing the floor, loving the moments I spent with her.

"I do have some small memories 'bout few folks from long ago I can tell you 'bout. Don't worry, they good ones, Mary, don't look like that," I said, seeing Mary's eyebrows arch inward. "I rememba my mama. . . ."—I let the mop linger on the wood—"an' this woman—think she my auntie. An' . . . an' my brother, I rememba the most 'bout him." Mary allowed me to soak in the silence as long as I wanted. "You think I might know wat happen to him fo' I die?" I questioned Mary, stopping to look at her with my large, inquiring eyes. Mary moved her eyes away from mine to the food that lay before her.

"Sarah, I cain't rightly say. But you bin here long enuf to know how those things go. Don't gotta tell ya how those things just don't happen round here." I nodded, knowing that answer all too well.

"Well I jus' figure, all these folks we knows but cain't find, we sure'll find 'em in heaven, won't we Mary?" Mary laughed softly as she drew her hand quickly across the edge of her head rag, wiping off the sweat.

"Sure will."

In the quiet that followed, Mary started humming a tune. I listened to it long enough to realize I hadn't heard it before.

"Mary, what you singing?" I asked when I heard her humming a tune under her breath.

She chuckled softly, then responded, "This song's an old tune that was made up an' sang as fa' back as I can rememba."

"One of dem slave songs they sing in da fields?"

She thought for a moment. "Don't think so. Only memba my mother singin' it to me fo' she was sold."

"Where it come from?" I asked.

"From an' ole tale of a couple, man an' wife, who, on dey way to freedom, up'n found bunches of slave folk hidden an' trapped beneath a hideout dug deep in the ground right by the riverside."

"Slaves a runnin' to freedom?" I asked, engaged deeply in the short story.

"Sho'. The two ole folks freed all dem peoples, maybe hundreds of 'em, an' sent 'em 'cross the riva. Just so happened that afta the last of da peoples disappeared on the riva's horizon, befo' the boatin' man could come back fo' the old folks, they was caught."

"Caught? Why the song got to have them caught fo'? Cain't it be somethin' glad?"

Mary chuckled. "You gonna hear the rest of it?" I nodded.

"They drowned themselves hand in hand befo' the slave catchers could kill 'em."

"That's a sad song, Mary."

"Well, many say when a slave be a runnin', the spirits of da two ole folks come back an' warn the slave when danger's awaitin'. Don't rightly know if'n it's da truth or not, but it goes somethin' like dis:

"Ole man Tom an' his good wife Liza
(None round here done seen any wisa)

When trouble's a lurkin', they calls a safety to yo' side
In da darkness of the night by the ragin' riverside
So's when you's a fearin' for your good ole freedom
They'll up'n find you an' carry you to freedom."

CHAPTER

5

THE FLOOR WAS ALMOST CLEAN.

Just a little bit of scrubbing over here.

I finished the task with a sigh and picked up the rag. Edging the door open to the small study, I glanced uncertainly into the room. Missus had told me to dust all the desks in the house. Was this one included?

Inching the door a bit farther forward, I brought the rag to the edge of the desk and began wiping it, carefully shifting around what I had to in order to clean the whole surface. Edging around the desk, I bumped into something standing against the wall. I began turning, but my body went still with excitement. In front of me was a large bookcase. And there were so many books! Surely I could peek into one of the primers. . . .

I scolded myself immediately over the thoughts that rushed through my mind and turned quickly back to the desk and the rag. But just as soon as the scolding stopped, I felt my feet creeping toward the shelf once more. I peeked over my shoulder and listened carefully for any sound. No one was near, and no one would notice if I sneaked just a quick look at the books. What possibly could that hurt? Nobody would notice!

I reached toward the shelf, my heart beating in my stomach. The burning feeling of danger shot through my body, but I paid it no heed. A small bowl of sugar cubes sat in front of a colorful book. Looking over my shoulder again, I hid a cube in my dress pocket and then nudged the bowl to the side to reveal the book. I slowly tipped the dusty book out toward me. I pulled it down and cracked it open an inch or so, then read the first word on the page I turned to. With satisfaction beating even louder than my fearful heart, I shut the book and slid it back in its place.

I can read!

Those were the first words that formed in my mind as my fingers slid down the spine of the book once more.

"What in the devil's name are you in this room for?"

It was the worst sound I could have heard. Missus's voice startled me so much that my hand jerked, hitting the bowl of sugar cubes. It tumbled through the air as our eyes followed its motions, my heart beating harder with every rotation.

The bowl's edge struck the wood floor and shattered into a miniature ice storm of sugar and shards of porcelain.

"You fool! My cubes! Were you stealing my cubes? And my china! My precious china is shattered to pieces! What's gotten into you, you stupid slave? Insolence and disobedience have consequences. How dare you! Charles, Charles, come quick. Come now!"

Before I could attempt an explanation, Masta Charles came running into the room. Seeing me, he rushed over, grabbed my arm, and pulled me out past onlookers whose eyes told me that trouble stood in my path. I bit my lips with dread as I listened to Masta shout nasty words while he dragged me out the door with Missus right on his heels.

Once outside, he told the overseer what to do with me. The overseer forced me past the beating tree—the punishment arranged for the worst of deeds done—to a fence. He tied my hands tightly to it and ripped my blouse halfway down my back, revealing my half-grown chest. He removed his bullwhip from his holster, and swung. The tip bit the air with a *crack!* Panic rose within me and began to swell. I tugged at the ropes that bound my wrists together; they sliced even farther into my skin like dull knives. My heart raced.

Crack!

The tip of the whip whistled through the air until it landed swiftly on my back. The sting of the first impact blurred my mind. I didn't even hear my own scream until the second strike rattled me, the one making me pay for my "insolence." Three. Four. Five. Six. My screams turned into whimpers of pain as my flesh seemed to find its way into a fiery hell. The struggling stopped: My body, strong and rebellious a few strikes before, hung limp and helpless. My hands had quit tugging to free themselves from the ropes binding them to the fence.

As he continued to beat me, I ceased counting the number of times the whip struck my back; my screams were now simple gasps. My eyes were squeezed so tightly together that I saw white stars in my mind. Large tears jutted from my eyes and dripped off my face, attempting to wash away the pain. All I wished, and all I wanted, was for it to be over. I prayed to the beat of his whip for the Lord to have mercy on me. Time seemed to stand still. There was only me, the pain, and that whip.

And then, it ended as abruptly as it had started, though the pain settled in quickly afterward. Fifteen lashes for breaking the china bowl and trying to steal the cubes. It was strange justice, but the only justice we knew: the justice of the slave master. The overseer untied my hands, letting me fall in a heap onto the fertile soil, and simply walked away. His work was done and he had done his job well, beating my bound young body as he had. But the pain didn't walk off with the man holding the bullwhip. It held me hostage and stayed with me even as Mary knelt by my side. She was a blurry mass to my drifting consciousness. She whispered to me, told me that it would be all right. It was as if her words were my gateway to heaven. I fainted dead away.

"Morning? He wants me back to workin' by mornin'?" I couldn't believe my ears. Lying on my stomach on a pallet the next day, Mary dressed my wounds once more. She shook her head slowly, angrily, with worry lines creasing her forehead.

"Mary, I ain't gonna be healed enough to work!" I exclaimed. "I'll jus' get beat again, this time fo' not doin' my job!"

"Shh, hush that talk! You'll be fine, chile, you will. This stuff here I put on yo' back'll heal ya quicka; it's somethin' my mama showed me, an' her Native mama befo' that. You'll be a little weak, but you'll be able to work."

The tears came again as Mary rubbed whatever it was she had on my back. It stung at first, and I grimaced as the herb-filled salve penetrated my open wounds, but it settled into a coolness that eased the pain. She told me that Missus hadn't watched; the whipping was too much for her to bear. Missus believed my lesson had been learned, and she was willing to give me another chance in the Big House.

How lucky I must be! I thought. In my mind, I dreamed of wrenching a bullwhip out of the overseer's hand and charging towards Missus, beating her coward self down. But I was smarter than that; my heart was better than that. I let my emotions simmer, then buried them inside with everything else.

"Tucker," I said, looking up to see a man standing by Daniel. He seemed to be thrown in some generation between Mary and me. He was a small man—quiet, thin boned, but quick and strong willed. His eyes had a faraway look to them. To me, his spirit seemed to be locked in a place I couldn't dream of touching. He had no one close to him I knew of, besides the respect of an older woman who lived on some plantation a day's travel down the road.

Tucker sought Daniel's company often and shared meals with me and Mary from time to time.

"You doin' all right?" Tucker asked me, smiling softly into my eyes.

"Sho', Tucker. I'm doin' okay." He nodded slowly, and took a long breath. "But I'd be doin' a little betta if you could tell Daniel to stop all that pacin'. It's makin' me nervous." I shot my eyes back over to my brother, whose shoulders were tense and whose lips were dangerously pursed. Hearing me, he stopped in place and softened the angry arch of his eyebrows. As Mary ran out to collect something else for my back, and Tucker left to continue the work he had temporarily abandoned, I turned all my attention to my brother.

"Daniel," I said softly, as if that one word would tell him I was all right.

My brother leaned down even closer, his eyes only narrowing more.

"Sarah, ain't nobody gonna be whippin'—"

"Shh. Daniel, don't talk like that! I got this for you." I handed him the sugar cube I had painfully recovered from my pocket. He stared at it without reaching out a hand to take it.

"That what you get whipped fo'?" He asked.

Dropping my hand that held the cube onto the pallet, I nodded solemnly, then added with a slight pause, "Least, that's what Missus say." In the silence that followed, I hid my secret about reading the book and not getting caught. If I had been caught for that "sin"—if Missus had walked in just a minute earlier and seen me attempting to educate myself—I would have been punished far more severely than I hoped ever to be punished.

I held out my hand to him once more, but he shook his head. I interrupted his thoughts.

"Ain't no need wastin' it now. Since I already have it, eat it! Or else I'ma feel even worse!" A slight smile curled the corners of Daniel's mouth.

"If you say so." Breaking off half of it with his teeth, he put the other half into my mouth. But the sudden stinging I felt drowned out the sweetness of the sugar. Mary had reentered the cabin and was touching my back with something in her hands. I squirmed under her touch.

"You a real smart girl, Sarah, but you need to learn to think befo' you act, honey, you hear?"

"Yes, Mary."

"Either way"—she stood up and walked around to look in my eyes—"you be a strong girl, Sarah, real strong and brave."

CHAPTER

❧ 6 ❧

THE MORNING AIR FELT A BIT BIT TOO COOL FOR EARLY springtime, but I knew it would warm up quickly. It had been almost a month since the sugar cube incident; the remaining wounds from the whip had scarred over. I had long since been back to work. The breeze filled my lungs as Daniel and I headed toward our religious gathering on Sunday morning. We neared a large shack in the middle of the woods, not too far from the Big House. It wasn't much of a building, but the men of the plantation kept our church setting decent. Everyone had gathered outside the shack, since it was used only when the weather made it necessary.

Daniel and I approached the small backless benches that had been carried out of the building.

"Hey, Mary," I whispered as we passed her seated figure, looking for seats. There were none left open.

As Daniel and I made our way toward the back to stand, a young man moved from his seat, offering me the place with a smile. I refused it and turned to walk with Daniel, but my brother had slipped into the shadows. The man offered the seat once again. I recognized him somewhat;

I didn't know him too well—there were quite a few slaves here—but I believed I might have seen him in the fields, or maybe doing carpentry work with Daniel.

I inched my way in front of the seat, nodding to the young man, and turned toward the woman who stood at the front. But my mind kept dancing back to the smiling man, wondering why he was standing so close—so close that our shoulders brushed. I locked my gaze in front of me.

Sundays were to be our free days, God's day. Masta gave the field hands half the day off. The house servants had less freedom, and oftentimes some of us were made to work. After all, housework never ended. But morning hours were always mine to have.

Our church had different preachers on different days. Masta picked a black overseer who had been a good "lamb of Masta's church" to make sure we weren't plotting, and he gave the permission for others to preach. Most of the preachers, however, knew how to dodge the rules. They would use biblical stories to create messages of joy and freedom for us right under the overseer's nose. "Slave language" is what Daniel and I called it.

As the woman finished singing, "an' we be free," I heard a deep amen resound next to me. People sat as an older man stood up and walked to the front.

"Now, we gots a new voice wit us today. But befo' that, I got a few words fo' ya." He went on to share news from other plantations and a Bible verse Masta always prepared to have shared with us. On this Sunday, Masta had chosen a few verses from first Peter, chapter two. The man recited the verses from memory and added his own statements where he thought it necessary.

"The Bible say be submissive to yo' mastas wit all respect, not only to them who is good an' who is gentle, but also to them who is unreasonable. Fo' what credit is there if, when you's sin an' is treated bad, you endure it wit patience? But if, when you do what is right an' suffa fo' it and patiently endure it, then that's what God find favor in, an' we's all lookin' to please God."

I leaned back and listened as closely as I could, my attention frequently drifting away to the chirping birds playing above or the young children stifling giggles just across from me. I remained awake but drifted into a heavy daze, playing with my imagination. The amens were lulling me into another world; they were taking me to another place where the chants were of a different language. I could hear a strange beat; there was a drummer tapping out fascinating rhythms while sitting, quite at ease underneath a large, beautiful, exotic tree. . . .

My small hands clutched the African cloth that hung over the beautiful legs of a tall woman. Mama Mijiza moved from one foot to the other, slowly at first, then faster and faster. She was soon spinning into the center of the circle. I grabbed Sentwaki's hand, staring with awe and longing, praying that I could be as free as Mama was right then, letting the wind feed her hungry body with nothing but . . . but . . . Africanness.

The next thing I knew, I was spinning too, spinning in Mama's arms in the center of the circle. The beat released the thoughts in my mind and I knew I was flying. . . .

A round of clapping and joyful yelling pulled me from the spell of my deep daydream. I left my hazy pictures of what life probably would have been like for me as a little girl and fell back into reality. Looking up, I drew my eyebrows into a puzzled arch. The young man who had been standing next to me had taken over the preacher's place. I let my mind focus on what he was saying, careful not to drift off into my old world again.

"Yessuh, we got'sta work hard, yes we do so's when we leaves this place, an' we knock on that door to heaven, the good Lord'll look us up'n down, say sho' nuff, Mrs. Patsy"—he gestured to a slave woman who sat in front of him—"you's can come on in here to my kingdom! That's where your freedom lie."

Mmm, freedom.

The word rolled off the young man's tongue in a seductive manner. He was saying that working was the only way to freedom, but I set that thought aside for the moment. There it was again: freedom. I could taste it!

"Amen, yes, uh-huh." Everyone around me chimed in with their own amens.

"But if'n you's ain't workin', says if you's ain't workin', the Good Lord'll look you up'n down, say 'Nope' an' He'll close that door."

He continued and I listened, dwelling in the essence of his words of freedom, trying to understand what all he was attempting to say beneath his phrases. Then, as the heat of the speech began to subside, I found myself staring into the eyes of the young man, locked for the better part of a second in an odd gaze. Although brief, it brought up a deep feeling that rose from within. Perhaps it was a mere second, but that second felt like an eternity. But I forced the moment to end, and heat rushed to my dark face as I quickly looked elsewhere, trying to dismiss the glimmer I saw in his eyes.

I bet that's a glimmer for freedom, I thought, trying to ignore the feeling in my gut telling me otherwise.

Following the sermons, everyone ate what little they had and talked with one another. I stayed with Mary, keeping an eye out for Daniel, who usually disappeared to talk with others and to do whatever else he did on Sunday afternoons. A little while later, Mary left me to return to the Big House to finish her day's worth of work.

I searched for Daniel for a long while and finally seated myself outside the shack. I hated looking for him; it always gave me a nervous feeling in my bones. So when he came up behind me and placed a hand on my shoulder, I let out a short sigh of relief but began questioning him immediately.

"Daniel, where you bin? You ain't told me I'd hafta search for you this Sunday! Why cain't you eva let me know where you at or where you go to? I told you I don't like lookin' for you! C'mon, let's go."

"You a bit cross today, ain't you? I'm fine, Sarah," Daniel said, half-smiling.

I relaxed a little when I saw his smile—a warm, unusual smile that lit up his face.

"Don't worry so much 'bout me. You need to be worryin'

'bout that Missus of yours layin' her hands on you!"

"Don't talk like that, Daniel! You know good 'n' well you could be beaten an' sold befo' the day is out, talkin' like that."

"John!" He said, ignoring my comment and addressing the man who joined us as we headed back. It was the young preacher man who had given me his seat.

"Those was some words you shared today. This my sister, Sarah." The man turned his eyes toward me.

"B'lieve I done seen you round some, but ain't met you the right way," John said, gazing at me. The glimmer had disappeared, and I pushed my curiosity away with it.

"I ain't neva shook no one's hand befo'," I said, placing my sweaty palm in his. He chuckled, bobbing my hand firmly up and down.

"Well, look atcha now, shakin' hands like you bin doin' it all yo' life." I gently pulled away from his grasp and occupied my hand with brushing away a bug that had landed on the back of my neck.

"You preach befo', John?" I asked him.

"Naw, not befo'. Why?"

"You'se got a good mouth on you." He chuckled. ,

"Well it's 'bout time. John bin talkin' 'bout speakin' fo' the people fo' a while," Daniel told me.

"You understand everything I say?"

I frowned and crossed my arms. "That some kinda s'prise to you or somethin'?" I asked.

"'Course not." His reply seemed to laugh at my immodest tone. I grunted.

"You ain't got no question fo' John, Sarah?" Daniel asked me. I listened closely to Daniel's words. He wanted me to test the man and he knew it was just a matter of time before I would.

"Well, then, sho' I do. John?" I asked, looking up at his teasing eyes.

"Yes, Miss Sarah?" he asked.

Miss Sarah. I boldly returned his gaze.

"Y'all was talkin' 'bout us workin' hard, reachin' heaven when we pass on, you know? But where in God's mind or God's book fo' that matta do it say we gotsta work hard fo' Masta? I mean, nobody like doin' this day in an' day out. That's what I would think, unless I'm wrong," I said, curious. We were far enough from everything not to be overheard.

"Naw, you right—," he replied, but I continued, cutting him off.

"But they all say amen like y'all's speakin' the truth. Why that be?"

"Ya, John, why that be?" Daniel mocked, with a laugh.

"You hush!" I said, swinging my hand at his arm.

John answered, "You knows we gotsta watch what we say in front of the ova'seer."

"Guess I can see that. But I reckon he ain't the only one you gotta watch what you say in front of," I replied in a matter-of-fact way.

"'Course not, it ain't jus' them. Some of us on slave row be runnin' to Masta, tellin' him what we sayin' against him."

"An' how you s'pose to tell which've us is loyal, an' which've us ain't?" I asked.

John laughed. "You testin' me, Miss Sarah? 'Cause seems to me you knows these answers already."

"Sho' she is," Daniel said, reaching into his pocket for some wood and a knife.

"Naw, ain't no point in testin' you or tryin' to prove a point. I jus' wanna know!" I responded as my shoulders rose and dropped in a shrug.

"Well, there's some of us that meet sometimes—secretly, of course. We talk 'bout things like that—you know, who we can trust, what we know 'bout Masta sellin' any of us off, an' otha things like that. We risk Masta catching us fo' the truth to be told. Those who unda'stand the truth talk wit us lata on, kinda like me an' you are doin' now, till we rightly understand the news 'bout otha plantations an' so's we can share otha things among us. Them peoples who ain't loyal be thinkin' on Sundays we talkin' 'bout workin' fo' the white man."

A deep laugh passed from John's lips as he continued quietly but insistently, "No, sah! We talkin' 'bout workin' hard."

"Workin' hard so's we can reach the op'n door to freedom?" I asked softly, using some of his words from the church service. He nodded, impressed.

"Yeah, that's right. Workin' hard so's we can make it through our own freedom doors," he said, eyeing me closely.

Working toward freedom sounds good, real good. But how?

"Well all right then, mister," I said with a nod his way. He responded with a loud remark.

"Looks to me like we got ourselves one smart gal round here! Take folks fo'eva to understand some've these things."

John winked at me but turned before I could say anything about it, walking off in another direction and whistling a tune I couldn't recognize. I could only imagine the words that went with it. A smile crept up on my face, though I refused to let it stretch too wide.

I didn't notice Daniel's smirk until he remarked, "He's only five or six years older'n you, Sarah." I shook my head and tried to wipe the smile away.

"Ain't interested in nobody. Got otha things on my mind," I said with a firm nod toward my brother.

"Like what?" he asked, still smiling.

In my mind, images of books, schoolhouses, stacked words, and ink scratched onto paper ran wild through my mind, but there I bid them stay. Instead I replied, "You talkin' 'bout me, but you ain't heard me say nothin' 'bout you an' that Birdie." I glanced over at him. He was rubbing the small stubs of hair on his chin with his fingers, looking as if a secret had been exposed. Birdie was a laundress owned by a city slave owner not far from the plantation. Daniel sneaked visits to her when he traveled with Masta around her way. I had never met the woman.

"Ain't nothin' to say," he said unconvincingly.

"You got nothin' to say? Nothin' at all?" I asked. "I should tell her that."

He simply laughed, but after a while, he said, "She a good woman, Sarah."

"I s'pose," I commented, keeping my eyes set in front of me.

"What's that s'pose to mean."

"You don't fool me. She ain't the only one got yo' attention," I replied.

He sighed, his eyes bouncing back and forth between the work in his hands and my face. "Now, you know that ain't the truth. I kinda like her," he said, his face darkening a bit. "An' Mama like her, anyway," he said after a short while, with an edge of persuasion in his voice.

"She doesn't know her," I said simply.

"Heard enuf 'bout her to figure," he replied.

"Well," I said, shrugging, trying to beat back the hints of a smile at the corners of my mouth, "sounds to me you'se softenin' up!"

Daniel chuckled. "You ain't got no decency at all," he replied, throwing his arm over my shoulder.

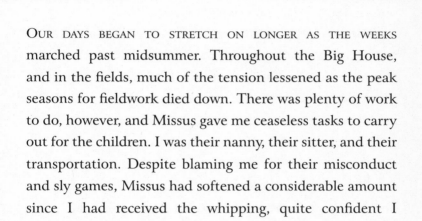

CHAPTER

❧ 7 ❧

OUR DAYS BEGAN TO STRETCH ON LONGER AS THE WEEKS marched past midsummer. Throughout the Big House, and in the fields, much of the tension lessened as the peak seasons for fieldwork died down. There was plenty of work to do, however, and Missus gave me ceaseless tasks to carry out for the children. I was their nanny, their sitter, and their transportation. Despite blaming me for their misconduct and sly games, Missus had softened a considerable amount since I had received the whipping, quite confident I was permanently put in my place. I saw my work as an opportunity; dividing my concentration between keeping order and educating myself, I raked their conversations clean for anything new I could learn.

Sometimes on Sunday mornings, or mornings when Missus took the children to the city, I stole away to places on or near the plantation that I had found when I was younger. When I went to church, it became habit to search for John, under lowered foolish eyelids. He made it a point, over the weeks, to slip by Daniel's side on some of those mornings, unannounced. He came and went like the tide; some weeks he wouldn't be there, some weeks he would, and after a while, Daniel left us alone. When I talked with him on those days after church, it felt like I was digging inside of myself to find the places and the treasures that hid from me in the fields and in the Big House. He'd never stay long, however, and I settled it in my mind that he had only a small place in the back of his mind for me. When I could, I turned from what my heart whispered and set my mind onto letters, rules, and other school knowledge.

But there were other times—when I took the two little ones outside to play, or when I dumped waste from the House before heading out into the fields later in the day—that he'd just appear. With a passing word or a lazy smile, he'd fix a gaze on my face that I'd turn away from without a single change to my countenance, but with a pleasure under my skin.

That glimmer I had seen in his eye that first Sunday, however, had never returned, and I held myself back from expressing something that stirred deep down in my soul. I called it a good old friendship and turned my mind off to the notion of anything more. My heart was mine to keep.

Early one Sunday morning, I found my way up a hill a good distance away from the Big House. It was plantation property, but the land here wasn't being used. When I could on Sunday mornings, when fatigue didn't strap me to my pallet, I'd steal away here to watch the sunrise, to take in the peace. But most times, I'd escape here after church when I wasn't needed in the Big House, or when Daniel bid me to leave him be, sneaking past the watchful eyes of slave row. Mary was the only one who knew.

I climbed up to the top and stretched out on my belly, the grass tickling my ankles. Shutting my eyes, I felt all my concerns seep out of my body and disappear on the wind. A calm energy that felt like God spread through me.

"Thank you fo' this." I spoke softly to the heavens.

That hill was my hill, or so I loved to believe. Here, I got away from all the struggles of a slave's life. The birds and animals felt it, as did the plants and trees. It was my turn to share in God's beauty. I squinted my eyes against the late-summer sun as I imagined distant mountains that stretched so far into the heavens, they had to be free from bondage and suffering, hate and sorrow, mental and physical pain.

I wish I was a bird or an angel so I could sprout feathers and wings and simply fly away, gliding, free as the wind!

"Wouldn't it be somethin' to stand atop them trees?" A deep voice shook me from my daydreams. I hadn't even heard his footsteps, yet John was seating himself by me, admiring the beautiful scene.

"You follow me up here? I know you did," I said, turning to him.

"Nope! Got up real early, an' the wind jus' a carried me here, to this place."

"You tellin' the truth?" I asked.

"Wouldn't tell *you* nothin' otha than the truth." And I could see that glimmer in his eyes that I had let slip from my mind.

I turned and began scraping the dirt from beneath my fingernails. He bent his knees up with his legs out wide and tossed his arms over his knees. I stole another long glance in his direction and studied his upturned face. His complexion was a rusty brown with a hint of red and a dab of honey—three colors that melted together in harmony. John had thick jaws and a large face that fit well on his long but broad neck and his tall body. His nose spread wide when he sat deep in thought, and his lips were like two pieces of clay perfectly molded together. His dark eyes curled at the corners.

"There ain't nothin' more beautiful than God's work. Us here, we God's work, jus' as them white folks, but they done gotten away from God an' doin' good an' took 'vantage of his work. Done made us slaves. Slaves the makin' of human folk, not God's makin'." He nodded at his own words, adding, "but them folks ain' bad." John's deep voice held a hint of wanting to escape from this white man's world—I recognized it as the need to run away, to be free!

"You always gotta preach?" I asked him without turning his way.

"I ain't no real preacher," he said softly.

"Sure sound like it," I responded, but he didn't hear, or perhaps he didn't wish to respond. I looked from the scenery to John then back again. There seemed to be a bond between the souls of the trees and animals and his own soul. Something in my head wanted him to go, to leave this hill of mine. But some other part of me fought it. It felt right.

"You bin up here befo'?"

He shook his head.

"Shoulda brought someone up here with ya," I said matter-of-factly.

His lips split in a subtle, soft smile. "An' why's that, Miss Sarah?"

I shrugged. "Don't seem right, you'se up here an' its jus' me."

"I like talkin' to 'jus' you,'" he said, leaning back on his elbows and tracing the skyline as outlined by the trees with his finger. I let my resistance melt into the silence. We sat there for a long time, listening to heaven whistle in our ears.

"You eva sailed the wind befo'?" he asked me.

I laughed, then replied, "Sail the wind? You mean, fly?"

"Sho'."

"Cain't no one fly, John. Only my ancestors could do that. They had big ole wings," I said, sitting up and spreading my arms out. "They'd dark skin like mine, an' determination like them birds up there!"

He laughed, his eyes sparkling in the sunlight. "So you know 'bout flyin'."

I settled back down, a heavy thought having just run through my mind. I chose to entertain it.

"Naw. If I knew 'bout flyin', I'd've flown on back when they took me away. They stole me away from my home where the sunsets filled up the skies like you neva seen, away from a family I was born to, and 'cross oceans a thousand times bigga than these cotton fields, all the way here."

I didn't know where the words came from or why I

chose to speak them to the man by my side. I didn't talk of that faraway past to anyone but Mary, sometimes Daniel, and I pondered all these things as I felt John's eyes rest on me. I felt his serene gaze absorb my words, my expressions, even my unspoken thoughts. He remained silent for a few minutes, until he finished weaving together whatever he needed to in his mind.

"You bin here a long time?"

I nodded. "Bin here fo' most my years. But . . . but when I come up here these days, to this hill"—I gestured to the sight before us—"when I come up here an' see this, I get some kinda feelin' deep in my bones, like I'm rememberin' it all, John, like . . . like I could step back into that yestaday so easily." I stared out into the sunlight, watching the wind pick up fallen, misplaced leaves and stray seeds and other pieces of nature that longed to find their way back home. They never made it far.

I dug my fingernails into the skin on my arms and turned back to John.

"But the fact is, it ain't that easy. So I leave all those thoughts 'bout where I come from alone most times. It was like anotha life."

John nodded. "You rememba much?"

"Not much—I was real little. But some things—strange things—like names; I rememba names betta than I rememba faces! How you reckon that?"

John shook his head. "I dunno. What names you rememba?"

I looked at him with a small smile, feeling very much

at ease. "There was . . . I rememba a little boy—reckon he was kin to me, my brother. When I see him in my mind, the name Sentwaki jus' jumps into my head."

John repeated the name. "Reckon I see why you rememba it. That ain't a name you fo'get."

I nodded at him with a smile. "Ain't talked 'bout none of this in a long time, John. I listen to my talk, sound like some story out of a book or somethin', nothin' else. Nothin' else."

My smile drifted away, and I could feel the faraway look return to my eyes. "I did fo'get so many things. Reckon that's fo' the best. Lot of things my mind tells me happened, I jus' cain't b'lieve, 'cause they seem so bad an' I was so little. . . ."

"Then, fo'get 'em, Sarah. Ain't no need fillin' a mind like yours—"

I cut him off. "Naw, John, it ain't like . . . it ain't like I can jus' fo'get. I . . . I have some bad dreams sometimes. Don't come often, but when they come . . ." I let my voice trail off, not wanting to complete my thought.

"What about?"

"I dunno most times. Things my mind has fo'gotten, my heart remembas when I'm sleep. I don't rememba them much, but I know the heavy feelin' inside when they come. I . . . I . . ." I frowned at him, at the spell he seemed to have cast.

"Sound like nightmares, almost," he said softly, filling in the silence that had fallen.

I averted my eyes, becoming aware that I was with someone I had just gotten to know.

"Don't know why I was sharin' all that. That's all jus' stuff that cross my mind sometimes. I didn't really have to share it."

He chuckled softly. "Don't know why I was jus' sittin' here listenin' like that. Reckon I like listenin' to things that take me away from here. Didn't really hafta let them words touch me somewhere on the inside, but I did."

A smile graced my lips, and I shook my head at his playfulness. "You need to leave me be up here an' go on 'bout your business."

"We was talkin' 'bout flyin' an' sailin' the wind, don't you rememba?" he asked.

"Don't matta much. I cain't fly, John."

"'Course you can. You see that bird?" He pointed a finger up toward a black bird circling the trees.

"Sho' I see it," I replied.

"Close your eyes, an' see yourself up there floatin'."

"Me instead of the bird? That's pretendin', John."

"No, there's a difference," he said calmly. "Pretendin' ain't real, but imagination's as real as you can get," John explained.

"I imagine things, John, but you act like I'm s'pose to be a small gal actin' like I'm some bird!"

John replied, "Who tole you imagination is fo' little ones, Miss Sarah? It's a kinda freedom on its own, don't you know!"

I sighed, but John ignored my resistance.

"Well I ain't leavin' till you try it, so it's all up to you."

I laughed. "All right, then."

He pulled himself up to sitting, closed his eyes, and leaned against my shoulder.

"Don't look at the bird an' wish you could fly. Act like you up there an' do it yourself." Amused, I shut my eyes too and did what he said. Slowly, I felt myself rising. Then I leaped up, floated, raced to the treetop, and flew into the sun's rays.

But our imaginings were interrupted by the sound of rough footsteps. We both turned to see Masta Jeffrey angrily making his way up the hill. He was the oldest of Masta and Missus's four children, somewhere near Daniel's age. He seemed like a young boy in my eyes, reckless but uncertain, and I kept out of his way as well as I could.

It must be his rare time to check up on all us slaves. I wondered about his sudden, odd appearance as a fear settled in my gut.

"Git away from that gal, boy!" The words erupted from Masta Jeffrey's lips as he approached the two of us. I stole a glance at John, his face set, almost calm-like, but his movements exaggerated in a clearly defiant manner. A frown broke through my blank face as Masta Jeffrey's boot came up and caught John's side.

"Move it!" he hollered, without even glancing over at me. I was frozen in place. Without flinching, John lifted himself up, moving as slowly as possible, and paused where he stood his ground quietly, quite obviously taller than Masta Jeffrey. He stared into the air. Anticipating the worst, I bit my lip in confusion, my fear growing.

"Didn't I say git, boy? Git away an' stay away. Too

much work to be done round here on my father's place for this kinda thing to be goin' on. Go on now."

John turned his back after running his eyes across mine, which held questions I had no answers for. As John walked down the hill, Masta Jeffrey began a loud rant, to me, about complaints his mother had of poor work being done in the house.

"You are a house servant?" he asked, glancing back to see John's form still receding. I nodded but kept my gaze lowered, internally begging for that form to climb back up the hill.

Don't leave me here with him!

Afraid of moving, I sat there waiting for Masta Jeffrey to finish what he had to say. But he was silent, and I knew he was waiting until John had completely disappeared.

"You don't have to be afraid of me, darky. Look at me," Masta Jeffrey demanded. I kept my eyes locked on the grass as if looking up would blind me for the rest of my life. He stepped closer to me. I pulled myself into a smaller ball. My heart was beating rapidly.

"I said look at me," he spit out again. His voice didn't have the same harshness it had when he was talking to John, but it remained forceful. I looked up, afraid that if I didn't, he would lash me with his whip, or . . . worse. He smirked as we made eye contact. I quickly brought my eyes back down.

What does he want?

He bent down toward me. Startled, I tried to scramble backward, but a tree stood in my way. He bent lower.

"I said you don't have to be afraid of me."

How could I not be afraid? In truth, I knew it then. I knew exactly what he wanted. It was the way his eyes dipped over my small frame as if I were a slice of cake on a fancy platter. But the fact was, I didn't want to know. As many times as I'd heard the whispered talk in slave row about young slave women being impregnated by their masters, I knew that just didn't happen on our plantation. Mary and the older woman had been here for years and never had that problem. Somehow I could not bring my mind to latch onto the idea of this happening to me. And yet, that very thought kept appearing, hauntingly, in my mind.

Why doesn't he have his way with me right now? What's he waiting for?

Maybe . . . maybe he wants something else? But what?

He bent nearer.

I was caught—a bird in a net with nowhere to go and no one to help. It was then that the urge to fight awakened in me, and suddenly, I was afraid of what I might do if he bent any closer. I did a dangerous thing, following a stubborn impulse that raced through my bones—those bones that remembered the feeling of having been my own person those many years ago. I lifted my eyes again and looked directly at him.

Take that from me, I dare you.

The feeling, the glance, and the words they signified lasted only a split second, but it seemed to be just enough.

A different sort of look ran through Masta Jeffrey like a

snake, and he took on the manner of a small child caught in a lawless deed. He rocked back slightly but regained his composure in a matter of seconds.

I scrambled up in panic, wondering why I'd allowed myself to let my feelings bleed so easily through my actions. Surely he'd do something now. I had to get away. . . .

I was on my feet, and I turned to run, but his hand came quick and fast around my arm. I tried jerking away, but he tightened his grip.

"You listen close, you better keep your mouth shut about me coming near you. This ain't anybody else's business." The craze and excitement over the undone deed seemed to be melting away. He patted the whip at his belt and loosened his grip on my arm. I pulled free and ran.

"You understand?" he hollered after me.

I wanted to scream back, *No, I don't understand! What do you want? Tell me, so I know!* But I kept running, and wouldn't turn back.

I stumbled down the hill, scrambling when I had to. I couldn't stop; I feared that if I faltered, he'd come storming down the hill behind me. I could have run back to my quarters and grabbed Mary in a tearful hug. But that was the direction I had seen John saunter, and I wanted to be alone. Nearing the woods, I dropped behind some bushes to listen for footsteps behind me. Straining my ears and hearing nothing of the like, I ran to the stream in the woods and cradled myself underneath a tree, trying to distract myself from the fear and confusion I felt inside.

With my finger, I drew the letters of the alphabet on the tree bark, and traced words I needed to hear.

No, I will not cry.

I rested my hand, leaned back against the tree, and sat still and quiet, allowing my thoughts to channel themselves into a low, monotonous hum.

CHAPTER

❧ 8 ❧

IT HAD BEEN TWO WEEKS SINCE MASTA JEFFREY CONFRONTED me, two weeks of anxious thought and nervous work. I tried to bury my fear beneath my composure, but at times, I'd find Mary scrutinizing me. She said nothing, however. I feared that at any time—when I was walking back alone to the cabin at night or cleaning an isolated room in the Big House—Masta Jeffrey would find me and force himself upon me. But that didn't happen.

I hadn't seen John in those two weeks, except for glimpses of him in the fields, where I worked in the afternoons, and when he preached one Sunday as if nothing were amiss. He was not there afterward, and I had no intention of searching. I thought he must've taken what Masta said seriously, and with good reason. It seemed to me that everything that brought me joy was taken from me.

It was Sunday once again, and after an exhausting week I was back at the waterbed. Missus called it a stream, but it was deep like a lake. It had its rushing waters at times and another bank that stretched to the length of about two or three of me. With my rags of clothes hanging on a tree branch close by, I had entered the water, prepared for the chill. The day was unusually cool, considering that we were at least a month and a half shy of the fall season—the picking season. One of the days in this season had snuck up and turned me fourteen before I even noticed.

A group of trees stood directly between the stream and the back of the Big House, giving me the benefit of privacy. The cotton fields stretched out on the opposite side of the Big House. From where I was, I could spot anyone approaching long before they could see or hear me. There were no rules against slipping into the water; none I heard or knew of.

Slowly releasing my hand from the bank, I began kicking and paddling, doing my best to keep my head above the water. By now, I was pretty good at it. I'd discovered the stream when Mary took me with her to gather some herbs and fruit for cooking when I was much younger. A wild apple tree stood at the edge of the water. Masta and Missus had a small orchard of apples, but this tree grew the largest, juiciest apples of all. I remember climbing up to pull some of the fruit down for Mary. I fell into the water and couldn't get back out until Mary, frantic with worry, found a rope to drag me out. I walked away shaken, shivering, and determined to be able to fight my way through the water myself. I resolved to teach myself, and that I did.

On this Sunday, as I made my way toward the bank, I suddenly had the sense that someone was nearby. Moving closer to the bank and lowering myself until my mouth was underwater, I looked around and spotted no one. Assuming my intuition was wrong, I started to turn back.

Then I saw him.

The outline of his tall body was all I needed to tell me that John was there.

How long had he been there? Had he seen my naked body in the water?

I knew he wasn't that close, perhaps not even close enough to recognize that it was me. But a feeling of exposure made me shrink from his sight. His back was against a tree, feet crossed at his ankles, and he was fiddling with an object in his hands.

Carefully inching my way out of the water, I moved out of his line of vision. I grabbed my clothes and quietly struggled into them, still dripping with water. I ran my hands through my short hair to shake away what droplets I could. In order to leave, I had to cross back over to the other side of the bank. Silently, I made my way over, keeping my eyes on John's figure. As much as I wanted to see and talk to him now, I knew I couldn't; Masta Jeffrey's threats rang like bells through my mind. One inch, two inches. I crept along.

Reaching the other side, my heart leaped with both relief and sorrow. I had escaped. But I looked away from my feet too soon, and my left foot clumsily snapped a twig. My whole body went rigid as John's head snapped up. He looked right at me.

He turned my way and I waited there, knowing the best thing I could do was leave, to run. But I didn't, I just stood, holding my breath. Doubts rushed to my head from two Sundays ago.

What does he think of me?

I knew I had to go, but my feet wouldn't budge. Why was my heart always so stubborn against what my mind told me was right? I thought again about leaving, but it was too late. With a few strides, John was standing right in front of me.

"Your heart's speakin' loud today, ain't it?" he said quickly.

I wanted to scold him for reading my thoughts so clearly, as he had done many times before. Without looking at him, I responded softly, "You don't know nothin' 'bout my heart speakin'." I made a motion to leave.

"Don't . . . ," he started, reaching out for my arm. But I held back.

"You know what Masta said," I told him, my eyes set like stone on the ground, resisting the urge to meet his.

"Masta ain't here. He gone off into town," John said quietly. I didn't even have to ask if he was talking about Masta Jeffrey or not—that was the only Masta on both our minds. His voice seemed to coax me into looking up at him, but I wouldn't.

"Sarah."

"What?" I asked as I crossed my arms and stared up at him with the emptiest look I could muster. He held on to it tighter than I expected.

"Did he . . . did he do somethin' to you? He hurt you?" John's voice was heavy, but it seemed patient. I lowered my eyes and said nothing, the fear of confronting Masta Jeffrey again and him carrying out his intentions swelling like powerful winds inside my chest.

"Sarah . . ." But he stopped, waiting, as if the very ground beneath his feet would rumble when I spoke.

I pursed my lips and looked back up at him. "Naw," I said simply.

John gave into the silence that followed for just a moment, before concluding that I was not convincing enough. "You ain't cryin', but I can see tears runnin' through you like a storm." He said the words calmly, but I could hear an unsteadiness lurking beneath them. A wind blew past my face. I heard the water move behind me and a single bird chirp. Everything seemed to be saying, "You better not tell, Sarah, you better not." *Tell what?* I had nothing to tell. Or did my heart know something my head didn't want to accept? And did John know something I didn't want to believe? I itched to get away, to escape confronting the very thing that frightened me when I worked in the Big House, anticipating the worst. But my feet remained firmly planted.

"He didn't do nothin', John."

"He didn't do nothin'? That the whole truth?" He questioned me calmly, but I heard a hint of mockery and anger, whether imagined or not.

"Naw, it wa'an't nothin'. Jus' a lotta talk comin' from him." I paused, then frowned into his eyes.

"But you already know what he wants. . . . You already know. . . ." I frowned deeper. What right did John have to stand here and question me like he was? Was he blaming me for Masta's intentions? It was my turn to show anger, and it leaked from my thoughts, misdirected, and seeped into my words.

"He didn't do nothin', John. That's the truth—ain't nothin' else I can say! But I don't understand. What you gonna do anyhow if Masta come to me askin' fo' what we both know he wanted? You gonna lash him with his own whip?" I was waiting for him to walk away—I wanted him to—to leave me to my solitude with my own fears and my own doubts.

But he stood there battling with the frowns in his cheeks, figuring how to reckon with his own pride, a stripped, bare pride that was being tested, scorned, and drained away, drop by drop, like blood from a slaughtered pig. My heart softened. He was as much a victim as I was, and he seemed wise enough to know that. "John, you really hearin' me? I'm telling you the truth. Don't you believe me?"

He nodded slowly, sadly. "'Course I do."

"Well, you ain't tell Daniel 'bout Masta Jeffrey, have you?" I asked softly, the anger dipping out of sight as quickly as it had come. He shook his head slowly, his eyes distant, staring through me.

"Don't want you to tell Daniel 'bout Masta even talkin' to me on the hill that day. You won't tell 'im?" His gaze was returning back to focus.

"Sarah, there's some things—"

"John, I know Daniel. Don't want him gettin' beat an' killed ova somethin' that ain't even happen. He's different from you. He ain't gonna . . ." But seeing the look that passed over John's face, I hesitated, having second thoughts on whether or not my brother and John were as unalike as I thought. He seemed to be struggling, as if his mask

69

of passiveness wasn't fitting quite well. I dragged my eyes away once again and drew circles in the dirt with my foot.

"I'm scared, John. Think Masta might change his mind an' leave me be? Think he might change an' be like his father, who don't mess with none of us like that?" I searched his eyes for an answer, for security, for a place to hide from reality. But nothing of the like lay there. Instead, I saw the truth that he would never bring himself to say.

Sarah, there's nothing I can do.

But instead of expressing what we both knew was true, John lifted his hand to my face. He paused for a moment and then soon began running his fingers across my cheek, wiping away a water droplet that had escaped from my hair. I let his fingers linger there and brush against my skin until they settled under my chin, lifting it slightly. Then he let go.

"A mind cain't rest on those things too long, Sarah. It's dangerous fo' a man. But I think you oughta know, I bin tryin' to figure somethin' out." His face was changing, masking the pain and replacing it with a sort of lighthearted look.

"Bin thinkin' an' thinkin', then finally figured there ain't nothin' really to figure out," he continued. "I found that I feel different, like I'm gone from the world when you're—"

"John,"—I looked up abruptly—"Masta say stay away. He was serious; you know that. So please, jus' please, there are otha slave gals here. . . ."

"Sarah, not even a fool could scare me outta feelin' what I'm sure I feel." I had nothing to say. His words traveled through the chambers of my heart. I let them roam.

"How you find me out here, John?" I asked him, feeling deeply relieved that he hadn't walked away from me long before, leaving me fearful and alone. "Don't no one know I come down here! I know you wasn't lookin' fo' me!"

"Followed dis right here!" he said, patting his chest.

"What's there?" I asked.

"Somethin' that's been a beatin' an' a listenin' to you fo' a while," he proudly replied. I put my ear close to his chest, then drew back.

"Cain't nothin' be there fo' me," I said with my arms crossed. "You a slave."

"I ain't no slave, Sarah." John's face had fallen as he said this, his voice painted with resentment. I looked at him with fear.

"Don't say that John, you know you's—"

"I said, I ain't no slave!" he bellowed, his voice now stern. "That's all up here, in yo' mind! Them folk call demselves Masta call us slaves, but only those who think they slaves is slaves. I ain't no slave. My mind don't belong to nobody."

I had never heard that before. Those words sparked something within me I had never felt. I found myself swimming in a world of thought, a world of imagination, a world of freedom I longed for, a longing that usually kept itself hidden out of fear. Now, with John standing right here, saying these words to me, I felt this longing of mine dancing on my face, clear as day.

"Well, I think maybe . . . maybe I ain't gotta be no slave either," I said, looking at him mischievously.

John laughed, trying to drown out the carriage wheels in the distance. Masta was back, and with that realization, many other facts came to me like a slap in the face. We were slaves. Our lives were worthless, built only to serve our white masters. Our days were rationed for them and them alone. There was no us.

The laughter ceased, and I silently left his side. He stood there for a moment longer, as if he held a treasure in his hand that kept falling through his fingers. Then he departed, and we slipped away from each other like one soul split in two.

CHAPTER

❧ 9 ❧

THE DAY WAS A HOT ONE, AND THE SWEAT TRICKLED DOWN MY forehead even before I could walk a half a mile from the Big House. Usually I had both of Missus's children for this routine stroll, but this morning, only young Missus Jane walked by my side. I was a bit glad; with her brother near her, the two would commence to racing down the road with me in hot pursuit, and they'd be proclaiming, "We gonna be late, Sarah, if you don't hurry up!"

The first few weeks after the incident with Masta Jeffrey, I lived in fear when I neared the Big House. But the days trickled into weeks, and I had no confrontations with Masta's son, not even a sign that Masta Jeffrey had ill intentions. So, soon enough, the storm passed. I finally grew to believe that for whatever reason, he had left me alone for good.

On this day, as we neared the road, I saw a figure pass, his round face lowered and his shoulders slightly drooped. He drifted past me without a word. It was the first time I had seen Daniel since he and Tucker had left to accompany Masta and his son on a long-distance trip. They had been gone for nearly a week and a half, and I had counted the days until their return.

I looked back at him, my eyebrows raised in question. *What was wrong with my brother?*

"Daniel," I said softly, keeping the corner of my eye on young Missus Jane, who continued on without me, "you all right?" He turned his head, eyes piercing me like two arrows. His glance was quick, and his nod was cordial, but the expression in his eyes turned my skin cold. There was an anger there that he immediately erased, then a lingering sadness. He turned away before I could say anything more, slyly stealing my heart as he went and setting it in his pocket.

I walked on, talking to young Missus Jane as she wished, but my thoughts swirled around my brother. We walked a few miles to a small, white wooden house. It was here that I was ordered to take young Missus Jane and young Masta Bernard. About eight children met five days a week in this tiny schoolroom.

Missus had decided to start them out this school year with a private instructor. She wanted to ensure the "best education possible." I'd caught pieces of conversation between Masta and Missus about having young Missus Jane attend lessons with her brother. Females only went so far in schooling, and Masta didn't want to invest money unnecessarily on her behalf. Missus seemed to have different plans for her daughter, however, and even though she wouldn't make them plain, she convinced her husband to keep young Missus Jane with her brother for the time being.

When we reached the door, young Missus Jane knocked

and slipped inside before anyone had come to open it. Without another word to me, she shut me out, leaving me standing on the step.

Heading a mile or so farther up the road, I neared a small gathering of slave children who were sitting around an older man. Seeing me approach, the old man nodded and fell straight into telling a story to the gathered crowd.

"I done knowed Liza was gone. Knew it befo' I felt de hushed silence hangin' 'mong slave row. Knew it befo' word was raised 'bout it. It was de way blurry images done formed in my mind's eyes, in my dreams dat night befo'. It was de feelin' my dream done gaved me. It was de way de wind rush thru my door, washin' my sleepy face. It was de way de mornin' birds sang with dat partic'lar melody. Dey knewed ha fate like I did. We alls knewed dat Liza was gone."

"Whatchya mean, 'Gone,' Uncle Bobby?" a small boy asked.

"Well, you wait, now. You ain't even heard 'bout da woman an' ha life yet."

"Tell us, then, Uncle Bobby!"

I stood leaning against the side of the man's quarters. Wrinkles covered the face and hands of this old man, Uncle Bobby. He was too old to work the land his master owned and was therefore left by his Master to do nothing more than waste away with time. The ten or so children who'd gathered about him were, on the other hand, too young to work. Most of them grasped small clay balls in their hands, signifying the play that had been suspended so they could hear Uncle Bobby's short story of the day. I had stumbled upon them one day while waiting for the Missus's children to finish their learning, and I'd been coming back ever since to listen to the old man's tales.

"Well, she was a tattle, she was. House hand that liked da fancy dings her Mizzuz done give ha fo' tellin' on folks an' makin' up bad stories to get dem slaves in trouble. Den on Christmas day the year she was all growed up, done walked outside wit all dem fancy stuff, even had fancy shoes! An . . . an . . ."

"An' what?" the children squealed. Uncle Bobby put his hands on his small hips, pausing for dramatic effect.

"Well," he said, throwing his seated legs out farther, "big ole clap a' lightnin' came an' strike ha!" His eyes bulged and his arms imitated heaven unleashing its wrath. The children, who had yelped with the scare, started giggling.

"Ain't no such thing happen!"

"Sho' did!" Uncle Bobby said with such a serious nod that the children quickly grew quiet.

"Lightnin' really strike her dead, Uncle Bobby?" He nodded.

"Well, I ain't neva gonna be like dat!"

I turned to head back up the road, chuckling at Uncle Bobby's story. As I walked along, searching for wild flowers for Mary, I heard someone calling my name. I turned to see Tucker.

"Hey, Tucker. Didn't notice you comin' up." I walked over to where he had stopped, just off of the road. I eyed him closely, searching for anything in his face that imitated the distress I saw in Daniel's eyes. There was nothing there that compared.

"How was the trip, Tucker?" I asked him, my anxious eyes still searching.

"Masta had us travelin' all day an' all night!" he said, wiping his brow.

"An' y'all ain't run into no trouble?"

"Well, naw," he said, gazing up at the sky as if remembering, "wa'an't nothin' unusual. Masta wa'an't in good spirits. Havin' some trouble wit his money. An', well . . ."

"What?" I asked.

"Well, we done seed a lotta sellin', me an' yo' brotha." He frowned. "Wa'an't no pretty sight." I sighed, seeing that Tucker didn't know what had come over my brother.

"Watchya this fa' from Masta's place fo'?" he asked, smiling at me.

"I was jus' gonna ask you the same thing, Tucker."

"Well, I sho' wa'an't sneakin' visits to hear that storyteller over this way."

I laughed. "Ain't sneakin' nowheres! I got to take Missus's children—you know young Missus Jane an' young Masta Bernard?"

He nodded.

"Well, Missus got them wit some tutor round here, an' I bin tole to get them there five good days a week."

"Ain't you s'pose to be wit them?" he asked, rubbing his beard with his thumb and forefinger. "That tutor must be two miles down the road from here!"

I bit my lower lip, and my eyes cut over to the old storyteller in the distance, then back to Tucker. "Wouldn't let me stay inside and, well"—a sly smile slid on my face—"that tutor saw me peekin' in on them an' tole me to stay away durin' their lessons." Tucker gave a whistling sound and shook his head.

"Yes, Tucker, you right. I didn't have no business up there. But cain't do nothin' 'bout that now. But what you up here fo'? You seem to be headin' down to the city!"

He put his hand on my shoulder, his eyes growing wide. "Masta gonna let me hire myself out! Gonna work fo' a blacksmith in town."

"Didn't think they did that much round here, Tucker," I said.

"It ain't that uncommon, an' see," he explained and said while leaning in closer, "I'se bin workin' wit him already. Late nights, sneakin' out there, then returnin' befo' dawn."

"How you sleep, then, Tucker!" I said with an excited whisper, considering how big a risk he had been taking. He shrugged his shoulders.

"Reckon money's betta than sleep. On our trip, we ran into the man, an' he done act like he ain't neva seen me befo' an' spoke to Masta on my behalf. They's business partners or somethin', an' Masta jus' up'n agreed!" he said with a final, satisfied nod.

"Thing is," he continued, "I can't earn my money no more. Gotta give it all to Masta. But at least I'll be getting away from this place from time to time, an' at least I ain't gotta sneak round to do it. I'm happy 'bout it."

"Well, that's good fo' ya, Tucker," I said, as he backed away.

"Sho' is!" he said, grinning. "Now I gotsta be gettin' on."

I waved Tucker off and walked on toward the schoolhouse, lost deep in thought.

The door to the schoolhouse opened some five minutes after I reached it. I watched in silence as the children skipped out of the room, one by one. Missus's children were usually the first ones out the door, but today I watched as the teacher, tall and slim, held young Missus Jane back until the rest of the children had filed out. Young Missus Jane's face was flushed deep red and grew even darker as the teacher bent over her to share a word or two. I walked closer to the building as the door shut, and young Missus Jane stood sullen-faced on the steps. She stared at the door for a few seconds, then turned to see where I was. Finding me with her eyes, she silently came to my side.

Heading back with young Missus Jane, I couldn't help but notice that all the enthusiasm had gone from her small body. She took her finger and slipped it in her mouth.

"Young Missus Jane, now, I think you'se too old to be suckin' on your finger like that." My words had barely tumbled out before she pulled her wet finger from her mouth and slipped her hand into mine.

"I got in trouble today," she said simply, squeezing my hand with hers.

My body had gone rigid at first, but then it melted, piece by piece, into the innocence of her gesture.

"Everybody do somethin' wrong sometimes. It's all right," I said to her softly. I glanced down at young Missus Jane's face and saw that blush in her cheeks was slowly seeping away. What I saw was a child, a little girl seeking to play and please and imitate what she saw around her.

I couldn't identify the feeling that raced through my bones. It wasn't one of affection, or love of any particular kind. It was, rather, a feeling of empathy, which lingered even after, as we approached the plantation, she yanked her hand from mine and fell into a different role. But even as her little feet thumped the earth while she ran to meet her waiting mother at the door, and as she screamed back an order that I should bring her something cold to drink, I remembered her small fingers seeking out my own hand for comfort. A small smile curled onto my lips.

CHAPTER

❧ 10 ❧

IT WASN'T UNTIL A FEW NIGHTS LATER THAT I FOUND THE TIME to talk with my brother. In the dark one night, as I walked back toward the cabin, I saw him headed off in the direction of his workplace, not five minutes from the fields.

Mary had returned to the cabin quite a while before, so I poked my face around the door to tell her where I was headed, gobbled down what little food she slipped into my palm, and headed to the place I knew Daniel would be.

I approached him and saw him with his tools laying about, a broken wooden chair leaning against his leg.

"Daniel, . . . it's late," I said quietly. Thinking he hadn't heard me, I called him again, but he didn't respond. "Daniel, you bin quiet lately—look angry a lot of the time. I'd feel better if I knew what it is makin' you act this way."

"Don't feel like talkin' right now," he responded, his attention fixed on his work. I took a deep breath and blew it all out at once. He wouldn't even look up to blink at me.

"Well, I'ma sit right here"—I found a spot on the ground in front of my brother—"and keep my sleepy eyes open if I have to through the night till you talk."

Daniel's face didn't change until, some moments later,

he looked up as if he expected me to be gone. "You still here," he said just as I began to doubt that he'd speak to me at all. I nodded over at him.

"Want you to promise me somethin'," he said, looking back down at his work.

"What's that?"

"Sarah"—he looked up again—"Sarah, promise me if Masta Jeffrey gets near you, you tell me." He stared into my eyes with a stern, unyielding look. I almost frowned, wondering if he knew about the incident on the hill those many weeks ago. The fear that had nearly subsided, for Masta Jeffrey hadn't spoken to me since, came rushing back as Daniel mentioned him.

"Daniel, I don't understand. What's Masta Jeffrey got to do with anything?" He was silent for a moment.

"I don't know. Jus' got this bad feelin' 'bout him."

"He do somethin' you ain't like?" I asked, trying to coax a confession that he knew about the hill. But he shook his head.

"Naw, jus' got that feelin'."

He doesn't know.

My heartbeat slowed with a bit of relief. If Daniel found out what Masta's son had said to me, I feared what his reaction would be. I didn't know how families dealt with the rape of their women—and I didn't want to find out. Perhaps if Daniel was bold enough to confront Masta Jeffrey, then Masta Jeffrey would seek me out for revenge! Perhaps he'd ask his father to sell Daniel, or beat one of us in the process. My heart was not willing to risk letting

Daniel know anything about the incident and Masta Jeffrey's intentions, even though they seemed to have died away. Daniel's anger seemed to flow too freely at times. He usually exercised the necessary restraint, but there were some things he'd risk his own life for.

I was glad he didn't know.

"Daniel, this got somethin' to do with you an' Tucker bein' gone all them days? What happened up in town?" Still shaking his head, he gazed over my shoulder into the black night, until he collected himself again.

"I've seen folks sold so many a times," he said with a hollow voice, "but never seen nothin' like this, Sarah. Never."

"Like what, Daniel?" I asked. I waited his silence out, my body sagging with exhaustion. When he brought his eyes to mine for a moment, the tears that had appeared for a brief moment disappeared from them.

"It touched me deep down somewheres, Sarah, an' won't seem to go away."

"What was it, Daniel?"

"Friend of Masta's wagon broke down. Masta told me to take the man on to town to do his business. Made Masta Jeffrey ride wit us. Skinny man Masta's friend was, with dark spots under his eyes an' evil barks in his voice. Knew I hated him the minute I sawed him . . ."

"Don't say that, Daniel."

"I hated him, I tell you." Daniel's eyes burned.

"Name was Knocks, an' he dragged a slave woman an' her son out to the wagon. He had bound her up an' put her in the back wit Masta Jeffrey. Her son, he say his name was

Lil' Lou, sat 'tween me an' Masta's friend. Knocks had tole her that Lil' Lou was gonna be sol' with her, jus' so she'd hush. But I knew it wa'n't the truth, jus' knew it every time I looked ova at that lil' boy. That boy jus' sat there, quiet, bouncin' with every ditch in the road. When we got there, to the sellin' block, Knocks dragged her up there in front of all those folk. She wa'n't smilin', naw, but she looked at ease 'cause her son was standin' next to her." Daniel brushed both hands up across his face and over his hair.

"Then the biddin' began. This man in the gatherin' crowd wanna buy her. Knocks put chains round her arms. Then some otha man up there sayin' he could use some young hands, an' they starts biddin' fo' that young lil' boy. There was no way they was gonna stay together, that mama an' lil' boy." He took another breath before he continued.

"That's when I sawed her face, horror drippin' from her eyes. She was starin' at Knocks as if she done seen a ghost. That's when things got bad, Sarah. They got . . . they got bad. She fell to her knees, right in front of Knocks, yellin' an' demandin' that he give her that child. He kicked her—his shoe went right in her face. Then he turned an' 'pologized to her new masta. But she wa'n't done. Shoulda laid there. Shoulda jus' laid there! But naw, naw." He was glaring at the memory.

"When she dragged herself up, face covered in blood, she say soft at first somethin' 'bout that lil' boy bein' Masta's baby. I heard it, 'cause I was lookin' straight at her like there wa'ant no one else there. I sat there feelin' hell breathin' close on my neck. She started poundin' near Masta's feet wit her fist an' screamin, 'You gave 'im to me Masta, why you sellin' yo' own chile.' His own, Sarah . . ." He stopped, and leaned his forehead on his palms. I sat with my face in my hands.

"Daniel, you don't hafta . . ." I began, my voice cracking, but he hardly heard me.

"Knocks was red in the face—every soul knew he was mad. An' that woman just kept screamin' those terrible screams. I turned away from the block fo' respect, an' my eyes ran across Masta Jeffrey's face."

He stopped short and looked fixedly at me.

"Sarah, I felt so dangerous sittin' there near him in the wagon, an' I think he knew it. He sittin' there breathin' heavy, and I think he was scared, but it didn't matta to me. Thought of you, thought of Mama, thought of that woman on that block, an' felt that wrongdoing swimmin' through Masta Jeffrey—jus' felt it as clear as day. Anger started bubblin' up. Cain't explain how it was when we was drivin' back. Some kinda terrible anger came a rumblin' up thru me an' bleedin' thru my breath. Couldn't even look at the two of 'em. Prayed to God Knocks wouldn't say nothin'. Prayed the devil wouldn't ask me nothin', wouldn't even move, fo' I don't think I would've controlled myself."

"Daniel, it's all right," I said softly. He was pinching his chin with his fingers, all the muscles in his face fighting against each other, searching for a little peace. The night was still and the silence made it even more so. Daniel broke it with a whisper.

"Sarah, you tell me, you hear? Tell me 'bout Masta

Jeffrey." I said nothing. Daniel stood up after a long while and lent me his hand. I took it, letting him help me up, and we walked slowly back to our quarters. The intensity of the moment stayed behind, burying itself where we had sat.

"You see Tucker lately?" he asked me.

"Ya."

"He tell you what he bin up to?"

"Sure," I began, dragging my feet with fatigue. "He tole me 'bout bein' hired out or somethin'."

"Ya, that's it," Daniel said.

"Somethin' special 'bout it?" I asked, wondering if he was using the conversation to take his mind off the pain-filled images in his head.

"Well, Sarah, there's some blacks that live round this part of Tennessee, free folks. Ain't many of 'em, an' them whites hate 'em, but they here. When slave folks get hired out, they make it easier fo' themselves to start blendin' in wit them freed folks, becomin' part of their organizations an' all."

"So you sayin' he's part of an' organization or somethin'?"

Daniel laughed. "Well, ya—somethin' like that. It's nothin' big. Tucker got a good mind on him, though. He didn't jus' hire himself out fo' the money."

"So what you sayin', Daniel? Somethin' important 'bout them groups?" I asked, feeling as if there was a message hiding beneath his words.

"Well, some of them groups—church groups an' things—guess you could say they give folks, slaves, hope."

"Daniel, I don't understand . . ."

He sighed, then pursed his lips. "Sarah, you know me. I'm jus'"—he shrugged his shoulders, and continued—"I'm jus' lookin' fo' somethin' else to think of. Somethin' of hope, you know? Somethin' that'll . . . help me escape it all." The silence swelled too large for me to keep quiet.

"Escape that burnin' feelin' on the inside, you mean, Daniel? That's what you mean, right?" I asked him, searching his face carefully. He licked his lips and placed his hand on my shoulder but said nothing.

"Daniel?" I asked, needing an answer.

"Yes, Sarah, that's 'xactly what I mean."

A woman's face flashed before me plainly, but I couldn't see it with clarity. The horror that had dripped from her eyes had come to life and built a mask for her to glue to her face. I glanced around and noticed ghosts that stood about—cold, silent, watching. The sky darkened above our heads and drenched the rest of us with rain. But not her: she stood dry, tall, proud, on that auction block. She was done asking, yelling, and pleading for her child. The woman had broken right out of her chains, snatched her son from the arms of her masters, and held him by his ankles, upside down. I heard words spilling from her, though her lips didn't move at all.

You ain't gonna have 'im. You ain't gonna take an' break an' kill this child befo' he even live decently. I don't care what otha blood he got runnin' through his veins, he's my child. An' if I cain't have 'im, the only one who will's gonna be my God.

I screamed, but a hand covered my mouth and a ghost

figure with no face whispered in my ear.

Sarah, don't you remember the auction block?

The images fell away quickly, and just as suddenly, I was somewhere else, skipping about arm in arm with a small boy who stood three or four inches taller than I was. We played beneath the glaring sun, hopped around trees, built structures in the soil, waded in the clear waters, until we were pulled without warning down, down, down through these waters and landed facedown in a strange cold new world.

A thousand feet dragged heavily against the ground. There were many sad faces—did they mirror my own? I fell into step with the weary bodies. Unfamiliar sounds, pale faces . . . I longed for nothing but my mother's voice and touch.

Another ghost whispered, *Sarah, you have got to remember the auction block!*

I saw a platform, a whip, and more of those monster-men.

Glistening black bodies were herded like cattle; freezing water splashed over bareness; oil smacked on breasts and backs with fingers that liked to roam . . .

I sat in the crowd, cross-legged, a small wooden toy in my lap.

Madam, would you be so kind as to lean your umbrella just a little bit this way, please? The sun is rather harsh today, and I'd like to feel quite comfortable, watching this spectacle. . . ."

Numbers two, five, and eleven were displayed before the crowd. Hands pulled lips apart to inspect teeth; fingers gripped muscles to place a price on able-bodied pieces of merchandise; eyes roamed up, down, front, back, determining who was in her prime for breeding.

Anger raged through my body like a wild animal. I ran to the platform, small hands pushing, small fists beating and beating at that monster-man. The inspector's face abruptly snapped around, and he tossed my small body back into the lifeless crowd. His eyes settled on mine—the look of a master who knew how dangerous he could be. I turned away from Masta Jeffrey then, screaming, and ran headfirst into another whispering ghost.

Perhaps now *you remember the auction block.*

The small wooden toy I had been grasping in my tiny fingers leaped from my hands, and grew until it stood eye to eye with me. It turned to flesh and bone, staring with my mother's eyes with features that mocked my own. The face was Sentwaki's, and it bore the look of calm, distracted patience. He brought a finger slowly up and pointed to his shoulder, holding tightly to my gaze.

Branded—he had been branded. Searing, smoking metal pressed into flesh. The smell filled my nose, a nauseating stench. Four letters had been carved into his skin, though he sat, as always, on his gray cloud. A tear slipped from my eyes. I was afraid to read the word.

Brother, where has all your laughter gone to?
Read it.
Brother, why are we in this place, so far from home?
Read it.
Brother, I don't want to be here. Take me back to Mathee, to Mama Mijiza . . .

Masta Jeffrey screamed in my ear, taunting with a whip held high overhead and demanding, *Read it, read it. I dare you, read it!*

S-O-L-D. The letters bounced past my eyes and chilled my spine.

Sentwaki, SOLD.

Ayanna, think of me. I'll think of you.

Sentwaki, brother, what do you mean? You're not leaving me, are you?

Yes, Sarah, that's exactly what I mean.

I stared after his body until the last glimmer of his shiny black skin faded into the distance, though I felt his spirit linger a bit longer, felt it mark the place he'd sat when he had seen the glow in my eyes for the last time.

I cried, my teardrops becoming rivers that carried him farther and farther away.

"Sarah. Sarah, honey, wake up." Mary was kneeling above me with tired eyes. She handed me a cloth and let me rub it across my wet face. My heart was wrapped tightly, and the tension I felt made my eyes spill more tears.

"Don't like 'em at all, Mary, not at all."

She sighed, climbing back into her own sleeping spot. "I know, chile. Hope you good an' out of that one. You still got some time to rest yet. Try to get some real sleep." I sank down beneath the rags that lay across my bed, trying hard to push away all the pieces of that dream my consciousness held on to.

CHAPTER

❧ 11 ❧

I DIDN'T ACKNOWLEDGE HIM WHEN I SAW HIM WALK BY IN the fields; it wasn't that way. Fieldwork was fieldwork, hard enough without any distractions. But the smile I had glimpsed in the corner of John's eye sat with me through the afternoon and the next day.

The air smelled fresh from rain that Saturday evening when I lay behind the cabin, remembering lessons I had overheard at the schoolhouse. After I was prevented from peeking through the window, I had found another way of listening in on some of the conversations that went on inside. There was a particular spot I'd stand at where, if I listened closely, the words from inside the schoolhouse would jump out at me and into my waiting, excited ears.

That evening, I spelled out words in the soil with a stick, putting them together and tearing them apart as I remembered.

"What you doin'?"

I jumped, quickly looking up to see John. I opened my mouth to speak, but words escaped his before I could succeed.

"Find me, wouldya?" he asked. With that, he disappeared

around the side of the cabin. I laughed and rose from the ground. But when I rounded the corner, he was nowhere in sight.

"John—" I stopped quickly as I saw him disappearing behind some trees a ways away from the cabin.

I followed for a good few minutes, pulling back branches and whispering his name. Then, coming upon a tall tree, I found him leaning against it.

"Tell me I ain't crazy chasin' you out here," I said, walking around to face him and hiding my smile.

"Here, blow on this," he said, holding a wooden object out to me. I grabbed it and sat next to him, blowing in it like he said. It made the strangest whistling sound. John smiled at my laughter.

"So, what was it you was doin' out there?" he asked.

I looked up, seriousness bathing my face.

"Wasn't nothing," I said simply after a few seconds of considering. I tried to turn my full attention back to the strange gift. He said nothing, but out of the corner of my eye, I saw him curl his lips against one another, waiting. I kept my mouth sealed as long as I could, stubborn against his silence, but finally, I relented. He knew the power of his silence, and he used it well.

"Can I trust you, John?" I asked, testing how ready my own heart was to share the fact that I was teaching myself to read and write. John leaned back, holding my gaze. A shadow seemed to pass over his eyes.

"John?" I asked again, waiting for his gaze to turn into an answer on his lips.

"I saw you, Sarah. I saw that look in yo' eyes an' knew you befo' I even knew yo' name. He was draggin' you out there. I coulda sworn it was me, that day, unda that whip." My cheeks flushed with color.

"Ain' neva seen nothin' like that look—nothin' like it. You were hurtin' befo' he even laid that whip on your skin. You spoke to me, that day. Said, by the grace of God, nobody'd break yo' spirit an' rip from yo' soul any dreams that was born there." I bit my lip.

"Now, you ask if you can trust me, an' I say, I'd sacrifice every piece've me befo' I eva see any person on this earth bring out that look in yo' eyes agin." I heard his words but locked them away in my mind. They were so real, they scared me. Instead of responding, I picked up one of his hands and asked him to hold it open. But he didn't do so; a slight frown appeared on his brow. I could see him concentrating, trying to form a decent question that matched his thoughts.

"Sarah . . ."

"Ya?"

"Ain't nobody bin . . . bin tryin' to break your spirit?"

I knew already what had crossed his mind.

"John," I said softly, looking into his eyes. He pursed his lips. "Don't think we should talk 'bout that, John."

"Sarah . . ."

"John," I responded softly, trying to coax him into letting his thoughts about Masta Jeffrey go for the moment. He looked away, shaking his head, and brought a patient face back around to me.

"All right. I ain't tryin' to talk of nothin' you don't wanna, Sarah. I won't ask again. I jus' . . ." I shook my head, then lifted his hand again.

"Nothin', John. Hasn't spoken to me or done nothin'. Now you gonna let me show you?" He stared at our hands for a moment, brushing his thumb against mine, and eventually opened up his palm. His eyes looked apologetic.

"Show me." With my finger, I traced the letters of his name in his palm, watching his face while I did. A smile was drifting out from behind the clouds of his pride.

"Bin teachin' myself to read, John," I whispered to him. His head moved back and forth, and he sat grinning.

"Can you grin any wider?" I asked him. He laughed this time.

"Naw, that's jus' . . . it's a good thing, a real good thing. Jus' hope you ain' goin' round tellin' folks . . ."

"John," I said, placing a finger on his lips to quiet him, "don't no one know. I ain't no fool."

"No, you ain't," he said. Both of us jumped when we heard a rustling nearby, then turned to see a field hand walking by us. He nodded in recognition without smiling and continued on his way.

That jolted me back to reality. "I best be gettin' on now," I said, and I stood up quickly, a bit fearful at the fact that I had so easily lost myself in a different world. John smiled softly and nodded, allowing his eyes to settle back on the wood and his carving tools that lay beside him.

CHAPTER

❧ 12 ❧

THE FIRST WEEK OF OCTOBER DRAGGED SLOWLY BY, AND WITH it came an inner battle with my learning. At this point, I had learned to read and write probably half as well as Masta Charles's little children, and that was no easy task. There was no teacher, only me and the lessons I picked up from the young ones. Every night, before I went to bed, I would take out a small section of newspaper that I had pulled from the garbage in the Big House and hidden under a loose floorboard beneath my pallet. It was on these sheets of newspaper that I'd draw imaginary letters with my finger, or with a stick, so that I could practice my writing. I'd even try picking through the words, reading what I could, and storing things I didn't understand for later.

Then, in passing one evening, I heard of a slave woman caught writing a letter to another plantation. I didn't know who it was she was writing to, or what the letter was about, but her master was deeply angered in it all and sold her far down south. What was it that had caused her master to sell her like this? Was it the mere fact that she had gotten educated in hiding? This concern stood out, and because of it, the news hit me with a dreariness I couldn't find the energy to rid myself of.

What, really, does this education mean to me? Is it worth the risk?

The weather turned sullen and gray and my thoughts in the fields dragged me to a place deep inside where the sunshine couldn't have reached anyway, a place where dreams were crushed beneath the soles of a heaven I could not claim—a heaven where I had the basic right to be and act and live as a human being. I felt suspended deep inside that place, when I woke in the mornings and when I walked into the Big House. The feeling remained through the children's bickering and reviewing of lessons at home. I stopped paying attention.

I felt miserable, and perhaps God knew so. He brought down sheets of rain that lasted an entire week. Thunder shook the sky and wrung out any sunshine in our hearts. And at night, the lightning scared many out of sleeping. I couldn't find John to talk to; Daniel and Mary didn't know about me learning. There wasn't anybody to convince me to keep going. So I succumbed to my doubts.

It was in that manner, running from the demons and images my mind was creating, that I ran into Daniel one morning as he was trudging back from the parked wagon. The storm was coming to an end, and a strange gift that came to me unexpectedly renewed my passion.

"Hey, Daniel," I said. "D'you hear what happened to that woman, the one try to educate herself?" He nodded, then shook his head, leaning in so I could hear his whisper.

"Bet that ain't even stopped her, neither. Hard thing to jus' up'n stop, learnin' is." An almost invisible smile caught the edge of his lips as his eyes danced around to make sure no one was close by.

"You know what I'd give to learn?" he asked, capturing the thoughts that had been running through his head, and placing them on his lips. I looked at him closely, wondering if he was educating himself, too. But his face showed no signs. I listened quietly.

"There's places you can go from this hell, Sarah. I've seen it in the city," he continued, his eyes wide and bright.

"What you mean?" I asked him, puzzled. He shrugged.

"Guess I'm just talkin'. But you remember that one day you asked me 'bout escapin' that burnin' feelin'?" he asked. I nodded. "Well, I met some folks know how to read an' write. An' I can tell, jus' a talkin' wit them, that learnin' sho' is one way to escape. Don't you think?"

"I think you talkin' a little loud fo' what you sayin'. An' all that's dangerous. Why even take them risks? What good does a little bit of learnin' do?"

Daniel looked over at me as if I were silly, a look that began to unwind the tight knots of doubts and tension within. "And that's not a risk worth its dangers, Sarah?" I grew aware of the noise our feet were making in the cold mud. I shrugged.

"Don't rightly know."

He laughed and waved me away, walking off to do his day's work—a day empty of the excitement of learning. I stared after my brother with wonder. Maybe learning was what I was supposed to do—what I was meant to do—if not for me, then for those who couldn't quite reach it.

The melancholy feelings and fear drained away from my spirit and sulked around like a sad shadow that knew it didn't have long to stay. Then, a new passion touched me somewhere in my spirit. Beneath my fears, beyond my doubts, that passion began to grow within me larger than before, a passion to learn I never thought I'd possess. I made a promise to myself: I would never give learning up.

CHAPTER

❧ 13 ❧

THE TWO OF US WALKED OUT THE FRONT DOOR. THE WOMAN I followed was some years older than me, and had a wise air to her. Her name was Zoey; she was a house servant—obedient, very tolerant, and tactful, quite different from me. She seemed to accept her lot in life without many reservations. I liked her well enough, however.

In my hands, stacked almost higher than I could handle, was a bundle of white sheets and clothes from the house. I walked behind Zoey, trying to keep her bobbing hair, braided straight down her back, in my sight.

"Zoey, slow down!" I demanded. She had a neatly wrapped bundle set atop of her head. With one hand holding the load, she was swinging her small hips back and forth as if hearing the sound of music, as she had seen me do before. She glanced back at me but kept her pace.

"Slow down, I say, 'less you wanna take my load!" I said to her. She slowed until her strides fell in with mine.

"Wish you'd hurry up," she said with more excitement than she mustered most days. "Don't you know what we in fo' today?"

"What you mean?"

"You ain't heard them yet, up at the Big House? It's Octoba 18."

I nodded, remembering. It was the day Masta got his plot of land—the day we were made slaves on his plantation.

"Why is it he always celebrate that day, you think?"

Zoey shrugged. "Don't know, but it don't matta to me. You know they always celebrate, an' they give us good an' fine food fo' dinner when they do."

There were a few holidays in the year that Masta and his family celebrated, and October 18 was one of them. For Christmas and New Year's, he and Missus would give us a resting period that lasted about a week after Christmas. That period offered me space to think. It was my relief.

Later that October day, I stood by Mary as she handed me some pots of food to take out for our feast. There were greens, cornbread, and bacon—bacon! I let the smell rise up and seep into my waiting nostrils, and shut my eyes for a moment with satisfaction. I looked over at Mary with a small smile.

"Look at this food, Mary!"

She chuckled at me. "Ya, and got y'all a surprise fo' later, too."

"What is it?" I asked with wide eyes.

"Said I got you a surprise. Ain't gonna tell you now what it is. You go on an' take that food down to Daniel an' the othas. I'll bring it with me lata."

"All right, well, let me help you at the sink, Mary," I said, setting down the food.

"Naw you won't. Go on wit that food . . ." Mary's

words trailed off as Missus's form appeared before us in the doorway. Naturally, I washed all expression from my face.

"You, girl," she said, pointing at me, "I'm going to take you out of those fields. You'll stay with the girls and Bernard, as usual, but you'll be with them through the whole day." I opened my mouth slightly to politely object, but Mary was shaking her head no with the slightest movements, so I simply nodded. As hard as fieldwork was, having the air and the space to think was my relief. I needed that, and Missus was stealing it away from me.

"Good. They seem to have taken a liking to you. I'll put a blanket on the floor near Jane's bed. You'll be staying in the girls' room."

"Sorry, ma'am?" Surely she didn't mean to say I was sleeping in the Big House? I looked over at Mary, but she acted as if nothing was happening.

Back when I first started working in the house, Mary told me she thought it would be good if Missus would let me stay in the house. Over the months, she stopped mentioning it, but I feared she still felt the same way. Perhaps, even, it was she who had asked Missus to let me stay in the house.

"What do you mean, 'sorry'?" Missus asked, catching my attention once more. "Can you not understand me? I said you'll be staying in my girls' room."

"Yes, but ma'am, I can't . . . I can't do that."

"Excuse me?" she said, taking a dangerous step farther into the room. "You do what I say!" she continued, her voice rising. She waited to see if I was bold enough to say anything more. A small fear had settled in my chest. I couldn't sleep in the Big House, so close to the heart of where our struggles lay. I couldn't sleep there, so near to the danger that had seemed to disappear over the months but that sat in the back of my mind in the form of Masta Jeffrey. How could I make her see that I could not stay there? I didn't know, but I had to try.

"Missus, I done everything you say, I listen closely, an' try so hard to do things like I'se s'pose to"—I paused, peeking at her stony face—"but . . . but . . . I cain't stay." She took two steps toward me and raised her hand to my face, but Mary stepped from the sink before Missus could strike. My breath was short, and looked fearfully at Mary. What would she say? Maybe she'd tell Missus that I'd love to stay, I was just talking a little out of my mind just then. Maybe she'd say I was a little scared at the moment, but after a day or so, I'd be excited to stay there. Instead, she said something quite different.

"Missus, ma'am, don't strike ha."

Missus turned to Mary with a different sort of look and hints of respect sitting in her eyes. "You hear her talking against me like that. She deserves a nice beat!" Missus said, waving her hand.

"Naw, ma'am, you don't undastand what she tryin' to tell ya. She have sleepin' spells, this one do," Mary explained, looking over at me. Her eyes told me to stay silent. "Wake up sometime jus' a yellin'. Have them bad dreams, she do. Don't happen all the time, but when them fits come on ha, she cain't help it, ma'am." I stood quiet, wondering if Mary knew the real dangers she was saving me from. Mary finished, and Missus looked over at me, her eyes running up, over, and through me to see if she could find any flaw in Mary's explanation. After a minute or so, her eyebrows curved down in a frown. She had found none.

"Would it be best she come earlier fo' they wake an' stay wit them till they's fall asleep?" Mary pushed. She was treading dangerous ground. Missus sighed heavily.

"Very well." Only then did she lower her hand.

"That's what'll have to do. Can't have a crazy servant waking up this whole house at night. My husband, Charles, wouldn't stand it. You come earlier, and make sure they fall asleep at night. But"—she looked at Mary for reassurance—"I don't want you sleeping here nights." With that, she left. I waited until the sound of her light step on the staircase died away. I turned to Mary.

"Mary—"

She walked over to the food I had set down, and placed it back in my hands. "Nothin' mo', Sarah. Take these on down there." She turned back to the sink and fell into a deep silence that forced me out of the room. I whispered a quick thank-you before I left the kitchen.

When I got outside, a good-size group of folks had gathered to eat. Their laughter and good spirits pulled my mind out of pondering why Mary had had such a strong change of heart. Instead, I busied myself with setting out the food and cider and handing out fair rations. I collapsed on the ground, afterward, to eat my own meal. A familiar voice caught my attention.

"Go on, set down ova here." An older lady was clasping John's arm, and the two of them were making their way over to the seated group. Another young man hopped up and helped John seat her as she welcomed all the greetings.

Looking up at me, she said, "So this be the one called Sarah. Done seen you round here some. John tell me you's a good storyteller." I laughed, remembering the stories I told John about broken memories from my past that I fabricated with pieces from my imagination, and sometimes from pieces of dreams that seemed tied to my life before the plantation.

"John, why you gotta tell . . ." But when I looked over my shoulder, John had already gone. I stared after him regretfully before turning back to the people around me.

Masta isn't here, so why's he running off so quickly?

The laughter and "nice" food pulled me back into the trance of the night. All of these folks gathered here shared a humanity that, on more days than we liked, was left buried beneath the work of the day. The small children ran around, evidence of raspberries on their lips. I shared a story that left the others smiling with a lightness I was glad I could bring out. Another man played a banjo made out of a gourd and some fishing string he told us he'd bargained for. By the time Mary quitted the Big House and headed our way, half of the folks had found their way back to their own quarters or to another small gathering elsewhere. Daniel disappeared away with them.

It was all for the better.

Mary carried a large pan in her hands—her surprise. It was apple pie. She didn't stay, just set the pie down, grabbed herself a nice piece, and left for the quarters. The rest of us devoured the treat and savored the laughter that accompanied sugary mouths and sticky fingers.

Heading home alone that night, a large piece of pie I had saved for Daniel sitting idly in my hands, I thought about John not staying at the gathering. Once again, despite the few times we had sneaked away together in the past few weeks—on the rare occasions when time permitted, on weekends, or on nights we could afford to sacrifice sleep—I found myself believing he had taken Masta seriously. I couldn't help thinking that maybe I wasn't even worth the risk. My heart told me I was wrong, but common sense washed over me. I licked my fingers once more and gazed up at the dark, starless sky.

I tried to avoid the shadows, but shadows come as blessings sometimes, and it was from them that John emerged. He slipped beside me and lightly pressed something into my hand, then took my fingers, one by one, and folded them against the object.

"This for you." A simple whisper in my ear and he was gone again, back into the shadows. I peeked into my hand to see a tiny wooden object. I couldn't make out its shape in the dark.

In the cabin, I studied the gift by candlelight. John had carved out an angel with wings, smoothing it out as best he could. Touching it softly, I drew my finger across John's perfect knife marks. I touched the curves in the face and cuddled its wings. After a few minutes, I set it on my pallet and marveled at the small wonder. I had told John about being free in my country. I had told him about Mama, Mathee, and how I saw her and felt her even now—as my angel. And now John had carved her. The design was so intricate, I wondered if God hadn't had a hand in John's project. It looked just like I saw her in my mind. The wings seemed to flow like a river, and her features reminded me of how beautiful my people were. My heart fluttered with a feeling that wouldn't ever leave my soul.

CHAPTER

❧ 14 ❧

MASTA'S HOLIDAY HAD PASSED US QUICKLY BY, AND THE WEEKS fell away as we molded back into our lives of labor. The day was cool, though I sat in the Big House. I was in the kitchen, cleaning, while Mary sat snapping beans for Masta's supper. The silence created space for my busy thoughts. Knowing it was unwise, I thought about what I was learning with little Masta and Missus.

Young Missus Jane ate a mo . . . mo . . . modicum of suga—no, sugar—from the bowl very furtive. No, that wasn't it. Very . . . furtively!

In the afternoons, the children would review their schoolwork from the mornings. I replayed in my mind their conversation from the day before.

"No, Jane," young Masta Bernard said, "furtively means softly."

"No, it don't. It means secretively, just like I said!"

"Boys is smarter than girls; therefore, I know!"

"No, they ain't!"

"Yeah, they are. Sarah, ain't boys smarter than girls?" young Masta Bernard asked me.

"I don't rightly know," I responded.

"Ah, 'course you don't know," he said, brushing my opinion away with a wave of his hand, "you ain't s'pose to be smart." He laughed. "Jane, boys are smarter an' that's that!"

"Nuh-uh. See? Look." Young Missus Jane held up a sheet of paper that her teacher had written on, and read the definition.

"Furtively means secretly. Miss Jane ate a m-o-d-i-c-u-m of sugar from the bowl very f-u-r-t-i-v-e-l-y!" she said. "Told you I was . . ."

My thoughts hushed abruptly. I had seen a quick movement below, just outside the cracked kitchen window. I knew nobody was supposed to be out at the water well at that time of day.

I edged myself to the window, trying not to raise curiosity in Mary.

There it was again—that movement from one bush to another. I had stolen a long enough glance to know that it was Tucker. His limber form knelt, waiting. I moved closer as another figure approached him from behind, though I couldn't see who it was. Tucker whipped around quickly, so the two figures were face-to-face. I could only barely catch their brief exchange.

"It's the preacher, is it?" came Tucker's soft voice.

"I ain't no real preacher. Only speak fo' freedom." The voice was very low, but I would know its bearer anywhere. John continued with his response. "It's tonight?" I heard no answer and could only imagine Tucker bobbing his head in reply.

"Where?"

"Empty cabin, mile east of the cornfield, an hour after work is done." That was the last sound I heard. Peering again through the window, I found that the two men had disappeared.

Glancing over at Mary, I eyed her carefully to be certain she'd heard none of the conversation. She hadn't. She was speaking to me, but my mind leaped about elsewhere. I got it in my head to find John, somehow, someway, before the day was out, and to find out what was going on.

I don't know what possessed me to follow my curiosity all the way down to the cornfield and to the empty cabin. I hadn't found John that day, and good reasoning told me to leave it alone. Through the rest of the day, I convinced myself that I *had* left it alone, and I went about my business without letting the kitchen-window conversation enter my mind.

But by the time nighttime crept upon the house and I sat rocking young Missus Jane's baby sister to sleep, all the thoughts I had locked away came cascading down in front of me. I fought with my spirit—that whisper in my ear persuading me to sneak down there, but the resistance was in vain. I realized after a while that from the moment they started speaking, I had already made up my mind to go.

I slipped between trees and crawled through open areas, praying that young Missus Jane would stay in bed. Young Missus Jane, I had found, was a sleepwalker, and Missus had asked me to stay later in order to make sure young

Missus Jane didn't get herself into a fix. Because I would only be there for part of the night, Missus ordered an older woman, a house servant, to sleep in the girls' room. But this night, I had slipped out a little bit early. On my way out, I'd knocked into the clock that sat in the girls' room and almost woke them up, but I'd stood frozen, listening to its ticking, and willed it to let me out the door.

The small, abandoned cabin finally came into my view. I stopped to study the surroundings, a bit nervous that I might have come on the wrong night. Whatever type of meeting this was, I knew it could not have been authorized by any plantation master, and therefore, they probably had a watchman waiting outside. But perhaps this was not the meeting day—perhaps no one was here! I shuddered to think I was out there alone. The warnings in the back of my mind surfaced, but then dissolved a moment later.

I had spotted him.

The cloaked figure sat behind the broken door of the cabin, hidden in the shadows. If he had not moved slightly, I don't think I would've seen him at all.

Staying out of his line of sight, I crept around the side of the cabin and kept my ears open to see if I could hear where the meeting was taking place. But I heard nothing at all.

But then the wind carried, a muffled voice to my ears. I swung sharply around. Behind me stood a small shack that was mostly hidden by a cluster of trees. Glancing around once more to make sure I hadn't been seen, I made my way carefully toward the run-down building. The closer

I crept, the louder the voices became. Crouching right in front of the shack, I could hear the voices—it sounded like men—but I couldn't make out their words. I crawled to the side and noticed a cracked wooden board above my head. Voices floated out to me from the opening, clear as day. The nervous feeling in my bones quickened as I lay on my belly, listening.

". . . cain't do this no longer. Gotta run sooner or later!" The weariness in John's voice was evident. His words brought a jolt of surprise to my chest.

"You know what happened to Billy, don't ya?" another voice whispered with a sharp edge of warning. I couldn't make out whose voice it was. He continued, "He ran off all in one piece, an' about three weeks later, came back in about three pieces. Hung his body up fo' show. Don't say you runnin' before you really know what you gettin' into. Ain't no room to be backin' out. Y'all know what happens when you get caught."

"Beg ya pardon, sah, but you gotta get caught first fo' that to happen." It was Tucker's voice that cut the man off. "We know the risks."

A long stillness followed. I couldn't even hear their breathing, but my breath seemed so loud, I feared with each passing second they would discover me.

Then the first voice spoke up again. "Well, if y'all gonna run, ain't no need draggin' otha folks with ya, like this man here. . . ." A deep grunt cut into his statement. It wasn't just Tucker, John, and that unknown man kneeling in the shadows speaking about escape. Someone else knelt with them. I prayed for the last man to remain silent, for his identity to remain concealed from me. But I knew who it was; I don't know how I knew, but I knew right away.

"This man here's the one who came up wit the idea," Tucker said softly. The other men seemed to be waiting for him to say more.

John filled the space. "Cain't stop otha folks from runnin' if they wanna run, sah."

The man sighed, and then asked, "Got anythin' to say?"

"Sho' I do," came the familiar voice of the fourth person in the shack. "When we goin'? Cain't go now—them slave dogs excited round this time. Heard somebody up at Bennington plantation up an' ran." My brother's words seemed to echo around me ten times louder than they really were. My mind raced, and with the pressure in my chest growing stronger, I was sure it would explode any minute.

John is running! Daniel is running!

"Naw, y'all won't be goin' now. It'll be cold, but I think it's best round Christmas." The unsteady, nervous silence that followed caused the tension inside to swell even greater. My heartbeat felt as if it would rip my limbs apart with its dangerous, heavy, deathlike thumping. I decided to leave and head back to my quarters.

Brushing away the bugs that had crawled up my legs, I tried hard to steady my shaking body. The November air was cold, and I was shocked.

Both John and Daniel running? That just couldn't be!

"Sarah, Sarah, what you comin' in so late fo'?" Mary asked me sleepily as I scooted softly through the door. I had thrown all my attention into running back to the quarters, as soon as I'd crawled far enough away not to be heard. Pausing at the door, I looked over at Mary lying on her pallet, hoping the night was too dark for her to see my solemn face.

"Sarah, you in late."

"Young Missus Jane," I said simply, kissing Mary to assure her I was all right, then walking to the water basin. I stood there a long time, hands submersed in the chilly water.

Mary doesn't know. Mary does not know, I reminded myself over and over, trying not to let the reality take hold inside me. But I failed. Every word I heard at the shack—every whisper and every imagined gesture and facial expression—kept playing and replaying themselves through my mind.

John and . . . and Daniel . . . are running? I wanted to feel anger, but fear pushed past instead.

"Sarah, somethin' wrong?" Mary asked, turning over to see me standing still at the water.

"Naw ma'am," I said as I hurriedly rinsed my skin and crawled onto my pallet. "Night, Mary," I whispered, but she had already fallen into that place of dreams.

Sleep was not to me this night; I knew of no such thing. I stared at the wall, confused, my eyes wide. I heard Daniel enter that night—heard him moving around with a slow steadiness. I watched him walk over to Mary and stare at her sleeping face for a long time. I knew, as I heard him lay down on his cover, that I wasn't the only one missing sleep that night. But soon enough, my eyelids shut and I was tossed back into the fiery pits of my nightmarish dreams.

There was a clock before me—a large clock. I stared, listening.

Tic-toc. Tic-toc. Tic-toc.

What was it I was waiting for?

Tic-toc. Tic-toc. Tic-toc.

Ah! It's time.

I crept through the woods and through the open spaces, retracing the familiar steps down to the broken-down cabin. I stopped in front of it.

Their faces bobbed back and forth before me, three male puppets with permanent smiles painted on their faces, swinging back and forth from string.

Who was it that stood there, controlling their movements like that? I had to know.

And suddenly, I was standing in the center of the dirt floor, lost in the darkness of the cabin. I searched for the faces, but all I saw were strings. Strings hanging from the ceiling, strings draped across the window, strings trailing across the floor, all attached, somehow, to the unseen, bobbing faces.

I must cut them loose!

I searched desperately for cutting tools and, finding nothing, fell into a deep panic. I ripped at the strings with my hands and bit into them with my teeth.

I have to cut them loose!

And, finally, they did come loose, these strings that had attached them to the Big House, to Masta, to Mary, to me. . . . All cut loose!

The bobbing faces stopped their nodding, the solemn looks returned, and they walked through the door, nodding a cordial farewell.

No, you can't leave me like this!

With arms outstretched, I dived through the door and walked right onto the ship, my legs almost buckling beneath me.

I crept around the upper deck, leaping, hiding, dodging eyes, bending low.

I followed the monster-man, who had covered his nose with a cloth, all the way to the door that led to the bodies.

It was meal time. Large spoonfuls of mushy provisions fell upon the bodies—our bodies. Chains rattled, a dangerous bustling about could be heard. No words were spoken; none were needed. The actions spoke for themselves.

What's mine is mine. This isn't real anyway. Wouldn't you rather die before me? So don't eat it. Let me have it. What does it matter? We'll wake up tomorrow, and our own sun will be shining on our backs.

A four-legged creature with a long tail ran across my feet and fell into the hole, fighting off mangled limbs and becoming buried headfirst in the stench.

That rotten smell of dead flesh, feces, urine, decay, and blood sent a wave of nausea rocking my body as I succumbed to a fit of gagging.

I became my four-year-old self, curled up and trapped in the midst of hell, my skin rubbing against a thousand bodies screaming questions aloud. *How do you lie there like that, in that same position, for hours, days, weeks? How is your soul not crushed beneath the weight? Tell us!*

Stop, I whispered.

I was transformed, this time landing in the skin of an older body. I broke through the chains of hell, feeling the tension growing thicker, hearing, now, the screamed answers to the questions. *I can do this because I've died already and cannot feel a thing. This isn't real. This isn't real! I can sit here like this because my mind has run away and locked itself safely in another world. And my heart, well . . .*

Stop it! I shouted this time, and broke free again. I pushed myself onto the upper deck and slammed headlong into silence.

Three men stood tall, side by side, their bobbing faces now attached to torsos and legs. Grand smiles adorned their faces.

But why are you smiling? I cut the strings. One of them held out something to me that was wrapped around his hand, but I couldn't see what it was. The three of them gestured in unison toward the sea.

I looked out over the edge of the ship. Black fins were circling around a figure that lay in the water. It was a man floating, dead, sinking. I saw the resemblance right away; the body looked like an older version of Daniel.

I turned back to the three men, their smiles haunting

and mischievous. The first one stepped up on the side, spread his arms wide, and leaped.

One down . . .

No, I screamed.

The second one stepped up.

Don't . . . I started. His smile widened, and I caught a glimpse of what had been wrapped around his hand. It was a chain. My eyes followed it, trying to find what it was linked to. Part of it wrapped around the wrist of the last man, meaning that if the second man jumped, he, too, would be pulled over the side.

I frantically followed the rest of the chain, tracing it straight across the deck, right to my own body and up to my neck. The two men leaped . . .

. . . and I was attached.

"Sarah, somethin' wrong?" I was moaning, but not loudly enough for Mary to hop up and wipe sweat and tears from my face.

"Ain't anotha dream, is it?"

"Naw, Mary, I'm all right," I whispered into the night, shifting under my covers.

"Sarah, somethin' wrong?" she said more urgently.

No, no, Mary, nothing was wrong. It was horribly right, just another piece to fit into the puzzle of sorrow that seemed to shape my life. Ayanna, of the Bahati family, the family of good fortune, seemed nothing more than a dream.

CHAPTER

❧ 15 ❧

CHRISTMAS, THE BEST DAY OF THE YEAR, WOULD BE ARRIVING in just a few days. Excitement came, but devastation chased it away. No matter how many times I attempted to cover up my anxiety, it seemed to peek through anyhow. No one seemed to notice, however, and I was grateful for that.

John and Daniel were leaving not a week from now, and they hadn't said one word to me about it yet. I figured they had their reasons for not saying anything. After all, they might not have had the heart to hang around a loved one who had just learned the news.

Regardless, I had assumed that they were just waiting a bit longer, seeking out a better opportunity to let me know. But as the days crept by, it began to seem that they weren't going to tell me at all, or not until the very last moment. Perhaps it was easier that way. I longed, sometimes, to be in Mary's position—oblivious to everything about the planned escape. But I had stubbornly followed my impulse to find out the secret, and I was paying for it now.

Because I knew, it was like swimming underwater; only with great effort was I able to pull my way through each day. I felt stuck in a place that was dragging me down. If I could just keep my mind on the children, housework, and education, I would be all right. But I couldn't. Daniel and John were both running.

By this time, Masta Jeffrey's threat from earlier in the year had been swept from my mind. Any time he appeared in my presence, he acted as if I weren't there, as was done with any servant, and avoided speaking to me at all. So when, five days before Christmas, he confronted me, I was nowhere near prepared.

It was late morning, on one of the children's longer days at the school, and I'd returned to the Big House. As I stood in the front hall, pushing a mop across the floor, I heard the door swing open behind me and somebody walk through. The footsteps slowed; whoever it was stood silent, unmoving. I glanced over my shoulder, wondering who stood there.

It was Masta Jeffrey. He was looking right at me.

I snapped my head back around, hoping he would go about his business. But a nervous thought was running through my mind.

What is he doing here, looking at me like this?

There was nobody but the two of us in the hall, and I could hear him walking toward me, every step like thunder to my ears. My jaw trembled as I tried to keep hold of my emotions. His shoes clicked nearer, and I feared what he intended to do—or what I was capable of doing. Surely he would leave me be in the front hall.

I turned. He was close . . . so close!

His hands came up, and he shoved my back against the

wall. I started to yell out, but his hand had already covered my mouth well enough to muffle the sound.

"Shh, shh," he bellowed in my face as my breathing quickened. I pushed him away, but he pushed himself against me again.

He's not gonna do anything. Not here, not now. Stay calm.

His face came closer, and I felt his hot breath on my neck.

"D-don't touch me." I dared to stammer out.

"Hey!" he whispered harshly, pinning his fingers around my mouth again.

He was taunting me. I felt the sweat dripping down my face, felt my tight lips fighting to hold in the words, the screams, that all my instincts, my anger, were trying to force out.

He's not gonna do anything . . .

I could have lifted my hands to strike him. I could have shoved him away. I could have scratched his neck or struck his face. But actions had consequences, and I tried instead to turn my head away from his.

A door suddenly shut upstairs, and the fire in Masta Jeffrey's eyes broke. As soon as he loosened his grip, I jerked away. My chest heaved up and down as any fear left in me ran steadily over into rage. I glared at his figure as he turned to walk away. But he turned back again, a sneer in his eyes.

"It's almost time." With that, he stepped out of the room.

All the breath I had held in came out in a rush, and the little bit of food in my stomach almost came with it. I stood against the wall to recover myself. I tried to tell myself I had controlled my actions well, but other emotions brought my hand to my lips. A tear tried to escape my eye, but I stopped it from falling.

I won't cry—no, I won't.

I picked up the bucket I had been using and dumped the water outside, and along with it, tossed the key that locked away my feelings. I walked to the kitchen to wash my hands but stopped in the doorway. Mary stood in my path, half facing me. The feelings I had tried to hide showed plainly on her face. I looked from her face to her busy hands. She was clearing the counter with one, and the other hung by her side, a butter knife clasped so tightly in her fingers that her knuckles were almost white. I stood there, calmer on the outside than I expected myself to be.

"I know you seen it, Aunt Mary," I whispered to her, barely moving my lips. "I'm all right," I tried to assure her. I tried to assure myself.

Mary opened her mouth but closed it before any sound could escape. She averted her eyes from mine and continued her work.

As soon as I entered the cabin and saw her, I felt my buried feelings surface. But I said nothing, joining her in her task instead. It was late when I came in. But at a time when Mary was usually preparing for sleep, she worked as if it were the middle of the day.

A long time passed before my mother said anything, and when she did, her words came out slow and heavy.

"I done seen it in him. Young, foolish, scared. Don't know what he's doin', Sarah," Mary said, looking at me now with tear-filled eyes. Her words seemed forgiving, but her eyes showed anger. She held her trembling lips taut, and looked away before any tears could spill over.

"Aunt Mary, he ain't got no right!" I said to her, shaking my head back and forth.

"Naw, naw he don't. Wish he was like his daddy. He ain' the best of 'em, but he gots mo' honor than that."

"Mary," I said, dropping onto my pallet, "he ain't done nothin' to me before, jus' tole me not to say anything 'bout what he was intendin'. That was a long time ago— back in summer. But he ain't . . . he ain't say nothing since! Why cain't he jus' leave me alone?" I asked in a whine.

"Don't know, chile. But I been seein' that in his eye. Scared even me, it did! Seen him born, an' . . . an' nursed that chile, I did. Neva tole ya. Came into dis world jus' 'bout the same time I lost my first child. A year or so befo' yo' brother."

I shook my head. "That don't mean anything to me, Mary, 'less you can stop him!"

Mary looked at me sadly and shook her head.

"Saw him grow up an' turn into one of 'em younguns don't listen to nothin'. Defiant one—always into some trouble. Always had a hard time tryin' to figure what's right an' wrong. An' perhaps, I'm afraid to say, he done figured usin' y'all female younguns like that ain' such a bad thing. Figure he ain't the only one thinkin' like that either. Most of 'em mastas I seen figure it ain' such a bad thing. Maybe he's jus' comin' round to that way of thinkin', chile." I dropped my head into my hands, a moan on my lips. I let the tears fall freely. Mary kneeled by me and placed a hand on my shoulder.

"Shh. Shh, Sarah." She rubbed my back for a moment. "You don't suppose I could hear what's goin' on in that head of yours?" I looked up at her with a frown, and she wiped one of my tears.

"You know what's goin' through my head, Aunt Mary. I can't do that, I jus' can't!" I searched her face, but it didn't change. It was sad, but wise and patient. "There's gotta be somethin' I could do, Aunt Mary! What's that gonna mean if I have his child? What's that mean, Aunt Mary? I can't . . . I can't do that. . . ."

She let my words run until my mouth grew tired. Then she spoke, cradling me in her arms. She tried stealing me away from the thoughts of slaves giving birth to children that were only half their own kind. She told me softly, through my whimpers, that it wouldn't be so bad. She told me our tears were a source of their pleasure. She said all I had to do was hold on to that blank face she had taught me. Just hold on. She mentioned the children I could possibly have—I would have. I couldn't take that. All I could think of was my homeland, and my mother there, her soft touch, her lips, her voice. I remembered her lifting me high in the darkness of the night, kissing my cheek as I squealed with delight, touching my belly, and singing softly the sweet tune of a mother's prayer.

I jerked from Mary's motherly touch. What exactly was she asking of me? How could she tell me to go along like this? It wasn't right.

"Sarah, we still have our lives, our own control right in here." She tapped her head. "They may try to claim our bodies as theirs, but our souls ain't, Sarah, our souls ain't."

Of course! There was the key. Our souls weren't theirs. Our bodies were, but our souls . . .

But no. What dignity lies in that?

One other possibility lurked in the shadows, waiting for that moment when I could see it clearly. Now was that instant. I felt my pureness stirring, that self which had an answer to all impossibilities, an answer I could embrace, could taste, could live.

"Aunt Mary, no! I can't do this Aunt Mary, I can't." I thought about all the slaves who had given birth, and felt myself rising from the pallet. I heard the yelling and screaming of those slave women and the shrieks of the babies.

"Sarah, listen to me," Mary began, watching me get up.

"Mary, don't you see?" I said with an expression of confidence, excitement stirring inside me. "Mary, he don't have no control over me if I'm free. Free, Mary, free!" Mary frowned at me, worried.

"What you talkin' of, Sarah?"

"Mary, I'm . . . I'm runnin' with Daniel an' John Christmas night, an' please don't try to stop me, 'cause whatever you say ain't gonna help. I been thinkin' about this for some time, an' I know now what I need to do. I made my decision that I'ma run with them." The words sounded good at first, hanging in the air with a sort of lightness I could feel. But suddenly, the words turned to ice and shattered before me.

Slowly covering my mouth with my hands, I stared apologetically at Mary, my heart quickening.

"Aunt Mary, I'm so sorry. You didn't . . . no one told . . ."

"Daniel's r-runnin'?" she asked, staring through me.

She must not have seen me nod, for she asked again, "My son . . . he's runnin'?" Even if I did answer, Mary wouldn't have heard me. I felt tears well up in my own eyes as Mary shut hers, her shaking hand coming to rest on her lips. After a few minutes of dead silence, I sat down again and pulled Mary into a hug.

Whispering in her ear, I said, "Neither of us s'pose to know that. I don't think they wanted us to know. I'm sorry for sayin' somethin' 'bout it, Aunt Mary, I shouldn't've done that." Mary shook her head as if to say, "Don't be sorry, chile."

Seeing her gaze return to me, I said, "But, Mary, cain't nothin' beat freedom. Even death is betta than this hell." She nodded quickly, wiping away a single tear, but she couldn't hold back all the tears that had begun to drip down her face. I sat near her and placed her hand in mine. She grasped it as if holding on could save her life and keep her son close to her.

When the tears slowed and finally stopped, she sat staring at the candle that was still burning.

"Mary, can I empty that basin?" I asked softly. I didn't know what else to say. Without waiting for an answer, I got up and emptied it outside. As I did, I heard her whisper softly, "That's my son for ya, always seekin' out freedom, jus' like his . . . jus' like . . ."

Just like his daddy.

I came back and we remained silent, the thought of Daniel's father running and getting killed sitting heavily between us. Mary picked my hand up again. Fresh tears were running down her face, but she wouldn't acknowledge them. She took a long, deep breath, then another and another. Finally, she looked over at me. Her eyes were red and puffy.

"We ain't gonna talk 'bout y'all runnin' no more," she said, softly. She continued, "I know Daniel had his reasons fo' not tellin' me, an' I sho' nuff respect that. An', baby, don't you get to thinkin' I'm gonna stop y'all. I . . . I . . ." She paused for a moment, then said, "Be safe, you hear? Y'all be safe." Her words resonated throughout the slave cabin. She stood, moving as if she had aged ten years, and blew the candle out.

She was ready to sleep, it seemed, or to try to at least. I settled across my pallet as I heard her do the same. But as soon as I had enough space for my own thoughts and fears to rummage through my mind, they did just that. I shivered. Mary must have sensed it, for I heard her softly call out my name.

"Yes, Aunt Mary?" I asked.

"Come here, chile. Lay ova here wit me." I hopped up

quickly and buried myself against Mary's warm body, like I used to when I was much smaller.

"Know you cain't sleep, so I got somethin' to ask you," she said quietly. "You got otha secrets jus' a hidin', don't you?"

"Other secrets?" I asked.

"I knows you can read and write, my chile," she said calmly.

"Mary, I ain' obvious, am I?" I said, afraid.

"Naw, don't worry yourself, chile. I'm the only one who know. I saw a piece of them newspapers stickin' out from under your pallet a while ago. I took an' saw some markin's on the pages. Figured right away it was yours. I was mighty stunned, but not fo' long." She sniffled. "You an amazin' gal, smart young woman, guess I should say, so different from the little gal I remember came here some years back. I shouldn't be the least bit s'prised 'bout Masta Jeffrey's business. Should've known, should've tole you, but at least . . ." She broke down crying again on my shoulder. Mary's heart had always been large, and tonight it felt as if it were crumbling in my hands.

"It's all right, Aunt Mary." She was sniffling again.

"I'ma miss you and Daniel plenty."

Aunt Mary's words echoed in my ear and took a seat in my heart as I listened to her sobs.

CHAPTER

❧ 16 ❧

CHRISTMAS ARRIVED QUICKER THAN MY SOUL WAS READY FOR. The fear that bit at every inch of my body when I awoke that morning was indescribable. Sweat dripped from my forehead to my eyelids and down to my chin. It was my dreams that had woken me, dreams of loud barks and blood smeared across severed limbs. Those dreams of death had stolen most of my sleep that night. Surely I was out of my mind.

Daniel's unusual behavior worried me. His attempts at kindness came out awkwardly, and he couldn't hold a complete conversation or keep his eyes focused on anything. I knew exactly why. Tonight was the night of their escape, and he was sharply aware that this day might be the last time he would ever see his mother or me. Along with that, he'd have to share the news with Mary, and then to me. What he and John didn't know was that I would be going too. I just had to be sure to keep my eye out for them all night long so I wouldn't miss my chance.

I had sewn a pillow each for John, Daniel, and Mary, during the little ones' school time. I used scraps of material I had been collecting from the Big House to add their names onto each one. I found myself running back to the pillows—the only proof that I had made my decision to escape. I wouldn't change my mind, I kept telling myself. I had decided.

During church, my spirit settled a bit when I saw John speaking to the mass of slaves. At first, my anger with John for keeping silent about running surpassed my fear. I stared solemnly and blankly and blocked out his words. But gradually, I began to notice something in his voice; a fervor rose from his words, and even though he spoke the same message he spoke most Sundays, I could feel the certainty behind it, and the weight of it all suddenly hit me. His words spun around and around in my head as my attention was swiftly drawn to him and my mind clung hungrily to his words.

Freedom, freedom, freedom, freedom . . .

The word pounded in his chest like fierce drumbeats, and I believe he heard me listening that closely, because suddenly, as his mouth spoke on, his eyes snapped around to mine and, like the sound of a gunshot, the pounding ceased, to be replaced by a feeling of uncertainty.

"What is it to be truly free? On this Christmas day, we gotsta get free from our sins—our sins of thinkin' Masta treatin' us bad—sins of thinkin' we don't need to be workin' fo' him. You gotta sacrifice one thing fo' another. We trade our labor fo' food, fo' homes, fo' clothes, an' most impo'tant, fo' the freedom of bein' wit they Jesus in this Christian religion. Masta an' Missus good to us; they got a good nature too. *My Missus,* graced wit the wings of an angel. *Jus' like my Masta too,* holdin' my eyes strong to the prize of what freedom really be. Freedom on Christmas day—it means escapin' into God's place, bein' grateful for all that done come our way, an' liftin' our voices in song. . . ." I looked away as those around me lifted their voices in song. His eyes had dug deep into my soul, trying to make me understand what he was saying, trying to explain his secret.

My missus, graced wit the wings of an angel . . .

He had spoken those words to me.

As his words died away, reality broke the daze I had drifted into. The fear of running burned fresh under my skin. John had made it perfectly clear: you had to sacrifice one thing for another. To him, that meant sacrificing what part of him said was freedom, running from me, for the physical freedom of being his own master. To me, that meant possibly even sacrificing life for the chance at freedom.

I slipped away and sat alone, waiting for the feast to begin. Christmas dinner was always much better than the dinner we were given on Masta's holiday. When the food came out, I barely ate any of it. I was starving, but I needed something more than food to fulfill me.

"You all right, Sarah?" It was Daniel. I didn't allow myself to look into his eyes, thinking he would see all the questions in mine. Eventually, I relented.

I looked down at my feet, then up into his anxious eyes.

"There a reason I wouldn't be all right?"

He stared back at me for a moment, considering my

question, then said, "Lots a good food, you know. You seen Mary? Gotta say somethin' to her." It was just an excuse to get away. He disappeared into the background of chatter, music, and dancing before I could tell him she was stuck back at the cabin with less of an appetite than I had. He tried to hide his anxious glance from me as he hurried off.

After hanging around awhile, I went off by myself, sat down, and stargazed a ways away from the Big House, alone on a concealed piece of land.

So what now? John ain't even gonna say goodbye?

And then, as if he heard my thoughts, John's rough, calloused, and warm hand slipped into mine, awaking me from my reverie. I turned to see John's eyes galloping across my sad face. I felt the same questions arising that I had felt with Daniel.

Where have you been? Why do you have to keep all this from me—me, Sarah!

I turned back to the stars, which were just as silent as he was. All I wanted to do was shut my eyes and steal away from the world with him. We were drowning, working for Masta, and scrounging for freedom. Why couldn't we just be?

When I faced him once more, I ran my eyes across his broad nose, and those eyes of his that curled at the corners—always observing and understanding. Would he understand what was on my mind tonight? I didn't see a hint of indecision in them, only many thoughts trying to gather themselves. I stared at the sky again.

"What you thinkin' 'bout?" he finally asked, breaking the silence.

"Nothin', really," I said softly as my emotions drifted between anger, fear, and the longing for freedom.

"You mighty quiet, you must be thinkin' 'bout somethin'!"

"Well, ya. Freedom. Freedom an' the stars," I said, trying to ignore the feeling stirring in the pit of my stomach.

"You know, don't you?" he asked, matter-of-factly, leaning back on his elbows. I wondered why I didn't find the question so surprising. He knew me well, and that I couldn't deny. Maybe telling him I was running with them wouldn't be as hard as I thought.

"Had a feelin' you knew," he said softly.

I looked away. "You should not've waited this long to tell me, John," I said to him. He nodded, curling his lower lip underneath his teeth.

"I shoulda tole you, sho' I should've, Sarah. But how you think I was s'pose to look in yo' eyes an' tell you that I was runnin'? You think that woulda made it easia fo' me to go?" he asked.

I said nothing.

"We was comin' back fo' you an' Mary. We gonna come back, Sarah."

Disappointment rose up from somewhere inside of me. *Why can't he ask me to run with them?*

The silence intensified and then died away again.

"You ain't comin' back. Ain't no runaway who got good sense gonna leave an' come back," I said plainly.

"Sarah, Sarah, that ain't true . . ."

"John," I said without a question in my voice, "got somethin' to tell you."

"Sarah, wish you wouldn't—"

I left him no room to continue. "John, I'ma run too, right wit you an' my brother." The words slipped out easily, and with them went the strain of holding my ambitions inside. But John was shaking his head.

"No, Sarah, no!" he said, turning to face me completely.

"What you mean, no?" I began as my thoughts stilled.

"Sarah, you cain't run with us. It's . . . it's not a good time right now. I'm comin' back, Sarah, I'm comin' back to get you; that's a promise!" A deep frown creased my forehead.

"John, you hearin' what you sayin'? You thinkin' 'bout what you tellin' me, John?" I asked. I shook my head with frustration when his demeanor didn't change, then turned the other way.

"Sarah, look at me." I obeyed him, not wanting to believe he was telling me not to run.

"I will come back for you, Sarah." I sighed heavily into the night. Did he want me to think him coming back for me was a nice thought—him returning to slavery after reaching freedom without me. After months, maybe years, of me waiting with anxiety on my shoulders. After . . . after I'd had Masta's baby?

"Sarah, jus' . . . jus' wait fo' me."

I stared out into the night as those words drifted from John's mouth, and set two fingers on my lips. Something was building up inside me that made it hard for me to simply accept his words, and I let it grow. I felt his tension.

I met his gaze and shook my head. "John, you ain't got the right to stop me from runnin'. Don't you want me there too?" His normally patient demeanor tensed considerably.

"Naw, naw, Sarah, that ain't it."

"Then, what is it? You know how much freedom means to me."

"Yeah, I do. I jus' . . . we had it planned, Sarah, an' if . . . it'd be safer if . . ."

"That you speakin', John, or someone else? 'Cause I can't tell. This ain't your choice. Don't no one promise a life where nothin's gonna happen to me 'less my body an' soul are free. How you gonna stop the whip from strikin' my back when you gone, John? How you gonna keep me here if the Masta wanna sell me? An' what if somethin' happens to you? You'd think I'd rather be here than with you, holdin' your hand?" I paused, then continued.

"I had freedom once," I said, looking away sadly. "Cain't you imagine how it feels, taken from freedom you already had; freedom you already felt an' touched an' tasted? I think of what it must've felt like, in that freedom. Your mind is yours, your body is yours—everything, yours! An' one day, jus' like that, you don't own nothin' anymore, not even your own feelings. I want that again—I wanna know that feelin' again." My face grew warm as he began to speak. I felt part of that freedom I spoke of just being with him.

"But, Sarah, I done told you I can make you free. Just let me get there first. Let me make sure it's safe for you," John said again, trying to persuade me.

"You ain't sat to think 'bout what you sayin', John. I

know how dangerous it is, jus' as you do. Who are you to take that decision of runnin' from me?" I pulled my hand away from his and rubbed my arms. I felt the cold around me. "I ain't no slave. That's what you tole me. But every day, I get up, an' everything I see an' hear an' do tells me I'm a slave. John, it ain't your place to persuade any slave that wants to run not to run."

"You ain't any other slave, Sarah!" he replied, pushing his fingers into my knee. I sat silently, wondering how this night would end. John was edgy and nervous, and I hated seeing him like that. His eyes remained clouded with secrets and frustration. I moved nearer and rested my head on his shoulder, feeling his chest broaden in a deep breath. He exhaled and slowly placed an arm around my back.

"John, you ain't really hearin' me, are you?" I asked softly near his ear. He didn't answer. Instead, in a calm tone, John said my name.

"Yeah?" I asked, mimicking his calm tone.

"If God gave you two wings and tole you that you could only use them for one single thing, what would it be?"

Gesturing to the sky, I said, "Well, I'd fly away—far, far away, to the heavens maybe!" I assumed he was dropping the subject, and I made an effort to lift his spirits. But I was wrong.

"If I had two wings," he said, "I'd take them wings an' cover you, completely, till not an inch was visible, so you'd be protected, from everything."

A teardrop slid down my cheek as I raised my head.

"I see you, Sarah, I see you when you know there ain't

many folks who'd care for you in this evil world. I see you an' have seen you for a long while wit your spirit obviously not intended fo' this world. Don't know how to 'xplain it, but you remind me of Aunt Pearl—you rememba, my grandma?"

I nodded. "Said she didn't want no masta's name, so she had us callin' her Bell, Gramma Pearl Bell. She said if she could be anythin' otha than herself, she'd be a bird, an' birds reminded her of bells when they sing." He sighed.

"You jus' like her, headstrong an' everythin'. She used to be proud to speak of freedom when those in her presence shook with fear at the word. Don't know if they ain't understand it, or if they was jus' too scared to talk 'bout it. But not her, not her. An' there's just somethin' . . ." He shook his head and looked down at the ground. When he lifted his eyes back up, a tear glistened in one of them. His sincerity made me turn away, his words touching me deeper than any slave should allow. Soon, I would find that out.

The wave washed over me then. I felt the truth of it all stare me right in the face as thoughts of Masta Jeffrey swam through my mind. I had to tell John. The topic of Masta Jeffrey was one we had agreed not to talk about, but even as the months drifted by and my fear of being confronted had died away, John would sprinkle conversations with questions that hinted at his deep-seated fear and his realization that he had no control over what Masta Jeffrey chose to do with me. John's sly questioning never caught me off guard, however, and my answer was always the same.

"He hasn't done nothin', John."

"Sarah, Sarah, you tellin' me right?"

"John, we said we ain't gonna talk like this. He hasn't done nothin'."

He'd nod, gathering up his fears and tossing them back into the deep waters they'd come from, and pretend to forget. But tonight, concerns about Masta Jeffrey seemed to be the farthest thing from his mind, and I began to see that I'd have to remind him of those concerns, and of how real they were.

"John," I said softly, turning completely to face him, letting his arm fall off my shoulder. I wrapped my arms around one knee. "Got somethin' to tell you. Scared to tell you, but I know I got to." He peered at me silently.

"He came back again, to me." I hesitated, every bone in my body begging me not to tell him what was on my mind. John sat up straighter.

"He? You mean . . ."

"Masta Jeffrey, ya."

He looked at me, his breath becoming more rapid, and his eyebrows arching. "But, Sarah, you . . . you tole—"

"I know what I bin sayin', John, an' all that's bin true. But he came to me a few days ago. Didn't do nothin' but scare me this time, but said he'd be back real soon. That's when I knew I gotta go with y'all. I gotta. I ain't gonna stay here an' let no masta of mine breed me 'gainst my will." I blinked up at him. The corners of his eyes no longer laughed like they always did: They were screaming down at me.

I continued. "John, you know that's the difference here

between bein' a slave an' not bein' one, an' I ain't got no choice 'less I'm free. I think 'bout runnin' north to freedom an' gettin' caught; I'm scared, I'm really scared, but that's what I gotta do. Ain't got no soul here, John, no dignity. I ain't no little gal now, an' Masta Jeffrey, he see that. If you go an' come back for me after you done reached freedom, you be surprised when you see me workin' in the fields with a light-colored chile strapped on my back. That the kind of bondage you comin' back to rescue me from? 'Cause Masta Jeffrey sho' ain't gonna wait that long, an' I thought . . . I thought you'd figure that yo'self." A tear slid down my face as I watched him sitting there with a balled fist raised to his tight lips.

"John, let me . . ." I began, raising a hand to him, but rage broke through the chains of calmness that had held him there on the ground, and he abruptly stood up. I hugged my knees as he walked over to a tree, which he struck with his fist.

He staggered back and fell down next to me. I wrapped him in my arms and squeezed him close. He forced a long breath of frustration out of his mouth.

"Cain't stand it like I thought I could. All these months, I tell myself ova an' ova they cain't control us that way. No matta what happens, no matta what, we still got our minds. But . . . Sarah, figure I bin jus' a lyin' to myself. I'd die befo' that man put his hands on you like that," John said with a vengeance in his voice that seemed foreign.

"John, don't talk like that. I'm runnin'. He ain't gonna have that chance." He squeezed his eyes shut and leaned more weight into my arms. I ran a hand across his forehead.

"You gotta run," he repeated, pain in his voice. I knew he was searching for other possibilities, but no others were good enough. I knew, because I had already searched my own mind.

"We . . . I could . . ."

"Naw, John, I'm runnin'," I said with finality in my voice. He sighed again, deeply, and we fell silent for a long time. I listened closely to his breathing, my breathing, and then the union of our breath, a small measure of warmth and bliss that pierced the nighttime chill.

John sat up straighter and began fooling with my hair.

"What you think Daniel gonna say?" he asked me.

"I don't know, but he ain't stoppin' me, either," I said softly. "Don't think he would stop me. It's jus' I want my freedom, that's all," I whispered more to myself than to John. I felt my nervousness at the thought of our escape silently creeping up on me as the minutes ticked on into the night.

I'm really going through with all this!

The two of us filled the sullen spaces with whispers that blended into the night.

"Wanna know somethin'?"

"What's that?" I asked.

"Cain't no one stop me from namin' my joy Sarah."

"Ayanna," I whispered. He smiled again with wonder.

"Ayanna . . . yeah, Ayanna. You wanna dance?" Something in his question spilled over like a warning, but I had too many worries to think much about it. Excitement lit up his face. The worry I felt swam from my mind, for the moment, as John pulled me up into his arms.

"Put me down!" I said forcefully in his ear, but he paid me no attention, satisfied by my laughter, until we neared the festivities once more. He set me lightly on my feet and guided me to the center of the music and dancing, where some of the slave folk busily plucked at banjos while others beat out rhythms with sticks.

It had to be the magic of the night—the music, maybe, or better yet, the spirit of the young man I danced with. With a step or two in time with the music, I was suddenly free: free as the wind, the stars, the birds, and the angels, just free! I was in a dream, swinging, flying, and spinning, around and around, in delicate motions with two hands on my waist. Then I was floating in my own grace, deftly defying gravity itself, like the wind, and I was spinning and spinning, back into his waiting arms. Indeed, I was not a slave. There was no question of that. The seconds were minutes and the minutes were hours. The world twirled away and it was just the two of us dancing—flying! Then we were still again, lost in a world far from the shuffling feet and smiling couples moving about us. His dark brown eyes shone brighter than the stars that laughed down upon us. His face came close, his nose resting softly against my own, and his lips took mine . . .

Then came the crash.

So dazed, I couldn't understand how one minute, John had brought me back down to the ground and was pulling me close to him, and in the next, I was lying on the ground with a stinging sensation on my left eye. The reality of the cruel world I was in came crudely back into focus.

The white man had slapped me down and kicked John to the ground. When John looked up, his lip dripped with blood, which concerned me more than the blood running down my own face. He moved his hand toward his mouth and slowly sat up. But his eyes were closed, and I feared the devil I would find when he opened them. The music subsided like a symphony of birds suddenly hushed by a poacher's voice, leaving nothing but scowling silence.

"All y'all, get." Those were the first words he spoke. Hardly anybody moved as Masta Jeffrey, who had stumbled into the middle of the gathering, staggered forward, drunk. A few voices rose among the small crowd, kindly asking Masta to let us be. But another harsh yell from Masta Jeffrey sent slave row—many of whom stumbled with drunkenness—dragging their feet away from the dancing grounds.

"You were supposed to stay away, weren't you?" Masta Jeffrey said with a slow drawl after he felt enough of the others had gone far enough away. He kicked in John's stomach. But no answer came out of John's mouth, although he was fully conscious and able to talk. His eyes were open, but his focus lay intently on the ground. My heart stood still.

"I told you, didn't I? Didn't I, boy?" I looked on with growing horror as John dared to lift his eyes and stare straight into Masta Jeffrey's with a scowl on his face. His nose flared out wide as if he smelled poison. John was doing more than treading dangerous territory: He was throwing himself to the lions. He shouldn't look Masta in the eyes like that, and he knew it. That was equated with a crime against God! Whether or not he thought of himself as a slave, he knew how Masta viewed him. Was he trying to get himself killed before the night was over?

"How dare you, you stupid animal!" Two more blows landed in the middle of his face, and with a terrible cracking noise, John's now-disfigured nose flowed blood. But he made no noise of pain and held fast to his death gaze. I brought my trembling hands to my mouth in horror. I couldn't tear my eyes from the blood that dripped in procession from his nose to his lips to his shirt as if it, too, wanted to escape what was coming next. As John lifted himself again, Masta beat him back down with his foot. This continued as I winced, using every ounce of my strength to stop from crying out. I looked around wildly and watched an overseer make his way over to the scene.

What is John thinking? Doesn't he want to escape?

With the overseer's help, Masta dragged John's body to the beating tree. I wrung my hands dry, but John didn't struggle at all, which was both a blessing and a curse. They tied his hands to the rope and ripped off his shirt. I alone could see the pain on his chest, burning like fire—pain telling him he had to strike back—if not for himself, then for me.

I wanted to run away so as not to bear witness to this, but I knew Masta wouldn't let me. If anything, he was beating John to anger me.

What have I done? My soul was crying.

Behind me, I heard the hushed whispers of slaves. "Naw, Lord, not on this day. Please, not on this day!"

Masta Jeffrey turned around and told them, "Get!" Then he turned to me, and I watched a grin slowly light his face as if the world sat idly in his palm. He told me to stay where I was, and it sickened me to think that he could find humor in his cruelty.

The overseer yanked out his bullwhip and raised it high.

What could I possibly do?

One, two, three . . . The lashing continued, and John's eyes rolled back in their sockets, so I could only see their white, but his lips remained firmly set. I felt every lash as if the whip were striking my own skin. I couldn't stand it. My body seemed to take on a mind of its own as I jumped from the ground and ran to Masta Jeffrey. I begged him to stop, apologizing for disobeying his orders. He raised a hand, and the overseer paused, the whip raised high. Masta Jeffrey grabbed my arm. I almost screamed— almost—but John's red eyes now stared at me, and with that I knew I needed to stand as tall as I could for him. My eyes tried to persuade him not to go against orders; he would not be less of a man for just enduring a little more of Masta's brutality.

"This, nigga," Masta Jeffrey blurted out, "is because you disobeyed your Masta." Turning back, he motioned for the overseer to continue to beat John's back, and he held me in place so I could see the chaos I had created. I wished that he would just strike my back instead. Only then would I feel less pain.

Around strike fifty, I couldn't count anymore, let alone look. An eternity seemed to pass before he hit the bleeding mound of flesh that had replaced John's back for the last time and Masta forced me to look. Masta Jeffrey dragged me away as Mary and a few others ran to help John. But Mary's gaze never left mine, even as Masta dragged me far enough away so that no one could hear his words. He then dropped me on the earth. His grip on my arm was very painful, but it was nothing compared with the pain I felt in my heart.

"Did you tell him?" His breath was nauseating, reeking of strong liquor. "Did you tell him?" he asked again.

With every jerk, I bit my lip harder, tasting my own blood.

"No, Masta, I swear . . . I swear it, Masta. I didn't, Masta." He patted his whip, his lips still close to mine.

"You better be sure, gal, you better be sure . . ." I was sweating now, despite the cold, and fought desperately to hold back the tears.

Our tears were a source of their pleasure.

Yes, I was a slave in his eyes, but I would not let him see me cry.

Then I heard a sound in the distance, a sound I prayed his ears would quickly pick up on before he could start fooling with his pants.

"I told you not to hang round with this here slave dog."

"Yessah, Masta." There the sound was again, and yet again, but he ignored it. He shoved me down further and pressed my arms into the ground.

"Gonna show you what—" The noise came again, now louder, closer. Masta Jeffrey staggered backward in his drunkenness and turned his head toward it. The woman's high, shrill voice called out his name once more, and this time it could be heard clearly.

"Jeffrey, son, where are you?" He looked back over at me, his lips curling into a half-conscious smile, and threw up the contents of his stomach onto the ground so close to me, I almost threw up myself.

"Cain't trust you," he said, staggering backward.

He repeated the accusation twice more, then turned back toward the Big House, stopping several times to vomit.

I stayed there on the ground contemplating what had just occurred. I was alone, and only then did the fit of sobs rush through me like a storm, soft but angry. I was glad I had been spared Masta Jeffrey's body, but I wondered why everything had to happen the way it did.

But I was not alone. Daniel approached silently and helped me up. On seeing him, I started, "John . . ."

"He gonna be all right."

With a soft cry, I buried my head in his shoulder and cried some more. How was I supposed to get out of this? How were we going to get out of it?

CHAPTER

17

DANIEL HAD TAKEN ME BY THE THE ARM AS WE HEADED BACK to the cabin the next morning. I was too ashamed to drag my sleep-deprived eyes around to look at his face. I felt as if everything was solely my fault.

"It ain't yo' fault, Sarah," he said, reading my thoughts as we entered the cabin.

"We shoulda talked it out wit you," he whispered.

Confusion settled over me. "You shoulda talked it out?" I repeated.

"Ya. Shoulda talked a long time ago 'bout you goin' wit us."

"You knew I was thinkin' 'bout goin'?" I asked, my heavy heart finding solace in the idea that he knew.

He nodded. "Knew that's wat you'd say to us, at least."

"How? Was it—was it Mary?" I asked, my face drowning in tears. His face showed no signs of surprise.

"I talked to Mary 'bout it," he said. "She said you told her 'bout us. She never tole me you were thinkin' 'bout travelin' wit us, though, but I jus' knew."

"But, Daniel, how'd you know?" I asked.

"How couldn't I, Sarah? You my sister."

I wanted to respond, but I felt too drained.

John was in a pitiful condition. He could barely walk, and he surely couldn't run. His insistence on running despite this would've torn my heart to pieces if I had been there to hear him plead; but I wasn't. The only two with John that night were Mary and another elder woman. They both let him know that he wasn't going anywhere until he healed. The older woman told him he shouldn't have disobeyed Masta in the first place.

"Wa'n't no way I'd give up the best day in the year I got to spend wit the person who keeps my heart safe an' warm an' protected fo' me. Gotta give up that day jus' to make sho' I don't go too far wit her?" Mary told me those were his words to her when she was putting her healing medicine on his back.

"If you had just saved this day, though, and obeyed Masta, then you would've had all the world with her," Mary had whispered to him.

When Masta's family left for church and the overseers were slacking off their jobs, I went to see John.

"Looks like things is switched round, huh?" John asked, trying, as he always seemed to do, to find some humor in downright bad situations. Not moved at all, I shook my head, standing with my arms crossed over my chest. He had covered his back with a rag before I came in, trying to hide all the blood, but it showed through anyway.

"What's wrong?" John asked me, a question requiring no response.

"If I . . . if I hadn't danced with you," I said, "I would not've gotten you in any trouble."

"Sarah," he said, "why you sorry? I should be the sorry one! I'm the one brought you out to that dance floor. Anyway, what's done is done an' I can truly say you the best danca I eva met!" he said, with a soft laugh. I wasn't fooled. I saw right through John to the disbelief deep within him. Last night was his night—his time to escape—and that moment had been snatched from under his feet. But, as he tried to make me feel myself again, my tight, worried, and anxious face relaxed a bit. We were alone, so John told me what he wanted us to do. I kneeled down beside him as he sat up to face me, his pain, which he did his best to hide, clawing at him. The fresh cuts covering his bare ankles revealed that the overseer hadn't aimed well for John's back. His nose was roughly bandaged with a bloody cloth.

"Sarah, you still gotta run."

I turned my head slightly to the side. "Now, you the one tellin' me to run. Guess that mean I ain't got no choice." John closed his eyes slowly and then dragged them back open, and I saw a determined look in them.

"That's right. Daniel an' Tucker know clearly what to do; we bin meetin' at diff'rent places talkin' 'bout it, gettin' information from free folks Tucker knows. We was careful 'bout it all, more careful than you'd think.

"Your brother gonna tell you what you gotta know, what we's all learned 'bout . . . 'bout stayin' alive. So if fate has it that you left alone, you gonna know 'xactly what to do. And as fo' me, well, I figure I'ma run jus' as soon as I'm healed up an' things go back to normal after y'all run."

I nodded. Daniel and I had planned to meet that night near the broken-down cabin where they first planned the escape.

John continued. "But I got some things to tell you anyway, things I want you to know."

I sat and listened closely to John's quiet words. He shared, mostly, basic facts on how to survive the winter weather and how to stay moving in the right direction.

When he was done, I took out the pillow to give to him.

"I have somethin' fo' you, John, but you cain't have it till you promise me somethin'."

"An' what's that?" he asked.

"You 'member that sermon you gave yesterday?" He nodded.

"You called me your Missus then. I was listenin'—I heard you. Said I was graced wit the wings of an angel. Well, you got to promise me you'll heal yourself up quick, 'cause you the one wit them angel wings." I touched his neck softly. "But can't no angel wings grow on an unhealed back. I say God's my masta, but you the beauty that sparks this feelin' in my soul. I'm gonna reach freedom, I tell you. But I need your promise before I go."

He chuckled, but I raised my eyebrows. "That's a promise, then?"

"Sho' is, now what you gotta show me?" I'd snuck him the pillow I made for him. He took it slowly, surprise showing on his face.

"What you think? You like it?" I asked him after he made no response.

"Don't know if I like the pillow betta or my name sewn on the front. Sarah, you can read!" he said, as if learning that information for the first time. "You know how good that make me feel?" But his whispers of gratitude and affection brought another stream of tears running down my face.

When would I see that face again?

John looked over at me and, wiping my eyes with his thumb, spoke in a soothing tone. "Sarah, listen, you gotta be strong. That's important or you ain't gonna make it."

"Is holdin' everything inside bein' strong?" I asked him, my voice more critical than I meant for it to be. He bit his lower lip.

"For some people, I guess it is."

"You ain't gotta hold everything in, John, not with me. I ain't fooled. You runnin' was the freedom that you wanted."

"No, Sarah, listen to me. Runnin' ain't freedom. Runnin' is puttin' your life in danger's hands. Runnin' takes you to freedom," he said, lecturing, as he loved to do.

"An' either way," he continued, "reachin' the freedom land's only half of my freedom."

"What's the otha half?" I asked, puzzled. He pulled on my earlobe playfully.

"Freedom an' you; freedom wit you," he said, as if that fact was as apparent as night and day. I sighed. Any other day, my heart would melt and my eyes would glisten. But not today. Today I felt worse with every word he spoke.

"You smart, smarter than most who let their smarts hide behind fear; but you gotta be strong, real strong."

"But, John, what if I stayed here an' . . ." The funny look he gave me cut sharply into my words.

"I know it wa'n't long ago I was tellin' you that same thing, but I cain't even think of you not runnin'. You told me yourself that you wouldn't let Masta Jeffrey come near you again." The firmness of his voice made it clear he wasn't changing his mind this time.

"You told me constantly that the thing you wanted most was freedom. You told me that you would take two wings and fly to freedom. Even if you did stay, I wouldn't let that devil touch you," he said, lowering his voice. "Like I said befo', I'd kill him first." His statement buzzed through my ears like a warning.

"But, John, he wouldn't, 'cause we could . . ." His heavy, unyielding gaze silenced me.

"*Education*. How you spell that?" He asked. I crossed my arms.

"We talkin' 'bout runnin', John, don't go an' change—"

"Sarah," he said calmly, "how you spell it?" I spelled it for him.

"*Freedom*. How you spell that?" I spelled out *freedom* for him too.

"*Love*. Spell it." I spelled it out slowly, lingering on each of the four letters. A true smile lit up his face.

"An' you can write these things, too, you told me."

I nodded.

"Can you write a book 'bout those things?"

I smiled. "Not yet, John."

"Well, how you eva gonna do that? How you eva gonna teach folk like me if you don't get yo'self to freedom?"

I sighed and let his words hang in the air. I tried to let them pass with the moment, but they seemed to have awakened something deep inside that had been asleep for a long time. I ran his words through my mind once more.

How you eva gonna teach folk . . .

It hardly seemed appropriate and I tried to wipe away the strange thought, but a small smile came to my lips as I wondered if I'd ever be educated well enough to actually teach other folks.

"So, now, what you got to say, Miss Sarah?" I looked up at him, thanking him with my gaze in response. I brought a hand to his head and patiently and slowly wiped away his sweat, his tears. I cleared my mind of all else, for I knew that our farewell would be a permanent good-bye.

John heard my thoughts. He grabbed my hands and pulled me to him.

"John, I . . ." He shook his head, stopping me midsentence. Despite the anguish I knew he was suffering both physically and emotionally, he enveloped me, as though he could squeeze out all our pain. I could feel his bare chest moving slowly up and down and his heart beating. I don't know how long he hugged me, but I wished it could have lasted forever.

Softly, he said, "I'll see you again, Sarah, I promise." It sounded good, so sincere, and his eyes held nothing but truth. But disappointment wasn't an option for me: I'd had enough of it. So I let that statement pass through one ear and out the other. But if I listened, I could hear his words banishing all the fear inside of me with that one simple promise.

"I ain't

no slave."

MARY KNEELED, HER MOTHERLY FIGURE STOOPING LOW AS SHE prayed, beckoning God onto our paths. Like her figure, my hands trembled slightly as I listened to her pray. Beneath her words, the prospect of freedom rang loud. She prayed hard to our God, asking that he not abandon us as we fled, that he carry us safely along on our journey to freedom, wherever freedom was.

Two quick days had passed since Christmas, and that evening burned fresh in my mind. Masta had given us the period from Christmas Eve to New Year's off, as was normal for each year. The watch on slave row had lessened considerably; John's punishment proclaimed itself in the air forcefully enough to stop any breaking of the plantation rules.

But nothing would stop our escape that night.

Mary stood as she finished her last plea to God with hands raised toward the heavens, and embraced Daniel and me in hugs. We all wept as she smothered us with an extra layer of love, the best form of protection she knew.

Mary stepped back and turned to me. "I almost fo'got," she mumbled as she brushed tears away. Out of her pocket pouch Mary pulled a tiny bundle of material: a small quilt she had made from scraps of various colors and patterns, saved from the making of Missus's clothes. On it, Mary had sewn a very detailed picture of a woman and a child holding hands. She placed it in my waiting hands, and I ran my thumb over the design.

"When you find time to do this?" I asked her, trying to force a smile to my lips.

"Don't you worry 'bout that. You got it in yo' hands—that's what's impo'tant." With anxiety eating at every part of me, and nervousness racing through my blood, it was hard to hold back any of my emotions. I threw my arms around Mary's neck in appreciation. She patted my back and then turned to Daniel.

"Daniel." She said his name softly. I saw Daniel's eyes creep up to his mother's face. A look passed between them, a look only a child could summon up on parting with his mother, and she with him.

"Mama, ain't no person could touch my heart like you done."

She frowned, fighting with her feelings.

"Chile, you don't call me Mama fo' nothin'."

A terrifying thought sprang to the front of my mind. "What if Masta come fo' you, Mary?"

She turned her untroubled eyes toward me. "Sarah, all y'all's gotsta worry 'bout is gettin' safely away. Done talked 'bout that wit yo' brother. Y'all don't worry 'bout me, I tell ya. Ain't no whip gonna strike my back. I bin wit that family a long time! I'se know what to say an' what to do. Jus' like when Isaac up'n ran . . ." She stopped for a moment and cradled her arms. "Jus' you don't worry. I'll be all right." She brought her lips to my forehead and kissed me gently.

"Mary, you knows you should be comin' wit us," Daniel said as I opened my sack to finger all the items once more, to make sure I was prepared.

"Shh, hush that talk! Ain' comin' witchya. You knows that. But go on, reach freedom, my chillen. And when y'all do, tell me, I'll hear you." I turned toward Daniel, and our eyes met. I dropped mine quickly, remembering our conversation about Mary earlier that day.

"Daniel, she say she don't wanna go. Can't make her go."

"Got an idea jus' in case she change her mind. John's gonna run soon's he's betta an' things settle a bit. Tole me he would take her with him."

"But Daniel, you sound so sure she gonna change her mind."

"Think she gonna make the best choice she can."

The same conversation must have been running through Daniel's mind, because he turned to Mary again and said, "Want you ta still think 'bout comin' when John gets away."

"Daniel," she said softly, reaching up to place her hand on Daniel's cheek. "Ain' my place. My place is here. I ain' no runnin' person. This ain' no heaven, but it ain' so bad fo' me. I'se used to it—only thing I known." It seemed as if Daniel was struggling to bury his worry as Mary nodded firmly and embraced us once more.

"Y'all take care of yourselves, now, you hear? Don't get

caught. I couldn't stand all that." She sniffled. "Y'all don't let me slip from your thoughts, hear?"

"'Course not, Mama!" Daniel and I responded. As we stood around in silence, waiting for our cue to sneak away, I gasped and ran to the loose floorboard under my pallet, remembering the pillows I had sewn for the two of them.

"Got these fo' y'all!" I said with excitement, watching Mary take hers and squeeze it to her heart. I watched Daniel closely.

"Sarah . . . Sarah, you can read? How long you bin able to do this?" he asked me, slipping his small pillow into his sack, his eyes filled with curiosity.

But I had no chance to explain. A soft hoot outside the door drained every thought from our minds and every word from our lips.

My heart leaped into my throat as I gazed back at Mary one last time. The tension in me caught the words I tried to say to her.

She must have heard it in the air anyway, for she whispered back, "Love y'all."

The shutting door echoed in my ears. We crept away into the night.

CHAPTER

❧ 19 ❧

WE STARTED OUR JOURNEY WHEN THE FULL MOON WAS BRIGHT and shining high in the sky. I had never been so afraid in my life. The more we ran, however, and the quicker our pace became, the more my fear grew into determination.

The trees grew thicker as we ran, and occasionally we had to slow a bit to find paths around wet areas or small lakes. We were running from Tennessee to Ohio. There were no strict plans after that. Our first destination, however, was the river.

The air was a bit chilly, but my mind, exhausted from running over Daniel's instructions, was soon distracted by the unfamiliar, scary sounds in the woods. I jumped at the noises, envisioning slave dogs and patrol groups with pistols searching for us. In truth, unless Masta Jeffrey came seeking me out sooner than I expected, I figured we had at least a few days' worth of time before Masta realized we were gone. But when the holiday elapsed, the true danger would begin.

I imagined, sometimes, that I saw John's dark body fleeing next to me. I drew on the image for a sense of security. A few times, I lost sight of Daniel's or Tucker's silhouettes. Frightened, I'd softly call out their names. I knew where I was headed: the landmarks and the signs nature offered helped guide the way. But I didn't want to separate from them.

As he also had other times that night, Daniel appeared by my side like an answered prayer. The sack, strapped to his back, bounced up and down as he neared me. Hidden inside it, as in mine, was some food, three gourds of water, his few belongings, and extra clothing. Mary had lined the clothes we had been given with a warmer layer of material. Each of us had shoes on our feet and a hat pulled low over our heads.

"I'm all right," I told him, but the words were half a lie. My feet, squeezed tightly into my shoes, had begun to ache after a few hours of running and creeping through the woods. My face had been scratched by tree limbs and sticks. I was frightened of the shadows that hung around us, and already discouraged. Perhaps the idea that we had escaped hadn't quite settled in my spirit yet.

We pushed on.

The sun broke that first morning long after I had hoped it would. We had run for hours on end, with only a few rest breaks for water. The anxiousness that had built up in me that night settled into a weariness I felt in my body. My clothes were damp from the midnight frost.

We found a resting place and tried to drift off to sleep so we would have the energy to run the next day. But our bodies had been so accustomed to working during the daylight hours that, instead of sleeping, we crouched in the shadows and spent many hours staring fearfully out into the daylight. I dozed off a few times, as did the others, but it took a few periods of rest to get used to the pattern.

Night came once more, and we fled again with haste. But by early morning, before the sun came out, my body had all but given out. We sought, and soon found, a small cave nearly hidden by some underbrush that could just hide us all. We filed in, and I sat back against the rock with a long yawn. Tucker looked over at me, his eyes revealing his exhaustion.

"You all right?"

I nodded, grateful for his comforting presence. His eyes remained on me, examining me to see if what I had said was the truth. Finally, he reached over and looked at my thumb, which I'd cut when I had fallen. Daniel was pulling out of his sack the last pinch of the first corn cake Mary had prepared for him.

"Hand all bloody-like." Tucker said.

I shrugged loosely. "Said I'm all right."

Disregarding my words, Tucker ripped some cloth from his shirt and tied it around my finger. I clenched my teeth and looked up at him appreciatively.

"We should be at that riva soon enough. Gots a lil' ways mo' to go, but if we all rest good an' long, then we's can make it befo' daylight tomorrow." I nodded at Tucker as my brother settled down next to me. He put a piece of corn cake in my hand, and I rested my head on his shoulder.

We had run for two nights without trouble, and I grew calmer and a little more confident as I shut my eyes that morning. All of a sudden, a strange feeling struck me. *I'm running to freedom!* A small smile drifted to my lips. We had escaped and were headed for freedom! I saw in the back of my mind Masta Jeffrey's face distorting as he wondered why his "plaything" had run away. Then another thought came, one I had tried to suppress. I imagined John lying on his pallet, praying hard for us. I returned the prayer.

Sleep was waiting for me this time, and I fell into its arms readily. Exhaustion won out over fear, but the three of us slept fitfully. If I had known that this would be the last time the three of us would be together as we were, maybe I would have savored sleep more. But I didn't know.

CHAPTER

❧ 20 ❧

NIGHTTIME FOUND US WITH THE STRENGTH TO MOVE ON. WE dashed out into the starless and foggy night in silence, reminding each other to stay together. All too soon, I was stumbling along, sore and nearly breathless, not yet used to so much nighttime exertion. I shook off what I could, however, since we had barely begun.

After hours of running, we stopped for a few minutes to catch our breath and to feed our grumbling stomachs.

Daniel tried to lift my spirits. "Sarah, when we's get to that riva, an' ride ova on that skiff, we ain' gotta run so much. Can walk a lil' mo'."

"You tole me already, Daniel," I said, pulling my aching foot out of my shoe to rub it, "but I don't mind runnin'. It's takin' us to freedom!" Daniel's red eyes didn't light up at the word. Instead, he glanced hesitantly behind him, over to Tucker, who was leaning against a tree sipping his water, and then back at me again.

"Dunno if Masta gonna send afta us or not. Figure he will, but cain't say if they already found us out or not." I looked down at the ground, trying hard not to think of what he was saying, and busied my mind with putting my shoe back on.

"Sarah," he said, looking back over at me, "if we—"

"C'mon, we gotta keep movin'!" I said, standing quickly and walking over to Tucker. There was no room in my spirit to hear any disheartening words. "Hope we don't hafta stop agin till we get to that riva," I added as the two of them fell into step close behind me. A silent prayer escaped my lips. We were going to make it.

We had to stop again, despite our desire to reach our destination as quickly as we could. It took us another day's worth of rest before we reached the river. By the middle of the night, we were out of sight of each other. We each had our own pace, and our own method of slipping into the darkness when we heard any sounds of danger. Because of this, and in order to move as quickly as possible, we planned to find each other at the river if we did happen to become separated.

At long last, the river came into my view. It was still far off in the distance, but near enough that I felt relief—a relief that was very short-lived.

I jumped in fright, almost tripping over my own feet as I heard the sound I had anticipated but dreaded at the same time, the sound I had prayed we would not hear.

The dogs!

Before I could catch myself, I had fallen to the ground, reopening the wound Masta Jeffrey had given me under my left eye. The ground seemed to rumble beneath my fall, as if trying to lead the dogs right to the spot where I lay. I tried to scramble up, but I tripped and fell again in my panic.

One second . . . two seconds . . . it's almost over. They're coming to get me. . . .

Someone, either Daniel or Tucker, pulled me up and pushed me onward. I couldn't tell who it was, but I could feel the terror in his trembling hands, before he disappeared into the woods.

My heart raced as I began to run even before I was steady on my feet. Before I knew it, I bounded faster than I ever thought possible, leaping over roots and dodging branches. I could get away—I *would* get away. As my legs ran, I looked around for Daniel and Tucker, but I saw no one. I was alone.

Get to the river.

My thoughts spun faster in my mind.

Get to the . . .

A single dog had barked once more, as if it wasn't quite sure whether or not it had found our trail. But the noise was terrifying.

I stumbled but then scrambled on my knees until I could get my footing again. Branches ripped at my clothes and skin like overgrown thorns reaching to stab the life out of me. But I didn't feel them.

One dog began to whine and was joined by another. They were getting closer.

Then I came upon the river so suddenly that I would've splashed right into it if not for the large tree there to stop me. The tall tree loomed over me with its outstretched branches, welcoming me like the arms of a protector. It roots stretched down into the dark river.

An ancestor.

Mary had told me that whenever a person was in grave danger, an ancestor was always there to help, you just had to find them.

I heard horses in the distance, a sound that shook me inside as I stood on the embankment, leaning against the tree. I steadied my breathing as I pulled off my shoes and hat and stuffed them into my sack. Stealing glances behind me, I buried the sack loosely beneath the muddy sticks and leaves piled near the part of the tree trunk that sat outside of the water, so that I could retrieve it quickly when I needed to.

The trunk was too wide for me to grasp, so I lowered myself down into the water by holding onto a thick limb. The river was so cold! Small chill bumps ran up and down my arms, but fear of what lay behind pushed me farther down into the water. I frowned, my free arm reaching farther down to find a lower branch. Just as I heard another bloodcurdling bark, my arm smacked against the branch I needed. I grasped it with both hands and lowered myself further. The water rose to my chin.

I searched in vain for the skiff that should have been waiting there for us. Even though the moon hid behind the clouds, enough light peeked through for me to search the dark banks of the river. The skiff was nowhere in sight.

Now what?

One of John's warnings flitted past my mind.

"If you eva gotta cross deep waters, make sho' you shed yo' clothes."

"Why?"

"It's wintatime, Sarah, an' them rivers hold all the cold you could imagine."

Another shiver ran up and down my body. In my haste, I had forgotten to strip my clothes from my back, and I had nothing else to dress myself in. They clung to me as I struggled to stay warm and alert.

I waited. Time ticked very slowly as I listened to the barking of the dogs. My heart was beating so loudly, I knew the dogs would find me for sure! They seemed to get closer with every breath I took, so I made every single breath a prayer to God to keep me hidden. I could've easily slipped into the peace and quiet of the river forever. . . .

Suddenly, their barks turned into angry growls. My heart quickened, but I knew they could not have seen me. They were far from where I stood in the water. But had they found Tucker? Or . . . or my brother?

Holding my breath, I turned my head and peered around the tree, but I could see nothing in the night. What I heard, however, stilled my heart.

The night carried to my ears a loud grunt, almost a yell. One of the dogs yelped loudly in response. I listened closely to the broken shouts of the voices in the distance.

". . . got somethin' . . . Let's go!" The sound of the

galloping horses came hauntingly nearer.

".... stabbed my goddamn dog, one of 'em did. Find 'im!" The drawl came from a commanding voice. I couldn't tell how many others were with him, scurrying around in the shadows. I inched as low as I could and peered around once again. Still I could see nothing. I was frozen with fear. Then a thought sprang to my mind.

Sarah, get across the river.

I ignored the impulse. I had to know if whoever had stabbed the dog had been found, or if he had safely hidden himself away. My answer came almost immediately.

"There one goes! You seen 'im? Stop!" I couldn't make out the rest of his words; they were lost to the night. But whoever had been discovered surely wouldn't turn himself in that easily. More shouts echoed into the night. I shivered in the water as the woods grew still again.

Suddenly, there was a loud rustling followed by two gunshots. A shout bit through the air. A scream almost emerged from my lips. My heart squeezed tighter than my grasp on the branch.

I could hear them questioning the fallen man, his shot body most likely at the mercy of the whip.

".... you headed, boy?" a new voice echoed through the air. I knew right away it was Masta Jeffrey. His presence chilled my bones more than the cold water did. Why was he out here? Mastas didn't usually chase runaways themselves.

I strained my ears against the yells that reverberated through the woods, but my heart refused to identify the person who had been captured. Another question from the slave catchers rang through the air. I shuddered, anticipating the worst.

What if he is conscious and he reveals our plans and our route of escape? What if they catch me next?

But only silence followed the questions that I could no longer make out. Whoever it was, he was not answering. Whether it was a conscious choice to remain silent, I could not tell. I wanted my spirit to relieve me of the sound of dying moans, to rid me of the images in my mind of dripping blood and hounds' teeth ripping through soft skin, tearing hopes and dreams apart. But instead, my spirit again whispered, *Sarah, get across the river.*

I looked out over the river, hot tears springing steadily from my eyes, and tried to steady my mind so that I could think.

"Swim," I mumbled softly, needing to hear my own voice. "Swim across." I could've stayed. I could've hidden and prayed for God to cover me with his big wings. But I was far enough from them to make it across without being detected, and my spirit was urging me to cross.

I shut my eyes and took a few breaths to try to focus. But as soon as I did, the image of a mutilated body ran across my mind. I almost spilled the contents of my stomach.

Who is it that lies sprawled on the ground? Who?

I shook the question away and pulled myself up to stand on an underwater stump. Easing the sack from under the brush, I tied it tightly across my back and shoulder. I was supposed to keep my belongings dry, but I had no choice but to carry it through the water with me.

I fought my way across the strong river, which had to be as deep as at least two of me. The temperature of the water seemed to have dropped dramatically since I had first entered. I moved farther along, my arms and legs working with each other. Using what I had taught myself back at the plantation, I kicked and pulled and kicked and pulled myself through the water. At times, water filled my mouth so that I felt I would drown. But I fought my way back up, back to the air, all the way to the other side. It didn't take as long as I had expected, though crossing on a skiff would have allowed me to keep myself and my belongings dry.

After finding a spot to shield myself, I collapsed on the other side of the river, exhausted and cold. My body tingled, but I knew that if I stopped there, I still risked of being caught. I rubbed my palms together and lifted my body slowly off the ground.

Walking on, I searched desperately for a place I could hide and rest, but after walking for some time, I fell back to the ground, forlorn and shivering. My legs felt like iron rods—I had to stop. A small barn lay ahead. I crept up to it.

There was no movement inside or out, and the door hung loosely on its hinges. Inside, I saw empty stalls, empty feeding rooms, and piles of hay. Thrown in the corner were three large horse blankets. Whoever the barn belonged to had either been gone a long time or abandoned the place entirely. I needed a place to rest, and that's the only warning my body followed.

I crept into the smallest, darkest room and buried myself beneath one of the blankets, surrounding my hiding place with hay. Only then did I notice that my cold, wet clothes still clung to me. As my heartbeat returned slowly to normal, I stripped the clothes from my body, wrung them out, and struggled my way back into them. Pulling the blanket tightly over my shoulders again, I curled myself up in a ball, like a child.

Rocking back and forth, I tried to empty my mind. But I couldn't. Before I could stop myself, the smell from the horse blanket nauseating me, I vomited.

I shook harder, wanting to cry out loud to rid my mind of the capture. Who was it that lay dying in woods? Had he really been by my side just yesterday? I closed my eyes, and when I did, I dreamed of ropes of blood grasping my ankles, grabbing my heart, reaching for my neck . . .

I awoke suddenly, trembling even harder, my eyes swollen from the tears.

Where am I?

I noticed sunlight bleeding through the walls of the barn as I came to my senses. I felt warmer on the outside, but inside, I still didn't feel quite right. I lifted myself gravely, then gasped when I saw two large eyes staring at me. I had concealed myself well, even though I'd been in a terrible state. Only eyes searching for a hideout could have found me—or the observant eyes of a small child.

The little black boy didn't move or jump, even when

he noticed me staring back. I was unsure of what to do. I looked from his eyes to his little hands, which clung to a jug. I rose, unsteadily, from my hiding place.

"You tell somebody 'bout me?" I asked the boy with a frown and with a harshness I hadn't meant to let escape my mouth. He still stared back at me, his face unchanged.

"Mama say take this to you, an' don't tell nobody I done seen you." He eyed me carefully, not budging until I had reached out after a long moment's worth of considering and grabbed the jug. As soon as I took it, however, he turned and ran to the door, his bare feet thudding softly against the ground. But then he whirled around and ran back over to me.

"She also say if she was gonna sneak to the barn like she does sometimes an' fix me some of that dried-fruit pie I like, but ain' s'pose ta have, she wouldn't do it tamarra night. She tole me she won't come here then 'cause them horses be back by then." I nodded slowly, my mouth slightly open, as the little boy crouched down near a large crack in the side of the barn and squeezed his small body through.

Sinking back into my perch, I tried to reason out whether or not to stay, whether or not I was in danger. Bringing the jug to my lips, I let the warm, sweet milk trickle down my thirsty throat and over my cracked lips. I emptied the jug halfway and buried myself beneath the blanket to do some more thinking, but drowsiness grabbed me, and my eyes were soon closed again. Once sleep came over me once more, the whispers began.

Don't cry for me, Sarah. When you reach freedom, I reach freedom, too, and so do all of us in bondage.

I awoke with a start, peeking out to see who had said those words to me. I longed for the ghost to reveal himself, but he didn't.

That's what exhaustion does to you, Sarah, I thought to myself, closing my eyes again.

I'm alone, aren't I? I thought, but I allowed my mind to share with me the comforting words I longed to hear.

No, I'm here. Mary's soft voice rippled through my mind.

I'm here too! It was John.

Shh, my child. It was Mathee, Mama.

This time, sleep came full and hard, and in my dreams, the ropes of blood began releasing their hold on me, laying out a path to freedom. At the end of that path stood John, arms open wide.

CHAPTER

❧ 21 ❧

I SLEPT FOR ALMOST TWO DAYS. I WOKE UP SEVERAL TIMES TO find small plates of food and jugs of liquid stashed by my side. As soon as the light streaming through the barn walls began dying down that third night, I stole away from the safety of the barn. After running for about a mile, I kneeled and emptied out my sack while there was still a little bit of light in the sky. I noticed a good-size rip near the bottom of the sack. *Anything could have fallen out!* But I hadn't the time right then to examine my belongings, the small bundle of which I pushed back into the bag. Instead I inspected my clothes and food supply. The dried meat Mary had packed was almost gone. The half piece of corn cake was spoiled. I tossed it away. All that remained was my small pack of nuts and dried fruit, and a gourd and a half of water. One of the three small gourds I had was cracked beyond repair. The clothes were still decent, however. I had a second pair of yarn socks, my hat and shoes, which I had let dry out in the barn, and another pair of pants. I tied the pants around the rip in the sack and pulled it all around my body once more.

I recalled Daniel's words as I ran on.

"Look fo' the biggest star in the sky when you'se lookin' to go north. Or when it's cloudy an' you in the forests, figure which side the moss grows. Most times, it grows on the north side of trees."

"All right."

"You can build a fire?"

"Sure! Mary taught me long time ago."

"Good. When you run outta food, gotta use what you got round you fo' eatin'. Fish in the waters, ducks, wild fruits—whateva you can get. May even have to steal a hog or two." I nodded at him.

"All right. How long it gonna take, Daniel?"

"Could take us a short time or a long time. Mattas what we run into an' how good we follow that path north. Now, there's folks an' places that may help us out on the way. Gotta know what to look fo'. Folks I talk to—folks who help us escape, Sarah—they say when we pass on by a house gonna do us some good, there always somethin' there that show us they safe folks."

"Somethin' there like what?"

"Couldn't say. But they tell me we'll sho' 'nuf know. But we gotta keep our eyes open. Might run right by them or miss them all if we ain't lucky. If that happens, we gonna hafta run most all the way."

"Wish you was here, Daniel," I whispered into the night as I let the lonely feeling inside me help carry me faster through the night.

I learned some things I never knew how to do before, running on my own. When I heard wild snarls echo through the woods enough times, I decided to take the time to learn how to climb quickly up a tree. I tumbled down the first few tries and fell hard to the earth. But the bruises hardened over. I practiced until I got good at it, then utilized this to keep myself safe.

I also had to teach myself to safely get a contained fire going. It was easy for people to spot fires, though, so I'd hide while it burned down to the last embers, then sneak back to the spot to roast whatever meat I had on a spit. But gathering food was a lot harder than I had hoped. Daniel had told me that he, Tucker, and I would catch and kill some of the small animals we ran into on the way—that's what runaways most often did. But being as neither of them was with me, catching the animals was quite difficult. I would get lucky sometimes and find rabbits or other small animals already dying or freshly dead. But that wasn't very often. Mostly I just depended on the berries and other fruits I picked along the way. After eight nights of running, the food Mary had provided me with and that I had collected with Tucker and Daniel began to run very low.

But I ran onward.

I was alone, and I was diving into a world beyond reason. I had been searching homes that I passed for hints or signs that would convince me I had found safety. But nothing seemed safe enough, and as desperate and tired as I felt sometimes, my mind would whisper small messages, reminding me that nothing, absolutely nothing mattered more than survival.

At night, I took to clutching large sticks or rocks and knew that if the worst came to be, I would not be afraid to use them. I began to wonder how much easier my journey would be if I had a gun. Perhaps I wouldn't have to spend hours chasing food I knew I would not get my hands on. And perhaps the whispers of the night wouldn't scare me so much.

The solitude tore at me. I longed for a hand to hold, and some days I sat shivering with fear, afraid to move on. I longed for words of assurance from Mary, good advice from John, and the knowledge that neither Daniel nor Tucker had been killed. But none of that came. There was no one but me scraping my way through what seemed menacing country.

It didn't take long for my supply of meat to run out. I tried to continue running, in hopes of getting lucky and finding something edible that would fill my empty belly, at least enough to give me the stamina I needed. But a growling, constantly hungry stomach made me weak. I caught nothing, and the fruit I found was not enough. I was desperate, and knew I had to risk danger to save myself from starving.

"'Scuse me, ma'am," I said, walking up to a woman who stood alone, taking care of laundry. I was making myself vulnerable to the daytime on the outskirts of a plantation. The woman looked up kindly at first, but seeing me, she became irritated.

"What you want?" she asked, turning her eyes away again.

"I'm goin' back to my masta's plantation. He gave me

leave, an' I been travelin' some days. Would like it if I could have some food." I looked with pleading eyes, searching for the kind soul I knew had to lie beneath her irritation. She looked at me sharply and tried to walk away, but I followed her.

"What you want?" she asked again without looking back at me. I could see she was afraid—afraid I was a runaway. For most of what I'd seen and heard, harsh punishment would be given to any slave who helped a runaway. So I lied to the woman. I had to.

"Ma'am, I need some food, that's all. I ain't . . . I ain't no runaway or nothin', I jus' . . . ."

"Go!" she whispered harshly, spittle flying in my face. I could see her fear playing across the creases in her forehead. "Go away. I ain't got nothin' to do wit you." She hurried from me, beyond where I was willing to venture, out into the fields. I stared after her mournfully, my hunger buzzing in my ears. I crouched down and disappeared back into the woods.

But someone followed me. I squatted beneath a bush, watching a male figure creep into the woods. Once well out of view of the fields, he stood up to his full height and stared in my direction.

"There's dried meat hangin' in the buildin' near the outhouse. You should take wat you need, miss, an' get goin' quick." The man stood, waiting for me to come out of hiding. But I didn't move. I stayed hidden and watched him walk slowly back toward his work.

I tried listening to my reason rather than my hunger.

I knew that certain slaves existed that would take it upon themselves to tell on runaways. These slaves sought only to appear loyal to their masters so that their plight as a slave would not be so bad. I knew I looked very suspicious. The man seemed sincere, but I didn't know for sure.

What if this is a trap? What if someone is there, just waiting for me to come out of hiding?

I didn't feel good about this, but I needed food. The day slipped by, and I found a new place to hide about half a mile from the plantation, though I was too nervous to fall into full sleep. I knew I couldn't run any farther without food in my belly, and so I waited.

When night came, I hastened over as quietly as I could to the area near the smokehouse the man had pointed out. I squinted through the dark to get a good view of it. All seemed still and silent, but the fact that the door hung open made me cautious.

Aren't smokehouse doors almost always kept shut?

I sat back against a tree, still hidden in the woods, but only a few paces away from the clearing. All I needed to do was get in, cut however much meat I could hold, and run back out. But anyone who saw me could grab me by force and throw a sack over my head, or even knock me out with a rock or stick. So first, if there was danger lurking, I had to get rid of it.

I emptied my mind of the longing for food, and focused. I opened my sack, laid a piece of fabric over the top for the meat, and held it close to my body. I took out my knife, then found a few small stones and a large, thick tree branch that I was able to carry. Backing farther into the woods, I threw the stones, one after another, as far as I could to the left of the smokehouse, then watched with quickening heartbeats as a figure emerged from the shadows near the house and disappeared in the direction of the sound.

Just what I thought. He had been waiting for me.

Taking my chance, I ran as low and as quickly as I could to the smokehouse and passed through the doorway. The smell of meat hit me instantly. How hungry I was! Without wasting time, I found a piece of meat that didn't look so tough. But my small knife wouldn't cut quickly enough.

Panicked, I glanced back toward the door. Nobody was there—not yet, at least. I searched desperately, walking through the hanging meat, for tool I could use.

A butcher knife!

I picked it up, and sliced the meat I had chosen into portions that fit into my sack. I was almost there. Just a couple more strokes.

I paused to wipe away sweat that had dripped into my eyes, took another worried glance toward the door, and steadied my shaking hand. I would make it out, I would.

When the last piece snapped free, I almost let out a cry of thanks to God. But I still needed to escape. Moving to the door, I glanced out, to see if the man was anywhere in sight. Grasping the large stick, I darted out. But the night remained silent as I slipped away from the smokehouse and traveled on.

By the time I was far enough away that I could stop and eat what I had taken, anger was rushing through my body. I tore viciously at a large chunk of meat, tying the rest of it up for later. Whom could I trust? The man who had told me about the smokehouse had betrayed me. So what stranger could I trust? I could trust my loved ones, but at this point they seemed like nothing more than memories in my mind. I was angry at how close I had come to being captured back into slavery by a person who knew how it felt to be bound in bondage.

I washed these thoughts away as best I could with a sip of water from my gourd.

A few nights later, I came to a little house in the woods. I had slept in a ditch close by and come upon it soon after I awoke. There was no plantation, no corn, tobacco, or cotton field, just a small garden and the house. But what especially drew my interest was a basket that sat in front of red shutters, adorned with a cloth that almost glowed in the evening light. Dusk had just fallen, so it was still early, but I saw no movement or light inside the house.

"Might be food, Sarah," I whispered to myself as I crept up to the basket to peer inside. But just as I did, candlelight flickered behind the cracks in the shutters. I darted a few feet away, then heard a rustling, followed by the shutters flying open, just missing the basket. A white woman, whose hair was tied neatly back, dumped bread and other food I couldn't see into the basket.

"I wonder, dear, if they'll notice these leftovers. We

can't eat them. Might as well leave them here for whatever can get to them." The words seemed to have been directed over her shoulder to someone in the house, but I saw her eyes dig deep into the night. I listened carefully to her words, then waited until a few minutes after the shutters had closed before I advanced toward the basket.

As I reached into it, the shutters opened again, and this time, I had no chance to hide. I could have run, but some instinct kept my feet planted as I watched the woman, whose head was turned, say "Dear, do you think they're hungry tonight?" But when her head came around, she gasped and took a timid step back. I simply stared at her, convinced that this had to be one of the safe houses Daniel had spoken of—it had to be.

She recovered quickly, and approached the window again. She nudged the basket closer to me. "Go 'head," she said in a gentle whisper, "you're safe." I stepped closer but remained partially obscured in the shadows, ready to depart as quickly as I could if I needed to. But the woman was now wrapping the food in the cloth, and she held it out for me to take. I stepped up, grabbed it from her fingers, and backed up to the spot I had left. I watched her a bit longer, and she watched me just as closely. Her hands were busy with something, and eventually she lifted a wet cloth to me. I stepped closer and gently took it from her.

"Wipe the dirt from your eyes. You can, well, . . . this is a safe place to stay for a day, if you need to," she began, softly as a cricket's breath.

"Thank you," I whispered, and turned to dart away,

even after she called, softly, after me. I left her sight, but stayed by the house to see what she would do.

"Well, anyway, dear," she said, calling behind her back again. "The weather's not warming up any. Figure it may get pretty cold." As she said that, she lifted a small blanket through the window, a blanket small enough to serve as a coat, and placed it on the windowsill. Then she retreated, closing the shutters.

I grabbed the blanket and ran on.

CHAPTER

❧ 22 ❧

THE WEATHER DID TURN COLDER, AND I HAD NO SHELTER. THE ground was my floor, the biting wind my walls, and the sky my only roof. The day was a routine, a monotonous drone of walking, creeping, running, eating, and sleeping. With the strain of this routine, my continual efforts to keep a decent food supply, the burden of constant fear, and the cold, my body grew tired.

I don't remember when the fight began, but suddenly, my mind and body were battling against each other. I was getting weaker, but I didn't want to accept it. My body would ask me if I could keep this up. But why did it matter if my body could or not? I had to. It was as this fight raged that another one of my dreams came, sneaking up on me in the silence of daytime, when I slept, and leaving me sweating heavily, even in the cold, the tears on my cheeks and the heaviness in my chest shoving me further into a gloom that was hard to find my way out of.

Some days, the loneliness ran so deep, I had to fall asleep to conjure up memories and the faces of loved ones. I sought them out for comfort, but their distant faces were from a yesterday that seemed almost like a dream. What was real was my escape, this running.

During those brief moments that hopefulness would slip up to me, I allowed my mind to wander to places I had not yet seen, to a life that sat waiting for me on the other side of this struggle to stay alive. I daydreamed sometimes about sitting in a classroom with other students, answering questions and reading books—daydreams that occasionally seemed so real, I longed to disappear forever into them. Education seemed to be an odd incentive, but thoughts of it spurred me along when nothing else could.

I knew there was a large river I had to reach, a river much bigger than the one I had already crossed, one I couldn't possibly miss. If only I could make it there. But where was it?

The days turned even colder. I began coughing and sneezing, but I stumbled onward. My chest rattled and my throat was sore, and I had headaches that left me kneeling for hours at night as I tried to relieve myself of them.

Then, one night, as snow fell steadily, heaven must have decided to turn all the elements of nature against me. Down came icy rocks, hurled my way as if the skies were taunting me for the slowness of my pace. I dropped down and tried to shield myself, but they came crashing upon my back and shoulders. I fought to get up again, to seek shelter. My throat burned while the rest of me shook with cold. With the surrounding land mocking me as I stumbled over its bumpy surfaces and my own feet, I searched for refuge from heaven's assault. Then I saw it.

Fire!

A fire blazed wildly amid the snow. I ran for it, mustering strength I didn't know I had. But the closer I got, the farther away it ran from me, until I stopped altogether and watched it disappear in the wind.

No . . . I'm seeing things.

Weary, as if carrying a full-grown person on my shoulders, I walked on, beaten by the rocks of ice and blinded by the wind and snow.

Then I saw the ledge.

Perhaps it would offer shelter—but, no! I shut my eyes tightly, trying to banish the mirage from my mind. But when I opened them again, the image had not disappeared. I felt a bit of relief. I was going to make it. My body lunged forward, racing in blind pursuit. But as I ran, I tripped over a mound, a large rock, and the impact hurled me straight to the ground. I lay there, cringing, crying, and realizing how blinded by snow and defeat I really was for the moment. I was sick, alone, and freezing. It was my time, I just knew it. I could hear the drums and the voice of Mathee, Mama.

Look up, Sarah.

Her voice in my ear came clear and absolute. I looked up and there was the ledge, waiting for me. It was a thick frozen slope jutting out over the ice: another ancestor.

I pulled myself up and stumbled on until I reached the slope and collapsed underneath it in a fit of coughs, huddling against the ice. My eyes narrowed, searching for something, anything, anyone, to save me. But the more I strained to see, the more difficult it became, until I closed my eyes altogether. I tried to force a prayer through my lips.

"God . . . I . . . help me. . . ."

My head throbbed powerfully, and I couldn't think clearly. I had just enough energy to put my sack under my head for a pillow and curl my body into a ball. But that didn't help. I could not stop shivering.

Then the coughing began again. The painful fit seemed to last forever, but soon enough, it died down. When it did finally end, and I opened my eyes, I saw tiny spots of blood splattered on my cloth and on the ice around me. My insides were freezing. Was this how it was going to end for me?

My head beat like war drums. I began to lose feeling in my limbs. I wanted to cry out, but I couldn't find my voice. It was a struggle to simply stay conscious. This was the end of my journey. I thought of all who loved me and wished I could pull through for them. I saw their faces: Mary, Mama, Daniel, John. But I couldn't. I felt the little warmth I had in my body seeping out of me. At least I didn't have to die a more painful death. At least I would die with my pride still intact.

I was back, back in the motherland. The cloth, the pots, the drums, Mama's hut—they were all there. I walked through our

hut, touching everything I could—the baskets, the jewelry, the walls. I eagerly sniffed the scents that filled my nostrils—Mama's perfumelike fragrances, the strange scent of Sentwaki's bow, the meal being prepared in an adjacent room.

How did I get here? What had I been doing? I couldn't remember. It felt as if time had been suspended and I had been carried back to the place where life should have left me alone.

Everything was so vivid, so real, all except for the light. There was a brightness I couldn't touch that emanated around me. Had I died and returned to my place of birth, as I had prayed for when I was younger?

Outside, the sun shone brightly, its rays stretching far across the land, traveling in and out of homes, forming shapes among the treetops. And yet a chill hung within the brightness. Then a touch. Dark skin, beautiful legs, neat curly hair, large lips. It all came into focus.

Mama Mijiza.

Mathee gave me a bucket to take to the lake and fill up with water. She wasn't any older than I remembered, just a few years my senior now. Then I remembered. The white men, the guns: they had taken her life. Mama Mathee, so young and vibrant, so loving. They had taken Sentwaki and me away from our mother, dragged us across wretched seas, torn my family apart. Angry, I glanced up at Mama's face, but she simply placed a strong finger over her lips and held my hand.

With Mama Mjiza by my side, I walked barefoot through the village, watching little ones scurrying over feet, women gathered at the monger posts, little boys leaping through the grass and racing through skirts, thighs, and shifting hips. They were all as I remembered them to be. The smiles melted hearts. The loud chatter filled the streets. The crying babies were gently rocked by the village hand merged as one.

I walked past the memories to the water's edge. Splashing the water over my face, I felt renewed. I let the memories of another life wash away.

But when I brought my hands back down into the water, it was no longer clear blue. My hands were now submerged in a water that was thick, deep red.

The scent of blood permeated the air. I tried to snatch my hands from the bloody liquid, but it curled up toward me, animate, and grabbed my arms, pulling me down into it.

Images flashed before my eyes. A small, smiling African girl twirled around in circles, as if dancing. Then her face was awash in pain. White men fired guns into the night, their bullets plunging into the depths of an African heart. An innocent heart. My mother's heart.

No, no!

I was awake, but my eyes weren't open. What I thought to be tears slowly ran down my face. But I felt my fingers wipe sweat from my head. My eyes opened, barely, and I could just make out a figure sitting over me. I shivered and fell back into a deep sleep.

I plunged deep into the blood. And as soon as the red waters consumed me, I felt my legs jolting, running. I was fleeing, stumbling, running away from barking dogs and the pale-skinned monster-men. The devils.

I was soaked in blood. I looked down and saw that the blood was my own, that it spewed like an angry fountain straight from my heart. I gasped in horror as I let my own blood run through my fingers.

Am I dying in death? How is this possible?

I looked up and found myself staring into the face of my mother. She gently lifted her two hands and placed them over her heart. They rested there, soothing me so that I felt peace and warmth enter my own heart. I looked down to see my hands pressed against my chest. As I withdrew them, and she dropped hers, I saw that the blood was gone. A slight smile passed across her face. Then, with a wink, she began her ascent, light as a summer breeze. After crossing the threshold that stood between the two of us, her body scattered into a colorful array of warm breath and energy, and Mathee flowed over me. I shut my eyes tight, breathing in the love that was seeping into my bones—the strength, hope, and warmth. *Oh, the warmth!*

I was healed.

CHAPTER

❧ 23 ❧

WARMTH BROUGHT ME BACK TO CONSCIOUSNESS. AS I LAY
waiting for another episode of shivering, I slowly became
aware of my surroundings. I didn't think I was in heaven—
it felt far from it—but I wasn't dead, either. My body was
wrapped in a damp quilt, and a thicker covering was set
on top of that. I studied my surroundings as my eyelids
fluttered half open.

Where am I? How did I get here? What time of day is it?

The room was small and simple, with walls dressed in
animal fur. The setting had a calming effect on me; I had the
impression that I was in a safe place, but I couldn't say for
sure. One thing was clear, though: this was no Big House.

I found, my eyes wandering, that there were no windows.
I couldn't tell if it was night or day. I tried to sit up, but the
drumming in my head began its pounding ritual, though
much less intensely than before. So I sank back down into
the softness.

I must have fallen asleep again, because I opened my
eyes to find myself staring straight into the small, green eyes
of a strange-looking man. In the candlelight that leaped
across his face, I could just make out his light brown skin

and straight and loose black hair. My dream flashed past me: barking dogs, guns, and . . . white men! I'd run from the same men I was lying here staring at now. But he didn't look like the others . . .

Fear still struck my chest. I pushed against my hands to scramble up, bracing myself for the headache that was sure to follow, but his words restrained me.

"Stay . . . need sleep . . . need food . . ." His words weren't harsh or demanding, and he had mentioned the one thing that chased the doubts away. Food! I fell back into the pillow as my stomach growled in response to the thought. It was then that I noticed the bowl sitting on his knee, steam rising from it. I looked up into his sincere eyes and let the aroma penetrate my nose. I turned with longing back to the bowl.

"For you," he said, taking my arm to help me sit up. Once I was settled, he held out the bowl and I took it without pause. But with another moment's consideration, spoon grasped in hand, I looked around, curious.

"Where am I?" I said in a weak, cracking voice.

"Eat first, then talk," he said. Without any further persuading, I began my meal.

"Careful. Hot," he said, pointing to the bowl. But I paid him no mind. Spoonfuls of the soup filled my mouth, and some of it even dripped down my chin.

"You like?" he asked. I nodded.

"Rabbit," he said simply. All too quickly, the food had disappeared. I stared mournfully into the bowl. Slowly and patiently, he pried the bowl from my fingers. Without a word, he stood up from the side of the bed. I stared after him, watching his small, nimble body retreat from the room. His black hair was braided down his back. Soon, he returned with another bowl of the soup. I smiled up at him as he handed me the bowl. His lips remained set, but his eyes smiled down into mine. He sat down again.

"You talk now?" he asked after I finished the second bowl and settled back with a full belly. I nodded.

"Where am I?"

"My home, in Kentucky. Found you out there almost dead. Very bad storm."

"But how you find me out there?" I asked, listening closely to his accent.

A small smile curled on his lips. "Just listen close to inside," he said, patting his chest. "Somethin' say go, I go. Find you. Carry you back here."

That explained the feeling I had of floating through the air.

"I thought I was dyin', freezin' to death," I said.

"Freezin'?" he said thoughtfully. "Yes, you freeze. But you live. Not your time to go, to . . . to die." He looked at me kindly, waiting for another question.

Suddenly, a haunting thought crossed my mind.

What if this man is dangerous? What if he makes deals with slave hunters? What if he knows who I am, where I had run from, and intended to take me back?

"Shh," the man said, cutting into my thoughts so sharply, I wondered if he could see the words spinning behind my eyes.

"You safe with me," he said with a smart nod. "You safe here."

My heart told me I was safe, but my mind convinced me that his words weren't enough. I tried to wash my face with a blank stare and to come up with a lie that would make me less conspicuously a runaway and enable me to escape his home. But sickness had left me weak and broken-down. A tear almost fell from my eye as I struggled to take possession of my feelings, which were tumbling every which way.

"Shh," he said again, leaning over to pat my shoulder as I sniffed back the fear.

"All I know, you lost from home. Gonna get better here, then return. Know nothing else. Gonna keep you safe until you ready to go." I eyed him carefully, then nodded trustingly at him, still unable to gather my emotions. I let the swelling feeling of gratitude show in my gaze.

"Ain't neva seen no white man help folks like me." I pointed at his hair. "Ain't neva seen no white man wit skin as dark as yours an' hair like that befo'!" I said.

He laughed and then replied, "You not seen many things in world. I'm no white folk."

I looked at him with a frown.

"They call me Indian. Forced family away." The lines that ran across his cheeks and forehead deepened.

"Who forced them away?" I asked, feeling the sadness behind his weighted words.

"Folk you talk of."

"Why you didn't go with them?" He turned his eyes away from mine.

Instead of responding to my question, he said, "We here long, long time before they come. We try to tell them land cannot be taken. Land not . . . ah . . . not property to be owned. They steal and call it 'my land' anyway. Foolish folk. No understanding. I not understand them. They no understand me," he said, raising his hand to pat his chest. Then he lifted his hand and pointed at me. "And they no understand you."

I nodded, solemnly, and covered my mouth when a cough escaped my lips. He helped me lie back down. Then he stood up.

"You need water. Be back."

"Thank you, sah," I whispered, hoarse. When he returned, I was drowsy again, half-asleep, but full of questions nonetheless. After I let the water run down my throat, I asked him what was on my mind.

"How long've I bin here?"

"Day four today," he said. "Your fever—very bad. I hunt around here and help folks like you long time," he said, leaning closer. "Know things out there in the earth, on trees, in bushes and woods—things that heal. But strongest medicine not work for you. Something else heal you. You wanted alive."

I sighed, distantly, and closed my eyes. I was drifting back into sleep, but he continued.

"Yesterday the worst day for you. Nighttime, you burn up with fever. I don't sleep one minute so I keep you cool.

You sleep, toss around all night, and speak words sound like 'Mathee.' Your skin so hot at first, but when sun touch sky, fever fly away. Your face brighten, and the fever gone for good."

I listened abstractly to his words, finding it more and more difficult to keep my eyes open. I didn't want to fall back asleep; I wanted to stay awake and alert, even though I trusted the man.

". . . sitting by your bed too, tired . . . talk to you. He keep talking to me, say he know you make it. . . ." He was standing, and walking away. His last few words met my ears as I fell deeper into sleep.

". . . that fellow here . . ." He had opened the door.

". . . came just yesterday . . ." His voice sounded distant, as if he were telling me a bedtime story.

". . . sleep good." The door shut, and I was asleep.

My heart skipped a beat as soon as I opened my eyes, the memory of the hunter's words echoing in my ears.

He had said ". . . that fellow here . . . just yesterday."

I threw my legs over the bed and sat up, trying to compose my thoughts. But the movement was too quick, and I held my head in my hand, begging the pain that had erupted to leave me quickly. As it did, my thoughts began to run wild.

He's here.

"Who?" I whispered to the empty room. Images of

Tucker's smile and the gaze of my brother's eyes passed through my mind.

"Who?" I asked again, standing, then moving quickly toward the door. I had to stop, and leaned against the wall to steady myself so I wouldn't topple over. But I shook it off and headed again toward the door. But before I could reach it, the door swung out wide. A young man stood there, eyes red and tired, mouth open just slightly.

Without a moment of hesitation, I had my arms wrapped solidly around him, my tears spilling into the sweat that dampened his shirt. He lifted his arms up and encircled me in a hug in response. So many silent words passed between us, so many unexpressed feelings. Over and over, the image of my brother lying dead in the woods had haunted my mind, drawn out so precisely and realistically that I had thought for certain I had lost him. And yet here he stood before me now in this room, life pulsing through every strong heartbeat I could feel against my body.

I still sobbed into Daniel's shoulder as he led me back to the bed. He sat down by me. I had questions upon questions, but it all was too overwhelming. I wanted to tell him how seeing him relieved every piece of my heart, and yet, it still didn't feel right. Now I knew for certain: Tucker was the one who had perished in the woods. My tears of gladness and disbelief became, in an instant, tears of mourning. Daniel felt the shift. He whispered softly, "He was brave, Sarah."

"Daniel . . ." I fell into a light coughing fit, feeling dizzy and light-headed from the exertion.

"You still weak, Sarah. Go on back to sleep. I ain't goin' nowhere." The voice was soothing, and it seemed to restore strength to my body. I let my tears carry me toward rest.

Just as he had promised, when I awoke, he was seated right beside me, my head still on his shoulder. I lifted my neck, stretching it out, and looked over at Daniel. I wanted to jump up and hug him again, never letting go. But instead, I turned to look at him. Daniel's face had grown thinner. But behind his eyes lay the same soul I had known for most of my life. I opened my mouth, but he cut in before I could say one word.

"The hunter's a safe man, Sarah, if you hadn't figured. This place is one of them safe houses I done told you 'bout." His words were unsteady but they were informative, as if he sought a subject that would be easy to talk about.

"Sho' seemed like it to me, Daniel, but how you know?" I asked, fighting to keep myself calm. I fiddled with my fingers, trying to find some way to drain the excitement of being able to talk to my brother, who for weeks I had believed was dead.

"Was runnin' an' saw the blinkin' lights. I was 'bout gone myself—tired an' jus' so weak. Sat in front of the house to make sho' I wa'an't jus' seein' things. Sat there fo' 'bout an' hour an' saw the lights blink twice again. Knew it as a sign."

I nodded. "I believed him when he tole me."

"Oh! Got somethin' fo' ya." From under his arm he pulled my sack and handed it to me. The tear had been roughly stitched up.

"Hunter fixed it up fo' ya. Say he gotta know how to take care of hisself out here. Nice man."

"Sho' he is." We talked on. The hunter had entered to check on us, and he showed us that we were actually settled below the house, under a trapdoor.

Soon after the hunter left, Daniel fell asleep. I watched him as his eyes closed, then took the sack he had given me.

I was tired as well, but I needed to make sure that all my belongings were still in my bag. I dumped its contents onto the bed and unwrapped a large hair rag that held my belongings. My hand ran across coins wrapped in fabric. I bit deep into my lip, remembering the moment Tucker had learned of my intention to escape with them. A strange grin had slid upon his face as he nodded with satisfaction. Then he pulled a bag of coins out of his pocket and handed me two.

I put the coins to my lips and whispered a prayer, trying to rid my spirit of the unsettled feeling I had. But sadness overcame me, and I quickly rewrapped the coins. My needle and thread were still there, as were Mary's gift and the smaller cooking utensils she had provided me with. My hand ran over the other items as I searched in vain for the little wooden angel John had carved for me.

Where's my angel? John's angel? Ain't no way I made it this far without it! But I must have done just that, for the small wooden guardian was nowhere to be seen. I sighed, afraid of what me losing it might imply. It was gone forever; had I lost John forever too? Or was he already thinking about and planning how to get to freedom, how to get to me? I shook that thought from my mind but just as soon as I had, the image of Tucker came to my mind. The scent of blood in the woods the day he was caught still lingered in my nose, his friendly face now swamped in death still painted on the back of my eyelids.

"Sarah?" I jumped as I felt a hand on my shoulder and heard Daniel's voice.

"Daniel! I was just thinkin' . . ."

"What's wrong, what's the matta?"

I sighed. "Had a dream 'bout my mama back from where I came from."

"Another dream?" He asked, his eyebrows arching with concern.

"Oh, nothin' at all like usual. It was a good dream, almost like she—like she healed me herself." We were silent for a moment before I continued. "Made me think of Mary for a moment."

As if my words were an open invitation, Daniel jumped right in to voice his concerns. "You know, I bin thinkin' hard 'bout her, Sarah. I didn't know what was gonna happen to you, an' I was worried to death 'bout Mama. Figured maybe it was me s'posed to make her come."

"Daniel, don't do that. Already told you, cain't make her do nothin' she don't wanna do. She'll be all right. She will."

Daniel nodded slowly.

"Sho' do miss her, though," I said after some time. "An' Tucker . . ." His name slipped from my lips before I had time to think. Daniel turned from me, gritting his teeth.

"Daniel, I didn't know who it was they caught," I said softly. "Thought it was you."

He angrily kicked at an object that lay on the ground.

"Damn!" he said under his breath as he got up to pace the floor. I wanted to comfort him, but the same feeling was eating at my own throat.

"I don't undastand, Daniel. He was so quick—fasta than the two of us. Why . . . why was he the one got caught?" Daniel came back over and sat next to me, anger and sadness etched into his face.

"Don't think he was tryin' to run, Sarah. Think he was tryin' to hide. Maybe he . . . maybe he wanted to save us." I took his cold hands into mine.

"Daniel, there was nothin' you could do. Nothin'!"

He shook his head. "Ain' a betta man I knew. I was the one mention runnin', an' he put his foot into it right away. He knew folks who could help us 'cause of that job Masta let him have. Helped us set it up an' everythin'. An' now look—he ain't even gonna reach freedom."

"Tucker's in freedom, Daniel," I said softly, "jus' a different kind." I began to cry, but Daniel brushed my tears away with his hand.

"But it ain't fair!"

"Naw, it ain't," he said, "and you don't know how much it meant to me to know you was here an' safe."

I nodded, attempting to stop the tears so my headache wouldn't return. "Reckon I'm carrying part of him in my heart so when I do reach freedom, he'll be there too." I said. "And Mary, Mary's in here too."

"Of course she is," Daniel said, but with little assurance.

"Don't worry 'bout her, Daniel. She all right." We were silent for a long while, and that silence brought on sleep once more.

CHAPTER

24

THE NEXT DAY ARRIVED, AND DANIEL AND I CONTINUED RESTING in the hunter's home. We weren't too worried about getting captured there, for we were certain that the ice raining down outside would stop our pursuers—if we were still being persued—in their tracks. But by nightfall, the storm had passed. A thin blanket of snow hugged the earth. The hunter explained to us that the coldest part of the season was now over.

The following evening, as we bundled up and gathered food and water, the hunter tried again to persuade us to stay one more day.

"Need more rest. Get weak with no rest!" But the hunter's words fell on deaf ears. Daniel had explained to me that he couldn't stay in one place too long. His desire for freedom ached too strongly. Just as soon as he felt it was safe enough to travel on, he did. But as daylight crept to a close, the hunter's words rang rather louder than before. Another day's worth of rest seemed more and more necessary. I confronted Daniel.

"Daniel, think the hunter kinda know what he's sayin'."

"What you mean, Sarah?"

"I mean to say we need anotha day. I need jus one mo' day of rest."

"Aww, Sarah."

"Daniel, its jus' a day. I'm gonna stay."

Daniel assented, and we stayed on another day, to the hunter's delight. We waited until the sunlight began to wane the next evening to prepare for our continued escape. We had clambered through baths and prepared for the next phase of our journey. We'd emptied the crumbs from our sacks, and refilled them with fresh food. The hunter had given us clean water in gourds, as well as a few words of advice. With that, we thoroughly thanked the man for his kindness, whispered words of parting, and disappeared into the night.

"Sarah, we ain't splittin' up. I ain't goin' through that again. Stick close." And I did. We had many good nights for running. We did have to wait out some dark nights, however, huddled in a cave or some other shelter. This happened on starless nights when the moon was hidden behind clouds and we couldn't see the moss on trees to find our way.

On one of those nights, Daniel said, "Sarah, we can keep goin'. Even if we ain' goin' 'xactly the right direction, we can find our way back tomorrow night. Cain't really travel too far off from the right way." Frustrated, he frowned out into the darkness.

"Daniel, like I tole you at the hunter's, be patient. We gonna make it." He sighed with irritation, but I wasn't fooled into thinking he was angry with me. I could tell my presence on this journey brought him comfort he could not take for granted, just as he was a comfort to me. It was easier to ignore pain that had overcome my body when I felt him slip his arm through mine.

That particular starless night slipped into daytime, but sleep eluded us. The noises in the woods were loud, and it seemed we had stopped near a burial ground. The sound of weeping and prayers filled us with uncertainty. We prayed that we were hidden well.

The day drifted by us without incident, however, and we ran that night, immersed deeply in this dreamlike world of escape, runaways bent on nothing but survival.

One evening, as rain poured down, soaking us, Daniel and I crouched low to make our way down a steep hill. Too late, I saw Daniel's foot slip. He slid quickly down the hill, through the mud, and slammed into a fence far below. We had run straight into the back of a home. I covered my mouth, realizing how loud the squeal I had let slip was. It took me some time to get to the bottom, and when I did, my brother was nowhere in sight.

Suddenly, I heard a rustling on the other side of a fence. A dog began to bark. I watched with growing fear as a light came on at the house and the door opened. A tall figure clutching a shotgun stood in the doorway. "Who's there?" the man bellowed in a menacing voice. I scanned the area for my brother. The man edged slowly down the steps, the gun pointing straight into the night, and asked once more who was out there.

I jumped when his shotgun went off, and again when a hand grabbed my mouth tightly from behind. I looked around in surprise to see Daniel pulling me along on the other side of the bushes, as silently as possible. I couldn't look back, but a few minutes later I heard the man curse and the door slam shut behind him. It was then I noticed the blood on Daniel's hand.

"Daniel, you hurt!" I whispered.

"Shh. I ain' hurt. Jus' got us some food." Indeed, he had. In his other hand was a dead chicken. In the daytime, we found a secluded place, and I fixed up the meat for us both to eat. What a blessing it seemed to be! Our food supply had been low, and we weren't quite sure how much longer we'd be running before reaching our destination.

It was only a few nights later that we reached the river that would take us to free land.

CHAPTER

❧ 25 ❧

WE HAD FOLLOWED THE HUNTER'S CLEAR DIRECTIONS AS WELL as we could. He had explained that there were a few marked trees on the bank.

"Find any one tree with mark. Wait. Nighttime come, make this sound." The hunter cupped his hands and hooted three times.

"Folk will help you cross. They not come first night, wait. They not come second night, wait. They not come third night, must cross different way."

We ran a mile along the bank until we found a large tree that fit the hunter's description. Daniel told me to hide while he kneeled and cupped his hands.

"Why?" I asked him simply, leaving my feet planted.

"Jus' in case this ain' right an' there's some trouble."

"But, Daniel—"

"Sarah, jus' hide!" I headed into the woods but kept my brother in sight. He cupped his hands, made the sound, and waited.

The night remained still.

Daniel made the noise again, then waited for a while, until finally, there was movement in the tree branches right above his head. I watched my brother freeze and look up. A figure climbed down and knelt next to Daniel. I stayed still and silent as I watched them converse. When at last they stood, Daniel motioned for me to join him.

Running over, the first thing I noticed was the man's features in the moonlight. He had dark hair and nostrils that lay uniquely on his face. He darted forward, expecting us to follow him. We did so without exchanging a single word.

He led us east a couple of miles along the riverbanks. He made a few motions, and another figure, what looked to be a black man, emerged from the darkness, hauling a small boat behind him. After the boat was put into the water, we climbed in, heads bent low, still without speaking.

The boat seemed capable of holding seven or eight people, so our load of four seemed rather light. Before we pulled off, our guide asked, "No one else?" Daniel shook his head, and we drifted out onto the river.

I couldn't help but wonder where we were going. My thoughts must have been heard, because I received a forward response from the rower. I was surprised to hear that the rower's voice was that of a woman. I couldn't make out her features—it was too dark, and the brim of her large hat shielded her face from our view.

"When we reach the other side, you two good people will be on free land!"

Free land. Free land.

I repeated the words in my mind, but they didn't feel as light as I'd thought they would. I let them resonate, but I couldn't seem to grasp them. The tense silence only grew greater as I searched for words. I could see in Daniel's face that he was doing the same. I was the first to respond.

"Free . . . free land? You mean, that's it, we won't have to run no more?" The words felt refreshing but almost unreal, as if at any moment, someone would reach out and snatch it all away. But my eyes met Daniel's and the true feeling of freedom—a sensation we had never before experienced—peeked out from our souls.

"No, you still gotta keep your eyes wide open an' be as careful as eva. It won't be over yet. There was a hunter, sent word of you to us. We tried to make it so's you will get safely to Ohio, or to Canada, if you choose to go on farther. Not a day east of here, a family's waitin' to carry you off," she said, her paddle not missing a stroke.

"Then . . . then we're free?"

"Almost," she replied.

I squeezed Daniel's hand in excitement.

"We ain't there yet, Sarah," Daniel cautioned.

"I know, but we close! We close, Daniel!" I could barely sit still.

The boat glided on, and it was very quiet aside from the animals of the night. But as we moved farther from the bank, I wrung my hands with nervousness. If we were spotted, there was no way out of this situation. Each of their strokes pulled us both closer to freedom and farther out into the open. For nearly three hours, Daniel and I sat anxiously as the man and woman took turns rowing the boat. Daniel had offered to help, but they had refused him graciously. The way the two silently interacted, I wondered if they were devoted to each other like a man and wife.

Finally, we came in sight of the shore. We had reached the other side! I felt my spirit hovering above the boat, and I was gazing down at myself, at Daniel, at our rescuers. Perhaps my spirit had to see it to believe it. We were rowing toward freedom!

The boat hit the shore harshly, jerking me into reality. My spirit still hovered as my body moved timidly to disembark. Both body and spirit faltered as I tried to keep my balance. Panic gripped my heart.

Where do we have to run to next?

The two of us stepped off of the boat. My feet sank into the mud, and I closed my eyes for a moment, feeling like a bird released from a lifelong cage.

We were on free land!

The river's constant motion became louder behind me, urging me to sprout wings and fly above the treetops, to gaze upon the land of freedom, my new haven, my new home! And then Mathee appeared. Her image came quick and sharp, piercing my mind as if to say, *This is real, Ayanna, this is real. But you must keep moving.*

The woman stepped off the boat with us and held us close so she could whisper in our ears. "Rememba, run straight east," she said, pointing at the line of trees. "In a night or two, you'll find the house. It's painted white, an' the shuttas are red. Go to the barn and part the hay. If you find two gourds of water an' two blue pallets, you in the right place. Mind you, be safe." With no further instructions to give, she hurried back to the boat. They had just enough time to reach the other side before the sun rose. They tipped their heads to us in unison, and we whispered, "Thank you."

I was ready to run, but I closed my eyes, remembering.

Tucker. Do you feel it Tucker? We all free, all of us, free now. You ain't gotta worry.

I heard Daniel mumble his name too, as if he was thinking my thoughts. I turned to him, smiling. "He knows we free, Daniel, we free! We *free!*"

On this side of the river, the woods were less dense and there were many more open areas with nowhere to hide. That was all the more reason to be careful.

During the day, we hid in the shelter of the thickest woods we could find, then ran again at nightfall. Just as it began to drizzle, we found the house. It was simple to spot, and the barn contained just what the woman had told us it would. Daniel's plan was to take the water and to hide out behind the barn until dawn, as a precaution.

I squeezed Daniel's hand, and all sorts of ideas started forming in my head.

What if we're caught? What will Masta do to us? Will he send us down south? Will he kill us as an example? What will he do to Mary if he finds out that she helped us? What if . . .

"Stop frowning, Sarah. Stop worryin'," Daniel said, interrupting this wave of thoughts. "Ain't nothin' gonna happen to us. Look how far God done brought us."

Still, later on, as the rain poured down hard, I dreamed of the plantation and the horrors it held.

"SARAH, SARAH, WAKE UP!"

"Slave catchers?" I shrieked to Daniel.

"No, not at all," he said calming me down. "You seem worn out!" he continued.

He was right. My eyes were swollen from crying, and my nose ran.

"We 'bout to leave!" Daniel said, excited. It was fully daytime, and he stood over me with brimming excitement.

"What you mean, 'bout to leave'? We jus' gonna walk up to the door an' say we ready to go?"

"I already talked to the folks, Sarah, while you was sleep. They the McCarthys." My brother helped me up. "We already in Ohio. Now we 'bout to go to one of the cities."

"Oh," I said with a sigh of relief. We entered the house through the back, and I met the elderly white couple. Mr. McCarthy opened up a cupboard and took out some decent clothes for both of us. He handed me a newer pair of pants and a shirt, to keep up my disguise. Then Daniel and I went off to bathe.

Mrs. McCarthy had cooked us a full meal of hot grits

with bacon and eggs and milk. When we were finished, we headed out back, and Mr. McCarthy, dressed in a suit, led us to the couple's carriage. The two horses were already bridled.

"We ridin' in this?" I asked anxiously.

"Yup," he responded. "I talked to your brother, and he says he knows how to drive a carriage pretty well."

"You mean, we don't have to run no more, an' . . . an' we don't have to hide?"

"Well, now, I didn't say all that. Your brother here, he's my servant, my driver. Started working for me about half a year ago. His name is Pete." I looked at Daniel to see if he was comfortable with his new identity. He nodded at me.

"An' what do I do?" I asked.

"You'll have to hide," he said, motioning for me to follow him into the carriage. My face fell.

"Hide? But sah, we on free land."

"Yes, you are, my dear. However, it still can be a bit dangerous for folks like you and your brother." The strain I had felt while running crept back into my bones.

"There's hay here in the back part with these barrels. See this small groove in the bottom of the carriage?" I looked to where he was pointing.

"This is where you will be, right here beneath the hay and between the barrels," he told me.

"For how long?" I asked, saddened. I had hoped to get a glimpse of my freedom land.

"It should take about two and a half days' ride to reach where we're headed. We'll stop at a few houses at night.

Occasionally, though, when the roads are clear, I'll let you come out."

"Sah," I began hesitantly, "there . . . there ain't another way I can get to where we headed? Don't make a lotta sense to me bein' in freedom an' we still gotta hide." The man sighed, stopping what he was doing to look over at me.

"You sound disappointed, but I assure you, you are but a few leaps from that freedom you're looking for. No hiding, no running, and certainly no more wagon rides under piles of hay."

Still, that's two and a half days stuck in hay! I thought. But I reminded myself of other things far worse than this we had experienced during our escape.

"Where we goin' in Ohio? Or we goin' all the way to Canada?" I asked, though I had no knowledge of Ohio and its land.

"You're full of questions, aren't you?" he said with a smile. I looked down at my feet, embarrassed. Daniel had already taken the reins.

"The farther north we go, the safer you are," he said softly, "but I don't anticipate taking you all the way to Canada." That was as far as he wanted to go to explain the specifics.

As we were talking, Mrs. McCarthy came out and proceeded to help me into the carriage. With the touch of a mother, she handed me a small clean rag to lie on and wished me good luck before she disappeared back into the house.

As soon as the hay covered the last inch of my body, I

felt boxed in, shut out from all light, with barely any space to move at all. It was hot, and the hay scratched my skin as the carriage rolled and jerked onto the road. How I wished I knew how to drive a carriage!

With the ride being bumpy, it took quite a bit of effort for me to stay underneath the hay. After a while, the rag that Mrs. McCarthy had given me did little to cushion my back. Every joint in my body began to ache, and waves of anger passed through me. I felt like a caged animal as I imagined the coolness of the air whisking by the carriage and the beauty of the trees and the land. Did this part of the country look like the land around the plantation down south, or was it more like Africa? What would be the problem with sneaking a little bit of fresh air into my lungs? The ride had been long, and the odor of hay and wet wood nauseated me. The thought of widening the small air pocket I had for my nose and mouth was very tempting.

Just as I was about to part the hay, I felt the carriage slow, then come to a stop. I quickly erased the idea from my mind. I heard the voices of Mr. McCarthy and Daniel. I longed for them to remember me and free me, but just as the thought crossed my mind. I felt the pressure of a hand, as the coffin of hay split in two and Daniel reached in and pulled me up out of my grave.

"You're soaked, Sarah!" I didn't hear him, for the sunlight welcomed me with a blinding ray. The air brushed across my face and cooled my body. A welcome chill ran through me. I took a few breaths and stretched my muscles, absorbing both the feeling of emancipation and the scenery. But all too quickly, the rest stop ended and I was back in my confinement.

We drove on.

We had been traveling for almost two days. At the first house where we stopped, Daniel, or Pete, wasn't welcome in the home and I couldn't even show my face. Mr. McCarthy said it would be safer if I just stayed hidden. So I remained locked in my coffin until we stopped later that evening. Daniel pulled me out of the carriage and sneaked me into the servants' cabin, where we would stay the night. Mr. McCarthy brought barely enough food for the both of us, apologizing as he left. We began our journey again as the first signs of dawn competed with the waning night.

On what would be the last day of our journey, I had been allowed to escape my hiding place for the last two hours because we had seen no one as we rode down a quiet road. But eventually we heard carriage wheels approaching in the distance.

"Quick, get back down!" But I had already retreated into my hiding place.

As the other carriage neared, I heard Mr. McCarthy whispering to Daniel, though I couldn't catch the words. Not long afterward, Daniel pulled the reins to stop the horses.

"Where you headed, sir?" My heart began pounding with fear as I listened to the stranger speak.

"Dayton," Mr. McCarthy responded.

"Where you comin' from?"

"Just a bit south of here," he said just as assuredly.

"Who's this?" The voice sounded testy.

"My servant boy," Mr. McCarthy said with no hint of nervousness.

"You know, there's a few slave ads out, sir," another stranger said, joining in the conversation. "On one of them, there's a boy, 'bout this one here's age." I could feel my heart jump into my mouth! Was this the end of our long, hard journey?

"This is my servant, sir. He's been working for me. I don't know what fugitive you have in your ads, but this here is my servant boy," Mr. McCarthy repeated, taking on the persona of a man who knew how to keep his servants in their place. I heard one of the strangers grunt sarcastically. There were only two of them, as far as I could tell. I continued listening to their conversation.

"How old is he?" the stranger asked, resuming their line of questioning.

"Around seventeen or eighteen, I assume. He could be twenty," Mr. McCarthy replied evenly.

"Your master gave you freedom, boy?"

"He doesn't have to answer your questions if I don't tell him to," Mr. McCarthy said defiantly.

"Excuse me, sir, but I'm talking to this boy here. He'll answer me if he knows what's best for him," the stranger answered arrogantly. "Boy, did your master give you your freedom?"

There was a pause that seemed to last an eternity. Our future rested on Daniel's lips. One wrong word or gesture and the men could wreak havoc on us. I could imagine Daniel looking toward Mr. McCarthy for permission to speak. Obviously, Mr. McCarthy granted it.

"Naw, sah, I was born free." I had expected Daniel's voice to waver, but it was just as strong and direct as Mr. McCarthy's.

"Where's your parents, then?" the stranger spat back.

"My papa got shot, sah, long time ago, an' my mama died at childbirth. She was young, an' Mr. McCarthy here . . ."

Where was Daniel getting all of this? I was amazed at the control and maturity Daniel maintained.

"What's your name, boy?"

"Pete, sah."

Pete what? In my head, I could hear them asking that, but they never did. Instead, everything was quiet again until they mentioned something about the back of the carriage. I held my breath as I prayed to God I had hidden myself well enough.

"You got anyone else riding with you?"

"No, sir, I don't. But we are in a hurry."

"What for?"

"My wife, sir. She came down with some sort of fever, God help her, and we had to come all the way up here to Dayton to get that medicine for her. Know it's a small town, but they should have what we need," Mr. McCarthy answered.

The silence lasted too long. I waited for the slave hunters to throw the hay from my body and snatch me back into bondage.

Then I heard, "All right, let's go. Be sure to tell us if you hear about any of them runaways, sir, especially those three separate slave gals in the ad. It shouldn't be hard to catch a slave wench." The strangers laughed at their own words.

"I'll let you know if I do."

"Good man," they responded.

I listened with a light heart as the sound of horse hooves disappeared behind me. Just like that, they were gone. We were off again, but this time I stayed under the hay without the agitation I had before. The stuffiness and foul smells didn't seem so bad anymore. We were now headed toward a dream, a dream called freedom.

Echoes

of

Freedom

CHAPTER

❧ 27 ❧

QUICKLY ENOUGH, WE REACHED DAYTON, A CITY IN MONTGOMERY County, Ohio. Mr. McCarthy carefully directed Daniel down streets and through busy crowds. I heard so many people moving about on the streets that I felt certain someone would notice me. But it seemed that no one did.

From what I could hear, this wasn't anything like the country roads or the plantations that we had just left. I could hear other carriages and wagons riding by us frequently, and the loud chatter of people caught me off guard.

We soon arrived at the home of Mr. McCarthy's good friend, the doctor. In the privacy of the back of the doctor's house, Daniel helped me out of the carriage and into the home. Mr. McCarthy and his doctor friend stood waiting for us. If I didn't know any better, I would have sworn the stranger was a slave catcher, because of the way he eyed us; that is, until he opened his mouth to speak. His demeanor changed as he relaxed his gaze, and by the time Mr. McCarthy spoke, the man was smiling.

"This, here, is Dr. Billingsworth," Mr. McCarthy said.

"Come, sit," Dr. Billingsworth said to us, gesturing to a small table in the back. His accent was nothing like the doctor's who came by Masta's place to get drunk and talk about us slave gals. It sounded, rather, like Dr. Billingsworth had studied reading and writing and the spoken word for a long while.

"You won't meet too many men of this kind. Dr. Billingsworth buys slaves, then sets them free." I stared at him, and he chuckled at my surprised expression. Helping runaways to freedom through hospitality and kindness was one thing, but to buy them and set them free was quite another.

Picking up where Mr. McCarthy left off, Dr. Billingsworth said, "That's right. As soon as you two step foot out of my home, you will be just as free as any free black man and woman. But neither Mr. McCarthy nor I can help you then. In fact, it's vital that this meeting here be immediately forgotten upon your departure, if you understand me." The two of us nodded with a seriousness which confirmed that we understood.

"There are a few black communities not too far from here. Settle, find jobs, and take every opportunity that arises to become landowners. I suspect some of the townsfolk will provide you with housing until you can handle things on your own. Do you understand?"

I nodded in silence, afraid that if I spoke, this dream would turn to dust and blow away with the wind.

"But first," Dr. Billingsworth continued, "you two must change your names. As of right now, you're my property until we fill out your free passes."

Unconsciously, I had expected something like this to take

place. I sat silently, but inside, I shook with anticipation. Dr. Billingsworth pulled out two pieces of paper and placed them on the table. He then proceeded to seat himself across from us. Mr. McCarthy chose to stand by the table.

"Do you remember when you escaped?" he asked.

"Sometime after Christmas, sir," Daniel answered.

Dr. Billingsworth laughed and shook his head.

"Not anymore," he said as he scribbled something down on the paper. "Let's start with you," he said, pointing to me.

"I bought you in November of last year, 1821, from Kentucky and freed you on this day, February 17, 1822."

1822! I had no idea I had been running that long.

"But—why November?" I asked.

"Well, now, if I bought you on that day, you could not have still been on your old master's plantation. You could not have escaped when you did. You see?" I nodded, and he winked at me.

"Exactly. Now, next is your name. You can't have the same name, so—"

"Anna, sir," I said, cutting him off midsentence. He looked up, surprised, holding my determined gaze.

"I want my name to be Anna," I continued confidently.

"Well then, you, dear, shall be named Anna." He scribbled the name on the papers and the pass.

"Age unknown." He said more to himself than to me.

"Sah, I do know my age. I'll be fifteen come springtime."

He brought a finger to his lips in contemplation. "I find

that not many know that. I'm glad that you do." He smiled while he rose to retrieve another sheet and then resumed writing. A few minutes later, he began to mumble under his breath, steal a few glances in my direction, and make further notes.

"Somewhere between fourteen and seventeen years of age . . . bushy hair . . . black eyes . . . five feet . . ." He finished scribbling for a few seconds more in silence.

"Well, there's your free pass," he said, finally holding up one sheet, "and your certificate of registration." He held up the other. "As of 1807, Ohio legislation brought forth a law requiring Negroes to carry free passes and to register with the county clerk nearest to their settlement."

I frowned. "So, you the county clerk, then, too?" Dr. Billingsworth smiled a tired smile.

"Some questions, Miss Anna, are better unanswered." With that, he swiftly brought his pen down upon the page once more.

Daniel was next. Dr. Billingsworth explained to us that he bought Daniel in May of last year from some plantation in Mississippi when he was down there on a trip.

"And your name?" the doctor asked.

Daniel turned to me, his eyes asking for my assistance.

"Um, Joe, maybe?" I said. Daniel frowned, unsatisfied.

"What about Paul . . . or Sebastian?" Daniel said, stumbling in an attempt to find a name, something he had never contemplated before. I shrugged my shoulders.

"Yeah, Sebastian," he said finally, turning back to the doctor, his voice gaining confidence.

"You sure about that?" Mr. McCarthy, who had been silent the entire time, asked Daniel.

"Well, yessah, I assume Sebastian will do me just right fine."

"What about our last names, sah?" Dr. Billingsworth looked up and smiled at me.

"Well, since I 'owned' you last, it would be Billingsworth; that's what it is on these free passes. But you two are now free people. You can decide your own last names."

"We can decide? But what if people ask us, sah? What we s'pose to say about our plantations, or our mastas or . . ." Questions rushed through my mind.

"Slow down a bit there, miss," he said.

"If anybody asks that much, it's safest to stay quiet and pull out your passes."

"But, sah, ain't you puttin' real life mastas on that paper who ain't eva known us in our entire lives? If so, wouldn't they find out soona or lata we ain't really from those plantations, that you didn't really buy us?"

He was silent for a few seconds. "Anna, you are on free land. If it does so happen people question you, free passes would do the job of keeping you here, in freedom."

"Yea, but sah—"

"Sarah." Daniel tried to end my questions, but Dr. Billingsworth was intent on settling my fears.

"Anna, you needn't worry about the names of the people I put on your passes. They are all friends of mine involved with my work. They help people like you and Sebastian here.

Now, I can't promise that nothing will happen; there's always an escaped slave who is found and taken back. But you two have come this far and reached this place called Freedom. So, embrace it." Dr. Billingsworth looked sincerely into my eyes.

"In the meantime though, here, take these." Dr. Billingsworth handed us the passes and certificates in neat envelopes. "Do not lose these, and carry them with you every time you come to Dayton or any other public place like this, you hear?" We nodded.

"Well, then, on to our next matter of business. The state of Ohio requires that any free Negro post a bond of five hundred dollars upon arrival into Ohio." My eyes grew wide with concern. Five hundred dollars! Did the doctor know we had no such amount? Would he send us away, to another state? Perhaps our journey had not ended! Daniel simply sat, awaiting more of an explanation. "The money is of no concern, however. It's been posted on your behalf. The bond takes care of families; therefore, you two must be brother and sister."

Flooded with relief, I said, "That's not too hard to remember."

Dr. Billingsworth smiled and rose from his seat. "With that, all legal matters are settled. Now I want you two to wash off, and then I will give you your clothes. You, Miss Anna, won't need a man's disguise any longer." After we washed off, Dr. Billingsworth handed me a faded blue dress and Daniel a simple shirt and full-length pants, something Daniel had not had since he was a boy.

As we approached the door, Dr. Billingsworth placed a few coins in Daniel's hands.

"It's nothing much, but you may need some on your way out of the city."

"Yessah. Thank you, sah." Daniel said. With that, the doctor and Mr. McCarthy nodded their good-byes to us and the back door shut. As we made our way into the street, I took a whiff of the air and closed my eyes. When I opened them again, sunlight illuminated my vision as I stared out at the world stretching before me. I was a free black woman on the streets of Dayton, Ohio.

CHAPTER

❧ 28 ❧

"Can you feel it tinglin'?" I asked my brother after we had walked at least a mile from Dr. Billingsworth's place, each listening to our own thoughts in silence. I had peeked over at my brother and seen hints of a smile playing with the sides of his mouth. Daniel looked over at me and caught my contagious grin.

"Ya, you can feel it, that freedom feeling," I said. He laughed—a sound I hadn't heard from him in so long!

"It's funny, I feel so light, I could jus' float up an' away!"

"Well, don't float too far, brother. You'll get spotted quick as lightnin' with these woman holdin' their chins so high," I said, throwing my sack down. Daniel stopped and watched as I straightened out my make-believe full skirt, lengthened my back as tall as I could, tossed my chin high in the air, and sauntered down the empty street as if no one greater ever lived. Daniel chuckled loudly and lifted my sack from the ground.

"Don't do that. You ain't like that," he scolded, though he was still smiling. I looked down at my shoes and rubbed my feet against the dirt.

Free land. We were . . . we were free—free folks!

I watched as a tear soaked into the soil next to my left foot, and another fell on top of that. He walked over to me and placed his hand on my shoulder. We stood quietly, more serious now.

"Daniel . . . Daniel, we in freedom. All them years, we slaves on a plantation, an' suddenly, we jus' . . . we jus' free!" I covered my mouth with my hand, laughing and crying with elation.

"Daniel, we . . . ," I started, seeing him stand there simply as if he didn't get it yet. But suddenly, he had embraced me in his arms like he used to when we were much smaller, spun around once, and fell into my arms. I laughed as he backed away, every line creasing his face bathed in a joy I thought had left him. I pulled my arm around his waist, and we fell into step, our hearts lighter than they had ever been.

But soon enough, a solemn, subtle feeling raced past my joy. I stared at the sky, wondering, silently, why John and Mary and Tucker couldn't have been there to share that moment along with us. I looked over at Daniel. The same expression had fallen over his face.

We neared the busy section of town, and everywhere I looked, I saw signs with words scribbled across them. I admired the place with interest. Unlike Daniel, I hadn't been to a town since I had been brought to America as a small child.

I pointed to a sign and whispered to Daniel, "Look, it say *shop* and *fish* and *townhouse*." I digested the letters like a hungry child, reading every written word I could. I hadn't read anything in so long!

Daniel pointed in the distance. "See those taller buildings?" I nodded. "They's factories, I b'lieve."

I contemplated that. "Sebastian, how hard you think it's gonna be to find us jobs?" I asked, making sure to use his new name.

"Can't reckon, sista. We ain't got a place to stay yet."

"You think they got large schools here?"

"Don't know that, either. But I think first we should worry 'bout findin' an makin' a livin'."

"Been thinkin' about a school, or learning, ever since I left that plantation. I sure do hope they got one."

Daniel and I walked the entire afternoon pretty much unseen—or, rather, unnoticed. We passed wagons driven by black men. We saw a small fishing dock with boats tied to it. White ladies in large dresses and bonnets made their way past us. Daniel and I laughed in secret at how many of them fit the exact description I had illustrated earlier. Most of the time, however, Daniel was lost in thought, and he spoke only when he needed to point out a landmark Dr. Billingsworth had told us to look for. As the afternoon slipped away, the bustle of people around us died down, and Daniel and his hope seemed to grow wearier as daylight faded. We both tried to dismiss the rain lightly falling upon our shoulders. The prospect of freedom wasn't dimming, but the question of how to manage that freedom seemed to be weighing on my brother's mind.

"We shoulda come to our part of town by now, Sarah," he said with some irritation.

"Anna," I responded.

He glanced over at me, the same irritation settling into his eyes, and retorted sarcastically, "Anna."

"How we s'posed to know when we get there?" I asked Daniel. He shrugged.

"All Dr. Billingsworth said was, we'll know."

"Well, then, we haven't gotten there yet, Sebastian." Daniel grunted in response. We walked on in silence for a couple of minutes until Daniel spoke again.

"Sarah—"

"Anna!" I almost yelled.

"It don't matter, Sarah! Ain't nobody round here!"

"We still in town, Sebastian. You don't wanna mess up one day in front of the wrong people."

He sighed. "Anna, we're gonna hafta stop soon. It ain't safe to walk in the dark, I don't s'pose."

"Stop where?"

We had walked beyond the boundary of the town, and found smaller buildings and a bit more trees. The rain was now steadier and harder, and darkness had sprung upon us.

"You think we can lie down for the night somewhere, maybe under a tree or somethin'? Then we can keep goin' in the mornin'," I suggested to him.

"I guess so," uncertainty ringing in his voice.

"We bin doin that all this time. One more day ain't gonna matta much."

So we walked quickly on until we came to a large tree standing alone in a clearing. Using our old clothes we had insisted on keeping, we made two sleeping spots and dozed off. We both clutched our sacks and drinking gourds as if someone would come at any moment to snatch them.

I awoke to the feeling of my wet clothes clinging to my skin. It was still raining, and I shivered from the cold, as memories of our escape flashed before me. What was it that had awakened me?

I looked in Daniel's direction and, as my eyes adjusted to the darkness, was shocked to see him swinging a sack through the air. Hearing the loud scream of pain that followed, I looked closer and saw a small figure twitching on the ground. Daniel was standing over him in attack mode.

"Daniel?" I whispered, forgetting his other name and not daring to move from where I was lying. "What happened?"

"I dunno, Sarah, it happened so quick!" He raised his voice over the moans and groans coming from the person on the ground.

"Heard a shufflin' sound an' swung at the dark. I hit 'im, but I think he just a boy."

Daniel bent down toward the figure, but the boy began screaming again, this time yelling, "Get away from me! Get away! Mama! Mama Bessie!"

At that instant, a flash of lightning lit up the sky. Sure enough, the boy on the ground was very young and clearly black. Daniel had backed away, but I kneeled by the little boy and, despite his screams, placed a cool hand on his sweaty forehead. He tried to shrink away.

"Sarah, what are you—"

"Shh," I whispered to the little boy while stroking his hair, interrupting Daniel.

"It's all right, we ain't here to hurt you." His screams subsided a little. "My brother just thought you was here to hurt us." The boy sniffed and nodded, wiping his teary eyes.

"Why you out here in the middle of the night, anyhow? Where's your folks?" I asked him.

"Please don't tell ha, please don't tell ha I was out here! Don't tell ha . . ." But he fell silent at the sound of approaching footsteps followed by a woman's voice. Daniel and I both jumped in alarm, and he reached down abruptly to grab our belongings.

"Sebastian, it's all right, we got our papers. We free folks."

A plump black woman approached the tree. In her left hand she held a lantern that she raised high to see what she had walked up to. The worried expression engraved on her face shifted from the little boy to Daniel and me. Without taking her eyes from the two of us, she spoke to the child.

"What I tell you, boy, 'bout comin' out here this late after dark? It ain't safe, Ned, it just ain't safe." Ned began to cry, so the woman lifted him up with her free arm. Glancing at him, her eyes grew softer, but the tone of her voice didn't change.

"What business you two folks have out here this late? What happened to my boy?" she demanded. If she was the least bit scared, it didn't show. "Well?" she asked again as I stood still, trying to think of what to say.

"I'm Anna. I done walked here. Me an' Sebastian, here, done walked all the way here from Dayton." Daniel reluctantly stepped into the light.

"What are y'all doing out here?" she demanded to know in the same harsh tone.

"We was lookin' for the closest black neighborhood we could find so we could settle down. We been freed."

"Y'all married?"

"Married? No, ma'am. This my brother, ma'am."

"Well"—the woman paused as if lost in thought, then turned and said—"you betta follow me, then. We can talk somewhere warm where it ain't raining. Bet y'all are a bit hungry, too. It's late, an' you cain't trust folks that closely round here. But a good woman don't turn her back."

For me, her offer was as sweet as sugar and honey, but I knew to Daniel, it was a step into possible danger.

"Sarah, I don't know about this," Daniel whispered to me as the woman began walking, but I simply followed her, knowing that Daniel would, too. I knew what danger smelled like, and the scent of this was not so sour.

But as we followed the woman, we stayed alert, ready to flee if necessary. The lantern light flickered, and in the shadows that sprang forth I imagined I saw snarling dogs and men lying in wait to snatch the two of us. I moved closer to Daniel.

How much longer is this walk?

Finally, we came upon a fairly large wooden house. We could just make out the clothesline in the yard. We moved along to the far side of the house to where three wooden steps led up to the front door. We followed the woman up the steps and inside. In the darkness, she lit three candles, and we soon saw that we were standing in a small room with a soft, long chair in front of us and two other, smaller ones to our left. There was something undeniably familiar about this place: It felt comfortable, almost home-like.

The woman silently placed the little boy on the long chair and gently tugged off his wet shirt. I could feel the water dripping from my own clothes onto the clean, wooden floor. She handed the boy a small towel and said, "Dry off your feet and legs. You've got a lot of explaining to do in the morning, boy." Ned's lower lip quivered. As if blind to his expression, the woman took off his pants and slipped a nightshirt over his head.

"To bed for now," the woman ordered, smacking him on his bottom.

"Yes, ma'am." Ned skipped away, relief showing in his movements.

Then she turned her attention to us. "Step on into the light, now, so I can see you good. Take these," she said, handing us towels. We began drying ourselves. "Well, I'll be. Y'all are young folk."

I nodded.

"Where y'all say you from? Where you live? How come you out there in the middle of the night, sleeping under a tree? Come in here and talk."

We followed her into what was the kitchen, where she sat us down and began busying herself at the sink.

"Ma'am," I said, "wish we had some kinda story to

tell, but really ain't got nothin' much to say. Figured—"

Daniel broke in. "Figured Ohio was a good place to move to for free black folks. Hope to settle down round here an' get jobs an' all."

While he spoke, I studied this woman. Mama Bessie was large, with shapely hips, naturally painted large lips, and eyes that seemed to see everything going on around her all at once. She wasn't smiling, but her expression was kind and genuine.

After listening and scrutinizing Daniel and me with long glances, she set out plates of food. My stomach had been churning with hunger, so the food was a welcome sight. She sat down with us, and we prayed over the food. I felt her eyes lingering on us as we devoured the meal. I noticed how still and quiet the room had become. I began to ponder over what more I could say, but as soon as I was ready to open my mouth, she spoke.

"Looks like you need a place to stay." Daniel looked up at her with imploring, excited eyes. "My name is Mama Bessie. Y'all have reached one of three Negro neighborhoods on the outskirts of Dayton. People come around here all the time with different stories and different pasts. I take them in just long enough for them to get on their own feet and earn enough money to buy or build a house."

"Is that why this place is so big?" I asked, before turning my attention back to the last of my food.

Mama Bessie nodded. "Yes. Church scrape up just enough for me to do what I do here. I have women stay here when they got no place to go. Give 'em three weeks to find some kinda stability. But mainly this place here is for them children. So many younguns don't have any kin. Their parents are dead or gone. So this is their home. Grow up here until they get jobs and get enough money to live on their own with a family and all. That's how it is here."

"You say women and children," I noted. "What about Sebastian?" I could tell from Daniel's face that he'd been wondering too.

Mama Bessie nodded, studying Daniel for a moment.

"You sleep here tonight, and tomorrow I'll give you the names of folks who have places to stay in exchange for labor."

"I sho' would appreciate that, ma'am." His eyes flooded with relief.

"All right, then," Mama Bessie said.

"Ma'am," I asked, "you say I got three weeks here?" Instead of answering, Mama Bessie leaned back in her seat and looked at me searchingly. Under her gaze, I felt as if our identities had been revealed. If she suspected anything, however, Mama Bessie kept it to herself.

"I can tell y'all have had it rough. Anna, there's another woman who lives here; her name is Florence. Does most of the work around here I can't do. There's some pay—it's not too much. But we could use some help. Now, there's plenty to do around here. Little children spill through during the daytime when folks out working. What you think?"

I smiled at her. "Sure wouldn't mind, ma'am. Thank you, ma'am. This means a lot to us," I said as she stood up.

With a nod, Mama Bessie turned to Daniel. "You can come on this way, you'll be sleeping over here." Mama Bessie led him to another room.

Their voices lingered a while longer, then Daniel called out, "Goodnight, Anna, an' thanks, Miss Bessie. We really 'preciate this."

"Oh, it's nothing, child. But don't call me Miss—it's Mama Bessie."

"Yes, ma'am, Mama Bessie," he said, making the correction. I could hear the words *Mama, Mama Mary* echoing all through his voice.

I began to consider how fortunate we had been to find Ned out by the tree. *No. Ned found us. We were blessed.*

Mama Bessie returned a few seconds later and led me down a hallway.

"Y'all look like you've been travelin' for a long time," she said softly to me.

"Yes, ma'am, we've been. Traveled a long way."

She led me up a staircase and along a hallway, until we reached a white wooden door.

"Here, let me see if there's space in here for you. Don't worry, though, we gonna find you a spot."

"Ma'am." I stopped her before she opened the door, my inquisitive spirit biting at me with another question.

"Yeah, honey?"

"I wanted to know why you taking me in like this. I mean, you don't even know nothin' about us 'cept what little we told you."

For the first time, I saw a small smile creep upon Mama Bessie's face. She closed her eyes for a few seconds, then looked back at me.

"Well, child, the world tosses to me what it fancies,

and I give back what I can. God done brought me through so many trials to get this place so I can help others who are in need just like I was. I been around a long time, and I know the face of trouble. I can smell it from far away. Now, I don't know what y'all went through before you got here, but I don't smell or see any trouble on you, nothing like that. So you here now, and in the name of God, I give my home to you." Her smile widened, and she placed her hands on my shoulders, "Plus, you different. I know your spirit."

Then she slowly opened the door of the end room and showed me a pallet to lie on. "Don't forget, it's Mama Bessie, you hear?"

"Yes ma'am. I mean, yes, Mama Bessie."

The room was too dark for me to inspect just yet: I could barely even make out my pallet, which sat right underneath the single window. The moonlight that seeped through the curtains, however, allowed me to find a place to set down my belongings.

"Thank you, Mama Bessie," I said again as she headed back out into the hallway.

I climbed into what was my new bed, in my new home. Closing my eyes, I felt my thoughts carrying me back to the dark roads of our journey. My lips began to tremble, and a teardrop escaped one of my eyelids.

Gratitude. That's exactly what I was feeling.

"Thank you . . . thank you . . ." The trembling grew greater, and I couldn't form God's name. But I felt sure he heard my spirit.

Then, unexpectedly, tears cascaded down my face, and my bliss was lost in a bottomless rage and overwhelming sadness. I thought of John. Slavery, my yesterday, was still his reality. Had he escaped yet? Was he headed toward freedom? Or was he bent low in the fields, buried in agony? Was his patience persisting, or did this hour mark the beginning of an irreversible revolt? Could he feel the tension in my chest that brought his name plunging through my lips in a harsh whisper?

Look ahead of you, Sarah, not behind.

"John?" I whispered.

Education, Sarah.

I thought his name again, allowing the burning to return, for the time being, to its shadow inside of me. I lay exhausted on a tearstained pillow. But then Mary's image appeared, and it brought me a feeling of peace. My tears were replaced with a smile as I blessed her and thanked her.

The crickets chirping outside my window turned into song. The large tree at the river's edge, the icy ledge, the healing hands: All these things that had helped me during my escape brushed past my consciousness. My ancestors . . . my family . . . Mama Mijiza . . . they were all singing to me . . .

Freedom, freedom, yes, freedom!

CHAPTER

❧ 29 ❧

As I lay on the pallet, I thought I heard singing, a twist of odd notes mixed with a beautiful melody.

Am I asleep?

I wasn't sure. I opened one eye and saw that the curtains had been drawn back to bring the sun's rays down onto my pillow. They struck my body with warmth. I imagined that I would be turning fifteen pretty soon, maybe in a month or so. Then a cold breeze rushed over my body, so I wrapped myself tighter in the quilt. When had my mornings ever been this peaceful? It was almost as if an angel had come to gently awaken me.

The singing that relieved me of my sleep stopped. I heard some shuffling around the room. A figure appeared over me.

"Anna, you up yet? I'm Florence." I opened both eyes. The high-pitched voice had come from a chocolate brown light-skinned girl. She was tall and fully filled out. Her smile gleamed in the sunlight, and her eyes seemed to giggle at me. Florence looked to be a few years my senior.

"It's Ah-nna," I said with a soft yawn, dragging out the

first *a* to emphasize the ah sound I intended my name to have.

"Anna, Anna. That's a nice name! But get up, would you! We have work to do, but Mama Bessie said I could show you around. Well, c'mon! Your clothes are right there. You see 'em? Mama Bessie put 'em there for you. Wash—the pump is outside. Dress. We'll eat when we return."

I slowly raised myself up as Florence, whose open personality was already becoming apparent, talked on and on about Mama Bessie's place and what I needed to do to get ready for my day. Slipping on the clothes, I admired the purple dress that fit me almost perfectly.

"You ready yet? Well, let's go!" Florence continued to urge me on. I followed her out of the room.

"Wait. Sebastian . . . where is he?"

"Sebastian?"

"Yeah. We arrived here together. Have you seen 'im?" I inquired of her.

"Oh, yeah, Mama Bessie sent him down to Rodney's a few blocks from here." She smiled. "Are you ready now?" I smiled back and nodded.

The Hadson neighborhood stood as a solitary place in the center of an expanse of fields and woods. Florence mentioned, though, that a few houses were scattered here and there between this neighborhood and Dayton. She also informed me that a wagon ride up to Dayton would take just around an hour. Walking away from Mama Bessie's, I noticed that her place was indeed the largest around, and for good reason. Young children scrambled all over her house and the grass out front, laughing and playing. The dirt roads were like veins, branching out to other houses. Most of the small homes I saw were wood and cabinlike, with the exception of a few brick structures.

As I listened to Florence talk about the people and experiences of the neighborhood, I observed my surroundings. A few homes had small gardens with flowers and vegetables, and some even had trees. Everyone lived relatively close to one another. As we walked farther on, I noticed the roads becoming denser with people bustling around. Wagons rode rapidly past us.

"This is the business part of town. Ms. Tina over there." Florence gestured to a woman selling goods. "She invented something to make people's teeth whiter. Usually she sells door to door, but today she must be doing good business out here on the street."

When we were passing Susie's Stitching Shop, I glanced around me. My nose detected the scent of fried fish. The smell made my stomach grumble. Sure enough, we came upon a dark-skinned man with a thick and curly moustache and beard who stood over pans in which pieces of fish sizzled in grease.

"Come an' get yo' fish," he called. I smiled distantly at the man. His demeanor reminded me of John. My mind broke away from Florence's chatter as the image of John walking by my side with his hip bumping up against my own held my attention hostage. I felt unburdened as I saw him point this way and that, the light in his eyes reminding me that we were in freedom. I allowed myself to hear his voice, and as I did so, the commotion all around me ceased to be.

Look, Sarah! We done found a black community existin' all on its own. How 'bout that?

But then the magic broke. I loosened my gaze from the fish seller's and quickened my pace, feeling a warm sensation in my cheeks from slight embarrassment. I needed to shake my mind free of those thoughts, so I decided to ask Florence what had been swimming around in my mind since I awoke that morning.

"Where's the school up here?" I anticipated her leading me toward my dream. Instead, wrinkles creased her forehead.

"School? What you mean by that? Blacks don't have a school. They say we don't need it." I felt dizzy, like the wagon wheels spinning by.

"So, don't no one here learn their numbers an' letters?" I asked, left wondering how I would continue learning what I had taught myself on the plantation. It had never been in question: I had expected to reach freedom and continue learning. Now that hope was crushed.

"Seem to me white folks up in town just don't like to see no black folks learning. Folks here in Hadson would be crazy if they even got close to that school. That's just how it goes up here." I listened with anger and a growing feeling of uneasiness in my belly.

"You mean, I come all the way to freedom an' there ain't no school?" Disappointment washed over me.

"You had a school where you come from?" I shook my head, turning from her. She didn't understand.

"Well, I'm sorry, Anna, that it ain't perfectly how you like it here in Hadson, but there just ain't many places for us that's exactly how we like them to be."

"I know. I just really wanna learn," I said with a sigh. How free could freedom really be without that opportunity?

"Well, in all truth, Anna, I always believe that if there's something you want that bad, there's always some way to get it. Don't be so down! It ain't that bad here." Her sincerity warmed my heart a bit.

"Where you from, anyway?" she questioned.

"I'm from Tenn—" I began, but stopped short.

Where am I supposed to be from?

"Kentucky." I let the word tumble out of my mouth as I made a vow to stay aware of what I was saying. I prayed Daniel was doing the same.

"You sure about that?" she joked, laughing. "Where your folks at, if you don't mind me asking."

"I lost most of 'em," I said, hoping to change the subject.

"Lost? You mean, they passed away or something?"

"No, no, they was sold."

"Sold! So you was a slave," she said matter-of-factly. I nodded.

"An' you was freed?"

Not really wanting to lie to Florence, I simply nodded again. *Maybe someday I'll tell her the truth.*

"I mean, you just don't see many slaves living here," she said. I stole a glance at her face to see if she had guessed the truth that easily. It didn't seem so.

"I ain't no slave," I said with a frown, cringing at the title I had run from.

"No, I didn't mean that. 'Course you're not. It's just, most runaway slaves and freed blacks from the south run to Philadelphia, or they travel all the way up to Canada 'cause they think it's safer. I reckon it is. A while back, I saw a slave that ran up here taken all the way back down south. I also heard of another man, one who had never been a slave in his life, taken down south too."

Florence's words set a deep, unsettling feeling under my skin. Even though I had known danger could be so close, even though Mr. McCarthy had spoken to us about this, I still suddenly felt afraid.

Florence must've noticed my tension for she questioned, "Anna? Anna, don't worry. Ain't nothing gonna happen to you. You freed anyway!"

I dismissed her words, letting the worry sink deeper.

"Anna, I'm serious," she said, tapping my shoulder with her long fingers. "I won't let it, that's a promise." I relaxed a bit, acknowledging her smile. The two of us would be good friends.

CHAPTER

❧ 30 ❧

DANIEL AND I HAD BEEN LIVING HERE FOR A LITTLE OVER TWO and a half months, and we were falling quite well into our new lives—new homes, new ideas, new goals.

I continued my work at Mama Bessie's house, taking care of the children, doing laundry, and cleaning. That was the trade between us: Mama Bessie offered us a home, and I helped out. Daniel lived half an hour from Mama Bessie's but would make it his purpose to come see me at least twice a day. Daniel had a temporary job fixing items for neighbors around town. Most days, he would get up early in the morning and walk down to Dayton to find another, steadier job, after having little luck in finding one in Hadson. Eventually, with the small amount of money he raised, he was able to borrow the materials he needed to build himself a wagon and rent two horses for travel. I prayed daily that Daniel would find that job soon, one that was close by and that paid good money. It worried me to see him gone all day, returning at dusk, just to go help out in some field. For now, that was his job, but it was what he called "slave work," and he told me he didn't come all the way to freedom to go back to a field.

"This ain't no heaven fo' blacks," he would constantly tell me, and it seemed he was right. Every once in a while, we'd receive news about trouble in the city—trouble between some free blacks and the whites who lived close by. The only way for blacks to avoid this trouble was to stay out of the way. In my prayers, I asked God to keep my brother out of that kind of mess.

What I wanted in this free land was rather different from what Daniel wanted. I wanted to learn. The desire started as a subtle feeling that would hit me while I did chores in the house, reminding me of my days back on the plantation with the children. While I did chores around the house, I took to praying for the opportunity to go to school. But the community had no black school, and I had no idea how to go about satisfying my growing desire. I continued to practice on my own, however. When Daniel stole time in the evenings to sit and talk with me, and Florence if she chose to be there, I'd practice reading the newspaper and writing, using whatever tools I could find. Every time Daniel rode to Dayton in his wagon, I gave him special requests.

"Would you keep an eye out fo' any paper and ink that don't cost too much, and actual books in the city? Get a newspaper, too, so I can find out how many schools there are round here. And find out what the white schools are like, and look for any black schools close by. And . . ." My questions about the city's opportunities were endless. So one day, Daniel decided to avoid all the questions and, with Mama Bessie's consent, took me with him.

We rode all day long as he showed me the church and the stores of the city. Then, as we rounded one of the corners, I spotted it, a lone white building that immediately caught my eye.

It was the school.

How I knew this, I did not know, but I knew. My skin tingled with excitement as I stared, dreaming of all the possibilities that lay behind the walls. I started to hop out of the wagon to dart across the field, but Daniel grabbed my arm, holding me back.

"Anna, you gotta be careful round here. You cain't jus' go round everywhere you please. That ain't our property."

"But it's a school, Sebastian. It's school property," I said, aching to get a glimpse of what a real education looked like up north.

Daniel crossed his arms and frowned at me, saying, "Don't matta what kinda property you wanna call it, it still means blacks ain't allowed." As we drove away, I tried to see into the large windows that lined the walls of the one-room schoolhouse. I spied narrow tables and long benches. As the building disappeared behind us, I felt a deep longing. I wanted that education. It was unfair for me not to receive the chance these white children did.

We spent the rest of the day looking for jobs for my brother. Daniel would walk up to a door with a sign that stated Work Needed and get turned down at each place. At one stop, a short man with grayish hair came to the door.

"What do you want?" he asked gruffly.

"Yo' sign say Artisans Needed," Daniel responded.

"Who is it?" A female voice rang out from within the house. The man leaned back and addressed his wife.

"Some black kid think there's work fo' him here." The woman behind him giggled. I watched Daniel's hand, held behind his back, form a fist.

"Better tell him how it is out here, Freddie." She laughed again as the man looked back towards Daniel.

"Does that sign say Niggers Wanted?" The fist clenched tighter.

"Didn't see that, sah."

"Then why's you here?" With that, the door slammed—just another one of the many Daniel encountered that day. It was all enough to drive me mad. He didn't even receive respect as a second thought. I admired him for keeping hold of his temper and for his determination. From what I had heard and what I had seen, aggression from a black person was not taken lightly here, in any situation. The law was not on our side.

This *was* no heaven for black folks. I had to keep reminding myself this, especially as my prospects for learning began to dim. Reading signposts and copying newspapers was one thing; true education was entirely another. Perhaps that dream was meant to die. Maybe it was far too unrealistic.

As the months stretched onward, the freedom and all its dimensions came into plain focus. There was work on weekdays, church on Sundays, and young folk gatherings on occasion. I busied myself with what I could to escape my restlessness in not fulfilling my passions, and my discouragement. I found myself wondering why the bells of my freedom were not ringing very loudly, and soon came to the conclusion that I was missing out on the thing I longed for the most: my education.

Florence, who had become a constant presence in the lives of my brother and me, was our eyes and ears until we could stand on our own. And even then, she was always there. It was as if she had been waiting for us to show up in the Hadson community. She was two years older than I was, a young woman filled with much energy and optimism.

In Mama Bessie's place, I felt like I had found a home among the children and the daily happenings. Even though Mama Bessie paid Florence and me a small stipend in addition to providing a place for us to live and food for us to eat, I felt, within the first few weeks, that Mama Bessie, Florence, and I shared something that ran deeper than this. Mama Bessie's rules on manners and hard work, most times directed toward the children, never fell short of my ears. But the children always made time for games and play—so much different from the life of the slave children on the plantation that I came from. Watching them brought a lightness into my heart.

Florence readily introduced me to the entertainment of the town. Sometimes, the church would sponsor festive celebrations that she often convinced me to attend. We'd meet other blacks from nearby communities. Some folks would travel all the way from Indian villages looking for a new place to settle.

In my trips from Mama Bessie's to the town center, I found that most of Hadson's residents were young people who put a lot of effort into work and building businesses. I met folks who had been free for most of their lives. Courting was common, and from what I saw, simple marriages and the raising of families were common.

Occasionally, there'd be gatherings out in a clearing near the Hill, as everybody called it. There was a lake with a large tree on the right bank and a huge hill on the left. The clearing sat in the middle of a circle of trees, and a platform had been built there. The young townsfolk used it for dancing and fun every once in a while.

"I think we should go," Florence said to me one evening as we cleaned up the last of the dishes. I had no desire to go, so I fussed, telling her I didn't wanna be around any music and dancing, but she wasn't having any of that. I eventually figured I could stay at Mama Bessie's and explain my feelings to Florence, or I could just go. Lord knows I couldn't begin talking about John without tears and anger, so I chose the easier of the two options.

"Sebastian coming?" Florence asked as we dressed for the gathering.

"Don't know. But why you concerned?" I asked, eyeing her with curiosity. She shrugged my question off.

"No matter."

We reached the Hill in a matter of minutes, and Florence began introducing me to people I hadn't met.

"That fiddler up there, you see him?" She pointed to the man on a stool at the front of the clearing. He was sitting in the middle of a raised platform that had been built for the musicians. "He's blind, but just listen. He can scare away a storm with all that fiddlin'!"

We walked on and greeted others. Daniel eventually found us and lost himself in conversation with Florence. As they talked, a wave of loneliness washed over me, and I felt removed from all the music and laughter and dancing. My mind was far away, wondering if John had run yet and if he would he ever find me here and how long he would he look for. I thought about how I would know if something happened to him.

"Anna!" Daniel called out to me, excited.

"Yes?"

"Come on. We gonna dance like we did when we was younger. You rememba?" My heart warmed as it always did when I saw a real smile on my brother's face. Daniel grabbed my hands and pulled me all the way to the platform. We spun and moved and shuffled, laughing all the while. A little out of breath, we stopped after a while, and I stumbled back over to Florence.

"Enjoyin' yourself, huh?" Florence said with a grin.

"Well, you got some lookers over there," she said, nodding to a spot under a tree where three young men sat. I glanced in their direction but quickly turned my eyes away. Florence asked my brother if he was too worn out for another dance.

"Well, now, if you're offerin' your hand, I don't reckon I have much of a choice but to take it, do I?" Daniel teased her.

"Don't flatter yo'self, Sebastian."

I laughed, enjoying the sight of the two of them walking off toward the music. But as the music played on, I felt my solitude tugging at the seams of my clothes. My attention began to drift to the fellows under the tree and as it did, an anxious feeling rose inside.

His eyes were smiles in themselves, and they were planted on me. They belonged to the tallest of the three young fellows. He brought another wide smile to his lips and nodded my way. I nodded back but gave him no smile in return.

I didn't come to the gathering for this.

My eyes fell back on the dancers, but my mind stayed with the young man as I noticed him stretch his limbs and walk my way. I stood my ground as the man came nearer to me, but I watched the musicians.

"Hello, miss."

"Hello," I said, without looking his way.

"You new around here?"

I nodded.

The man stood by me, silent for a few moments.

"Well, I'm Henry," he said finally, stepping in front of me and holding out his hand. I looked at his palm. His hands were large, high yellow, and seemed soft. I shook it, more for observation's sake than to be cordial. They were soft—even more of a reason to keep my space.

John's hands are rough.

"Well, now, you've got to have a name too."

"Anna," I replied.

"Well, Anna, I bet that you have some beautiful eyes. Wish I could see them. You think, maybe . . ."

I looked up at him, half-amused. His grin grew wider. Mine disappeared.

What does he want?

Suddenly, Florence came up beside us, breathing deeply and sweating, but also grinning.

"Henry! I see you've met Anna," she said between breaths. "You know, she told me she hasn't danced much." I turned angry eyes at Florence, but she didn't appear to notice.

"Naw, that cain't be," he replied, shaking his head. "I saw her floatin' around the dance floor like she knew exactly what she was doin'!" He took my hand in his.

"Would you do me the pleasure of giving me this dance?"

But Henry's words never reached my ears. I caught two words: "floating" and "dance." My heart fluttered. How silly of me to have come here. The wrong person was standing in front of me.

"Anna!" Florence chided, distant like a ghost from another world, "did you hear Henry?"

"Oh, ah . . . ya. But I'm . . . I gotta go back, Florence," I said, taking my hand from Henry's grasp and stumbling past Florence in a daze.

"It was nice meetin' you, Henry," I said with a single glance toward their puzzled faces.

Florence threw her hands up in the air as I began walking away.

"Anna, where you going?" she called to me.

"Well, see, I saw Sebastian headin' down to Rodney's some time ago, an' I was plannin' on goin' with him, so I just . . . I gotta go. You stay an' have fun. Don't worry about me."

My brother had left to go to Rodney's, but that wasn't where I was headed. My heart ached, and I knew that I needed to be alone with my thoughts, with my prayers, with my tears.

John, why did you have to dance with me that December night?

My heart felt heavy, and my tears flowed freely. The further I separated myself from the Hill, the stronger my fear and doubt became.

Will I ever see John again?

CHAPTER

❧ 31 ❧

LIFE STRETCHED ONWARD AND WITH EACH NEW DAY CAME a new sense of hope. Amid all the working and cleaning and meeting new people, I would occasionally find a piece of myself, something distant or from the past, that had been missing. This sure was freedom, but I was still bound to images of the whip, families torn apart, and screams heard in the darkness.

The whip haunted me. I'd lay awake at night hearing it echoing in my mind. I'd see John, lying there, bloody, sliced up, unmoving, his eyes wide and unblinking. My mind created so many questions at night.

But as time advanced, some of the more brutal images faded, and my doubts and fears became less pronounced. The feeling of being free in my homeland was very distant from me, but my soul drew the connection between then and the present. My dreams vacillated between images of the plantation and thoseof Africa.

For the five months we'd been in the Hadson community, I awoke early each Sunday morning, hours before anyone else in the household. Like the old Sundays when I was in slavery, I found my place of peace: here, it was on the hill by the lake. I'd sit there and watch the sunrise, the same one I saw back on the plantation, except now the sunrise smiled upon a free girl. Sometimes, as I sat there, consumed by the essence of the moment, I would imagine my mother seated next to me. She would close her eyes, lie down by my side, and hold me in her arms, whispering secrets about what different dances meant, about nature and its gift to humanity, and about womanhood and the beautiful art of happiness beyond circumstance. She talked about my brother, Sentwaki, and of things I had forgotten. I would lie there, letting my thoughts and memories spin in my imagination.

Some Sunday mornings, I would hear footsteps. I knew they weren't real, but I allowed myself to hear them and the voice I longed for. *"You eva sailed the wind befo'?"* I'd try to, but I could never sail like I did back on my hill, back when John was with me.

In Hadson, church started later in the morning. After visiting my special place at the lake and traveling through the images of my mind, I would try to slip back into the house before it erupted with activity. Florence and I, and any other woman who happened to be passing through, would grab the children's clothes and iron until our hands were sore. Mama Bessie would fix breakfast and call the youngest to the kitchen to eat first, followed by the other children, with the older ones eating last. After everyone was washed, dressed, and fed, we would head out to church.

This morning was no different. Florence and I stood side by side, with a child grasping each of our hands, and walked down the dusty roads. The church sat slightly behind the home of one of its members. It was a small wooden building with two windows on each side and a cross placed above the door.

Many people were in attendance, even those who didn't come to church regularly, because today marked the church's tenth anniversary. There were not enough seats for everyone in the building, so many stood in the aisles. Fortunately, Florence and I had arrived early, and we found our normal seats in the second row. Since there were so many children, one of the women of the neighborhood had been asked to take them to a nearby house and do a separate sermon. Mama Bessie called it the "children's church."

As Florence and I seated ourselves, little Ned came running up. He was always a delight, so curious about everying, and I had to admit that I favored his presence over those of the others.

"Miss Anna, let me stay wit you an' Miss Florence, pleeeease!" I looked over at Florence with laughing eyes but kept my lips set.

"Ned, they have children's church today. That's where you're supposed to be." He pouted and crossed his arms. It was too much for me.

"All right, come sit between us. But you gotta be quiet. One little peep, an' I'm takin' you out!" I said to him as he hopped up between us with delight. I looked over at Florence, who was gazing at me with raised eyebrows, and I shrugged.

"We here today to celebrate what God Almighty done

fo' us." Church always opened with a prayer followed by singing. The church had one small hymnal written by a black man that had been brought from Philadelphia, where it had been published. Not too many folks could read it, however, so it sat out of view until after the service, which is when I would get my hands on it to read its words.

We lifted our voices high, filling the building with a joyous sound. During the sermon, Florence and I joined in with the amens and yesses that rang throughout the room. At the end, a deep plate was passed around to collect what money the folks in Hadson could spare. If someone in the neighborhood had a problem, we would stay and continue praying and praising until the plate was filled with enough money to get them through it.

Finally, the feast came. Tables had been pulled out and set up in front of the church to seat all the people, and the yard rang with laughter and talk. The size of the celebration compared with the festivities for the two holidays we celebrated at Masta's.

After the activities had simmered down, I wandered around, searching for Florence. I came upon a group of young folks who were laughing and clapping around a tree. Henry stood at the center of the group, holding a hat. How silly Henry looked to me as he squatted by the tree with a half-serious, half-amused grimace. He was shaking the hat this way and that, regarding whatever was in it with amusing intensity.

"Any more buyers? Say, Anna, give me a few coins an' I'll show you the trick! Reckon if you figure it out, you get your coins back, but if not . . ." Laughter burst from the group as Henry set his large lips in a deep frown and shook his head.

"You clever, Henry, but not that clever. I ain't givin' up no money to you!"

"I suppose Florence wouldn't want to try it?" he said as Florence approached us.

It was hard to hold back laughter. "Henry, stop!"

"I'll give you a coin!" Hattie-Mae, a young woman around my age who worked with her aunt in the stitching shop in Hadson, tossed a coin to Henry.

"Y'all ain't no fun!" Hattie-Mae said, turning to us.

"No, we just got sense, that's all," Florence responded.

"Well, that kinda sense ain't gonna get neither of you married."

Florence laughed. "You always talkin' about marrying, Mae."

"What else we suppose to be doing?" Mae said as she fluttered her eyelids.

Florence laughed, and I joined in, a little less heartily, keeping my thoughts to myself. Five months in freedom, and I had done little more than attempt to keep John's bobbing image out of the forefront of my mind. I was waiting for him.

"I'm not marrying nobody right about now," Florence said in reply. "It ain't no use. An' ain't nobody around here suitable for me nohow."

"Don't matter to me." Hattie-Mae said, shrugging and turning back to the fun.

As I looked around, my eyes rested on a slender figure in a nice-looking long dress that ruffled at the bottom edges and buttoned all the way up to the neckline. The woman's black hair fell loose and curly by her shoulders. Her arms were crossed, and her lonely stance called out to me. She was leaning against the church building a short distance away from Henry and the others. I made my way over to greet her.

"You from around here?" I asked kindly, walking up to her. She turned her head toward me. The woman was most likely a few years my senior. She had very light skin, and her eyes were an intriguing, waterlike blue.

Hearing no response, I said, "I'm Anna."

"Anita," she said simply, looking at me with almost no interest.

"You bin round here long?" I asked.

"I'd rather not tell my story. It's no different from anyone else's around here." She looked away, in the direction of whatever had been catching her interest before I started speaking with her. Her words sounded kind of educated-like. But I sensed irritation, an unkindness I didn't feel I deserved. However, just as quickly as the notion entered my mind, it left.

"Why don't you join us?" I asked.

"I don't prefer to," she said simply, holding strong to her rigid stance.

"Ah, c'mon. Those folks aren't that bad." She eyed me for a long moment, and then, still looking irritated, turned her head to the side.

"You're from the South?" She asked it like a question, but her matter-of-fact tone brought a chill up my spine.

"I was freed," I said, forgetting about making friendly conversation with her.

"I saw you reading in the church," she continued, as if she hadn't heard me at all.

"I like learning. Plan on getting educated someday." She laughed a laugh that turned my heart cold.

"And then what? You get educated, and then what?"

I frowned. "Gotta get educated first to know," I said softly, feeling very small next to her words. She pushed herself lightly off of the building, and stood at her full height.

"I wish you well, then," she said with a nod. Without another word, she turned on the heel of her boot and left.

"Don't worry about that one," Florence said, slipping up behind me and pulling me back to the gathering. I looked back, watching the young woman walk off into the distance.

I headed back to Mama Bessie's a few hours later, after we had cleared the church grounds. Florence was still in conversation, so I went back alone.

Once I was far enough away, I voiced my questions and agitation to the heavens.

"Don't worry about Anita too much," a deep voice erupted. I nearly jumped out of my shoes. I had thought I was alone, but Henry had quietly come up behind me.

Turning back around and starting to walk again, I said, "I don't think it's mighty nice to scare a girl like that."

"Ain't scarin' nobody."

"An' didn't nobody say I was worried 'bout nothin'."

"Ah, Anna, I heard ya. You might not have said it straight like that, but I can tell. She's like that with most everyone. Ain't much for social talking and all that. She live with old man Joshua some ways away from here. Got a right fine house, very large. Man got him a lot of money. Worked his way from poor to wealthy."

"She his daughter?" I asked.

"Naw, just been working for him for a while now. Maybe they relatives—I wouldn't know. She the closest thing he got to life, bein' that his wife died an' he stuck in that house from sickness. Anita don't make it her business to get out much." I nodded in silence. "She ain't too nice to folks, though most of us figure that's all she knows. So don't worry yourself with her."

"I ain't worryin'," I said, picking up my pace.

"Hey, why you walking so fast, Anna? Ain't I good comp'ny?" Henry asked, taking a couple of large steps to catch up with me. "You know, with those quick legs and that smart head of yours, I see life taking you a long ways!"

I looked over at him. "Henry, you tell me. How far can we go in this place called Freedom?" I still heard Anita's mocking comment about education, about the idea that education offered nothing for us.

"Well, that's easy! You find you a job, build a house,

start a family in this place, and live life just like that. My pappy told me, when he was still living, that that's the farthest life will take us black folks. . . . *Slow down,* would you, Anna? I can't think right, trying to keep up with you and looking at how pretty you are at the same time."

I felt relieved when we came to Mama Bessie's house. I turned to face Henry.

"You know what I think?" I asked him.

"What?"

"Well, sometimes, this place called Freedom seems to get me down when I think 'bout what I want the most. But I think life'll take you as far as you wanna go. You can have that job, that house, and that family. But if you wanna fly farther, then shouldn't nothin' stop you."

Henry laughed. "Well, then, guess you right about that. You gotta lay your eyes on what your really want," he said with more amusement in his voice than seriousness. I looked at Henry for a moment, saw the way he was laying his eyes on me, then frowned at him.

"You know, Henry, I've laid my eyes on education. I've seen it, I've dreamed of it, but it's not mine. It seems the white folk don't want me to have it. So that just goes to show, you have to do a little bit more than laying your eyes on it for it to be yours." With a smile, I retreated into Mama Bessie's.

CHAPTER
❦ 32 ❦

"I WONDER WHY THE DEATHS OF THE COMMON *BLACK* FOLKS round the city never make it into the papers," I said.

"Reckon you shouldn't think on that too hard," Florence replied.

It was a sunny Friday morning, and I sat near Florence reading the local papers. I had come across a section highlighting the loss of a certain servant to some kind of milk sickness. Continuing as I yawned, I found that the white woman had spent part of her day working for the school in Dayton. I stopped short and ran back over the words I had just read. A grand idea hit me then, and I quickly sat up.

"What is it?" Florence asked, immediately attentive.

"Flo, it says here that a woman servant they had helpin' out at the school ain't there anymore. She died." Florence's excitement waned significantly as her eyes fell back to the stitching in her hand.

"Flo, did you hear me?" I asked, wondering why she didn't see the possibility lurking behind the words.

"Yes." She dragged out the word. "But I don't see what that's got to do with us," she said, looking up again.

I frowned at her. "Florence, this my opportunity to do

what I wanna do! If I can get that job, an' help out for a couple of hours a day, I'd be in the school buildin' an' I could hear the lessons an' I could get my education . . ."

"Anna!" Florence bellowed, cutting me off. "I don't think you're really hearing yourself. What you're talkin' of is dangerous, Anna. The last thing those folks like is black folks with an' education. You know that!"

"Education's not banned here, Flo! There ain't no laws sayin' we cain't have no education!"

"But getting educated in white schools is against what they believe. An' you kno' their beliefs is more important than their laws. You know that. You can't do no learning there."

"Well, just don't look at it as an education, then, Florence. It's a job as a servant. They don't gotta know I'm learnin'." Florence shook her head as Daniel ran up to us and leaned against the wooden porch rail. I turned to my brother for the support I needed.

"Sebastian, when you headed to the city again?"

"What you ask fo'?"

"They need a servant fo' the schoolhouse, so I'm goin' to see if I can work." His silence and the serious expression in his eyes baffled me. Why couldn't the two of them understand what this meant?

"They askin' fo' a black servant, Anna?" Daniel asked me. I shook my head, and his eyes traveled from mine to Florence's. Florence shrugged at him as if to say, *She's your sister!*

"What's wrong with you two?" I asked, irritation

weighing down my words. "This a school—it's my chance! All I wanna do is keep learnin' wherever I can until we find a place that has a black school. Till then, the least I can do is listen in on lessons at the schoolhouse!"

"Anna, that ain't no school fo' us. It ain't safe fo' me, it ain't safe fo' you, it ain't safe fo' any of us." Florence mumbled in agreement. I stared hard at my brother as he looked sheepishly back.

"All right, then. I'll walk to the city," I said, standing. Daniel grabbed my arm.

"Now, Anna, don't go an' do that. Jus' listen to what we sayin'. What we talkin' of makes a lotta sense. An' besides, I bin askin' round fo' you, tryin' to find some black school somewhere."

My anger lessened a bit. "You have?"

He nodded. "If it's learnin' you want, we gonna find it. But don't go puttin' yo'self in no danger. Now listen, I came here to see if Mama Bessie'll let y'all come on wit me. I'm travelin' to the Gibson community. Got some business to take care of, an' I'm gonna need me some comp'ny. Should be back before dark."

"Think I'll stay. Got some cleanin' to do," I said, turning to go into the house.

"Flo?" Daniel said. I waited to hear her verbalize what she did and did not have to do that day, and finally agree to travel with him, and then I shut the door.

Inside, I looked at the newspaper again, and felt Florence and Daniel's warnings evaporate.

This is just too right!

As soon as Florence and Daniel were off, I washed up and put on my best dress. Finding Mama Bessie, I told her I was headed to town.

"To Dayton?" she asked.

"Yes, Mama Bessie."

"With who?"

"Just me, Mama Bessie, but its important business an' I suspect I'm already a little late." Mama Bessie put her hands on her hips and eyed me closely.

"Gonna let you go, but I want you to wait for Mrs. Eli an' her sons. They come through here once a week, an' I'm sure they'll be glad to give you a ride."

I agreed but asked, "When they gonna be here, Mama Bessie?" She looked past me to the window.

"Any minute now. Best be gettin' on out there." Suddenly, a smile formed on her lips.

"There a dark fellow you meetin' up with?"

"No, ma'am," I said, startled. "I ain't meetin' with nobody." But I could tell she wasn't convinced.

"All right. Would you buy somethin' for me?" she asked as we walked outside. Mama Bessie dropped a few coins in my hand and described what she needed. "You go on now, but come on right back here."

"Yes, ma'am."

The school was situated at the outskirts of the city, almost isolated from Dayton. It was surrounded by grass and a few trees on an acre's worth of land. This provided space for the children to play and run around in the mornings, and the separation between the school and the city allowed for fewer distractions. The building was smaller than the schoolhouse Masta's children had attended in Tennessee.

After thanking Mrs. Eli and her sons for the ride, I hopped out. I stood and took in the sight of the school building, then crouched in the shadows of the county jailhouse to think for a moment. The school seemed to call out to me, though the idea of approaching the place made me apprehensive.

What if Florence and Daniel were right? What if this is dangerous?

The questions came, but they settled uneasily somewhere out of my reach. This was my chance, my one chance to steal my education like I stole my freedom. Surely nothing could stop me in my pursuit.

After staring at the school a few moments longer, I decided to go to the stitching shop to buy what Mama Bessie needed. After this, I paced the outskirts of the city for nearly an hour, going into the general store and otherwise busying myself in order to blend in with the people bustling around me.

Eventually, I heard the faint sound of a bell ringing nearby, as though it were summoning me. I rushed back into the shadows of the jailhouse and watched as the young children spilled with enthusiasm from the school building. I waited there, following the last of the children with my eyes down the crooked, dusty path that led away from the school.

As the last of them disappeared from view, I emerged, straightened my clothes, and made my way up the path to the school door. It took only two knocks before the door was jerked open. A young, plump face appeared in the doorway. Her cheeks were flushed red, perhaps from the heat within or from a long day of teaching. Upon seeing me, the woman furrowed her brows together and straightened her back with a slight, almost unnoticeable step away from the doorway.

"There something you need, miss?"

"Yes, ma'am, there is. I noticed that you'd do mighty good, here, with a servant of some kind, ma'am. I could clean up the school buildin' an' take care of the windows an' the heatin' durin' the day an'—"

"It's a single room! What do we need a servant for? We especially don't need black servants in this school. We have the help we need, and it's best you stay away from the school."

"Yes, ma'am, but I done heard the woman who helped out done passed away, an' I know I got the experience fo' this an'—"

"Do you hear what I say? We don't need you here. The city doesn't need you here, and the city is what pays. Now go on and leave. These folks around here don't like to see you blacks near the school."

"But, ma'am . . ."

As if to further emphasize her words, she placed both hands on her hips and stepped farther outside, pulling the door closed behind her. She moved toward me so swiftly that I almost stumbled backward.

"I think I've said what I needed to say. Now you're going to have to go. They have work down in the city. Find some place there." I supposed I should have guessed from the start that the schoolteacher had no intention of listening to what I had to say, but I could not simply walk away so readily, still hoping, still feeling as if an education were possible. I stood on the steps, gazing around her at the building, the windows, the letters scratched conspicuously on the walls.

God, all I want . . .

"Go on now!" The woman said, interrupting my silent prayer and motioning for me to leave.

I walked slowly back along the path, feeling the teacher's eyes burning holes in my soul as I left. Sullenness crept upon me as my head pounded: I was hurt. But I kept my head raised high, my shoulders boldly pulled back, and my gait sure and focused. Her angry dismissal of me only made me more determined. I kicked up the dust and memorized the details of our exchange. Certainty hung in the air, and I hoped she could feel it.

I would be back.

But my thoughts of returning were suspended when I saw a finely dressed man turn onto the school's path. I lowered my gaze and quickened my step, attempting, with no avail, to pass unnoticed.

"Miss." I lifted my head and stopped short, as if surprised. The man was tall, and I found myself looking up into what seemed to be a light-skinned, handsome face, though his hat made it difficult to see him clearly.

"Yessah?" I responded nervously, glancing quickly away, and praying I could avoid trouble.

"Perhaps it's not my place . . ." The man had a strangeness about him, and I couldn't tell what his intentions were. So I stood there, awaiting his words.

"But, miss, I don't think you understand the rules here. Blacks usually don't come around this way." I nodded, waiting for more. His lips opened again, but after a nod, he continued toward the school.

A week or so passed, during which time I pondered long and hard my decision to return to the school.

"You're not still upset, are you?" Florence had asked me repeatedly in the days after our first, tense conversation about the incident.

"No, I ain't upset," I'd assure her, holding strong to my secret in my heart. I'd keep it buried with me until nighttime, when I found myself envisioning John sitting beside me and sharing words of support.

What do you think, John? Should I go back? What would you do?

I'd go back.

Of course you'd go back, John, that's how you are! But you think it's smart?

I think you're smart. Follow your heart.

And that was it. He'd disappear into the night.

Using these imagined assurances and my own instincts, I made up my mind.

I woke up early that morning, before Florence, and crept out the door. My absence wouldn't be so unusual; occasionally, I took walks before our morning work, when nighttime offered me little sleep.

I headed down the road, intent on running into a townsman traveling in the direction I was headed. Sure enough, a wagon rolled slowly by me.

"Sah!" I called out to him. The wagon kept rolling as the man waved his hand in the air, signaling to me that he couldn't stop.

"Sah, please!" I called again. Hesitantly, the wagon slowed.

"You goin' to Dayton, sah?" I asked, running up to him.

"Sure am, but ain't got no room in here."

"Sah, I really need to get to the city."

"Look, miss, I apologize, but—" He ceased his speech as I leaned over and pressed a coin into his hand.

"A quarter, sah. A whole twenty-five cents."

He looked at me, speechless. "You . . . you need a ride back here, too?"

"Just need to get up there, sah," I said, shaking my head.

He hopped out of his seat and helped me into the wagon. I rode by the man's side, silent, as he talked excitedly.

"You know what I can do wit this twenty-five cents?" he asked me. Not waiting for my reply, he listed what he planned for himself and his family. I could barely hold on to his words as my own plans spun around in my head, making me more and more nervous. The school most likely had two or three teachers, who, if I understood correctly, lived with different local families. I clung to the hope that I would meet a different teacher who would hear me out and offer me the job as servant.

About half a mile from the city, I asked the driver to let me off. Upon reaching the school, I let out a sigh of relief as I noticed the children darting in and out of the school building. Their morning had not yet begun.

My presence was not as obvious this time around. I approached from behind the building and knocked softly on the door, nodding vaguely at the children who stood staring at me. I was greeted at the door by a young boy a third my size, whose rosy red cheeks seemed to giggle up at me.

"Yes?" he asked innocently in his high pitched voice.

"I'm here to see your teacher," I said to him.

"She's not here yet. You wanna come in?" His hands were already on my wrist as he dragged me with enthusiasm through the door.

The noise, chatter, and laughter abruptly ceased. I looked around, caught off guard by the sea of white faces and empty stares.

"Why you wanna speak to her?" The young boy's voice rang out, breaking the silence.

"Fo' work," I said, trying to calm my nervousness by turning my full attention to him.

"Oh," he said, staring at me as the other children, now mumbling among themselves, began to leave the room. I watched them with contempt. They were just children—at least, more than half of them were! What could they see in me that was so revolting?

"You gonna learn, too, like we are?" I looked down at the young boy and suddenly felt a strong sense of appreciation for his naivety.

"'Cause if you are, then—"

"Tod, come on!" One of the older female students dragged him out of the building without glancing at me. He smiled at me as he left with her. I could not bring myself to smile back.

The minute the door shut, the laughter and games began again. I listened closely as I heard a group of girls reciting the Lord's Prayer, most likely for their lesson that day.

"Our Father, who art in heaven, hallowed be thy name. Thy kingdom come, thy will be done . . ."

Thy will be done. I repeated this in my mind over and over again.

Suddenly, the door sprang open, and to my dismay the same plump young woman I had encountered before trudged toward me. I stood a good two inches taller than she was, but she seemed to hold the air of a superior.

"Ma'am—"

"It's you again! Did you not understand me before? The children are here, and it's time for school. You must leave." As she spoke, I noticed the dark potbelly stove sitting quietly in the corner. Even that object, with its inattentiveness and silent obedience, was allowed to listen in on the lessons every day. Why couldn't I?

My eyes skimmed the room further. I saw the Bible lying on the teacher's desk; copies of a small book called

The New-England Primer were skewed across the tables and benches. I saw the chalk, the blackboard, and letters written with beautiful penmanship.

"Ma'am—" I began again, intent on saying what I had to say.

"You have no right to be here," she said, interrupting me in a harsh manner.

I'd had it all planned out in my mind. I had planned to make a strong case on my behalf. I would ask, again, for the opportunity to work in order to employ my skills and abilities in whatever manner was needed. This had been my plan, straightforward and harmless. But the plan was drowning beneath the walls that stood disdainful, all painted in white, and seemed to run away with the faces of the young students that popped in and out of view behind the window. I listened to the woman speak to me, just as Missus had a long time ago. The woman stood in front of me, her gaze demanding and arrogant. She was waiting for me to turn and leave, but I didn't move. I couldn't.

"I have every right to be here," I said softly, dismissing the screeching voices in my head that warned me not to stray from my plan.

A shadow fell across her eyes. "Excuse me?" Her sharp reply seemed to yank every bit of pride I had from my soul.

I want a job here at the school! Just give me a chance!

Those were the words than ran through my mind, the words I had every intention of saying. But that was not what escaped my mouth.

"I want an education."

The woman's face registered alarm and anger. She didn't look so young anymore, and she didn't seem so much in control.

"An education? Do you even know what that is? Black folks can't have an education. That's not their place! At least, not in the classrooms here in the city."

"I wanna do what the children here are doin'!" I exclaimed, digging myself deeper. Her mouth let out an awkwardly high, shrill sound.

She's laughing! My disgust lit a fire in me that hadn't burned since I'd escaped.

"I don't agree with any injustice against you people. But there are reasons why you reside where you do and we reside where we do. This is not a place for any kind of Negro. You have no idea what education is, and even if you did, you wouldn't know what to do with it!"

I looked at the children from the window. They seemed to have lost interest in the matter; they were lost in play.

"Just 'cause you think that, don't mean I still cain't get an' education. I can sit an' learn just like they can!"

The woman's mocking amusement disappeared. She glared at me, hatred biting at the downward curvature of her lips. "You think you're fit to do what they do? By no means are you fit. You think your pursuit of education makes you fit for it? No. You blacks should know nothing but to live life simply and stay out of trouble. You think education is for you? It's not. Education makes you people unmanageable, unruly, wild, and destructive. Concepts and words would do more to turn you against each other and against the good people of this city than they would to make you wise. There is no such thing as a sophisticated Negro. You think you're fit for an education? Well, you're not. It's not your birthright and it never will be."

Her words felt like the chains of bondage. They hit me like Missus' beating rod. It was Mary who had taught me how to wash my face of expression and to hang my head in obedience, but I suddenly could do none of these things.

"Education gonna be mine," I said without faltering. I stared hard into her eyes and pointed a finger toward the window. "I'm just as capable and free as they are!"

The words struck down the woman's last bit of patience. Her hand quickly flew across my face, and without any thought of the consequences, I let my emotions take over. I reached out my hand and grabbed her wrist.

For a moment—a profoundly still moment—I heard only my harsh breath. We stared at each other.

Then, unexpectedly, she broke her stare and looked toward the door. Her expression changed drastically from anger to an apologetic pout and, finally, to that of victimized shock. As reality settled coldly in my limbs, I dragged my eyes around to the doorway as well and saw the man I had met on my previous trip to the school. The white man's eyes were more inquisitive than condemning. His black hat was tipped to the side, and he stood very still.

How much had he seen and heard? How long had he been standing there? Had I lost my mind?

I felt my fingers throbbing and realized it was the

woman's pulse. Pulling back, I dropped her hand as quickly as I could as my heart beat furiously. It was I, dark skinned and threatening, who was out of place. The seconds ticked by, pregnant with anticipation. I had to get out before this nightmare turned dangerous.

With three quick strides, I approached the door, terrified. I didn't wait for a clear path. I didn't wait for arms to rise up and beat me to the ground. I didn't wait for the screams of alarm that surely would come. I closed my eyes and pushed through the door, expecting to run with full force into the white man's body. Instead, I almost stumbled down the steps as the passageway for my escape opened up without any obstacles. The children parted, clearing the way for me as I fled.

I walked fast at first, then broke into a run. I didn't wonder why the man wasn't following me. I didn't stop to ponder why the woman wasn't shrieking. I didn't pause to reflect on my humiliation. My one thought was to get away.

I ran from Dayton, the fear that I was being followed stopping me from looking back. Even when the school faded into the background, I could not slow myself down. When the ringing of the school bell sounded distant, however, I eased my pace somewhat.

Are they not following me?

Surely I couldn't get away that easily. Not only had I grabbed the woman's wrist, but a white man had witnessed it! Had they pitied me? Or was this a trick, so that they could take me by surprise later?

I ran on for nearly half an hour, until I was convinced that no one was pursuing me. I had forgotten what danger felt like.

I wrapped myself in my arms, attempting to squeeze away the sickening feeling that the confrontation had left me with. But the feeling simply turned into trembling and tears. The incident had touched a place deep down that brought back feelings from my escape from slavery. Fear ran through me, and I vomited.

I stopped by the side of the road to rest, letting the built-up emotions, the disappointment, and the emptiness fall over my shoulders. Hadson lay some thirty minutes ahead of me, and I had no intention of going back to Mama Bessie's in the state I was in.

But just as I had settled down, I heard wagon wheels approaching from a distance, coming from Hadson toward me. Jumping up, I wiped away the evidence of stress on my face and attempted to calm my spirit. Holding my head low, I began walking again.

The wagon rolled by, and my brother shouted out my name. I paid him no mind and kept walking with my head low.

"Anna!" He yelled again, but I bit my lip and hoped he'd just keep on riding.

The wagon came to a stop.

"Anna, how come you ain't talkin'? What's goin' on?"

"Sebastian, you go . . . go on. I got work to do at Mama Bessie's." My voice trembled subtly, but he heard it.

Leaping down, he took hold of my shoulders and got me to look at him.

"Sarah," he said, using the more familiar name he still preferred, "where you bin? What happened? You shakin', Sarah. What'sa matta?"

"The school," I said, softly.

He sighed. "You went to the school," he said, more to himself than to me. I stared at the wheels of his wagon in response. He bade me get in.

"Daniel, don't take me back to Dayton. I have to be gettin' back to Mama Bessie's an' I just cain't go back there, not right now."

He frowned and helped me into the wagon. "Why? What happened, Sarah? Tell me."

"It was jus' the faces an' the books an' the writin' an' the benches. . . ."

"Sarah, what you talkin' about? What happened?"

"She slapped me, Daniel, an' I grabbed her wrist, an' the man was there. He was just there, he just appeared."

"What man?"

"Some man had the door open, an' I rushed passed an' I . . . I ran!" Daniel gaped at me, then turned his eyes to the road. He picked up the reins and started back to Hadson.

"But you safe, you here. I don't understand, so they didn't do nothin' about it?"

My thoughts slowed back down. "I don't understand it either. I was right there. An' they just . . . they just let me go! What's that mean?" Daniel shrugged and pursed his lips. We rode in silence as my anxiety subsided a bit.

"You angry at me, I can tell," I said after a while.

"You scared me, Anna. You jus'—had me thinkin' things I don't wanna think. But you safe, an' I feel betta 'bout that. You wa'an't gonna give up your passion. I shoulda known you betta than that."

"You sayin' you woulda stopped me from goin' up to the school some way or another?" I asked, feeling mild anger rise again. From the schoolhouse to my own brother, they were all telling me it wasn't my right to pursue this thing called education.

Daniel turned a tired smile toward me. "You think I could make you do somethin' 'gainst what yo' mind was so set on? I ain't neva bin able to do that."

I smiled a little and sat back. "So you think it was right, me goin' up there?"

Daniel laughed. "I don't hafta tell you that. This yo' dream. What you think?"

"I think I jus' about lost my mind today!" I said, feeling a bit lighter.

He laughed and nodded. "Whateva you done, don't know how you done it this time, but if they ain't after you by now, don't think they gonna be."

"You don't think so?"

He shook his head. "You know what scare me the most, though?" he asked.

"What's that?"

"I think if you was told there was the smallest chance fo' you to get what you wanted, you'd go right on back agin."

He chuckled, but I closed my eyes instead, and sighed.

"You think, maybe, I want this education a little too much?" I asked him.

He sat thinking, then responded with a question that brought back the strength I felt I had lost that morning.

"I dunno. You think we wanted our freedom a little too much?"

CHAPTER

33

THE COLORS BLEEDING THROUGH THE TREETOPS SKIPPED WITH delight in my mind's eye. I was young, my small back resting against my mother's shoulder. I watched the shadows of very tall men pass in and out of view. My toes melted into the soil of my homeland.

It was a soothing feeling, more of a sensation than a memory. I sat with my eyes closed underneath the shade of a tree, sharing with Florence beautiful recollections I didn't even think I had of the place I'd left long ago. The moment was a respite from the tension that had still burned in my chest about the events at the schoolhouse. For days afterward, I feared a knock on Mama Bessie's door, and white men storming in. I was sure they would drag me out and throw me in the jailhouse for the rest of my life. But this never happened, and on this day, I let all my worries drift away.

"She had this walk, I remember, that always would remind me of a dance. She wore them long skirts, with a whole lot of colors. I remember 'cause I would always play with the jewelry on her ankles, an' those skirts would tickle my neck."

"What did she look like, your mother?"

I sighed, gazing beyond the setting sun. "Wish I could remember—wish I could explain with words. But, well . . ." I shrugged.

"Oh!" I said with a smile, remembering. "An' I had a brother, Flo. Always remembered his name. Always. It was Sentwaki." She repeated the name. It sounded strange on her lips.

"He was bigger than me—older, I think. Every memory I have, even if it's a small memory, he's there. Even when we came 'cross the waters, it wasn't till we was both sold on the auction block that he left me—for good."

"I wonder, sometimes, where he could be. When I see faces I don't know, I pass them by, wonderin' if I could be starin' in the face of my own blood brother."

She nodded. "That would be somethin'. You remember how it look like, where you come from?" she asked.

I sat and thought for a moment.

"You know, Flo, of all things, its hard to rememba that, too. I know the feeling I had bein' out near the trees an' the water. Oh, the water!" I laughed. "Clearest thing you eva seen. Stretched out far and wide. Beautiful water . . ."

We were still speaking about my past even as night crept up, Florence soaking in every word. The sound of wagon wheels racing by dulled the dreamlike sensation for a moment.

"Don't think I ever met no one like you," she said, standing up to stretch. "You say you from Africa, an' what a picture you paint of that place!"

I laughed, gathering up the children who had

congregated outside for play and sending them inside for bed. We followed them inside.

Later, when we headed to our room, I asked Florence about her family.

"Well, ain't nothin' much to it," she said, her eyes more dreamy and distant than sad.

"My mama and pappy was freed folks. My mama's folks was free, too, but she left them to move on here, to Ohio, with my pappy. We was living with some black folks in an Indian village. Don't remember much from there."

I smiled and ran my hand across her braided hair, which was tossed across her shoulder. "You have Indian blood in you?"

She nodded. "Yes. My pappy's daddy. Mama died before I could even walk, an' Daddy moved on here." She seemed to be considering that as we settled into our room. "You know, the more I think about it, I never really knew him that well either. I know he loved women—Mama Bessie told me—and I've always had a feeling my mama never liked that. He loved me, but he didn't feel responsibility for me. We came here, he an' I, and I met Mama Bessie, an' that was the end of it."

"The end? You mean, you neva saw him after that?"

She bit her lip, lost in thought. "Mama Bessie said I did. Once or twice." She shrugged. "He was young. Used to doing things on his own."

I nodded, understanding. An urge came over me suddenly to tell Florence about John. I opened my mouth to speak, but the words wouldn't come out right.

"There was somebody . . . I mean back south. . . ." I

felt out of place looking at Florence, feeling the coins in my pocket, dressed in freedwoman's clothes, wrapped in the dignity of calling my own self Masta. And where was he?

"Anna?" she asked, questioning my silence.

I started again, gazing down at my feet. "Back south, there was a man I knew. We was . . ." I stopped again. What right had I to speak of a time and place that seemed so distant from me, a place that still caged his soul?

"We was . . ."

"Good friends?" she asked.

I smiled over at her, burying the words back down in my soul. I couldn't share that with her, not now. I'd tell her about Mary instead.

"Yes. Had a good friend down there. Wish you coulda met him. Real good fellow. Then there was the woman that took me in," I said.

"Before we ran from that plantation, she had—" I stopped short as I noticed Florence's piercing eyes spring alive with questions.

"'Ran from'? You say . . . you say 'ran from,' Anna. I . . . I kinda always thought you ran, that you wasn't freed like you said," she said in a loud whisper.

"How you figure that?" I asked her, feeling my emotions shift from mild alarm at how easily I let the words slip, to gratitude for her understanding.

She shrugged. "Guess that's jus' something good friends can do."

"Flo, but you know . . ."

"I know, I ain't s'pose to say nothing about it. Don't

worry about me, Anna. I understand. Besides, you see me tell anybody yet?"

"Yet?" I teased her, laughing. She joined in.

"So, you from Africa. Then you run all the way here from . . . ?"

"Kentucky," I lied, sticking to what seemed safer.

"Kentucky. Which means Sebastian ran too?"

I nodded.

"Hmph," she said, sighing and sitting back in surprise. "So, that's why you call him somethin' different sometimes. Heard you call him Daniel a few times. An' he called you Sarah. Always wondered, but didn't ask no questions. Figured you'd tell me if you needed to."

"I didn't know we said those names so much! We ain't suppose to."

"Naw, don't worry. Anna, I'm around you two all the time. Y'all don't use those names too often. Jus' sometimes, you two get to talking an' forget. Funny, to me."

"I'm surprised you didn't ask no questions."

"Well, you cain't know *everything*. But what . . . how did you . . ." But her thoughts were interrupted by a slow, heavy knocking on the door. Florence hopped up, pulled the knob, and stood face to face with Daniel. She stared at him for a moment, taking in the anger in his eyes and his heaving chest. Sweat trickled down his forehead.

"You all right?" she asked him softly.

"Wanna ask you if I can sleep here tonight," he said.

"You talk to Mama Bessie?" she asked. He nodded.

"All right then, I'll move on to an empty room for the

night." She moved away to take what she needed while I looked hard at my brother.

"Sebastian, what's wrong?" I asked him. He collapsed against the doorway.

"Rodney's gone, dead. They killed him." Florence instantly stopped what she was doing and sank down next to him. I brought my hand to my lips, eyes still on Daniel. Rodney—the young man Daniel had stayed with upon arriving in the neighborhood—was gone.

"Stole some of the crop, that's all. Jus' stole some crop fo' his motha an' his brotha, an' they kill him. Mr. James say he would do it if he found out who it was. Rodney say to me the man jus' talk, that's all. But no. The man killed him. 'Course, cain't nobody prove that all of a sudden, but we knows the truth." I looked over at Florence, who looked at me with concern. She turned back on my brother, watching his movements like a hunter.

Daniel threw his hands up and let them fall on his knees.

"Don't reckon y'all think it's right, they jus' come round here killin' folks, huh?" His question went unanswered.

"Reckon decent folks would do somethin' 'bout that."

"No, Sebastian, that ain't smart," Florence said to him in a soothing tone.

"Look here, they gonna take a man's life fo' a simple thing like that? They give us every right to do somethin' 'gainst it. Ain't a decent law that exists sayin' no free man cain't defend, protect, and strike back fo' his own!"

I leaned back against the wall, letting his words settle into my own thoughts.

"Ain't our place here, Sebastian. Black folks ain't got no say in the law," Flo said.

"But—"

"Say, you want them to find you out an' take you back down south?" Florence asked even more softly, every muscle in her face working hard to contain her emotions.

Daniel's face snapped up. "How you know that?" His lips were trembling.

"No matter, I asked you, is that what you want?" she asked. "'Cause I know this place, Sebastian. I seen people taken 'cause they mixed up in the wrong mess an' get found out. You cain't do nothing now. Best let it be!" Her words cut sharp and forcefully through the room.

"Just let it be, huh?" he retorted, sarcastically.

"Uh-huh," she responded.

"Cain't just let it be."

"Yes you can, too!"

Daniel was silent. He knew Florence was right. Florence placed a hand on his forehead, running it across his short hair.

Florence left a little while later and, as Daniel fell asleep sprawled across the pallet I usually lay on, I lit my candle and sat thinking thoughts that chased the sleepiness away.

After a little bit, I pulled out some old newspapers I had. I dipped my quill in ink and scratched the word *injustice* through one of the columns. Daniel stirred and lifted his head.

"That you, Anna?" I gazed at my brother—his swollen

eyes, dry, pursed lips, his furrowed brow—all evidence of weary, gruesome dreams.

"Yes. Was just thinkin', Daniel," I whispered to him. He grunted, turning to lie on his back and resting his eyes on the ceiling's wooden planks.

"Thinkin' 'bout what?" He asked.

"Thinkin' of what I'm gonna do when I get my education."

"What's that?"

"Gonna write me a trea-tise."

"What's that, Anna?" he asked with a broken yawn. Lately, he had fallen more into the habit of calling me Anna, even when we were alone. He seemed to like the name.

"Those things that folks write when they wanna talk about somethin' that means a lot. Figure I'ma call it my Treat-ise on Injustice."

He closed his eyes again.

"If it's about Rodney, I . . ."

"Shh. Not jus' about him. Rodney ain't the first unfair death we seen since we been here, Daniel."

"So, tell me 'bout it," he said with another yawn.

"Well, I ain't really wrote nothin' yet, Daniel. I told you, I need to be educated fo' I go writin' somethin' like this. I don't—"

"Jus' tell me what you thinkin' of."

I sighed. "All right. I was thinkin', how far black folks really gonna go here? Are we eva gonna have the rights otha folks got?"

"That's a question we all got," Daniel mumbled.

"Well, seems to me we got the same things goin' on up here that's goin' on in the South. Only difference is, we ain't under no whip an' ain't nobody gonna beat us fo' thinkin' fo' ourselves. But we ain't treated like people, Daniel. Been listenin' around, heard someone say we ain't even got a right to this black community, though we call it our own. Say they got the power to jus' take it from us—an' why not? We don't seem to have a real place in that city of theirs. We cain't defend ourselves in the courts. We s'pose to give five hundred dolla's jus' to live in this state, Daniel—you think them folks had to pay money like that?" I shook my head and looked away from him.

"What if . . . what if all of us young folks around Hadson—all the folks workin' an' raisin' families—what if we all got to learnin' an' all started understandin' all they important papers an' laws, an' all started protestin' on paper. That would be somethin', wouldn't it? That's how otha folks are heard—that's how they make their points and convince othas to believe them. Why would it be any different fo' us if we did the same? What you think would happen?" I asked, but left him no room to respond.

"I've bin thinkin' 'bout why they ain't want us learnin' in the South. They were scared of what we would do if we had some learnin'. Here, learnin' ain't against the law, but they don't want us nowhere near their schools. Maybe, somewhere deep inside, they scared of the same thing," I said with a dry laugh.

"Or what if . . . what if all the beatin' hearts ragin' fo'

justice turned into real violence, Daniel. Me an' Florence sit here an' tell you the smart thing is to jus' let it be. But what if this happens jus' too many a times an' none of us can jus' let it be? You cain't be suppressin' that kinda energy fo' too long. How long can you hold folks back, 'specially folks who know they s'pose to be free, 'fore that need for justice starts turnin' into somethin' dangerous? Reckon somethin' oughta be done. But what, Daniel, what?" I finished my rambling with a low grunt and gazed over at Daniel's face, half-expecting him to have fallen back into his troubled sleep. But his eyes were wide open.

"Reckon you voicin' the thoughts of many folks round here, Anna. Didn't think you thought about it that deep. That idea bout folks learnin', though . . . you know, that seems betta than anythin' I eva heard, Anna," he whispered into the night. I shook my head.

"It's not so great. Ain't wrote nothin' but a word," I responded, dropping onto Florence's pallet. "But thinkin' 'bout all this, an' dreamin' of writin' somethin' on it all is the nearest thing I can do to an' education." He sighed and turned away, and soon enough I heard the steady rise and fall of his breathing. I fell into sleep just as swiftly and my ideas of freedom weaved in and out of my dreams.

CHAPTER

34

REVOLT. REVOLT. WE SHALL REVOLT.

The words passed through the sea of black bodies like a fierce wave from the ocean outside. I pushed the two bodies on my left and right aside, and stood up to see who had spoken. The darkness that hung was thicker than heavy smoke, but I could see quite clearly.

Revolt. Revolt. We shall revolt.

No one had spoken those words aloud. Instead, I could see the words creeping through the bodies; I could sense the collective feeling breathing as if it were alive. The ship tipped heavily one way, and the bodies shifted with it—that ugly sound of human chattel sliding across the wooden boards of the bottom of this slave ship melting into one long, deep breath. The ship dipped back the other way, and the breath taken was released in a loud boisterous hum that seeped heavily through skin past eardrums to soul, the pain that lay beneath it sharp enough to kill.

I want out! Let me get away! I screamed.

The hatch above us opened. A barked order reached our ears. *Up deck! Now!*

They came slowly, bare bodies blackened by birth: bumping, thumping, limping, sulking, dragging themselves up. Old bones gave out, legs collapsed, but the monster-men prodded, as if nudging animals from their cages.

But there was a light up there. What did it mean? After all that time in the darkness, did freedom await us? Was there an ending to this horrid reality called hell?

Then the sunlight hit our eyes. The pain stabbed at our bodies and minds, swirling steadily between our brows but bringing with it a lightness that touched our souls. Whiteness! It was the light of hope and faith, a sign that we were being freed! Our bodies would be rid of these chains. Our minds would be rid of this prison. Our hearts would be rid of this horrendous burden!

But once we emerged onto the deck, our dreams and fantasies plummeted back to reality. The whips and rods awoke from their resting places. The whiteness we had believed was pure now oozed from the skin of those demons. It wasn't whiteness, it was redness, it was hate, it was un-God-like terror, it was the monster-men, who had fooled us out of a freedom.

On deck, a drum sat waiting for us.

Dance! A shouted order that the whips helped us understand.

Dance!

Soft shuffling, low humming that drifted from souls rather than throats; prayers to sprout wings and fly—these were our dance. The dance became louder, quicker, the beating suddenly taken over by someone who knew how to speak through the drum. I looked for something familiar to hold on to in his gaze, but I saw only emptiness and . . . rage.

His eyes were screaming, *Let me die, then let me fly, fly back home, just let me try!*

And his drum spoke: *Do you, do you, do you feel it?*

We danced faster, our feet beating stronger, drowning out the pleas and whimpers and screams of the young women who had been dragged to far corners of the ship while we danced. They were ripping through the womb of our land, and it was too much for the moving bodies to bear.

Do you, do you, do you feel it?

We danced more rapidly, our limbs moving more freely. We refused to be animals herded and prepared for slaughter.

Do you, do you, do you feel it?

Then the fire stick was raised to the skies to stop us, but we wouldn't stop!

It clicked again, but we couldn't stop!

This time, the fire stick spit flames into the air. Clubs came out, knives were drawn, fire sticks from both sides shouted insults at one another.

Revolt! Revolt! We must revolt!

Screeching voices, tumbling bodies, wide stares, and bloodcurdling screams filled my ears and eyes. And we wouldn't stop it!

Frantic monster men, leaping bodies, explosions, and high-pitched screams floated through the air. And we couldn't stop it!

And there beside me, a young girl standing over me, skin shining rich in the sun, slipped carelessly out of the air. She had a hole in her chest. Her eyes, her frown that gripped the edges of her jawbones, her fingers that groped for the point of impact—they all seemed to lock themselves in place, suspended.

The bullet tore through my own skin, and I fell down into the hole below, down, down, down, watching as three pairs of bare black legs were sent dangling, hanging, swinging back and forth above me. . . .

I hit the ground, a blanket of snow, and rolled aside quickly as a procession of angry townsfolk stormed forward in protest.

Pitchforks, flames, and guns clasped by bodies adorned with farmers' clothing were raised high to the heavens. They marched on to witness the reincarnation of a body left rotting in the fields, the stolen crop now the bars that bound the man's body in place. Townsfolk screamed, the murderer at the forefront, scarecrows in the dark trying to remove the bars and the body; but to no avail. Through death, he was speaking to them.

Do you, do you, do you feel it? I've had enough.

The marching continued, but the pitchforks, flames, and guns turned to documents, pieces of parchment. An awareness arose that the quick-witted tongue and well-read mind could help win this battle and bring success to this revolt.

But let me do it, I can do it!

I stared at a single white face in the crowd who had hollered those words. He stared back, his white face turning chestnut, turning deep brown, turning a purplish black.

I am ready! Let me do it.

There was a crack, a hush that was suspended over the crowd, and the man lay dead.

No, no! I want out! Let me get out!

This time it was Daniel kneeling above me, frantically calling my name.

My eyes came open.

"Daniel," I said, rubbing the tears away.

"You all right? Is there somethin' I'm s'pose to do?" he asked me, his eyes tired but filled with concern.

"Naw, Daniel, figure I'm all right. Jus' . . ." I sat up, trying to remember how and where I used to bury that heavy feeling my dreams gave. My last nightmarish dream had been months before, when I was escaping from the plantation. I had allowed myself to forget what the dreams felt like.

"You bin havin' many of those, Anna?" he asked me.

I shook my head. "Haven't had any, actually. Maybe Mary was right. Maybe I will get rid of 'em for good after some time."

Daniel got to his feet. "Hope so. Cain't stand seein' you like that."

Daniel disappeared for the next few nights after the incident, which about worried me into my grave. He'd sometimes

302

leave us for a day or two, but never four and five nights at a time. I spent each evening he was gone racing down to Hadson and asking around for him. I'd always end up at Rodney's house, coming face-to-face with an older woman.

"You seen 'im today?" I'd ask her.

"Naw, haven't seen him."

"You heard from him?"

"I haven't, Anna," the woman would say with a light pat on my shoulder, "but I promise you he's all right. Don't worry so much. He'll be back."

And then one night he did come back. As Florence and I sat in the kitchen plucking turkey feathers for the next day's meal, I heard some noises out on Mama Bessie's land. Running to the window, I peered out and saw him making conversation with another man and three women. Florence brushed her hands against her dress and looked out, too, watching with growing irritation at the five of them laughing and carrying on. She strode back to her stool, roughly seating herself again, and began yanking at the feathers with annoyance. Her tension felt unforgiving.

"What is it, Flo?" I asked her as I pulled open the door. She shook her head and kept her eyes on her work.

"Sebastian!" I yelled as the others drifted away. I ran and caught him in a hug but pushed him away again.

"Why would you leave us like that without sayin' nothin'?"

"Work," he simply said, smiling.

"Sebastian, you actin' quite strange. Now, I ain't gonna ask 'bout yo' work or nuthin'—ain't my business to know.

But you cain't do things like this!" I explained to him, sternly. He laughed away my comment and made for the door.

"You think this is funny, Sebastian? We ain't seen you for the past few days! You act like you don't care!"

He turned back and apologized. "I know I bin gone fo' a few days, Anna, an' I'm sorry I didn't say nothin'. Didn't know it would be that long. But don't go sayin' things like that, that I don't care. This is me, the same me you've known foreva." Then he shook away his frown.

"An' anyway, I got some news fo' you. Where's Flo?" He walked through the doorway and stood tapping fingers against one another, smiling at Florence.

"Hey, miss." His giddiness broke the shadow that had come along and sat with us as we waited for his return. But Florence said nothing.

"Flo," he said after a few seconds, stepping towards her.

"Don't wanna hear no 'Flo' from you, Sebastian."

"Flo, I bin gone fo' a few days, that's it. What's wrong?"

"I don't fool with folk less they serious. Got my mind on other things, other dreams, an' don't have no time for your foolishness."

He laughed, but uneasiness darkened his expression.

"What you talkin' of, Flo? Came all the way down here to see you an' my sista here. . . ."

"It's your ways I'm talking of. Gonna disappear for all them days an' come back like this!"

"Like what?" he asked, seeming genuinely puzzled by Florence's mood.

"Like you was out there, Sebastian!" she said, pointing out the window and looking squarely into his face. He fought not to drop his gaze.

"When I be with somebody, that's who I'm gonna be with. Ain't no games an' fooling with me. An' jus' as sure as you wanna be laughin' an' huggin' an' prancin' around with those other girls, there is no Flo in that, you hear?" she said, almost spitting the words out.

"Flo, it's just funnin' . . ."

"And I say, no sir!" She slammed the turkey down on the table, and feathers flew every which way. She left the room as quickly as her mood allowed.

Daniel followed her with his eyes, saying nothing. For a moment, he looked like he'd been struck, but it wasn't long at all before his face melted back into a light, amused calmness. He turned back to me, his eyes asking for an explanation.

"If that's what she say, that's what she means!" I said to him. He shrugged his shoulders to show it meant nothing to him, but he couldn't help stealing another glance out of the room.

"Sebastian, you gotta understand, you can't jus' leave like that," I tried explaining once more.

"Sorry, Anna. It's jus', wit Rodney gone . . ." He stopped, looking away for a moment, clearly fighting away the anger he felt.

He turned back to me, his lips curled upward, and asked, "That why she so mad?"

I chuckled. "Don't think so. Looks like you got more eyes fo' women than she likes."

"I don't see it that way!" he exclaimed.

"Then maybe that's what's wrong." He sat in silence for a moment as I continued my work. I had questions for him, things part of me wanted to know. Like, what was he involved in and where had he been? But I kept silent, knowing my brother would share what he thought was necessary and leave the rest in secret, where it belonged.

"Well, anyways, Anna, they knows 'bout you."

"What you mean? Who?"

"Well, I done took what you tole me 'bout you wantin' to write on injustice an' the laws an' all that an' tole 'em we got somebody here who gonna use education, someday, to make a difference."

My blood rushed to my face. "Don't like you doin' that, Sebastian," I said quietly. I didn't know where the fear came from, but it was there.

"Why not? You said this was yo' dream! You said—"

"I know what I said, Sebastian! But I don't have a cent's worth of decent writin' in my bones! I ain't writin' those things fo' the community, not yet. They just thoughts I wanted to share with you."

"Well, then, who you writin' an' thinkin' them things fo'?"

"Fo' me, Sebastian. An' for Rodney, I suppose."

"What good's that do?"

"Plenty. If I cain't get an' education, then I'ma have to make myself one. I might as well do it writin' 'bout things I see goin' on round here."

"But share it!" he said, the veins in his neck becoming very prominent.

"Sebastian, I'm not gonna do that jus' yet, an' I'd think you'd do me mighty fine to hush up 'bout it."

"All right then," he said, rising from the table and finding his way back to the door.

"You'll think 'bout it, though?" A sly smile slid across his face. "For me, Anna?"

"Go on, Sebastian," I said, waving him away.

CHAPTER

❧ 35 ❧

TWO ROADS LED FROM THE HADSON TOWN CENTER TO MAMA Bessie's. The longer of these stretched across significant pieces of land with natural sights that caught even the most unobservant eye. The shorter road was less eye-catching, but useful when a faster route was called for.

Walking into town late that afternoon, I had taken the longer route. I had nothing more to do that evening than to complete my tasks for Mama Bessie and the household.

I entered Mrs. Susie's shop to buy what Mama Bessie needed and to pick up my newspaper. The shop was always my last stop if Florence wasn't with me. Every week, Mrs. Susie's husband would bring me back a newspaper from the city, and I'd drop a penny in Mrs. Susie's hand in exchange for it.

"Thank you, Mrs. Susie," I said with a smile, placing the coin in the woman's palm.

"My pleasure, Miss Anna," she responded, placing the paper on the counter. As I grabbed the newspaper and turned to go, a sheet of paper slid from among the pages and floated onto the floor. I glanced up at Mrs. Susie, who had turned her back to me, and bent down to pick it up.

The words on the page were written in beautiful penmanship, and read:

*Longer roads tend to lead
to what is strongly desired.
If schooling is that desire,
then travel that road.

I can help.*

I glanced again at Mrs. Susie. "Mrs. Susie, you know somethin' 'bout this?" She twirled back around and saw me waving the page. Her face folded in a frown.

"Naw. Where it come from?"

"Jus' slipped from the newspaper!"

She put her hand thoughtfully on her mouth. "Reckon that ain't my husband's, neither. He can read some but cain't do no writin'—not like that, at least, an' he don't own no paper that look like that. What it say?" I looked back up at her, then crumpled the page in my hand.

"Nothin' important, it don't seem. Think somebody slipped it in there by mistake."

"Uh-huh," she said, returning her attention to the fabric that stretched across the counter.

"Good night, Mrs. Susie."

"Goodnight, chile."

I walked outside and glanced around me to see if anyone was watching, or if anyone looked suspicious. Mr. Jones, the neighbor Florence had introduced as "the man with the limp," walked slowly across the street, pushing a cart before him; two children squealed, hopping over a small puddle of rainwater; Ms. Tee sat still with her eyes closed, seated on the porch of her shop. Every person I saw seemed to be occupied with his or her own life, and no one took any notice of me.

I flattened out the paper and read the words three times over with both fascination and fear.

Is this a mistake, or was it meant to fall into my hands? What does it mean? Who is it from? And how did that person know I wanted an education?

It seemed too much of a coincidence for it to be a mistake. But then a thought struck me: What if this was a trap? Could it be that slave catchers had found me out and wanted to take me back down south? But the method made little sense. What was going on?

Or was the school after me, wanting to punish me for grabbing the teacher's wrist? But that had been so long ago.

Or, what if there was no danger? What if I was simply being offered the chance at learning—the education I constantly dreamed of?

Whoever it was seemed to know me well. But I quickly came back to my senses. I knew from my escape how cautious it was necessary to be. However much I regretted running away from the chance at an education, I didn't want to take the risk of walking down that road.

"I'm sure this is what my brother would do, at least," I whispered to myself, trying to shake off my disappointment as I took the shorter path back home. My curiosity, however, lingered alongside the fear.

I walked on, and the evening air felt good across my skin. When I was a good distance from town, I lifted my finger to the sky and traced out four letters, trying to distract myself.

J-O-H-N.

"Excuse me, miss." I jumped at the voice and spun around to see a figure approaching me with a relaxed gait from quite a distance away. My eyes darted around to see if anyone else was in sight, but we were the only two people on the road. He had to be talking to me.

"Who's there?" I called back, my heartbeat quickening. I now shuffled slowly backward as I squinted into the darkness to see if I could make out the person who was nearing me.

"Sah, you talkin' to me? You need somethin'? Do I know you, sah?" I said, continuing my backward movement.

"I daresay you don't, miss, but I'd like to speak with you!" The voice called back in a friendly and light-hearted tone. The accent, however, was unfamiliar to my ears. My feet stopped as I clutched the paper in my hands tighter. I stood where I was.

Could this be the note writer?

"I apologize for finding you at such a late hour. In light of my own daytime responsibilities, I had no other choice." His pace slowed as he neared me.

"I figured you wouldn't go down that other road. You're careful, then, as I supposed. You'll need that. Caution is important. You'll need that."

"Sah, I don't rightly know what you mean by that an' . . . an' . . ."

"That other road," he had said.

"The letter—that note. It was you who wrote it, wa'an't it? Who are you?" I called uneasily back into the night. I could see only the outline of his clothes, but from that I noted how well he was dressed. He wore a suit, boots, gloves, and a hat. I glanced behind him, but it appeared that he was alone. He approached me with a quick yet untroubled step.

"Don't be alarmed, Miss Anna. I would like to help you," the man said, walking closer, and stopping only when he was a few arms' lengths from where I stood. I still couldn't see his face clearly.

"My name. How you know my name, sah?" I stopped short and caught my breath. It was quite dark now, but some things about the man stood out almost instantly. He almost surely, from what I could make out in the dark, was a white man.

"Sah, I don't . . . I don't think you got the right person," I said softly.

"No, no, I believe you're the person I wanted to speak with. It's Miss Anna, am I correct?" he asked calmly. I could see that he was smiling.

I nodded slowly, then added, "Sah, I haven't done nothin' wrong . . ."

"No, heavens no! I daresay you haven't."

"But sah, you're . . . you're a . . ."

He stepped closer and gestured with his hand in the direction I had been headed. "Please, don't let me keep you from continuing on your journey. I'll walk with you in the direction you're headed, if that's acceptable to you. As I said before, I would just like a quick word. I want to help," he repeated.

I frowned and avoided the man's gaze, my heartbeat quickening once again. It seemed like he was here to do me no harm. But what was he here for? His letter spoke about education, but what could a white man possibly do to help educate me?

"Sah, reckon I don't need no help with nothin', specially from no one like . . . no one like you."

He chuckled softly, looking down at his feet. I crossed my arms over my chest and waited for him to respond. I admitted to myself that I was curious.

"I understand why you might say that. Please don't be alarmed. I really am not here to harm you. I think, perhaps, you'll be quite interested in what I have to say." The man had already begun walking before he finished talking, leaving me no time to think about whether or not I should follow him. I took a few long strides to catch up, though I purposely left a significant gap between the two of us.

"You read my note," the man said matter-of-factly without glancing my way.

"Yes," I said quietly, trying to collect my thoughts, which strayed between curiosity and doubt. I recalled my last attempts to seek an education. The odds did not seem to be on my side.

"Well, I understand that you desire to receive an education." His statement hung in the air like a question, but my lips seemed to be sealed shut. Surely he wasn't speaking of providing me with an education! I had sought out and gone to heavy extents to find something that didn't seem possible to obtain. How could this man suddenly change all of that?

"I've heard it from other folks, but I must hear it from you. Do you want to learn? Get educated?" His words jumped out at me again and circled before me. I sighed into the air with irritation. What right had this man to talk to me about something I couldn't have? The question haunted and mocked me.

"Sah, even if I do tell you what I want, I jus' cain't see how you gonna help me. An' why you wanna help in the first place? Seems to me I couldn't mean much to you. Never seen you before. Don't have nothin' to give you. What is it makes you come round this way talkin' of helpin' me?" I asked, giving voice to the doubts in my head.

"You keep jumping to my attention, and I've made it my business to understand your intentions, and to give you a hand in these affairs." He waited as I considered his words. I tried to ignore the hope and anticipation and excitement that were bubbling up inside me.

"Ain't nothin' much else I want more than to learn, sah," I said slowly, "but there's still somethin' unclear to me. Don't see how I can be 'jumpin' to your attention' as you say. You say you don't wanna do me no harm, but sah, quite plainly, your words makin' me a bit nervous." In my heart, I knew that was a lie. I was far from nervous: I was clinging to his words tighter than a baby to its mother.

The man looked over at me as he walked, and I averted my eyes from his.

"Well, you caught quite a bit of my attention up at the school in the city."

"The school?" I asked, feeling my heart dip quite suddenly into panic.

He nodded. "Yes. Twice, I believe, you came by, though I daresay it may have been more than that?"

"You were there?" His chuckle came again, warm like a summer breeze. I looked over at the man again, and this time met his eyes.

Those eyes. They looked so familiar.

The scenario flashed quickly across my mind once more: the schoolteacher, my hand around her wrist, the man standing at the door. He was the man I'd seen at the school!

"You were there," I said, biting my lip.

"Yes, I was. But don't alarm yourself. I said a few words on your behalf." His accented voice blended pleasantly with the night air. With those words, my panic diminished greatly.

"On . . . on my behalf? You mean, they never came after me because . . . because of you?"

He nodded.

"But why?"

"That's no important matter. There's a bit more, though. At a meeting not long back, I heard a young man mention a younger relative of his who had the desire to be educated. He shared with those gathered her ideas about a young man's death. He further explained her far-fetched dream of writing something significant on justice. Common sense allowed me to connect his description to the woman who was persistent enough to do what she did at the school." I could hear Daniel's voice, right then, sharing with the community my ideas on justice and about Rodney's death.

"But, sah, again, why you so interested in this? I don't have nothin' to do with you."

He shrugged. "I told you, Miss Anna. I want to help. I really have no greater reason than that. And there's something I want to share with you."

"'Bout gettin' educated?"

"Yes, about that." I listened to his boots click, every tap bringing a lighter feeling to my chest.

"I want you to be cautious with your education," he said simply.

"Cautious? Didn't think it was against the law fo' us black folks to learn nothin', sah."

"It's not, Anna. That's not quite what I mean. There's nothing dangerous, here, about learning. Education itself is something every person in Ohio should have the right to, and here, unlike the South, people don't take learning as a serious threat. Perhaps you'd be surprised to know that here in the North, there are quite a few places where black folks are getting educated." I was engrossed in his words and hardly noticed Mama Bessie's place materializing in the distance. The man was speaking with an attitude so unlike that of most of the white folks I had run into in the North that I figured if the nighttime had swallowed the color of his skin, and if it weren't for his accent and his sophisticated way of speaking, then perhaps I would've believed he was a black man.

"But at some point in getting educated, Miss Anna, you start to wonder what it is you can and will do with that education. Now, I've seen folks with a smart head on them who begin to use education in ways that make it dangerous."

"But gettin' educated ain't dangerous!" I said, feeling the need to hold on to the possibility that I might have that chance, and to defend it as much as I could.

"It's not the education that threatens them, Anna. Like I said, it's the way you go about using it."

"Who's 'them'?" I asked.

"Well, let's hope you don't encounter them. Most of them won't have much patience for you protesting against things you don't like or you using what you've learned from books to try to change the way black folks are treated around here. They will hurt you—they'll beat you, scare you out of it, and force you to use that education for nothing more than burying yourself under dreams that cannot be achieved."

"But who are they? Don't mean no disrespect to you, sah, but do you mean the white folks who make laws an' don't want nothin' to do wit us?"

"Why would they do all of this?" he asked rhetorically,

completely disregarding my question, as if to say I already knew the answer. "It's because you're the dangerous kind."

"The dangerous kind?" I asked.

"Sure you are, or have the potential to be."

"To who?"

"You've already told me that, Anna. Education is a tool—it makes you less ignorant and more likely to find ways to be heard. You have a determination that many others don't, as I noted from the school incident. I understand this about you, most probably due to the fact that I'm the same way."

I felt my guard melt away just a little bit more.

"But I believe it's my job to give you the warnings. A Negro becoming educated is just as powerful as a Negro discovering what true freedom is. It gives you a power some folks don't like and a voice that some people won't stand for. I can see how badly you want this, how it leaks from your actions and toys with your senses. But once you have that voice, you step into a dangerous world."

A heaviness filled the empty spaces that arose when the man's words turned to silence. Thoughts rushed in once more, and with them came the knowledge that the things he spoke of only mattered after I had already been educated. But I wasn't educated—I had no means of getting educated. Surely he knew that! Did all this talk really lead to something I could wrap my hands around?

"Sah, I appreciate what you tellin' me 'bout bein' cautious with what I choose to do after I get educated. But, sah, I ain't gettin' educated. You talk to me like you undastand us black folk, like you really undastand how it is to have thoughts of learnin' runnin' through you like your own blood, but it's nowhere in sight. Be lovely if I could have that opportunity to learn like otha folks . . ."

"No one said you don't, Anna."

"Sah, everyone been sayin' it ain't my choice." I felt passionate about everything I was saying. I needed him to hear me out.

"My respects in sayin' so, but ain't no way for me to learn here. Tried everything I could, an' I don't have anything left to try. I'm not quite sure if you're here to change that or if you just talkin' to me 'bout dreams of mine that cain't even come true." I listened to his breathing, waiting for it to turn into an answer on his lips.

"It sounds to me as if you're telling me to go ahead and say what I came to say to you." he finally responded. I said nothing.

"Miss Anna," he said slowly, "the education you want may take more than reading newspapers and street signs." His words were ringing like church bells around me and lit a small spark in my chest.

"You're . . . you're offering me an' education, sah?" He was silent, but his silence seemed to cloak possibility.

"Sah?" I asked again. He stopped in his tracks and turned to me. I stared boldly back, waiting, still, for an answer.

"I know a black woman who tutors. She doesn't much like to be mentioned—that's just her choice—but I believe I'll have a word or two with her."

"A . . . a tutor? You mean, I'm . . . I'm really gonna get educated? With a tutor?"

He laughed. "I'll speak with her, Miss Anna, though I have little doubt she'll work with you."

"Really? You speakin' the truth? But sah"—my face fell a little bit—"sah, what am I s'pose to give? I don't really have nothin'."

"Anna, I have little more to do with the matter than to give you the opportunity to meet and talk with the tutor. Couldn't expect anything for that, could I?"

I smiled. "Guess not sah, but I don't really know how to . . ."

"You're quite welcome, Miss Anna," he said, gesturing for us to continue walking. I followed, feeling as giddy as a little girl.

"Sah, who are you? You doin' all this fo' me, but I don't even know who you are!"

"I don't come around these parts too often and, ah, well, I'm a passerby, Anna. My identity lies in the darkness."

"But . . . what's your name?" I asked, intent on finding out something about him, afraid that if he walked away without leaving any evidence that he'd been there, I'd lose the dream he was offering to make come true.

"The name's Caldwell, and I assure you, I'm a friend."

"Mr. Caldwell," I repeated.

"Please don't ask around for me. That's the only favor I ask of you," he said. "If folks want to know how you're getting educated, tell them you found a tutor."

I nodded. "But sah, how will I know . . ."

He held up his hand. "Anna, you'll know. You'll get the news about meeting her and studying with her sooner than you can imagine. Now I've said what I had to say."

After a minute, he said, "Education is a beautiful thing. What you do with it, however, makes all the difference in the world." We came to Mama Bessie's, and he stood by the steps, sharing his last words.

"Well, sah, can you wait a moment and jus' meet Mama Bessie, the woman of this household? I want to tell her 'bout all the things you say, an' I want her to see your face—"

"Miss Anna, as much as I would enjoy that—"

"Please, sah," I said, already bounding up to the house, "at least wait one quick moment. Let me get her." I dashed into the house, leaving the man leaning on the rail at the bottom of the stairs. I ran inside, called out for Mama Bessie in an excited whisper until I found her, and dragged her to the door with me. But when we neared the spot where the man had been just a moment before, nobody was there. I stared down the road, but the man had disappeared before I could thank him properly.

"Mama Bessie, Mama Bessie, he was jus' here, he was jus' . . ." I started, an edge of disappointment showing up in my voice.

Mama Bessie smiled, and placed a hand on my shoulder.

"Don't matter, Anna. I got somethin' for you."

"What's that, Mama Bessie?" I asked, shutting the

door behind me as we turned and headed into the kitchen. Her grin was as wide as ever.

"What's got you grinnin' like that, Mama Bessie?" I asked her, giggling at her shining face.

"Man came by today to say somethin' to me. Asked me if a 'Miss Anna' was a 'resident' of my place. I told him you was. He gave me the name an' the home of some woman that . . . that . . ."

"That tutors, Mama Bessie?" I asked, standing before her with unbelieving ears.

She nodded. "You'll meet with her in 'bout a week's time. Gonna fix yourself up, go on down there. Take Florence with ya, if ya like, an' ask 'bout learnin'."

"Mama Bessie, you talkin' the truth?" I asked, knowing the question was unnecessary. I felt tears ready to spring from my eyes.

"Sho' is talkin' truth, Anna. You know that."

"Mama Bessie, who was it that came by? He was a white man, wa'an't he? Or somebody else?"

Mama Bessie simply shrugged. "He was a good man, Anna—that's all I got to say 'bout it."

"But, Mama Bessie—"

"Leave it be, Anna," she said simply, placing a hand gently on my cheek.

"I hear you talk of this dream, see you readin' whateva it is you can get your hands on. Now it's time you get the real thing. Gonna be learnin' now. You worked hard at fulfillin' this dream—an' cain't nothin' make me prouder. You'se a blessin' here, an' I'm glad the Lord done what he done."

With that, Mama Bessie left me standing in the kitchen alone.

"Learnin' . . . ," I whispered to the empty room.

"Me . . . me learnin'?" I questioned. I dropped lightly into a seat, and stared before me, allowing the feelings inside to run excitedly through me. I thought about the mysterious man and his gift to me, wondering if I'd ever find out who he really was. But the thought swam away as quickly as it came. All I could think of was standing by the schoolhouse back on the plantation, trying to listen to the lessons, saving newspaper scraps, reading the titles of the books in Masta's study.

"You hear that, Mary? You listenin', John? I'm 'bout to get educated! No more sneakin' around on a plantation tryin' to learn. No more just readin' words on buildings. I'm gonna be learnin'! Me—gettin' educated!"

CHAPTER

❧ 36 ❧

TODAY WAS THE DAY. I STOOD OUTSIDE MAMA BESSIE'S HOME
with a smile that nothing and no one could make fade away.
A new starched outfit outlined my figure. I had bought these
clothes with the money I had saved and money Daniel had
given me.

Today was the day I would meet Mrs. Rosa, the tutor.
It almost seemed silly to me that a woman who had lived
so close by on a secluded plot of land, just between Hadson
and Gibson, had, this whole time, held my passion.

When I told Florence about the matter, she immediately
decided to join me that day. She'd itched with about as
much excitement as I had. Florence reminded me so much
of Daniel—enjoying my joys, ready to stand by me when
I needed her, but steadily moving along her own path.
Florence's passion was in designing and repairing clothes,
but for right now, she chose to continue helping Mama
Bessie with the housework.

Side-by-side, Florence and I walked to Mrs. Rosa's
on that September day, a day I won't ever forget. Even
the breeze welcomed us as we walked. The house stood a
short distance from the road, but as soon as we saw it, we

ran all the way to the front door. My anticipation almost spilled over as I stepped up to knock, but Florence held me back.

"You sure this her house?" she asked me.

"Flo, I'm sure."

The hollow sound of my knocking echoed.

No answer.

"Knock again!" Florence whispered.

I did, three more times. I shook my head in frustration. It seemed we had walked all the way down here only to be disappointed.

"Well, Anna, . . ." But before Florence could finish, the latch clicked and the door swung open. In front of me stood a gorgeous black woman whose thick black hair lay in short, neat curls all over her head. She was a young woman, but seemed to be a decent number of years older than me. Mrs. Rosa was dressed rather nicely, in a flowing skirt that just touched the floor and a white blouse buttoned up almost to her chin. Her skin color was somewhere between my own and Florence's.

"Hi there, ladies." She smiled, showing two rows of straight white teeth. Her accent dipped beautifully out of her mouth and reminded me of a couple who had visited Masta's house many years ago, people who had traveled across the seas.

"What can I do for you?" she asked in a soft, warm voice that lacked the roughness of the language I had heard from people most of my life. I stood in place, speechless, gazing at this woman. There was a perfection about her—

her grace, refinement, and composure—that set off longing in my spirit.

How is it that this woman reminds me of Mathee?

I felt Florence nudge me gently in the back. Immediately, I straightened up and lifted my chin just slightly.

"You Mrs. Rosa?" I asked her.

She smiled. "Yes, I am. Can I do something for you?"

"Well, ma'am, I'm Anna. This, here, is Florence," I said. She nodded, waiting. "I'm here to see 'bout learnin'."

"Are you?" she asked.

"Yes, ma'am, I am. Bin looking for some kinda school for black folks since I came here but couldn't find none. Man found me the otha day, telln' me he'd help me get educated like I've bin dreamin' 'bout."

"What did he say?" she asked patiently, as if she already knew.

"He told me 'bout you an' 'bout what gettin' educated means. Don't know who he was. Was a white man, I believe. I ain't seen him around here none."

She nodded slowly, looking carefully at me.

"Ma'am, you . . . you know the man? You teach fo' him or somethin'?" I asked, my curiosity still biting.

She looked slowly from my face to Florence's and didn't answer right away.

"Well, now, I'm not one to answer many questions, but I can say this. I don't teach for anybody. I tutor sometimes, that's all." She raised her eyebrows. "But no more talk about how you ended up on my doorstep. It seems that there's other business to attend to, anyhow, concerning you wanting to learn. So, please, come in." Having deliberately washed the mystery from the air, she then took a step back into her home and motioned for us to join her inside.

There was something familiar about the place that caught my attention. The room's calming scent reminded me of something ancient, perhaps an herb Mathee had used to freshen up the air of our hut back in Africa. The room was large, warm, and pleasantly decorated. Portraits of fancy-looking folks with black skin hung from several walls. My eyes would have lingered on them, but something else caught my attention: two large bookcases at opposite ends of the room. They were filled with books. I gasped in wonder.

"You got a lot of books in here," I said, excited. Mrs. Rosa glanced at me, considering my excitement for a moment, but said nothing.

Florence and I sat down in chairs that had carved wooden legs. Mrs. Rosa pulled up a seat for herself in front of us. As we waited for her to sit down, I envisioned myself slowly running my fingertips across the books, then pulling one down, slowly opening it up, taking in the smell of the pages, and burying myself in the words.

"Anna," Mrs. Rosa said, prompting me to return my thoughts to her. There was an elegance about the way she sat that made me aware of my own posture. "You say you want to learn. Learn what?"

"Well, I guess I wanna learn to write, and to be able to read whatever I pick up."

"Can you do either already?"

"Yes, ma'am, I can read some and write a little bit. I reckon I don't really know what else I could learn in school. I suppose, maybe, I can get better with my numbers." I paused to consider her question more deeply.

What do I want to learn?

"Mrs. Rosa"—I looked her squarely in her eyes—"I've bin carrying this idea in my mind fo' a long time that one day, I'd be able to read an' have a real honest answer to why some things are the way they are. Figure I wanna be like those educated folks who use their minds all the time."

Mrs. Rosa looked at me for what seemed a long time. She got up, after a while, went to one of the bookcases, and began searching through books until she found the two she wanted.

Handing me the first, she pointed to the name at the bottom.

"What name is this and who does it belong to?" she asked as she sat again, placing a long finger on her lips and awaiting my response.

"P-h . . . Fil-lis . . . W-hee-at-ly . . . Filis W-heeatly." I thought for a moment, running the name through my head, but I knew no such person. "I dunno—I mean, I don't know, Mrs. Rosa," I said after I glanced over at her.

"Phillis Wheatley," she replied with no change in her expression.

"Oh," I said, wondering who the name belonged to.

"Where do you live, Anna? Who are your parents? Or do you live alone, or are you married?" she asked all at once, moving quickly to the next order of business.

"Parents? Well, I don't have no . . . I don't have any parents. I live with Mama Bessie, and—"

"She a slave!" Florence said, cutting me off. "I mean, she used to be a slave, ma'am. She was freed," Florence said as steadily as she could as she batted guilty eyes at me, "and came here earlier this year."

I glared at my friend, and she looked sheepishly away. I had not anticipated sharing that information with this woman. If anything, that fact might take away my chances of getting educated.

"A slave? How did you learn to read and write, Anna?" I stared down at the quilt, not answering the question. I didn't want to lie, but I couldn't tell the truth. Of what importance was that to her, anyhow? To my surprise, Mrs. Rosa laughed, a beautiful sound to my ears. I brought my eyes back up to see that her face showed admiration rather than distaste.

"Ahh, I know the answer well. You must be determined, Anna, and quite brave, if I dare say."

"I want an education, Mrs. Rosa," I said truthfully.

Mrs. Rosa nodded at me. "I can see that, Anna. All right. Now, do you have a job?"

"Well, I work with Mama Bessie in the house with the children. She give me a place to stay, an' a little bit of money each month that's mine to keep. But that's all."

Mrs. Rosa nodded and searched my eyes for something I prayed that I had. Finally, she spoke.

"Most folks don't know about me tutoring, and I prefer that it stay that way. There's no danger in doing what I do, I just prefer to have as few students as possible."

I nodded hurriedly. *As long as you'll teach me!*

"But I think, Anna, that tutoring you would be a pleasure. However, there is one thing I need from you." Inside, my spirit sprang to the rooftop, danced among the clouds, and shouted with joy. On the outside, however, I stayed as calm as I could, waiting for her next words.

"What I require is your dedication. I want you to focus on what I teach and to learn all you can. If it so happens that you are no longer interested in this education, I need for you to let me know. I do not tutor the blind."

"Tutor the blind?" I asked with a frown.

"I can't teach you if your eyes have closed to what I teach, rather. There is nothing wrong with that, it just means they have opened to something else. Do you understand?"

"Yes, ma'am."

"I can't tutor one who has no desire to be taught, especially around here. But I see the opposite in you and I believe that, if you can make it here by the time the sun has fully risen every Monday through Thursday, I might be able to tutor you."

I threw my arms around Mrs. Rosa and thanked her with tears in my eyes.

"And what about you, Miss Florence, what have you got on your mind?"

Florence had been sitting silently, smiling, but quickly responded, "Oh no, no ma'am, I don't want no education like that. I jus' sew, Mrs. Rosa, that's all."

Mrs. Rosa studied Florence for a second as I reveled in the moment. Then she got up and guided us to the door.

"All right, ladies. I apologize for having to rush you off, but I must be getting back to my business. Anna?"

"Yes?"

"I'll be happy to see you early in the morning next week."

"Yes, ma'am."

As Florence and I walked back to Mama Bessie's, my mouth ran fast with words.

"Flo, why didn't you ask her to tutor you right along with me? You told me yourself you wanted to learn!"

Florence shrugged. "I got other things on my mind, Anna, and when I said that to you, I didn't mean learning like this! I don't think I could do that."

"Why not?"

"It just ain't for me. There are other things in this life for me. But you don't understand how much it means to me to see you smiling like that."

My smile widened. Another answered prayer.

On Monday, I was up bright and early. When I knocked, it took Mrs. Rosa a little while to answer the door. When she did open it, a small child sat patiently in her arms. The little girl gazed at me with eyes that looked like Mrs. Rosa's.

"Hey, Miss Anna. Seems my baby's up early today.

Hope you don't mind, but she won't cause distraction."
She considered my puzzled glance at the child.

"I didn't tell you about Little Sue?" she asked, guiding
me through the door.

"No, ma'am."

"Well, then, this is her."

I waved my fingers at the small child, and she bent her
fingers back in response, silently and solemnly. Mrs. Rosa
set her on the floor with a wooden toy and led me to the
table set up in the front room to the right.

"How are you today, Miss Anna?" she asked, seating
herself.

I smiled. "I'm doing good, and very grateful to you," I
replied.

"You mean, you're doing well," she corrected without
hesitation while pulling out a small piece of paper and her
ink.

"Write your name for me."

A wave of fear hit me. Would she judge the way I
wrote? What would she think? But the anxious feeling
faded just as quickly as it came. I put my excitement
aside and focused.

I slowly drew the quill out and wrote the first letter. A.
Then I paused, thinking about the next letter: y. Then, a-n-
n-a. I wrote in large letters, glancing over at Little Sue upon
hearing her mumble words to herself that I couldn't make
sense of. I looked up at Mrs. Rosa quickly, waiting for her
remarks. She took the paper without any expression.

"Oh, Ayanna is it?"

"No, ma'am, just Anna."

"But you wrote Ayanna."

"I wanted you to know my real name, my . . . my African name."

Mrs. Rosa quickly glanced up at me. She seemed, in that moment, ready to share some secret with me, but she said nothing. Her eyes returned to the book she had been reading.

Another thought swam into my mind. "Mrs. Rosa, why ain't there any black schools anywhere? Newspapers say the city pays for white schools in different places, but I ain't heard of any black school funding."

Mrs. Rosa looked over at my seated figure and lifted two fingers to her lips as she thought about my question. "There are black schools, Anna. I haven't heard of any in Ohio, but there's a city—Boston—that has a school for black children. It's a little different there."

"But—"

"I think it's time we started that lesson of yours," she said.

I let my questions slip away, and we began.

It didn't take long for me to realize that the woman who tutored was quite different from the kind, relaxed woman who had answered the door when I first met her. No badly pronounced word, uncrossed *t*, or spelling error I made ever swept past Mrs. Rosa's scrutiny. Her lips remained pursed throughout the lesson, and every blunder of mine was met with a soft but firm "Try it again."

"An educated mind is a quick mind, Anna. Listen

closely the first time," she instructed me that first day when I asked her to repeat herself. In every passage I'd read or copy, she'd bid me to dig deeper and find meaning in the words that I couldn't find at first.

On that first day, Mrs. Rosa walked me through a lesson on how to put my thoughts on paper in an organized way. She jumped straight into reading, picking up books and directing me to read a few chapters aloud. When she had to attend to her child, she would give me an assignment so we wouldn't lose any time. The process was slow with her constant interruptions to correct me. It was plenty of work, but the excitement that pulsed through me never wavered, even as I stumbled through everything she placed in front of me.

What could be greater than getting educated as a free person?

Mrs. Rosa was drawn to poetry, and I found I liked it, too. One of the poems she selected was by a black man named Jupiter Hammon.

"I want you to read one of the stanzas in this poem, Anna. It's titled 'An Address to Miss Phillis Wheatly.'" She laid down a single stanza she had copied onto paper.

"Mrs. Rosa, you never told me 'xactly who Miss Wheatley was," I said, pulling the page closer.

"She was a black woman who had her poetry and writings published. Not many folks know about her, but I made it my business to learn what I could."

A black woman like me, published!

"Mrs. Rosa, how do you know all this stuff? How did

you get their poetry? They seem like great folks! An' yet, I ain't never seen their stuff."

She smiled a little. "You haven't ever seen, you mean. I have my ways, Anna. I have my ways."

I believe it was the moment Mrs. Rosa shared Miss Wheatley's story that my world began to expand. My mind spun with the idea of writing well enough to have books published, but Mrs. Rosa quickly chased away my daydreams.

"Read it please, Anna."

I nodded and bent over the page.

"'O, c . . . coe-m . . . no, cuhm you pee . . . pee-usss'?" Uncertain, I glanced up with knitted eyebrows at Mrs. Rosa.

"The *i* sounds like *eye*," she said without looking up, scribbling the word on a sheet of paper. I waited for her to continue.

"It means very religious-like," she explained.

"Oh. 'O, come you pie-us you-th: ad . . . add-ore . . .'"

"Try the other sound the *a* makes."

"'Uh-door.'"

"Know what it means?" she asked.

"I think so. Let me finish it. 'O, come you pie-us youth! uh-door the wise . . . no, wizdum of . . . of thy God in br-breeng-eeng thee fruhm dist-ant shh-ore, shore . . .'" I stopped, pleased at hearing myself speak the words, but Hammon's message left me a bit confused. I looked over at Mrs. Rosa.

"'O, come you pious youth! adore, the wisdom of thy

God, in bringing thee from distant shore. . . .'" She recited the stanza from memory, then waited for me to critique it.

"Sounds to me like Mr. Hammon's sayin' that livin' on that distant shore was a sin. Sounds like he believed it was God's wisdom that dragged loads of folks from that place through hell on large boats to this land, here." I felt anger simmering deep inside.

Mrs. Rosa looked up at me with steady eyes. "I'm glad you've learned not to simply read the words but to make sure you understand exactly what it is you're reading. That's important, Anna."

I looked down at the stanza again and back up at my tutor.

"Why would he believe that? You believe the words, Mrs. Rosa?"

"Many people believe that, Anna, even people like Mr. Hammon."

"But what about you?" I asked her, interested. But she simply picked up the paper.

"Right now, we're not learning about what I think. Here, let's look at this. There are rules in writing you need to learn."

The day continued like that. That afternoon, Mrs. Rosa gave me a book to take home. She told me to read the first chapter and write down any words I didn't understand.

I held the book tightly to my chest as I walked back along the path to Mama Bessie's. A small smile raced across my lips. I felt like someone new.

The second day arrived just as quickly as the first, and that morning I found myself knocking once again on Mrs. Rosa's door.

"Good morning, Anna."

"Good morning, Mrs. Rosa." As soon as I stepped inside, however, the morning's thrill drifted steadily away. As I stood in the arch of the doorway, I saw two other girls seated at the table. One was a good deal younger than I was. Her red curls jiggled as she turned to see who was entering the room. The young white girl smiled at me and waved. Anita, on the other hand, decided against lifting her eyes in greeting. She kept right on reading. I felt uneasy as I turned back to Mrs. Rosa.

"Anna, I also tutor two other girls," Mrs. Rosa explained matter-of-factly upon seeing the questioning expression on my face. "Each of you has one private day and then you have three days together. Come in and meet them."

"I've met Anita," I said quietly.

"Well, good. Anita Jacobs has been with me the longest. She's a wonderful young scholar." At that, Anita raised her eyes but didn't quite manage to look at me. I wondered why she had discouraged me from getting an education when here she was, learning herself! I looked at her set lips and resolved in my mind that she had never smiled in her life.

I silently sat down in the chair reserved for me, and

Mrs. Rosa sat beside me. The seating was as imperfect as could be: a four-person table that seated four very different people.

"This is Peggy," Mrs. Rosa said, touching Peggy's hand.

"Yes, I'm Peggy, and I'm ten," she said in a high-pitched voice.

"Hey, Peggy, I'm Anna," I said, not knowing whether to hold out my hand or nod her way. But she held her hand out to me and we shook hands like friends. I wondered why she wasn't in the white school I saw in Dayton.

"So that it's clear and there are no questions," Mrs. Rosa began, cutting into my thoughts, "Peggy's mother believes in equality. It's that simple. She also believes that Peggy will learn more quickly in a private setting rather than in a school with other students."

"Yes, I like my teacher," Peggy added, smiling excitedly.

Mrs. Rosa smiled and stood up to pull a book from her bookcase.

How I longed to dig in to those books!

She sat, crossed her legs, and handed me the book.

"We'll read while Little Sue is sleeping. Later on, I have assignments for each of you to work on." She looked over at Anita and Peggy to address them. "Anna's just learning to read. She'll start us out. When it's her turn to read, listen to the story and translate it into French."

I stared wide-eyed at Mrs. Rosa.

"I was born overseas, Anna. It was the first language I

learned," she explained. "We learn French, sometimes, just for fun," she said with a smile.

Nervous, I cracked open the book and began to read, picking through words, struggling to sound them out, and feeling all eyes glued on me. Mrs. Rosa was there by my side, helping me out, but out of the corner of my eye I saw Anita cross her arms.

I felt embarrassed, especially when I passed the book and heard Anita and even Peggy read with little effort. When my turn came again, I tried running through the words like Anita and Peggy, but I only stumbled worse.

"Anna, slow down. You don't have to read like that yet. Don't worry, it will come," Mrs. Rosa interjected.

But I wanted it to come immediately. As I sat through the writing part of the lessons, discouraged, I made mistakes I normally would not have made.

"Anna," Mrs. Rosa said at one point, "I want you to stay a little longer after we're finished."

I nodded as my heart sank.

The hours passed, and we separated in order to work on our own assignments. Anita seemed inclined to spend time watching or playing with Little Sue, and Mrs. Rosa appeared to like that. It seemed to me that Anita changed while she was with the little girl. Although she never smiled, the deadness that sat in her eyes would be replaced with a bright aliveness.

We sat for many hours at the table, reading and working with numbers, taking only a few breaks to get some sunshine or to eat, but the lessons finally came to a close. As Mrs. Rosa walked Peggy out the door, I sat silently, tearing my gaze away from Anita's as she slowly packed her belongings.

"I see you made it to your education," she said after a while.

"Yes, I did," I responded. "I don't understand why you'd tell me education don't do nothin'—anything—for folks, and yet here you are, learning yourself!"

She shrugged. "It's what the old man wants. He's a stickler for education—thinks everyone born has a right to it. I owe it to him." She headed toward the door but turned back.

"You don't need to push yourself so hard. You're doing well." With that, she walked out the door, tall, proud, and alone. My anger melted a little bit. She could be so harsh one moment, and then not so bad the next. I didn't understand her.

I sat silently, waiting for Mrs. Rosa to return, and stared behind her when she glided back through the door. "Anna," she said kindly, coming back to the table and setting Little Sue down on the floor, "you are a very smart young woman." I looked down at my hands. "And for that reason, I never want to see you comparing yourself against the other girls. Now, I've only known you for a few days, but I can see that you are gifted and quick-minded. Nobody started out reading perfectly—nobody. You hear me? Please look at me."

I obeyed her, lifting my head until our eyes met. "I know all that, Mrs. Rosa. Don't know what got into me today."

"That's all right. This is your dream and you take pride in that. But you have as much potential as anybody else." She placed a hand on mine and leaned in a bit closer. "Remember, not one of us other than you taught ourselves to read and write, and certainly not under the circumstances you were in." She smiled, a smile surprisingly filled with pride.

She went on. "Now, you keep learning and working hard. Keep your mind on you and what you are doing. Pretty soon, you'll be excited with all that you've accomplished. Have you ever stopped and wondered why you want an education, Anna?"

"Of course I have!" I responded, my heart heavy, torn between Mrs. Rosa's words and my fears about the overwhelming task—learning—that lay ahead. I didn't understand why I felt close to tears.

"And what are your reasons, do you think?" she asked quietly.

I took a long breath. "Mrs. Rosa, what you call an education, I call freedom. It pounds through my chest like the longin' a child has to fly away the first day they're thrown into the fields down south to work. I wanna be free in the mind so maybe, jus' maybe, I can bring some justice to this world." I stopped short, wondering why I had allowed my imagination to whisk me away like it did. I felt embarrassed. "Don't know if you understand me."

"Sure I do. You have a lovely way of putting things— very flowery, very real, like a poet!"

I laughed at her comment.

"When one is placed in a situation like yours, Anna, where obedience and autonomy mean serving someone besides oneself, there is a natural instinct to find ways to prove to society and to oneself that the seemingly impossible can be accomplished. It requires courage, faith, a strong desire, and belief in oneself. Not everyone has that sort of determination, Anna." Her words brought a smile to my lips.

"Mrs. Rosa, none of that would matta much if I wasn't sittin' here, learnin'. So, thank you."

She smiled back at me. "This is what I do, Anna."

Just as quickly as Mrs. Rosa's words of wisdom came, they subsided. She returned quickly to business, saying, "Now here, I want you to read this to me."

After that day, at the end of every group session we had, Mrs. Rosa kept me longer. I worked hard to do what she said, burying the desire to compare myself with the others, and struggled through passages, completed exercises with numbers, and practiced my penmanship. And when I began to feel discouraged, I thought about John—not the vision of him running or being whipped into submission or the blood and broken dreams or his sad eyes. I wouldn't even allow myself to think of him running and trying to reach freedom. Instead, I thought about him sitting next to me, contented, as I told him I was going to be just like Phillis Wheatley.

No, you gonna be Sarah. You gonna be Ayanna Bahati!

I heard his voice echo in my head. I was doing this for him, for Mary, and for Tucker. For Daniel and Florence. I was doing this for Ayanna Bahati!

CHAPTER

❧ 37 ❧

November came and left, and Christmas was soon to arrive, a Christmas I'd spend with Daniel and Florence. Mrs. Rosa excused us the last couple of weeks of December and the first week in January, but I continued studying through it all. December found the streets decorated in thin sheets of snow. The greetings from the folks in town left me feeling lighthearted. Winter brought a warm closeness to the community, and yet, the closer Christmas crept, the less happy I felt. An entire year had gone by since we escaped. It was my first Christmas in freedom, and John had not yet arrived. Was it safe to keep hope burning in my heart?

The cold brought Daniel home from the fields much earlier with less money. In addition, Daniel's thoughts about leaving Mary on the plantation, and about her well-being, started to spiral in the wrong direction. In the first few months we were in Hadson, he had commented about John's inability to find us, though he quickly promised never to mention his doubts again. But now I began to notice these very thoughts reentering our conversations. He never revealed his worries in front of Florence, at least not at first. It was to me his doubts would come spilling out, and I'd try to guide him back to reason as well as I could.

"What if she's still there, Anna, still unda Masta's hand?"

I shuddered at the thought and kept my fears to myself. "Mary's safe, Daniel."

He shook his head. "That thought of her still bein' there jus' ain't easy to live wit."

"Naw," I said, shaking my head, "but she's safe, Daniel. She's not worrying, she's not unhappy, because I'm sure in her heart she knows we safe."

He shook his head vigorously. "This is 'bout her, not us. Who's there fo' her? Who?"

I felt a tear slip without my permission. "You know she takes good care of herself, Daniel. But I miss her, too, miss her plenty."

He sighed. "I could've done so much more fo' her. Shoulda brought her wit us."

"Daniel, you done what you could. You know she wasn't coming. An' you know what John say. He gonna bring her."

His face darkened, and he turned to me with eyes that looked beyond my face. "An' what if . . . what if they don't find us, Anna. They . . . they ain't gonna find us. It's me. I'm the one need to go back to get her."

"Daniel!" I said, almost shouting. His face relaxed immediately.

"Anna, Anna, I'm sorry. I didn't mean none of that. That's jus' my anga talkin', Sarah. I don't mean none've it."

I tried to brush away his words. "Daniel, don't want you talking about going back. That's more dangerous than running. An' if John already run with her, she's not gonna be there if you got back anyway. So I wish you would hush up with all that talk!"

He came over to me, his emotions having settled back down, and looked me clearly in the eyes. "I'm not goin' nowhere, sista," he said, taking my words and placing them somewhere unknown to me in the storage house of his mind. I feared his thinking, though. If I had been irrational in seeking out an education, Daniel could be ten times worse in whatever he wanted to pursue. It would be impossible for a runaway returning south to find an escaped slave who was running north, let alone to avoid being snatched right back into slavery. I convinced myself that Daniel understood this. But the far-fetched notion of Daniel leaving left my spirit agitated.

Aside from this, however, December nights were rather joyful. After long days with the children and the housework at Mama Bessie's, I was able to spend more time with my brother and my best friend, as well as my learning. I tried my best to push my thoughts about John to the back of my mind, and enjoyed the company of these companions.

Henry began to come around more often. He told Florence and me that he respected our company, and would sometimes come up alongside us as we talked in Mama Bessie's yard and completed our chores.

"Here he is again, Anna. Wasn't it just last week we saw him hiding in the bushes, watching the two of us?" Florence said on one gray day, just loud enough for him to hear every word.

"Sho' wasn't me hidin' nowhere," he said, striding toward us. We all laughed, but Henry's chuckles were louder than ours, and off-key.

"Henry, don't you have a job?" I asked him.

"Sho'!"

"Well, shouldn't you be at it?"

"Shouldn't be nowhere but right here for right now, don't you think?"

I turned my eyes uneasily away from his and glanced at Florence, but she hopped up, saying she had a quick errand to run in the house.

I turned my eyes back to Henry. His upper torso and body sat awkwardly on his long legs, making him look taller and stronger than he really was. His hair was cut to perfection, and his smile curled his cheeks in so that they dimpled like a baby's. Henry was a nice man, but sometimes his friendliness made me uncomfortable.

"Don't suppose I could sit with you for a while?" he asked, standing over me as I turned my eyes back to my work.

"Won't be out here long, Henry," I said, the lie feeling unnatural on my lips. He sat anyway.

"Lookin' quite nice today, Miss Anna." I dug my eyes deeper into my work. I didn't want to hear that from him, not at all.

"You hear about Mrs. Brown an' her fits?" he continued, trying to share the town news.

"No, but I think I'd rather listen to my own thoughts, Henry," I said, quite serious. He took it as a joke, however, and laughed some more.

"Well, looka here. I'm good company. I'm not headed nowhere special. Let's listen to your thoughts together."

His jolly smile left me uneasy. I stood and gathered my work.

"We have a lot of work, today, Henry, that's gotta be finished before all the children wake up again."

He stood up with me, trying to shake away his disappointment. "All right, then," he said, watching me for a few moments as I busied my hands. "Gonna see you and Florence around later, then." He watched and waited.

"Sure thing, Henry," I said, then followed my heart where it had already disappeared: into the house.

CHAPTER

❧ 38 ❧

IT WAS MY FIRST DAY BACK AFTER OUR WINTER BREAK. OUR
session had ended, but I stayed a bit longer to talk with
Mrs. Rosa.

"You know what I think, Mrs. Rosa? I think the idea
of being free means a little more than escapin' from a
plantation."

Mrs. Rosa smiled and sat back in her chair. "How do
you suppose that, Miss Anna?" Mrs. Rosa asked.

"It's just a thought. I used to think coming here, to Ohio,
meant freedom all in itself. But bein' here, I figure it's more
than that. I think I've found some new freedom in learning,
here with you, an' I think I lost some old freedom in leavin'
people who meant a lot to me. Freedom ain't just—isn't
just—having the chance to be free from slavery."

"Sure, Anna. There are plenty of freedoms, different
freedoms for different people." She sat forward and leaned
her elbows on the table. "So, are you saying to me that you
don't feel as free as you think you should?"

I laughed. "Well, course I feel free. I'm not bound to no
whip any longer, Mrs. Rosa."

"Any whip, you mean."

"*Any* whip. Cain't complain much about that. But see . . ." I looked up into Mrs. Rosa's eyes, into the soft places behind the shell she wore while teaching. "See . . ." I began again, but held myself back. I looked deeper as she held my gaze, and found myself immersed in a world of understanding, even before my words about John had escaped my lips.

"What's missing from your freedom, Anna?" Her words were almost a whisper, as if she knew exactly what was stirring inside of me. I shook my head and bit my lip to hold the tears back.

"Anna, it's all right. What is it?"

I shook my head once more and bit my lip to hold the tears back.

"Mrs. Rosa, I can't. . . ." I fought to hold the feelings inside, but they had minds of their own.

"Go ahead, Anna. It's all right to feel as you do. It's all right to trust me."

I felt as if my own mother had spoken, inviting me to share and to heal.

"Don't know if he ever gonna find me," I said. Her silence was just what I needed. "His name's John, Mrs. Rosa. Got a few years on me. Had long, dark fingers an' skin different shades of brown. An' there was a mark on his chin always been there, always."

A small smile crossed my lips.

"Called himself John. They called him a slave, and me, I called him my joy. Had some past on some other plantation—didn't matter, though. Felt like I was holdin'—holding—the stars when he came around. We talked about heaven and hell and all matters of the day when we wasn't working. He listened mostly. It was my mouth that ran with questions and dreams and things that lay far beyond that plantation. He was real patient and quiet, and smart and funny when he wanted to be. 'Cept when he was serious—the ground under his feet would shake when he was angry!

"We flew past the bounds of that plantation many times without ever going nowhere! Just our souls and our minds." I paused, slightly embarrassed. Was I making any kind of sense? Mrs. Rosa nodded, and another tear slipped down my cheek. I continued.

"He never said I was beautiful, but he didn't have to, I guess. It wasn't about being pretty, naw. The way he did things—his silent gazes—that's what told me what was in his heart. Never said things like, 'I really do like you.' Instead, when I asked if he did, he'd take my hand and wipe a tear that left my eye. Didn't know my own tears could move anyone the way they did him. He wasn't never mean but always said 'xactly what had to be said. There was never a soul that could make me more angry! But that never stayed long. He ain't—he never had that controlling hand I saw sometimes in folks, and he . . . he was always there, somehow, in some kinda way," I said with a short laugh, basking in the memory.

"He carved me things and sang tunes in those fields I could hear from a mile away. They were sad. Said, 'I find my love at freedom's gates in heaben.'" I sang it softly, then let the tune fill the space in my mind for a moment.

"Always told me we wasn't slaves. Said it was all what you believed up here"—I patted my head—"in your mind. Said home was the heart, nothin'—I mean, nothing—more than that, nothing less. John had a dream, but didn't we all! His dream was called freedom." Ghosts from the past drifted by in the heavy silence. I longed to remain among the good memories, but my story had to continue forward.

"Masta said I was never to go near John, but John come around me anyway. Masta said he was gonna give me his child! 'No, sah,' John told to me, 'you gonna save yourself.' But that last night, John couldn't save his own self. Masta beat the skin off his back for comin' around me. Took his dream and left me with his broken body." I felt the pain, then, spurting out from my soul like blood. I hadn't really talked about John to anyone for nearly a year; I couldn't even bring myself to say these things to Florence. Now they poured out faster than I could control. I brought my hand to my forehead.

"Saw John that day I left. He said to me, 'I promise you, I'm gonna be as free as you; I'm gonna be free wit you.'" I opened my eyes and saw golden suns bidding me to go on, but I feared I had let out too much information.

"Mrs. Rosa, nobody really knows."

She nodded vigorously and looked away from me briefly, attempting to hold back her own tears. But when she faced me again, her cheeks were wet.

"Shh, Anna. I understand. You don't have to explain yourself, I understand."

I nodded. "But am I free, Mrs. Rosa? I got this freedom . . ."

"You have," she whispered, softly.

A weary smile came to my lips. "I have this freedom. I have this education. And I have his promise, Mrs. Rosa. Didn't wanna hear it, didn't want it to mean what it meant. But I heard, and I'm waiting, and I feel like I'm bleeding with all these days that go by."

She took my hands. That's when the rush came, the tears now spilling with sobs that heaved from my chest.

"Who's the one who makes these things happen, Mrs. Rosa? I know I ain't different from the rest of them whose lives are torn apart by that system of slavery. Death is what those slave holders want. Separation is what they want. They want us to hurt—to love an' forget. They want us to hide our feelings an' fear so that we ain't no better than dogs. People seen this all they lives. Don't see why my life would be different. So when I tell you I got this hope, it hurts even more to know that for all it's worth, I might not even see my John again." She watched me closely as my tears ceased and calmness took its place.

"He's a piece of your freedom, is he?"

I nodded. "So if he never comes, you'll never be free?"

I looked up at her, confused, wondering why even this had to sound like some sort of problem from a lesson that needed to be worked through.

"Mrs. Rosa, don't know what you mean. Didn't want this to be just another lesson."

"Everything's a lesson, Anna, even the things that feel like this. Now, look around you and see if you can answer my question."

I did as she said, and my eyes naturally fell on the books.

"Education is my freedom."

She nodded, but I felt unconvinced.

"So, you're saying he ain't part of my freedom?" I asked.

"You mean, *isn't* a part of your freedom."

"That's what I meant. He *isn't* a part of it?"

"I'm just sharing my opinion, Anna. I thought the same thing as you when I was younger. But what you feel in your heart is something quite separate from your freedom. It's just a piece of your heart. Maybe he's got that piece; maybe he'll have it forever. But that doesn't have to keep you from being free."

"I think I can understand that," I said, thinking hard about her words.

"And, you know, life's greatest gifts come from pursuing and holding on to what gives your life purpose. For you, right now, that's education."

I crossed my arms and sighed. "Guess that is a purpose, a purpose I can sure live with and be happy about. But John gives me purpose, too, Mrs. Rosa," I explained to her, readily awaiting her response. I found myself hanging on to her words with a strong respect.

"Well, let that purpose ring out in what you do! Let it drive you to make the most of the freedom you have."

I nodded. "I . . . I can do that. Sure I can." A few seconds' pause followed my words.

"I'm scared, Mrs. Rosa. Scared he ain't—he's not—ever gonna find me. Scared he might give up and settle. Scared he gonna be found and taken back. Scared Masta gonna kill him!"

She patted my hand to comfort me, though tears still wet her cheeks. "It's okay to be scared, Anna. Fear isn't really a bad thing if you can see it for what it is without letting it stop you from doing what you have to do. Put a word or two in for John, a prayer as deep as you wish it to be. But you have a purpose, so keep your head up as high as you can and keep your passion churning in your soul. You go to church," she said, needing no response, "so you know things are always going to happen by the grace of God."

I bit my lip and nodded.

"Now, I don't mean to always make something into a lesson—"

"No, it's all right, Mrs. Rosa. I think that if my mother was living, she would be the same way."

She smiled with appreciation. "But aside from all my words, there's not much more I can offer you, Anna. You"— she laughed a little—"you're like a good book to me. Every time you read it, you find something you never saw before."

I laughed with her.

"Mrs. Rosa, is . . . is Little Sue's father still around?"

"You mean, am I married, Anna?" she asked.

"That's what I mean."

"Yes, I am. But that's enough of that. I wanted to give you something, a gift I forgot to give you for Christmas." Mrs. Rosa walked out of the room and came back a few minutes later with a stack of bound sheets of paper that had been written on.

"I want you to have this. It's a story about different people's lives—about blacks in the south, blacks here in the north, and blacks across the waters." She handed the stack to me.

"You've been to all these places?" I asked her. She nodded, pausing for a moment to consider what was on her mind, and continued, "My father was from Africa, taken to France as part of the slave trade. Our family was freed."

I nodded but was shocked by the idea that she had lived in a world so far from here. "I guess that means you don't really agree with much of what Miss Wheatley writes," I commented, remembering some of the poems of hers we read about the land she came from.

"Well, no. I couldn't ever feel right saying my father's homeland was pagan, although back in France, they tried their best to instill that in me. Sometimes, reading what she wrote, I figure she knew that, but I can't say for sure. But that's beside the point. What she accomplished was amazing to me. That book you are holding is my dedication to her," she said, pointing to it.

"The book is fiction, but the lives of the characters are as realistic as I could make them. I don't plan on having it printed. I'd rather share my work with good people like you. So take it. Read it," she insisted. Her eyes suddenly glazed over with seriousness. "But you keep it to yourself, you hear? Don't let it get around . . . ," she dropped her defensive gaze quickly, "I mean, it's just a simple, small thing. Enjoy it, but keep it to yourself, if you will."

I took it as she bid, a large smile brightening my face as she led me to the front door to see me off. But I turned back. I had nearly forgotten to give her the gift I had for her.

"I almost forgot," I said handing her a box. "I kept this through Christmas, as you did with my gift. It's not much, but I hope you like it." Inside was a piece of beautiful material on which I stitched her name. I had thought she might hang it over one of her bookcases.

Surprised, she held the box, admiring its contents.

"Wanted you to know how grateful I am," I said simply.

"All right, Miss Anna. Please study hard!"

"Yes ma'am," I replied, stepping out the door.

Reaching home later than I expected, I found Daniel and Florence talking while Daniel built some object for a man in town. These small jobs brought him both joy and a bit of extra money.

As I approached them, their speech tapered off.

"You're friendly again with my brother, I see," I said to Florence.

"Don't really have a choice but to be friendly with him. He is your brother." She laughed at her remark, but Daniel's face didn't change.

"Just friendly?" I asked with a small smile, challenging her response.

"Well, sure, don't see why not," she said with a long

look at Daniel. His eyes didn't budge. I laughed. The two of them seemed to be growing closer, despite what they claimed. I felt as if I knew Florence so well, and if anybody was going to catch the attention of my brother, I would have hoped it to be no one else but her.

"How was the ed-u-cation today?" she asked.

"Well, there's Anita. She's very smart with her books and lessons, but she seems so distant, so far away from everything. She ain't polite at all one moment, but then the next, she's almost nice."

"Stop tryin' to figure everybody out, sis," Daniel said.

"Even if you tried, don't think you could figure that one out. Anita's been like that since I've known her. Just quiet, and off to herself most times," Florence added, turning around to face me. "What else happened?" she asked.

"Got this for a gift," I said, holding up the book, waiting for their excitement to show. Florence took the book and held it up for Daniel to see, then handed it back to me.

"This sho' is something nice, Anna," Florence remarked.

I smiled and put the book away for the moment and seated myself with them.

"Florence, you were in town today. Anything go on I should know about?" I asked her as I always did.

"Nothing much. Just helped out Mrs. Susie a little bit in her shop for a few hours. Mama Bessie had help in the house."

"Any new folks come by the shop?"

"Well, ya! A woman came by from Riverside. Say she heard about Mrs. Susie's an' needed some wedding dress.

Mrs. Susie gave the job to me!" she said, quite excited.

"A wedding dress? That sounds like a lot of work. What else went on at the shop?" I asked. I could tell I hit the right nerve. She soon lost herself in explaining her day, as was so natural for her to do.

"An' that foolish boy, Steve, came by again," she was telling me.

"Again?" I asked with a laugh.

"Sure!"

"That Steve would never give me any kind of attention," I said.

Florence laughed. "Well, you won't believe this, Anna. He . . . he asked me to marry him! Just up an' out of nowhere!" As she and I giggled, I caught Daniel's expression over her shoulder. He glanced up with a frown, then immediately looked back down at the wood in his hands. Florence went on, and as she did, Daniel's tools made more and more noise. I was amused at my brother's irritation, especially as I found him fighting with his own reactions to Florence's comments. I wondered just how deep his feelings for her ran.

". . . told him I ain't ready to be no wife, and I didn't even know him well enough, an' . . . Sebastian," she said, turning around to look at Daniel.

"I'm trying to talk to your sister, but I cain't hardly hear myself!" The banging grew softer, and she turned back to me.

"He told me to think about it, an' I said I would. Don't mean I am, but . . . but marriage, Anna?" She laughed again. "How can . . ."

Daniel suddenly stood up. "Since this conversation ain't for me . . ." He stood there with his belongings, anticipating a response. I said nothing. Florence looked back at him again, crossing her arms to see if what he had to say really made up for his interrupting her like he had. But he said nothing and walked out of the room.

"Don't think he wanted to hear all that, Florence," I said to her with a light laugh. She glanced over her shoulder, considering what I'd said.

"Don't know why it would bother him. It ain't like it's on his mind to ask me somethin' like that." Her lips spoke those words, but her eyes told me something different.

The next day, Daniel came back with a swollen left hand. He wouldn't tell me how it happened. But over the next few days, Flo told me that Steve had suddenly stopped coming around. She was amused, but she held her stubborn pride with my brother as long as she could. Despite this, I began to see something unraveling before my watchful eyes, something Daniel and Florence were trying to remain oblivious to but that was catching up to them nonetheless. Daniel was changing. He seemed to be drifting out of his socially playful ways, and spoke more and more of how things would be with a family of his own. It was all for the better, it seemed. And Florence was at the root of this change.

CHAPTER

❧ 39 ❧

"SEBASTIAN . . . SEBASTIAN, WHERE ARE WE GOING?" MY BROTHER pulled me down the street, heading toward the center of Hadson.

"I told you, Anna. You know them meetings in Hadson I go to all the time? That's where we goin'."

"Sebastian, I don't have any interest in men drinking an' talking loud about nonsense."

He laughed. "Why I gotta keep tellin' you? It ain't like that. You gonna see. Think you might 'preciate it."

Daniel and I had left Mama Bessie's that cold evening to head down to the community meetings that were held to discuss our responsibilities in our community. Daniel had invited Florence, but she couldn't go. She was preoccupied with trying to finish sewing her gift to the mother of a newborn baby. So, Daniel and I continued on to Hadson, stopping only to greet passersby on the streets.

Finally, we arrived at a small house hidden in between two larger, nicer-looking ones. Even in broad daylight, my eyes probably would have skipped over this building.

Instead of entering through the front of the house, Daniel led me around to the back and tapped lightly on the door. I saw two eyes appear and stare suspiciously out from the cracked window to the left of the door. I took two steps back.

"Anna, it's all right. C'mon."

The door creaked open, and we squeezed through. As I entered the dark room, I saw a young man standing in front of me. He was almost completely covered by a long coat and a wide-brimmed hat. Consumed by the darkness of the space, it was hard to see him well, but he seemed, as best as I could tell, to be most likely closer to my age than Daniel's.

"Smithson," Daniel whispered, clasping the man's hand and engulfing him in a quick hug, "This my sister, Anna. Anna, this is Rodney's brother." I shook hands with the man, who returned my gaze with a small smile.

"Go on down there," Smithson said, pointing to an empty wall on the opposite side of the small home, if you could even call it that. Daniel walked forward, yanked a carpet from the floor, and pulled open a trapdoor.

I gasped and whispered, "Why do we have to hide?"

"To be safe, of course. Don't worry, though. Ain't nothin' gonna happen, Anna."

Daniel helped me down the five or six steps and into a larger room, which was lit only by a single candlelight and filled with people talking among themselves. As soon as we stepped through the door, every face turned to us. The quiet that fell could have made the sound of a scurrying mouse seem loud.

"Sebastian," one person said, breaking the silence. The

first greeting was followed by many others. Daniel nodded his own greeting as we made our way among the seated guests.

"Brought wit me a good friend've mine. She came to listen, that's all."

People greeted me, and I shook their hands. There were many people in the room, most of whom I probably knew, but there was no way for me to tell. Most of them were clothed in a way that shielded their identities, as though this was a necessary precaution for being part of the gathering. One man stood up as I walked by.

"Anna," he said, kindly offering me his seat and kissing my hand. I thanked him and sat, noting how respect seemed to come so naturally to these townsfolk of Hadson.

I noticed that the conversation had erupted once more, as if there had been no disturbance. My mind turned to what people were saying.

"Naw, Alik, working in Dayton ain't the same as working here. If, somehow, we all got jobs here among each other, we wouldn't even have to deal with them white folks."

"How can you say that, Abram? How can you? You talking about work, something that provides what is needed for our families. We barely got any money down here. The only way to keep from starving and dying is by working in the city and getting some of that money."

"The white folks will kill us quicker than starving would any day, and you expect us to work for them?"

"Well, my folks are white. You work for us just like we work for you, sometimes, an' you know we wouldn't kill ya." Soft laughter broke out. Mr. Walker was a white citizen who lived on the outskirts of Hadson and kept himself well immersed in the black community.

The conversation rolled on, and I glanced around again, amused by the figures about me. I'd find myself staring at a pile of rags thrown over what I thought was a male body, when suddenly the sound of a woman's voice would ring out. No children were present, but there was a great contrast between the young folk and the old, and more often than not, people within the same age group had the same opinions. I had expected a couple of flasks of liquor to be floating around, but I saw none. An old woman sitting with her hair wrapped and her arms outstretched at the head of the room seemed like she might be getting ready to direct the whole affair.

As my eyes roamed a bit more, they fell on a curious figure crouching patiently in the shadows. He wore a tall, thin black hat that covered nearly his entire face. He had on black gloves, and the collar of his frock coat was pulled up around his neck. His demeanor made it appear that he might be asleep, but I had a feeling he was listening with an intensity greater than that of the rest. Something about him struck me as being out of place, but no one seemed to notice or care. He seemed familiar to me, but soon enough, my attention was swept back to the conversation as I heard a voice I recognized put forward an opinion.

"What about those of us who ain't got families yet? What you propose we do? Them jobs in Dayton is our best bet until we do settle down, because all these family businesses in Hadson ain't gonna do us no good."

I looked up to my left to see Henry crouched low in the corner of the room. I nodded to him as he turned his eyes to meet mine. I was a bit surprised to see Henry here. He didn't strike me as the kind of man to really take things seriously. He seemed so carefree.

"That's exactly what I'm sayin'!" Mr. Sandford interjected. "You all expectin' us to just up and quit our jobs fo' them folk, although we been workin' for them for years, ever since we came here! How you reckon with that?"

"Mr. Sandford, I done had two children killed in confrontations with those men they worked for. We need to split apart from them folks! Set up our own world in the larger community so we can get so strong together that they won't bother us no longer." I heard another woman laugh in a sarcastic manner in response.

"We cain't beat them by making our own little separate community! We strike with our so-called strong community, and then what happens? I'll tell you what happens. They strike back with twice as much force, as well as having the law on their side. If we don't interact with them, they'll just send folks here to Hadson to make sure we ain't starting no mess against them. They always gonna be in charge of us. That's just how life here goes."

At that, the room exploded with heated talk coming from both sides of the debate. I sat in awe as the woman who had said those words now got to her feet, trying to make her case while others pitched fits back at her, asking how in the world she could accept the fact that someone else was in charge of her life.

"Where's our freedom gonna come in, Bella, huh? If we accept them as superior, when are we ever gonna have our true freedom?" a voice rang out.

"Freedom? What's freedom if you're dead?" another asked.

"I'm sure the freedom of death is better than this bondage we in now, with no rights as if we not people at all," said a quiet man sitting with his chin on his knee.

"So, are you suggesting we all get killed? You suggesting we go fight back, raise torches, and burn Dayton down by candlelight? Every single one of us would get killed," one of Bella's allies responded.

A feeble voice broke through: "Ain't no need to raise your voice, we just discussin'."

"This ain't no discussion," another person added. "You got people sayin' we better off livin' as half men, inferior to them. Who in their right mind would believe that? How else are we supposed to get anywhere without fightin' back?"

"You mean how Rodney fought back?" the woman named Bella added, still on her feet.

"Rodney?" Daniel started, looking troubled by this. "Rodney was right to do what he done. Problem was, there wa'an't nobody there to stand up wit him. It would've bin a lot harda to kill fifty men standin' up 'gainst what they b'lieved in 'stead of one. But no one did; no one 'cept Rodney. 'Stead of talkin've how we need to understand our place underneath them, we need to start plannin' ways of bein' mo' like Rodney."

After Daniel's words, a dozen other voices followed. Then I heard humming, a soft sound at first that grew louder as the seconds ticked on. Soon enough, the room was completely quiet, save the persistent humming the old woman in the front of the room brought forth from her tired throat. For a while everyone sat in silence, shrinking back into their positions, listening with saddened hearts as the woman hummed to her heart's decree. Finally, all was silent as we waited for her to say her piece. I listened intently as she began to speak.

"Bondage . . . sufferin' . . . pain . . . heartache . . . slaughterin' . . . My eyes done seen it all. Where we stand among it all? You got them white folks and you got these black folks, and you got some red folks ova yonda. But it don't stop there. We say 'white folks' like it's some kinda poison, and they say 'black folks' like we vicious dogs. That ain't what defines us. There are white folks I know, kindest folks I done ever seen in my long life. It's all in here." She paused to bring her wrinkled hand slowly to her chest to tap her heart.

"Now, seems like to me we got folks of this here community claimin' we is lower and less smarter than them white folks. Let me tell you what. You wrong. Still, we got folks sayin' that freedom will only come if we take up our knives and guns and kill every single one of them in Dayton. Let me tell you what. You wrong. But that don't mean we ain't got to fight. And by fight, I don't mean killin' every white man you see. Fightin', for us, is understandin' that we is just as smart. Fightin' for us is holdin' our heads up high, showin' them we already know that all them 'niggas' an' 'apes' you hear comin' from they mouths ain't the truth. Fightin' for us is doin' the things we must to get somewhere an' to make some better place for the younguns here. Now, that's my word; y'all go on wit whats you want to say 'bout it." She paused, looking around the room, but she had lost my attention for the moment. An idea had struck me when I heard her speak her last few words.

"I got a question." I nervously forced my voice through the mumbling that had started back up.

"You—you say we have to make a better place for the younguns. How we gonna do that?"

A woman behind me lifted her voice in agreement. "Ya, what about the children?"

"Teach 'em the ways of livin' here without messin' wit the white folks," one voice spoke up.

"No!" another person called out. "We gotta teach 'em how to stand up fo' themselves an' fo' they community."

"I don't be raisin' my children those ways. Teach 'em to do whatever they gotta to raise all the money they can. . . ." They continued, and I leaned back, lost in the obscurity of my own thoughts.

Teach 'em, teach 'em, teach 'em, they said.

What if . . . what if I could teach them their letters and numbers?

But no, the idea was silly. I let it wash away with the rain that I could hear pouring down outside. Once again, I brought my mind back to the conversation and my eyes back to the gathered group. My eyes ran across the folks hidden in the shadows and stopped with surprise as they met the gaze of two eyes sparkling at me. I knew right away who the man was. The hat on his head tipped forward slightly, and after an exaggerated pause, he turned his eyes away.

He nodded at me!

I eyed him closely as he rose silently, an invisible man to the debating crowd, and brushed past some people to exit the room. Even as he walked out, he kept every feature of his body hidden with some piece of clothing. It took all of a few seconds for my curiosity to bubble over, leaving me tracing the man's steps out the door.

"Anna?" Daniel said, breaking off his participation in the conversation.

"Need some air," I whispered. I don't know what drove me after the man, the man who had called himself Caldwell, but I followed my spirit out the trapdoor and into the night. The disappointment hit me harder than the cold I felt when I stepped outside.

The man was nowhere in sight.

Heading quickly back home with my brother, I breathed in the cool, damp air.

"So, what you think?" Daniel asked me after a while.

"'Bout what, Sebastian?"

"Those meetins, of course."

"Figure they're a pretty good idea for the community."

"Ah, see there? Told you so. We need everyone's opinion," he said, looking at me with a smile.

"Maybe so, Sebastian, but . . ."

"But what?"

"I feel as if there's something else that needs to be done for Hadson, and I'm the one to do it."

"Something else like what?"

"Something . . . I don't know." I shrugged, letting my thoughts disperse themselves on the breeze.

"With all that talk of fighting back and working for them and all that, I just find myself wondering what else I could do. Something . . . different."

What was that something different? I knew the answer, but I kept coming upon the doubt that rumbled through my mind.

How silly, Anna, you're no schoolteacher!

I shrugged off the idea and walked on in silence alongside Daniel, the two of us allowing our own thoughts of Hadson to carry our minds on different paths.

CHAPTER

❧ 40 ❧

FEBRUARY SPRANG UPON US AND BROUGHT A NEW WAVE OF learning that had me up late into the night, working on a new assignment Mrs. Rosa had placed in my hands. I never complained: There was no reason to. I loved it. I was now feeding the yearning I had grown to accept as a slave, and I was never too full. By now, Mrs. Rosa no longer needed to keep me after the group classes, but usually I stayed anyway, burying my face in a book that I chose from one of the bookshelves. I could read anything if I wanted to, and Mrs. Rosa heard my thanks daily.

The lessons were my refuge, my escape, when I felt fearful or angry or saddened, and those emotions could sneak up on me at any time. I didn't understand the bond I felt between John and me. His absence only made me love him more.

Amid all of this, Mrs. Rosa was very proud of my progress, of how much my reading and writing had improved. Anita hadn't changed. She stayed quiet and was involved only to the extent she had to be. Peggy and I got along very well. I had never thought it would be possible for me to talk and interact with any white person as an equal, but I found myself doing this all the time with her.

Usually, at the end of the day, Mrs. Rosa walked Peggy a short distance up the road, where they'd meet her mother, so Peggy wouldn't have to walk home alone. On one occasion, Mrs. Rosa asked me to walk with them. We headed outdoors, and Peggy waved around a picture she had drawn in the two hours Mrs. Rosa had given her to complete it. We chatted about our day as we walked along.

"Anna, you didn't miss a single word Mrs. Rosa asked you to write down today—not one! You're getting really good at everything—maybe even better than me!"

"Well, I thank you, Peggy. But I couldn't do a lot of it without your help." She smiled, then, spotting her mother in the distance, took off running toward her.

When Mrs. Rosa and I approached the woman, she hugged Mrs. Rosa close and they exchanged warm words, like sisters would do. She then turned her smile to me, and I saw that she had dimpled cheeks, just as her daughter did. Her hair, pinned up into a bun on the top of her head, was brown, though, not red like Peggy's. We shook hands and she nodded cordially.

"Peggy tells me you're the new student. She says you learn quicker than anyone she's ever seen." I glanced at Mrs. Rosa, then back into the woman's friendly eyes.

"Thank you, ma'am."

"Sure. Maybe one day you'll be helpin' others, too, like Mrs. Rosa does."

My heart skipped a beat. "Well . . . well, that would be nice, I suppose." After we parted, the woman's words trailed behind me.

As February rolled along Daniel was becoming more and more involved with secret plans and community projects that took him from Hadson for as long as three days in a row. More worrisome, however, were Daniel's ideas about Mary's predicament. I still feared that he would pack up his belongings and return to the South without alerting me, simply to avoid the pain of telling me good-bye. He fell into heavy moods, sometimes, moods that took some getting used to for Florence, and lately, even I could not figure out what was in my brother's heart.

I shared my dread with Florence, leaving out the many details that made the situation as alarming as it was. She fell into an anxious state, regardless, and decided to approach Daniel about it all. I let her speak; I had learned when I was much younger that Daniel would share only what he wanted to share when it came to personal matters.

"Sebastian, what've you been up to? What have you been planning? We're concerned . . . concerned about you."

Daniel had stopped by briefly to visit with us, when Florence began to question him. He turned to me, but, seeing my piercing look, he turned back to Florence.

"It's my work," he said simply, intending to leave his explanation at that.

"Sebastian, you're not . . . leaving us, are you?" Her voice shook.

"No!" he said all too quickly. "Wouldn't leave a pretty

lady like you, an' my sista here . . ." He shook off his distant, gloomy demeanor, brought his hand over my own, and dared to look me in the eyes again.

"Anna, you know, I b'lieve I'm safest when I'm in your good graces, an' when you ain't worryin' so much 'bout me."

"Sebastian—"

He waved us off. "Gotta go! Y'all keep watchin' out fo' Mama Bessie, hear?"

My heart nearly stopped: His words sounded like a farewell of some sort. Florence, however, seemed content with his words, and returned to the house, chatting about something else. I barely heard her; instead, I watched my brother walk away from Mama Bessie's. His every stride seemed to sprinkle a little bit of emptiness into my soul. *But he said it's for his work!* I attempted to assure myself of this, but his leave-taking sat heavily in my chest.

Sleep was a mere thought, a dream in itself that night. I lay awake, clutching my covers, the feeling of lonesomeness eating at my gut. The darkness burned my eyes, which wouldn't close. They were frozen open from the cold feeling traveling through my body.

It had been a few hours that I lay like this, unmoving, when I heard a soft tapping on the door. Florence stirred almost immediately. I stayed put as the tapping continued. She rose like a corpse coming to life to answer it. She turned the knob, and as the door opened, I heard her gasp softly.

"Sebastian! What you doing here? How you get in?"

"Shh, Flo. My sista 'sleep?"

"Seems like it to me, but . . . Sebastian, why you here?"

she asked again, her voice sounding more amused than concerned. I heard him step into the room and walk over to where I lay. I shut my eyes before he got too close.

"She sleepin', I told you!" Florence whispered. I heard a long sigh escape his lips before he turned back to her.

Florence questioned him again. "What is it you need, Sebastain? It's real early, an' it's good to see you an' all, but you really ain't s'pose . . ."

"Flo, I'm leaving," he said quietly.

"What?"

"Jus' fo' a little while, not long. Be back in no time!"

"Sebastian, you—"

He interrupted her. "I promise, Flo. I'll be back." It might just as well have been John's voice making that promise.

"What for, Sebastian? You can't keep doing things without telling me what they are."

"I'm needed, Flo, that's all. It's just some business that's gotta be taken care of."

"That's it?"

"Yes."

"Why you ain't wake Anna to tell her?"

I didn't have to wonder why. My brother hated good-byes. He had already parted from me in his own way.

"She'll just try an' talk me down 'bout it, an' I don't want her to do that. Fact is, she's right half the time, but this . . . this jus' somethin' that needs to be done." The temperature in the room seemed to drop a couple of degrees. I was freezing.

"How long you gonna be gone?" Silence. "Sebastian, how long?"

"Don't know." I listened to my breath in the silence that followed and wondered what in the world was stopping me from jumping up and talking my brother out of going.

'Cause you know him, Anna. You know him a little too well.

"You don't know? Sebastian, how could you not know how long you gonna be . . ."

"Come with me, will you?" Daniel asked her.

"What? You want me to leave my work an' all?"

"No, Flo, come with me now, jus' till the rays of dawn break through the sky."

"Sebastian, I don't know if . . ." Her voice trailed off, and within the confines of a minute, I heard her shuffle out of the room, and the door shut.

But I couldn't let him go like that. I lifted myself from the bed, ready to dart toward the door and scream after him, but before I could move any farther, the door creaked back open. Daniel poked his head around. He must have known that I was awake. He felt it.

"Daniel, Daniel, please don't go," I whispered to him, my lips trembling, but he cut into my words.

"Anna, I'll be back." He said it with such finality that it felt as if he had shut my lips tight with his fingers. He stood a minute longer, embracing me with his eyes.

"Wouldn't lie to you, Anna. B'lieve me, I'll be back." With that, he stepped back out of the door and shut it, leaving me in scowling silence.

Mary was gone. John wasn't here. Now my brother had left me too.

I didn't sleep; I couldn't, even when daylight showed its face. Florence returned, the mixed emotions of contentment and sadness playing their own roles on her face.

This was going to be harder than I thought.

The morning flew past in a frenzy. I lay asleep, claiming sickness, not quite ready to walk out into the suffocating smiles and laughter of Mama Bessie's household.

Nighttime slipped back upon us; the entire day seemed lost in the stroke of an hour. Florence was back at my bedside.

"Anna, I spoke to Sebastian this morning."

Silence.

"Said he'd be gone for a while, but he'll be back before you blink!" I knew Florence well enough to know that she was covering her sadness with forced cheerfulness.

"Why he leave?" I asked, playing the part I had to assume.

"Work."

"There a reason he didn't tell me himself?" A routine question.

"Well, no, not really. I was up, an' . . . an', well, he said don't go about thinkin' he ain't as smart as you. Said to trust him like he trusts you; he knows what he's doing."

I coughed, but Florence didn't budge. I coughed again.

"Hey, Anna, you don't sound too good. Hope you're up tomorrow, though. I don't have to go to the shop, an' I miss my help in the house!" Then she was gone.

I wasn't up the next day or the next. Mama Bessie came up often with food and loving words of comfort. She, alone, seemed to understand that the chains that bound me to my bed were not those of sickness, but rather lack of spirit. She explained to me that word was sent to Mrs. Rosa concerning my condition.

It was the fourth day that I solemnly returned to the world about me. I was in this place called Freedom. I had things to do, a community I was part of, and an education I had to continue with. A week passed, and it was then that I saw Florence's real feelings, beneath her smiles and her claims that Daniel would be back soon.

I woke up early one morning, before the day's chores began, and found Florence leaning against the window, shoulders drooped, and her chin resting in her hand.

"Flo?" I called softly, pulling myself up. She said nothing. "Flo? You all right?"

"I ain't a fool, Anna. I know that kind of travel, for whatever work he's doin', is dangerous," she said, still gazing out the window. I sat silent, letting her roam around in her own mind.

"He told me when he comes back, he don't wanna see no evidence of me cryin' an' carryin' on. Said smile for him when he's away, an' maybe the wind'll carry him back quicker." I felt a pang of sadness. I felt myself clinging to Florence's words, knowing I shouldn't, but I couldn't help it. My eyes welled up.

"I know he'll be back safe. I jus' know it! I jus' wish he didn't have to go," she said, brushing a tear from her eye.

She sighed, ran a hand over her hair, and turned to me, a weak smile crossing her lips.

"You ready for a long day?"

Two and a half weeks went by, and my mood darkened. However sad Florence felt over Daniel's absence, she remained in high spirits, hopeful that he'd return unharmed. She didn't know his true purpose. He had gone back for Mary—I could see it all over his face! Florence didn't understand that there was really no such thing as a runaway successfully returning to the South and making it back to the North. She didn't understand how foolish Daniel had been to leave us.

I thought about this as I walked home on a Thursday evening from Mrs. Rosa's. Oddly enough, Daniel leaving seemed to muddle everything in my mind except my education. My desire to learn all I could only strengthened, and I put all my energy into it.

Words were my life. This life was my love. But did I love this life? It was so painful, so . . .

"Look, Anna, look what I made fo' him!" Florence was walking quickly up to me. In her eyes, I could see hints of redness, but where tears once had been I saw a childlike excitement. I took the small blanket she was holding.

"It's for Sebastian's friend's little baby. He made the little boy a wood toy, an' I figured I could do somethin' for the baby too. Sebastian gonna be so happy when he gets back."

"He ain't comin' back, Flo." I said harshly. The excitement seeped out from Florence's eyes. Her smile turned into a frown, and she spoke to me with an edge of anger in her voice.

"What's wrong with you, Anna? Don't know how you reckon that, but it ain't the truth. He said he'll be back, and you watch!"

I was about to respond, to tell Florence again that he wouldn't return, but it seemed useless. She wouldn't hear me out until time proved me right. I held back the tears with mature patience. This was the way things went: life brought people I loved close to me, and it often took them away. I'd have to find peace in that.

"This your brother. Don't you trust him?" Florence asked. I nodded slowly. "Then get yo'self together," she said, her jaw tight.

Florence took the blanket and headed back toward the house. The doubts in my own mind were screaming too loudly for me to hear the assurance in her words. I didn't think she was as angry as she looked, maybe just scared at what I had said. I turned my thoughts to Mary and whispered to her spirit.

"Aunt Mary, I don't know what to do. Pray for your son, Aunt Mary. Please pray for him."

CHAPTER

❧ 41 ❧

"ANNA, I WANT TO INVITE YOU TO DINNER TOMORROW NIGHT at my house. I would like you to meet my husband." Another week had come and gone, and I was at the now-familiar house of my tutor. I had tried my best to work through the day's lessons with poise, but I was distracted by the emptiness I felt. I had been readying myself to head back to Mama Bessie's when Mrs. Rosa invited me for dinner.

"You haven't talked about him much. What does he do, again?" I asked. She looked at me with a curious grin.

"Just about everything under the sun."

Reaching Mama Bessie's, I ran into Ned at the front of the yard, and he dragged me into the house, bursting with news of the events of the day.

"And Helen just had him hollerin' an' all. . . ." I let the boy talk until he was red in the face as I greeted Mama Bessie and helped her with dinner for the children. When he had finally finished and run back out to the yard to play, I told Mama Bessie about my plans for the evening.

"Well, go ahead, chile! I have the help I need tonight."

I thanked Mama Bessie, greeted Florence, and left for

Mrs. Rosa's house, whistling to myself to keep my thoughts at bay. Reaching her door, I knocked softly. The door came open in a flash, and Mrs. Rosa, abandoning her normal intimidating stature, pulled me along through the house to one of the back rooms. As soon as I seated myself at the table, a procession of knocks, an awkward little tune, sounded on the front door. Then I heard the door creak open.

"Hello!" a voice called out.

"One minute, Anna," Mrs. Rosa said as she hurried around the corner to receive her husband. I heard the door shut.

"Hey there, miss! I'm, ah, I'm looking for a stolen beauty, a rose of some kind. They told me I might find her here, somewhere in this house. I know I've just barged in, but do you think you can help me?" The man's loud and hauntingly familiar voice echoed throughout the house. Mrs. Rosa's laugh was carried pleasantly to my ears.

"Hush all of that, would you? You know we have company. Anna's here."

"Indeed, you told me to expect your best student. I'm certainly intimidated!"

I could hear their footsteps, and in a matter of seconds, Mrs. Rosa's husband followed her through the kitchen doorway. Looking at the man, I prayed that my true reaction didn't show on my face.

"This is my husband, Anna," Mrs. Rosa said, watching my expression with amusement. I followed him closely with my eyes, unsure of whether to hold out my hand. I was stunned: She was married to a white man.

However, as he walked closer, and finally stopped to stand behind a seat at the table, my initial thoughts stood still with a sudden realization. I knew him.

"Mr. Caldwell!" He smiled, warmly, and held out his hand. I stood quickly and grasped it. "It was you—you got me an education!"

"Well, now," Mrs. Rosa said, "I daresay I had just a little bit to do with that, don't you think?" She laughed, then disappeared for a moment to gather the dishes, as Mr. Caldwell and I sat down.

In the light, where his face was exposed much more clearly than before, I noticed how young he looked. He had a playfulness about him and a light in his eyes, which made me feel quite at ease in his presence. In the dark, it had seemed obvious to me that he was a white man, but here in the light from the table, I had to drag my eyes across his face twice before I settled on that conclusion, and even then somewhat uncertainly.

"Mr. Caldwell, I . . . I don't think I rightly understand. You two . . . That just ain't common. . . ."

"Miss Anna," Mr. Caldwell began, his lips curling upward in a smile, "you speak as if I were a white man."

"But, sir, ain't it the truth? It's quite plain—"

"Please excuse me for not sharing this—I didn't think it was necessary to correct you before—but folks do say it takes little more than a drop of Negro blood to make a person black." He dramatically held his hands up to the candlelight to find that single drop.

"You're a black man, sir?" I asked as Mrs. Rosa walked back in, placed the dishes on the table, and sat down. He nodded with an understanding smile on his lips at my shocked expression, which I didn't even try to withhold.

"Sure, that is, if you choose to see it that way." I gazed at him again, curiously, and almost laughed as my eyes began to see what I hadn't before. His lips were like Daniel's; his hair was cut short, but hints of a natural curliness seemed to be hiding there. He was a black man, but mixed almost beyond recognition.

"All right, now, that's enough surprise before the meal," Mrs. Rosa said as she prepared the table.

"Where's my Little Sue?" Mr. Caldwell asked as we began to eat.

"Asleep, like she ought to be at this time." But just at that moment, a noise that began as a low whine and quickly erupted into wailing drifted down to our ears. Mr. Caldwell threw his head back and laughed as if he'd never been more amused.

"Look at that! She knows when her father's home." Mr. Caldwell laughed a bit more and held Mrs. Rosa's gaze with pleading eyes until she gave in to his unspoken request with a sigh.

"All right, Caldwell, I'll bring her down. Listen to her. Sixteen months, and already carrying on like that." Mrs. Rosa left the table, and Mr. Caldwell watched her closely until she had completely disappeared around the corner.

"Don't let her fool you. She wanted Little Sue down here

just as much as I did," he said, leaning in and whispering. I smiled, and he leaned back once more.

"But anyhow," Mr. Caldwell said after his laughter died down, "I'm quite proud of you, Anna."

"Thank you, sir—"

"Call me Caldwell," he said, interrupting me.

"Okay, Mr. Caldwell."

"That's my household name, my real name. I don't often use it outside of here. It's dangerous for me. It's not so easy acting as if I were white in one world and black in another, but I've been doing it for most of my life. I'm sure you wonder why I choose to fall back into my role as a black man. It's not too common for folks who can pass, but I believe it's my responsibility, and it gives me a sense of pride, if I may say so. But I do what I need to do to appeal to society and make the mark I feel I'm destined to make."

"What mark is that?" I asked him. He looked over at me and raised his eyebrows.

"That, I am still working to understand. I spoke to you, that night some time ago, about the dangers of using education to make a difference in the lives of the people you see struggling around you, about using it to challenge existing systems. I've had my share of digging into that side of education and, well . . . " He fingered the edge of the plate in front of him and lowered his eyes. "Rosa hates this talk."

"But why would she hate it? Seems to me that's something noble."

He scratched the top of his head and shrugged. "Noble, perhaps, but all things come at a cost, Anna."

"That must mean you were in some trouble."

He nodded slowly but kept his lips shut as he stared past me.

"What happened? If it's all right to ask."

He snapped back to attention and chuckled. "You've got a lot of questions. It's no wonder my wife likes you so much," he said with another small smile.

"After Rosa and I married, the two of us undertook writings we thought could benefit society. We didn't really understand the dangers then. We were very young, and we made our way here from Europe. I had a little bit of money, inherited, and we traveled with that, sometimes under guises I'd rather not explain," Caldwell said with a frown I almost did not see.

"But we came here and decided to write about what we saw going on around us. Rosa's approach was more practical: She took in some students and edited my work. She and I thought we could do something about injustice and be a voice for the black people. Through me, we could carry it to the white society and make some kind of a difference. But we came face-to-face with the true nature of inequality. A few men took me, hid me, and showed me no mercy. I was beaten for days, and they threatened to sell me—to sell me, Anna!" He laughed, despite himself, a laugh that quickly disappeared behind subtle lines on his forehead and around his mouth.

"That's what gave me an intelligence you couldn't

learn in books. If I wanted to live out my dream, I had to learn to dodge the dangers and maintain a dual life. But"—he shook his head back and forth and stared hard at the table—"Rosa doesn't like remembering those times, as would be expected." He turned his eyes up to me, and I saw fragments of the past drifting plainly into view.

"We agreed she'd teach you, Anna. It was her suggestion, at first, for me to talk to you about it. Perhaps she doesn't want you to know this, but I don't think, in her heart, she wants you running down the same path I chose to run down."

"Well, Mr. Caldwell, I feel like I'm warned well enough."

He laughed and leaned farther back in the seat. "I'm not so sure about that."

"What makes you say that?" I asked quickly, ready to defend myself.

"As I told you already, I haven't seen many people like you. You have to be some kind of perfectly cut gem to come into this household, anyway, as a student under my wife. But there's something in you I see in myself. It's dangerous business, Anna, using education to make direct statements in society, and you don't have the benefit I have."

"And what's that benefit?"

"Different identities. Not that it makes it much less dangerous. Poor folks don't like educated people. But they'll listen, if you're not talking to the ones who know about your black blood."

"I don't really think that matters much for me right

now, Mr. Caldwell. I got my mind set on learning, an' I ain't—or, I'm not—thinking about too much else."

"Well, I believe that's where your mind should be set now."

I nodded. "But, Mr. Caldwell, you know, even after all you've gone through, sounds like you're still part of that dangerous business you talk of."

The gleam in his eye suggested he was holding back a secret, but I couldn't question him further. Mrs. Rosa came down with the giggling child and placed her in Mr. Caldwell's arms when she reached out for him.

"Only for a few minutes, Caldwell. She should be long past asleep." Mr. Caldwell glanced quickly at his wife, a pout in his eyes but a small smile on his lips. I watched him play with the child as Mrs. Rosa sat to finish her food.

Mr. Caldwell's conversation that followed lightened as we talked about the months I had spent with Mrs. Rosa since I had spoken with him the first time. We talked about Hadson—the people, the ways of life, the issues. Little Sue insisted on being handed from one parent to the other, until she fell asleep again in her father's arms.

"Mr. Caldwell, what is it you do?" I asked as we finished our meal. He and Mrs. Rosa shared a quick but significant glance I could only attempt to understand. Then Mrs. Rosa looked over at me, ready to speak on her husband's behalf.

"He's, well . . . Caldwell works with money. That's what he's good at. Actually"—Mrs. Rosa paused, and her expression shifted to a look that reminded me of our weekly lessons—"perhaps it's best not to explain much about that. Some things even I don't know about," she said with a small frown, turning to Mr. Caldwell. "But it's what we agreed to."

"Again, Anna, don't let her fool you. Anything and everything I do is done with her permission." They seemed to be speaking to each other, instead of to me.

"Most things, at least," she responded, her frown relaxing.

Mr. Caldwell chuckled and turned back to me, shaking his head. "Perhaps the simple answer to your question, Anna, would be that I take care of the financial matters of some of the businesses in and around the city."

I nodded, wishing for a better explanation but knowing I had already gotten the only answer I could expect.

"We live so that his work never intertwines with his family. He disappears from here the mornings that he's home, and he returns at night, as he did today. Not many folks know who he really is," Mrs. Rosa said, looking over at him.

"Or about us," she added. "Caldwell acts as white in Dayton and the other places he travels to, and he doesn't really come around Hadson very often." The baby shifted, and Mrs. Rosa sent Mr. Caldwell a look of dissatisfaction. But he had long since won the battle of keeping the child at the table with him.

"All the folks in Dayton think he's white?" I asked. There was another shared glance and a slight nod.

"So at the schoolhouse, Mr. Caldwell—"

"Yes, they think so at the schoolhouse, too."

By this time, we had finished eating, and I had been sitting back in my chair, my arms crossed.

"But, Mr. Caldwell, you saw how the woman treated me. Why didn't you . . . why didn't you stop that?"

"Anna, please don't be naïve," he said, my comment appearing to have touched a sensitive nerve. "To them, I am a white man. There are social rules that apply. Reacting strictly from my feelings could put me in the jailhouse, or worse."

I felt my cheeks grow warm, and I looked down at the table. "I'm sorry, Mr. Caldwell."

"No, don't apologize. I understand, Anna, I really do. I understood then, and that's what brought me rushing home to see what Rose thought about you. And I understand now, and that's why you're sitting here with us tonight."

We spoke on for at least another hour and a half. The two of them made me feel like I was part of something important, something loving and beautiful.

Soon enough, however, it was time for me to leave. Mr. Caldwell walked with me to the door, still cuddling Little Sue in one of his arms.

"Before you leave, I want to give you something I think you'll like. I know what I've been telling you about how to use education—all the warnings I've given—but listening and talking with you at the table, I have a strong feeling you'll appreciate this." As he spoke, he reached into his shirt pocket with his free hand, and pulled out a small booklet. But he had chosen the wrong moment to share it.

"Caldwell, not that, not now, please!" Mrs. Rosa said as she entered the room, almost pleading, watching him open the booklet. I saw his slanted writing covering the pages.

"I'm writing another book, Anna. I'm going to do this one right, though."

Out of the corner of my eye, I watched Mrs. Rosa shake her head.

"Rose thinks I'm a complete fool," he said, waving the open booklet her way.

"You are, Caldwell. Now put that away, would you?"

He forced out a theatrical sigh and slipped it back into his pocket, then turned to me.

"I would have loved for you to look at it, but"—he nodded toward Mrs. Rosa—"it seems I have little say-so in the matter. But, Anna, I've been attending those community meetings Hadson has every now and then. You know these—I realized you spotted me on one occasion." I nodded and he continued. "They have some interesting points that should be written up in a book of some sort. What do you think about that?"

"I think that's a fine idea, Mr. Caldwell."

He nodded, shut the book, and turned to Mrs. Rosa with a sly smile. "I'm finished, Rose. I just felt it was necessary to share that before she left."

Mrs. Rosa pursed her lips and said, "Sure, but I would like your views and your business to stay with you. It's not safe water to tread in, and there's no use in warning others about those waters just to show that you're wading in deep yourself."

He laughed. "I just showed it to her, that was all," he said. "And look! I think it's about time to take this little one off to bed. Miss Anna"—he held out his free hand for me to shake—"it was wonderful meeting you in an appropriate time and place. You are one smart young woman. I wish for you the very best."

"Thank you, Mr. Caldwell," I said, shaking his hand.

"You're more than welcome."

"Anna," Mrs. Rosa said, embracing me as Mr. Caldwell went upstairs, "it was a pleasure to have you over."

"Thank you, Mrs. Rosa."

"I know I don't really have to say this to you, but Caldwell, the real Caldwell, isn't a known man. He convinced me that he felt comfortable making himself known to you, and I was fine with that. Anita knows some things, and we have friends who understand, but that's all. I would appreciate it if you . . ."

"If I kept silent."

She smiled at me and patted my shoulder. "Get back safely, Anna."

And then, I walked off into the night, my stomach full and my mind inspired.

CHAPTER

❧ 42 ❧

I LISTENED TO THE CHILDREN SQUEALING AS I STEPPED FROM THE road into Mama Bessie's yard. I was reading as I walked, my head hung low over the schoolwork in my hands and my fingers running across a passage I couldn't understand. Nearing the porch steps, I lifted my head, then stopped instantly to stare wide-eyed at the figure that graced the entrance to the house.

He stood tall in the doorway, a new shirt hanging loosely but neatly over his chest. His eyes looked tired, but they fell on me. I stood suspended, my books finally slipping from my fingers and falling onto the grass by my feet. But I paid them no mind. His lips stretched a mile wide in a smile I had foolishly tried to wash from my memory.

My eyes remained glued to the figure as Florence brushed past him and ran up to me, proclaiming, "He's back, Anna! See? I told you—trust your brother!" Daniel came quickly down the steps and hugged me, but I held back.

"I don't understand," I said to him.

"Understand what?"

"What happened to you, Sebastian? I mean, you're . . . you're back. You shouldn't be back. . . ."

"I shouldn't be back?" he asked, puzzled, looking over at Florence for an explanation.

"She kept saying to me you wasn't comin' back, ever!" Florence told him.

"Anna? Why'd you think somethin' like that?" he asked with imploring eyes. Florence went back into the house, giving us some time alone to talk.

"You said you were going back to get Mary!"

He looked at me with a shocked expression. "Never said no such thing!" he retorted.

"Sure you did. You said you were going back south."

"Back south?" Daniel said. "You must think I ain't got no sense in the world, Anna!"

I breathed in the sight of him as blood rushed back to my face. "Sebastian," I said, "I was so sure you had left us for good! You said—"

"Anna, that was my anger speakin' when I talked 'bout my mama. Didn't have no real thoughts of goin' back there! I know I say things crazy-like sometimes, but you gotta know I ain't completely a fool. Jus' bin gone fo' some important work. Wa'an't gonna tell you befo', but I done got involved wit this group that help send folks runnin' from down south to Canada. This time we went right down near the border. It's dangerous round that way, but it sho' ain't as dangerous as returnin' to the South. Folks there be the nicest folks you eva met! Pay us a penny a day, say they knows we takin' off from work an' we gots families to feed, but they needed our help." He threw his arm around my shoulder.

"You got a lot of stuff to hold on to in that big heart of

393

yours, Anna. I told you, don't spend no time worryin' 'bout me! I'ma always be here." I nodded, breathing back my tears. He leaned in closer to me, a solemn look in his eyes.

"Maybe you should open that heart on up a little more, too, Anna."

"Sebastian . . ."

"Fresh fruit don't always stay that way."

His words brought back a memory from a week or so before he had left, when Henry had found me on my way back from Mrs. Rosa's. Henry insisted on walking with me the whole way back and offered me a taste out of his basketful of fruit. We had a good time, laughing like I would with Florence, but the fun rested in a place inside that didn't quite reach my heart. It never would.

"Sebastian, please don't. I thought you understood." His words had fallen heavy on my ears, evidence of his own doubts inside.

"I'm jus' talkin', Anna, don't mind me," he said, turning away and walking into the house.

Hours later, as night settled, Daniel and I walked out to the lake. He recounted the things he had seen and done while he had been gone.

"Lotta things I done seen, good things an' bad, gonna stay inside me fo'eva," he said as we stood by the water. After a moment, he said softly, "I hear Tucker out here, sometimes. There's no anger or sadness in him. He say to me, 'Be the big brother fo' your people. Don't you eva stop that fight fo' our rights.' An' I ain't neva gonna stop doin' that, Anna."

I sighed. "Mary wouldn't want you to."

"I know. You hear her too, don't ya?"

"Of course I do." I leaned over and rested my head against Daniel's shoulder.

"Mary's always gonna be with us," I said.

Daniel said nothing, but he stood tall, listening to the sounds of the night.

CHAPTER

43

"MISS ANNA?"

"Yes, Ned?"

"Why you always readin' those things?"

"What things? You mean, these books?" I asked the young boy, holding up the novel in my hands.

It was a Saturday morning, May 1823. Ned and I sat near Mama Bessie's garden, a wooden toy in his hand, and the book in mine. Ned was taking a break from his chores.

"But you do that stuff all the time! Why?" he stressed in a whine, his way of expressing that my time would be better spent with him and the rest of the children.

"It's important to me, Ned, that's why."

"But why? That like your job? You get money fo' readin' that thing an' writin' an' laughin' an' talkin' to yourself all the time?" he asked, innocently inquisitive.

I laughed. "No, no money, Ned."

"So why you do it, then?" he demanded.

"Because there's so many things in this world we don't know. Things we never even heard of. Things that . . . that teach us folk to be better people."

"Ain't that what Mama Bessie for?" he asked, quite serious.

I laughed again. "Books tell you things don't know one here in Hadson know! Folks teach us to be scared of reading and writing, Ned. But you know what?"

"What?"

"Being able to read and write is one of the most powerful things you can have as a black person."

"Why?"

I set my book down and looked thoughtfully at him. "It's the one thing can't anybody ever take away from you once you have it. It's the one thing folks don't want us to have because it makes us smart—real smart. As smart as just about anybody!"

"You mean, we be just as smart as even the white folks?"

I nodded, feeling the power behind the idea. I watched silently while Ned's eyebrows bent inward slightly as he allowed his thoughts to absorb my words. Finally, he looked up.

"Is that really so, Miss Anna?" His eyes pierced my own, trying to see if I was tricking him. As I watched him consider how beautiful education could be, a small light that had been growing within me flared.

"Sure is, Ned."

"Well, I wanna learn my letters an' numbers too!" he said almost immediately, with certainty.

"Can you teach me, Miss Anna?" The light was growing brighter. I looked closely at this young boy, a small seed waiting to blossom into whatever society made him out to be.

But what if his young mind were educated? What if all the young minds in Hadson were educated! What if . . . Thoughts about teaching spun through my mind as they had done a thousand times before.

"Well, Ned, I'm going to have to see about that," I said slowly and a bit nervously. Had I learned enough yet myself to be able to teach others?

"Okay!" he shouted gleefully, hopping back up to resume the garden tasks.

I went into the house to fetch him a pail of water, turning the idea of teaching the children of Hadson around and around in my mind. Once I brought Ned the full bucket, I found Florence and joined in helping her fold the clean clothes.

"Anna, you know, I don't think you can keep getting past that Henry for long. He's taken a real liking to you. He's the nicest-looking guy around here," Florence said. She'd spoken to me before about Henry and me spending more time together. I frowned at her, my fears about Henry's desire for more than a friendship now confirmed.

I tried to change the subject. "I don't think Sebastian would like to hear you say that."

She laughed and said, "Well, now, he jus' gonna have to deal with that, now, ain't he? But I know that man is splitting wood over you."

"I wouldn't say so," I replied, keeping my eyes on my work.

"Well, I sure do believe it! All he talks about is 'Anna, Miss Anna!' And you'd think he'd have stopped that by now with these other women runnin' around here tryin' to take his heart. But no, he's got his eyes set on you, an' you give him none of your time."

I shrugged. "It's not like you and Sebastian, Flo. We're friends."

"Not in his mind, you ain't," she said. "But since you don't believe me, you can ask him what he really thinks later today."

"What do you mean, Flo?"

"There's another gatherin' tonight. Folks from Gibson an' Riverside gonna be there. I'm sure your fellow will come by—I don't believe he misses a gatherin'—an' you . . . you gonna come with me."

I didn't reply as I placed a white shirt down on a blanket that was lying on the grass. I glanced up toward the road. A tall figure was approaching. I was surprised to see that it was Anita.

"I'll be back," I told Florence hurriedly as I walked toward Anita. I almost never saw her except at Mrs. Rosa's and, occasionally, church.

Something must be wrong, I figured.

"You need something?" I asked when I reached her. As usual, she stared past me, her eyes skimming everything but my face.

"Anita, you need something?" I asked once more, determined to get back to my work. She dragged her eyes around to mine.

"The old man is sick. I was told to come here, that Ms. Bessie would know what to do."

"How sick is he?" I asked.

"Quite sick, he . . . he may be about to die."

I gasped, and ran into the house. When I came out again I was pulling Mama Bessie behind me. After explaining his ailments, Anita stood and waited as I rushed back into the house with Mama Bessie to help her prepare what was needed.

"She care, Anna, she jus' care in different ways than you or I do," Mama Bessie said in response to my question about Anita.

"Child ain' barely eva bin out that ole man's house since she came up this way. Her soul seems so weary. Musta had it hard, that one."

I nodded, grabbing the small bag she was handing me.

"Now, you be careful with that. Ole Joshua jus' might make it yet."

"Yes, ma'am."

I made my way back out the door, holding her concoction.

"Here, Anita. You be careful with that, hear? Mama Bessie said he just might make it."

"Let's hope so," she said simply. I turned away, not even caring to grace her comment with a response.

"Anna." I turned back to see Anita looking squarely at me. Her face had softened considerably. It looked almost friendly.

"I don't mean . . ." I smiled, saving her the trouble of apologizing.

"It's all right, Anita. I'll see you when the week starts at Mrs. Rosa's."

She nodded at me, lingering for a few seconds more, then walked back down the road.

Just as Florence had predicted, the late-night gathering had young men and women streaming in from the Gibson and Riverside communities to partake in the dancing and fun. Gibson was some five miles south of Hadson, and Riverside lay just as far away to the east. The dancing and laughter could clear one's mind after a week's worth of housework or farm work.

But I would have gladly stayed behind had it not been for Florence's insistence that I put my books aside for the night. I hadn't been back to many gatherings, even when Daniel attempted to drag me to one. Tonight, however, I gave Florence the upper hand and put on my nicer clothes. Florence had sewn a dress for me a few weeks before, and I slipped it on, along with the only pair of shoes I had.

Outside, the breeze and music lifted everyone's spirits. Girls and boys were swinging to the beat of the music. And just like before, memories of my first dance came back. I was flying higher and higher in John's arms . . .

"Anna, stop gapin' at them, wouldya?"

"Gaping at who, Florence? I'm not gaping."

She laughed. "I know you're not, but those men may

think you are. And why is it you had to carry that book out here?"

I shrugged. "I came here. That should be enough for you!"

Florence laughed again as we made our way over to a small gathering of children. They were watching a couple of young men act out a story. As we stood by, watching, a tall man with a thick beard walked up to Florence.

"Hello, lady." Florence greeted her old friend from Gibson with smiles and chatter. After greeting me, he motioned her away so that they could talk awhile.

"You'll be all right by yourself?" she asked me.

"Sure," I said.

I watched her walk away. I watched as Daniel came running into the gathering, searching faces and stopping upon seeing Florence, who was fully engaged, cheerfully, in her conversation with the fellow from Gibson. I watched as he stood there a few seconds then sulked into the crowd of dancers and grabbed a partner, stealing petulant glances at my best friend. I watched as Florence spotted him, stormed over, and started a bout of arguing with him. I watched as their tension peaked and then toppled over into laughter, dancing, and full immersion into a world of love that had been slipping from my own space. As the two of them disappeared into the distance, I sat, turning my eyes to the young men acting out the play for the children. I listened to the children shriek with laughter and gasps, and allowed my thoughts to remain in that moment.

I laughed quietly to myself as one of the young men

whose identity was lost beneath a gray hat fell to the ground as if he'd tripped. A minute or so later, the children were clapping loudly, and soon enough, were being led away from the late-night gathering by older women. I leaned my head against the tree and fell into a light sleep.

All around me I heard a thumping sound, like feet hitting the ground in a rhythmic pattern. Someone was running. Someone was calling my name. Someone was trying to tell me, Let him go, Anna. Let John go. . . .

"Don't think sleepin' was part of the plan when we decided to have this gatherin' tonight."

I opened my eyes and let my surroundings wash away my short dream. Henry stood in front of me, removing the gray hat from his head and wiping sweat from his neck and shoulders. His usual smile broadened his face.

"You were good up there," I told him.

"Thanks!" he said.

"But, I was just about to do some reading."

"Anna, listen. Now, before you say anything else, you must know how lovely you look. I ain't sayin' that just 'cause I wanna, I'm sayin' it 'cause it's the truth, an' I done turned down three women to come dance with you," he said dramatically. "Now, all I'm asking for is this one dance."

He waited with his hand out as I looked at him and pondered. I tried to see someone who caught my interest, someone who made my heart flutter; but I had none of those feelings for him. Nor for anyone else here.

"You stubborn, Anna. It's just a dance!" he said again.

"I guess just one dance wouldn't hurt."

"Great!" Henry said, pulling me up by the arm and leading me to the dance floor.

The two of us took to the floor and moved about until we were out of breath. The jerky twists and turns weren't nearly as exciting and enjoyable as my dance with John. But it lifted my spirits a bit and cleared my mind for a good while. I gratefully took the punch he poured me, and we sat under a tree to rest. Not a word was said while we drank our punch and caught our breath.

"That dance, that was real good, huh?" Henry eventually said. I made a small sound in my throat to indicate my agreement, but this wasn't good enough for Henry. His comments turned into words I had not expected.

"What's wrong with me, Anna? In your eyes, somethin' in me must not be right. I mean, most ladies here wouldn't know what to do if they were with me, but you're different. You're like a stone that stands alone; you're here, but you're somewhere else at the same time. I've been watching you and the way you go about things, and I . . . well, I kinda like you, Anna. But you don't seem too fond of me. Is it somethin' about me? Tell me."

I didn't dare look up, because I was too embarrassed and too angry that I was in this situation. Instead, as I stared at the glass of punch in my hand, I thought about what I could say to make my point without upsetting him.

"Henry, you're a fine man. I don't know why you'd ask me if there was something wrong. That's sure not my place to think or say. But it's just that . . ."

"Just what?"

I looked up at him. His boyish face and manly demeanor caught me off guard. Florence was right: He *was* nice looking.

I reluctantly continued. "I . . . I guess I like you well enough, Henry."

His face lit up like a candle. For a moment, I knew I was staring into the face of someone other than Henry. I saw the fire of freedom in his eyes, I felt the meaning in his touch. I couldn't believe it—it was, it really was . . .

"Anna?"

"Uh-huh," I said quickly with an inaudible sigh. This wasn't John. The touch of his hand was cold, and I wanted to escape it, escape from this man I didn't know well enough. I looked out toward the dance floor, enveloped in my own thoughts as Henry went on about his life and his family.

"So, Anna?"

"Yes?" I said, turning back to Henry. I felt that it was time for me to go, and I searched my mind for a kind way I could leave. Instead, I sat politely still.

"Well, see, Anna, I was saying I'm glad I know now that you really do like me." His excitement brimmed. "And so I've been meaning to tell you how I feel. See, well, I've been thinking, come late summertime, we can get married and raise a big family of our own."

The words came smashing down like a stack of wood. This was all wrong—bitterly wrong. I jumped up so fast that I knew I startled him.

Did I just hear what I think I did?

"M-marriage? I'm just sixteen years old, Henry."

"Well, most these women here get married around your age. So, I thought . . ."

I glared at him with my arms crossed. He looked confused.

"Anna, thought you said you like me well enough?"

"Henry, *no!* Why . . . why do you have to go and ask me something like that? We're friends, Henry, we're . . . we're friends! That's all!"

The shock that showed on his face touched my heart, but not deeply enough for my words to stop spilling forth.

"Why, Henry? Why me?"

He smiled uneasily. "Why not you, Anna? Can't stay unmarried forever. Gotta have some kinda man to—"

"I can stay unmarried forever!" The words came tumbling out angrily, bringing reality to the feeling I had inside that I might not see John again. I brought my voice down to a whisper, avoiding Henry's eyes.

"I can stay like that, Henry, an' I will, as long as . . ." I stopped. I had to stop before I started crying in the presence of this man I called a friend. I felt upset and guilty at the same time. I longed for Henry to chuckle my words away, to say simply that he understood. That what I felt and what I had said were all right. I longed for him to touch my hand, to pat my back, and to let me cry out my grief on his shoulder. But none of that happened.

Henry's eyes were entreating, his jaw set. The shadow of hurt had fallen upon his features. I tried to collect myself and form an apology, wanting to make everything right in that moment and waiting to hear a word or two of comfort from him. Perhaps he wished the same.

Then he did begin to say something.

"Anna, maybe you should think . . ."

I pried my eyes away from his before he could say anything more, crying on the inside for all the things I felt and all the things I missed and all the things I could not say to this man.

I turned and walked away, but still I listened for the questions and shouted words, hoping they wouldn't follow, and hoping, too, that they would. They didn't. Henry stood his ground and let me be, which made running away feel even worse. I told myself I didn't care, that only John mattered. But John wasn't here, and perhaps he never would be. What was I leaving behind, walking away like this?

My walk turned into a run as I sought out a place of seclusion. I allowed my mind to wander, trying to alleviate the pain of John's absence. He'd been away from me for a long time. I began thinking about anything that would help suppress it: Mrs. Rosa, my work, Mama Bessie. Eventually, thoughts of John started finding their way back to where my fears helped bury them.

The wind began to blow hard, biting my face and loosening the grip of my emotions. I collapsed by the tree in Mama Bessie's yard and closed my eyes, dreaming of the man who held my heart.

CHAPTER

44

ONE DAY THAT AUGUST, I STAYED BEHIND AFTER A TUTORING session to talk to Mrs. Rosa about the idea that had been sitting in my heart for a long while.

"Mrs. Rosa, I've been thinking about something. I haven't said anything to you because, well, I couldn't really decide inside myself if this was something I really wanted, and—"

"Tell me what it is, Anna," Mrs. Rosa said, trying to calm my excitement.

"Well, I've decided that I want to make this happen, Mrs. Rosa. I want to start a school. Now, before you object, I just want to tell you that it won't be an actual school building, or anything fancy like that. I can't afford that, anyhow. I just want to teach the children at Mama Bessie's and any other children in Hadson who want, and have the time, to learn."

The thought had been taking shape in my mind, and the more it came into its final form, the more inspired I felt. This was what I had to do with my education. I knew it.

Mrs. Rosa's face melted into a large smile.

"Object? I think that's the most exciting and wonderful

thing I've heard in a while. It's one thing to learn, but to learn and then spread what you know is even better. Anna, how could I say no? It's taken you only a year to learn what it takes most people three or four. Of course, you still have so much to learn, but many of the residents of Hadson can't read or write at all, so you would be starting with basics anyway. What an idea! You just tell me what I can do to help."

I rushed back to Hadson, filled with joy and determination after my discussion with Mrs. Rosa about how to make my school a reality. A year ago I simply wanted my own education, and now here I was, ready to teach others—at an elementary level, at least.

When I returned to the house, I told Mama Bessie, who was in the kitchen cooking, about the plan. She immediately sat down with me to come up with the best time of day and best place to do what I wished.

"You know, Anna, ever since you went off learning like you are, I been prayin' you'd do somethin' like this. Now here you are, ready to teach these younguns round here. What a blessing you are!"

I grinned and said, "If I may say so, Mama Bessie, I'm doing this more for myself than anything. Some urge is just pushing me to do this."

"Well, Anna, it's something that needs to be done, an' God is telling you that. You keep listening, and this school of yours will go far."

I nodded in agreement. We talked as we cooked the rest of the meal.

Not a week later, I stood tall and ready as thirteen small boys and girls sat giggling and squirming on a quilt spread out on the grass outside Mama Bessie's. They ranged in age from five to twelve. Mrs. Rosa and I had put together a teaching plan for them, and now I was getting ready to implement it. Ned sat in the very front and seemed more excited than the rest.

"Miss Anna, we gonna be able to read like you?"

"Miss Anna, can you teach me to write my name?"

"Miss Anna, what if it rains?"

"Be quiet now so Miss Anna can start. If you don't listen up now, she's gonna send you back inside. You don't want that, now, do you?" Mama Bessie's voice echoed from where she sat mending clothes, under the tree. Thirteen no's blew my way as I beamed at them all.

Florence was also out there, keeping order for me as well as she could. Personally, I believed she, too, was out there to learn. What was more, I had convinced Anita to help me teach. She stood by Florence quiet but alert.

The idea was that three times a week, I would teach them for two hours, and I stayed as committed as I could to making those two hours beneficial to every single child. I thought back to when I used to peak into the school building back in Tennessee and tried to mimic the calm, composed manner in which the teacher stood and went about her work. I was surprised at how well the children kept their focus on the lessons.

The hour began with Anita and me writing the alphabet and having the children identify each letter as we told them the different sounds of each one. To make the task easier, we divided the children into two groups, with Anita and me each leading one. I enjoyed the lesson a great deal.

I had believed that breaking through Anita's solemness and convincing her to work with me would be difficult. But the first time I asked her to help me teach, she agreed with a nod even before I could begin to explain the idea in more depth. Her manner altered when she was out there, just as it did when she was with Little Sue. I marveled at the change but didn't comment on it. Florence noticed it too.

"That the same Anita I know?" Florence whispered to me the first day, enjoying the sight of a giggling cluster of girls surrounding Anita's tall form.

As the weeks went by, one or two more children from different families began to show up. The news of my "school" was spreading quickly, and I was excited.

One day I looked up, while the lesson was still in progress, to see I had some visitors standing off to the side. Henry stood looking out at the horizon, and Daniel was leaning against a tree, closer to where we sat.

I hadn't seen Henry since the dance a few months before. I had been pondering how to apologize to him for my response to his marriage proposal. I knew I had been wrong, and if anything, Henry had been looking out for me. Family was of great value in the community. I had to apologize, and now was the time. But when the final child skipped off, proud to have sounded out an entire word with my help, Henry was gone. So I walked up to Daniel instead.

"You mighty busy now, Anna, out here savin' the community by teachin' these kids, workin' wit your own tutor, an' helpin' Mama Bessie out all at the same time. Don't know no one else who could do it all!"

I looked down at my feet, smiling a little. "You make it sound like a lot, brother."

"It is, tho'," he said.

"I guess so. You know, Sebastian, I was thinking that one day, I could get a building for the school. You know, it's nice out here, but this would be more like a school if we were actually under a roof."

"Gotta go one step at a time, sis. You'll get that buildin', jus' like you got yo' education. You got this special way of bringin' to you what you really want."

I shrugged. "Some things."

"Yeah, well, you know, I'm thinkin' 'bout a house right now. We need a home."

He was right. He had been staying with Rodney's relatives, and I had been living at Mama Bessie's for a year and a half now.

"Talked to Henry," Daniel said to me, changing the topic.

I looked away from my brother, recalling our conversations after the night of the dance. I remembered Florence telling me the proposal wasn't so bad and that Henry really cared for me. She didn't understand, but Daniel did, and the only thing my brother had told me that night with a sad smile was that I was one stubborn woman.

"Said he's doin' jus' right fine. Got him a—"

"I've been meaning to apologize to him, Sebastian," I explained quickly, interrupting him.

Daniel put his hand on my shoulder and stared at me until I looked up at him. "It ain't my business, sis," he said with a soft smile. "Don't care if you like that wit all the menfolk you meet!" he said, laughing. The laughter quickly died, however, when I didn't respond.

"Anna, I jus' wanted to tell ya. We've bin here fo' some time. You gotta . . . you gotta live yo' life."

"I am, Daniel!" I whispered harshly, and then more calmly, "Sebastian. Brother, this is my life," motioning to the yard where I held my school sessions.

"I know that, Anna, but—"

"He promised me, Sebastian," I said softly, looking steadily into my brother's eyes. He swallowed, looking back at me, and I turned to walk away, making every effort in the way I walked and the way I held my posture to seem content with my situation. But I was fooling myself, and I knew it. What kind of chance was there that John would find me? I didn't know what I meant by telling Daniel what I did, but I buried the questions and let my concerns blow away on the wind.

CHAPTER

❧ 45 ☙

WITH TWO STRONG BEATS OF TWO MIGHTY WINGS, I WAS HIGH, very high above the shores of my homeland. The wind caressed my face and I was cradled in a woman's arms. African scent, black skin: Mama.

A woman with skin a little lighter, her body a little heavier, began to stroke my hair away from my face, her own brilliant wings sheltering me from the sun's rays: Mary.

Then I stood alone, watching the two women, radiant with light and love, smiling at me, telling me without words to remember my name, Bahati.

With a few beats of their massive, colorful wings, these bare feminine bodies disappeared over the seas and flew across lands, rejoining the trees, the plants, the earth, the animals. . . .

"Sarah!" I heard my name being called, pulling me back to Earth.

"Anna!" Could that be . . . was that . . . *John?*

"Anna!" The loud whisper jolted me awake, pulling me quickly from my dream. I jumped up in time to see Anita pulling open the door and running over to me. Florence had woken up and was staring wide-eyed at Anita. Panic spread like a wildfire through my limbs.

"What is it, Anita?" I asked as Mama Bessie walked through the door with her arms crossed and deep furrows lining her forehead.

"She can't find him, Anna, she can't find him! They're looking for him, but . . . but they can't find him! He came to Mrs. Rosa—"

"Anita!" I whispered loudly, trying to slow her thoughts down, feeling my own heart straining to stay calm. "Anita, who? Who are you talking about?"

"Mrs. Rosa . . . Mrs. Rosa's husband . . ."

My heart paused feeling the tension in her words. I pulled on my clothes, looking over at Florence and then at Mama Bessie. They stood unmoving, concern in their eyes.

"Anita, has Mrs. Rosa been harmed? Where is she?" Anita didn't answer, just stood with her hands around her arms, staring past me. "Anita!"

"She's fine, Anna. She wanted me to find you. She felt you were a part of this, and she needs your company."

I nodded, my heart feeling heavy.

"Anna?" Florence whispered from under her pallet. "Anna, let me see what I can find out around here, and I'll find you two. Where . . . ?"

Florence and I turned questioning eyes to Anita.

"We'll be at my house." Then Anita explained to Florence, as quickly as she could, how to get to the old man's place. Then Anita and I rushed out onto the road, where a wagon was waiting. She gestured in the direction of the driver.

"The old man I live with hired him out. You remember when I came over asking for the medicine after Joshua got sick?"

I nodded.

"He lived through that, but barely so. He's been bedridden to the point where he can't even get up and take his normal morning walks. But I explained to him what happened this evening, and he offered to help in whatever manner he could. He's a good man."

"What did happen, Anita?" I asked her as we pulled off into the night. "You said Mr. Caldwell's missing."

"He didn't come home when he was supposed to, last Thursday evening. Mrs. Rosa waited for two days, hoping he was simply tied up in travel or the like. But it wasn't that."

I clasped my hands together nervously and stared off into the night, afraid of what would come next.

"He came to her earlier this evening, Anna. He used the back entrance and their code to tell her there was trouble. She only saw him for a few minutes, but . . . there was blood on his face and hands."

I caught a sob that had tried to escape my throat, and listened on in silence.

"He told Mrs. Rosa he didn't have long, that he didn't know how the night would end. He said that she was safe— and that he wanted her to wait at home for him for at least a few hours. No one saw him approach the house—but he said he was on the run. Some person had been tipped off that through his work, Mr. Caldwell was helping runaways."

"What?" I asked in disbelief. "Was he really doing that kind of work, Anita?"

"I don't know, Anna. But regardless, Mr. Caldwell said they had no real proof. He said it was also possible that somebody had found out about his black blood, but he wasn't sure."

"But he was bleeding, Anita—"

"Anna, let me tell it all. A few folks had found his book he was trying to put into print under a different name, and traced it back to him. Some of his close friends were baffled by it all, but figured that they could protect him from whomever had it in their minds to attack him, but Mr. Caldwell said he knew better than that. He knew angry folks would come after him, would find him, and that's exactly what happened. He left Mrs. Rosa's just as quickly as he came, and now we don't know where he is, or . . . or if he's even alive, Anna."

"How do you know all of this, Anita?" I asked, disregarding her last comment and trying to keep my head on straight.

"I was there. Mrs. Rosa doesn't live that far from where I stay. The first night Mr. Caldwell didn't come home, she came by, asking me to stay with her and Little Sue until Mr. Caldwell came back home, just in case he needed her and she had to leave her child. I did what I had to for the old man but stayed at Mrs. Rosa's, thinking nothing of it. It had happened at least twice before, Mr. Caldwell not returning the night he'd promised and Mrs. Rosa calling on me to watch Little Sue. I didn't see him, Anna, so I can't say how bad he really was. But I could hear him fairly well."

"And you said there are folks looking for him now?"

She nodded. "I believe Mrs. Rosa already had a plan for this. There are a few men that Mr. Caldwell knows fairly well in Hadson, and Mrs. Rosa called on them to help look. I believe your brother's among them."

"Where is Mrs. Rosa now?"

"Where we're headed, the old man's place. The lot of us agreed that, even though Mr. Caldwell told her she was in no danger, it might be safer for her and Little Sue to stay somewhere else until he's found."

We fell silent and didn't mutter another word until we pulled up to the house.

"There she is," Anita said softly, nodding toward the figure of a woman leaning against the porch rail with a small child fast asleep in her arms.

We walked up the steps and stood on either side of our tutor. She looked frozen in place as she gazed out onto the old man's land.

"Mrs. Rosa," I said softly, placing a hand on hers.

She took a deep breath, blew it out, and turned to me.

"Anna, I don't know where he is. I don't know how serious it is." She glanced down at her palm, and I followed her eyes to see a small spot of dried blood she hadn't washed away. The tears I saw in her eyes made my own swell. Her hand balled into a tight fist. "A bunch of angry folks found out about his work, the things he wrote in that book of his, maybe even about his blood. I know they're after him."

"You know exactly who it is that's after him, Mrs. Rosa?"

She shrugged. "I know the type of men who wouldn't like the work my husband was doing. I don't know any names or faces, but I know the type." She turned to Anita, then to me. "But where is he, Anita? Anna?" I looked in her eyes and saw flames. They were threatening, something I had never seen in her before.

"Mrs. Rosa, they'll find him." But I knew that my words would be buried under the haunting images that sat in our minds.

Anita's house was very large and sat in solitude amid an expanse of wheatgrass that was hard to make out in the dark. I imagined that the old man hired workers to tend to the fields.

Once inside the home, we climbed the staircase to Anita's room and sat near the window. Mrs. Rosa tucked her baby under the quilt that was spread over Anita's bed. Anita herself sat anxiously in a rocking chair, and Mrs. Rosa sat on the bed with me, very still. The flames in her eyes had died down, and she sat looking out the window with a regal calmness as if she were gazing at her past.

She must be listening for his whispers in the wind, waiting for him to tell her that he's safe.

I sat by Anita, who had dozed off, and tried to figure out what I could say to Mrs. Rosa. I soon arranged words of sympathy and opened my mouth to speak, but Mrs. Rosa's soft voice broke through the air before I could.

"He didn't come home, Anna, until earlier tonight. Came and left before I could really understand . . ."

"I know, Mrs. Rosa. Anita explained it all."

"Not many folks in Dayton know who he is—that he's a black man striving for some social change. That's why we live like we do. That's why he can do so many things in the town, while acting as if he were white. That's why I stay away from making myself known to everyone. But he told you all of that already," she said, looking at me for the first time. Her eyes were strangely clear.

"This happened before, Anna. When we first came here to live in the North, we shared the dream of helping our people. I built false dreams around him, believing that the story of broken black lives and families being torn apart was something outside my own life and experience. It wouldn't happen to me. We were educated folks, and we thought we knew what we were doing." She wiped away a tear.

"But they took him then, and I was jolted back into the reality of life. It scared me, Anna, seeing him beaten like he was, hearing the disbelief in his voice that he had come so close to being sold down south. So, I built new dreams, especially when Little Sue came along, and found my freedom in something else. But Anna"—she turned to me—"Caldwell is my heart. He's foolish but brilliant. I don't know—" Desperate knocking rang out, interrupting Mrs. Rosa. Anita woke without hesitation and swept downstairs to answer the door. A few minutes later, she rushed back in, her face drowning in anxiety. Following her was a middle-aged man who labored under the weight of Mr. Caldwell's unconscious body, which he held in his arms. Mr. Caldwell's left shoulder was wrapped in a bloody rag, and a large gash ran from the top of what remained of his right ear, down his neck. My body shook, but I lifted Little Sue's sleeping body and took her out of the room, catching a glimpse of Mrs. Rosa's face before I left. She was already at Mr. Caldwell's side, her lips trembling and her eyes frantically examining his bruises and wounds.

I stayed with Little Sue, attempting to soothe her back to sleep when she awoke from her nightmarish dreams every now and then. When Anita came in to rock the child, I hurried to see whether Mr. Caldwell's condition had improved.

I watched silently as Hadson's doctor worked at Mr. Caldwell's side. A few of the young men who had searched stayed for a little while, then left, slipping back into the night. My brother was one of the young men who stayed.

Soon Florence arrived. She offered to sit with Little Sue until the child fell asleep so that Anita and I could be with Mrs. Rosa. She sat quietly, all of her attention focused fully on the still figure lying on the bed.

Life seemed to hold its breath in the room as the doctor operated on Mr. Caldwell. The doctor occasionally asked us to dispose of bloody rags he dropped in a bucket by his feet, and we did so anxiously, trying to replace our fear with hope. Hours passed, but they felt like minutes slowly trickling by.

As the first light of dawn came through the window, Mr. Caldwell opened his eyes.

"Rose," he called out weakly. Mrs. Rosa grabbed his hand in hers. The doctor respectfully left the room.

"I'm here, Caldwell. You're awake again. Stay with me this time. Stay here, please. Stay with me."

"Rose, Rosa, I made a mistake. I wasn't as careful as you told me"—he coughed, then continued—"as you told me to be. Why is it that we don't listen to the best advice a soul could give?" He tried to muster a smile as he brought his right hand up to her face and stroked her cheek with his finger.

"Caldwell, don't you worry about that now. The doctor—" She paused, and sniffed. "You're still with us. You're awake!"

His attempted smile fell away. "What did the doctor say, Rose?"

Mrs. Rosa only looked at him, her mouth slightly open. A few tears slipped out, and she squeezed her eyes shut for a moment. Mr. Caldwell coughed again and brought a finger to his lips.

"Don't do that, Rose. We all come here and we all go at some point."

"No, no, Caldwell, it doesn't matter at all what the doctor says."

"Rose, please, it's all right."

She nodded, wiping her eyes.

"Tell Anna to . . . to be careful, to think carefully about what she . . . what she chooses to do. This work can be dangerous," he managed to say through his coughs.

"She's right here, Caldwell. You tell her yourself."

I walked over and stood next to where Mrs. Rosa knelt.

"Anna!" He paused, and I saw his swollen eyes creep up to Mrs. Rosa's face. He was trying so hard to be his own, funny self. "Anna, we deserve justice and peace. Don't give up the fight for those things."

"Caldwell!" Mrs. Rosa scolded his fickleness, though a tender smile softened her face.

He coughed again, and Mrs. Rosa laid a hand on his chest. After a minute, he continued.

"We all fight in different ways. I heard you are educating youth, Anna. That's . . . that's a fight. Not so dangerous as my work, but . . ." He paused to catch his breath. I saw the veins in Mrs. Rosa's neck thicken.

"Caldwell, rest now, she understands."

"But," he continued, "important nonetheless. That's a wonderful thing, Anna. But be careful if you choose to do other things with . . . with your education. I don't want you to end up . . ." His words trailed off and he turned to Mrs. Rosa.

"Rose, you keep this one here nurtured with strong support. And Anna." He slowly raised his hand toward me. He was too exhausted to turn again and look my way.

"Yes, sir?" I asked loudly enough for him to hear me. My mouth was dry.

Hearing me, he dropped his hand and said, "You take care of my Rose and Sue, you and Miss Anita, there. I . . . I heard she's good with the little one. And for my little girl—Rose,

Rose please let her grow up like we talked about. Whisper in her small ear each night how much I love her. Let her know her father—its through her that I'll stay alive."

Mrs. Rosa whimpered, her free hand quickly rising to her mouth. "Caldwell, please! You're a strong person. Stay here, please, I know you can. I know it!"

"Strong . . . ah, well." Though he struggled to speak, he still tried to keep his tone light and good-humored. He closed his eyes for a moment. I saw Mrs. Rosa's hand tighten around his.

"Sometimes strength is letting go. They're . . . they're angered by the truths that I put out there, but at least I put them out, and that's . . . that's strength, Rose," Mr. Caldwell mumbled with his eyes still closed.

"Who's angry, Caldwell?" Mrs. Rosa asked, wiping away the blood that had trickled past his lips.

"No matter. They try to strike fear within us, but it doesn't work that way. We cannot fall into the hands of fear that easily."

"They're good for nothing, all of them!" Mrs. Rosa said angrily as she ran her hand across his forehead. Silence drifted in and sat for a while before Mrs. Rosa chased it away.

"You're wrong for this, you know, Caldwell, for writing the book, and putting yourself in this position. But in all your wrongness, there's nothing you could've done that would've been more right. I'd never sit here and condemn you for what you have done. But Caldwell"—she was crying now—"Caldwell we need you here. . . ."

"Rose." He struggled even with this simple word.

She touched her lips to his and told him to hush. His eyes opened once more, and he drew on his last stores of strength and spoke.

"Rose, they don't know about you or Little Sue. You will be . . . just fine."

"Caldwell . . . Caldwell, don't, please don't leave us."

He brought his finger slowly to her lips. "Shh. You've always been so strong, Rose. Stay that way."

"Caldwell . . ."

"Let me . . . let me rest, Rose. My work won't die with me, I promise you. My love for you won't . . . won't . . ."

Mrs. Rosa's breathing was rough and quick. She grasped his hand with both of hers and brought her face close to his as his eyes fell shut. She kneeled, leaned her head against his, and whispered to her husband through her sobs.

"Caldwell, do you remember the fields of flowers? The starry nights? Do you remember . . ." She climbed up to lie next to him and kissed his cheek.

"Caldwell." Her tears soaked into the blood on his shirt as her whimpers grew louder, and her whispers softer.

Anita took me by the arm, and we left the room.

Mrs. Rosa didn't tutor for the first few weeks after Mr. Caldwell died. Not many people knew Mr. Caldwell— or Mrs. Rosa, for that matter—but word passed quickly through the town, and the incident, however vaguely understood, sat heavily in the hearts of many people.

It was another injustice done—another injustice to talk about, to sweat over in midnight meetings, and to tempt the impulse to strike back.

A week after Mr. Caldwell passed, I made my way to Mrs. Rosa's house. I found her trying very hard to hold on to her reserved, strong nature. Even through her tears that she told me were always necessary in times of grief, she maintained her focus. There was food to cook and a baby to care for, and she had books to read if the loss weighed too heavily on her soul. Anita and I agreed to tend Little Sue when we could as a way of helping Mrs. Rosa. She opposed strongly at first, holding tight to her child as if she had nothing else left in the world, but Anita knew just how to pluck the child away. And, on her own, Little Sue began calling me Auntie Anna.

This assistance gave Mrs. Rosa the time she needed to gather herself. She started speaking of work, although she and Mr. Caldwell had saved a good amount of money. She'd speak of working as a nanny, or as a housekeeper in the city, but she pursued neither.

Without the structured schedule of tutoring at Mrs. Rosa's, I was not always certain how to proceed with my day. But my lessons continued informally. When Mrs. Rosa felt up to it, on the days I went to see her, she'd greet me at the door and would pull me over to the table. During those visits, we'd pour through lessons like we had before Mr. Caldwell's death. I also continued to run my own school in the yard, or in Mama Bessie's kitchen on cold or rainy days.

In this manner, three trying months slid by.

CHAPTER

❧ 46 ❧

SOMEHING ABOUT THE DAY DID NOT SEEM RIGHT. IT WAS ONE of those days when I could look up at the winter sky and feel something odd in my bones. I thought that maybe it was a touch of the sadness I still felt over the death of Mr. Caldwell. Or that I was fearful, given that injustice had struck so violently and so close to home. Whatever it was, I tried to dismiss the feeling.

Daniel had picked up a job with a local lumber company, but he continued transporting ice to the cities for extra money. He decided that morning, because his deliveries were light, that he'd take me with him to the city.

At one of the few stops he had all day, Daniel asked me to watch the wagon while he went inside. The streets were not busy, almost empty in fact, so I decided to walk around near the wagon, just to stay warm.

I don't know what possessed me to turn, pick up the discarded newspaper, and look at the half-soiled page. Perhaps it was my excitement in finding a newspaper I didn't have to pay for. But whatever the reason, one minute I was sitting idly, thinking of the nice school I would have one day, and the next, I was staring at the words that screamed at me from the page. I felt something unseen pulling the breath from my lungs like a ribbon from my hair. It read:

RUNAWAY
FOUND, KILLED

Negroman JOHN, runaway about 6 feet 2 inches in height, strong build, found and killed. Ran away from Williams's plantation, Tennessee. Runaway found by Horace Finch and shot dead in river on his property in Kentucky. Nov. 15, 1823, reward of $25 paid to Mr. Finch for death of slave JOHN.

I couldn't find my breath. I was only vaguely aware of Daniel saying my name over and over and of him steering me back into the wagon without calling attention to us. Then I passed out. I don't remember doing so, and when Daniel recounted it to me later, I denied the whole event. I didn't believe it; I couldn't believe it. Daniel spoke to me about the ad, later, and Florence came up behind him, trying to explain to me that John was dead, but I merely laughed in her face. She didn't know what she was saying, how could she know? She didn't even know John. It wasn't her that he promised he'd see again.

I told her this. "You're wrong. That can't be right, can't you see?"

I couldn't understand their blank faces.

"Daniel?" I questioned my brother. He knew for sure. But my brother simply told me that Florence was right. John was dead; it was the truth.

"But Daniel, how could you say this? *You? You* were there, Daniel, you should understand!"

"Anna, listen," he started.

"How can I listen when you won't tell the truth!" I shouted out at him, tears watering my eyes. Then Mama Bessie's hand touched my shoulder, and she handed me that paper, those false newspaper words, that thing straight from hell. And again, the words came, the truth, the comforting sighs, and this time—this time I listened . . . the veil lifted.

They're right.

I raced off into the starless night. The cold, shooting through my body like the white man's bullet, was a blessing. Maybe, just maybe, it would steal me away to death, too.

If Daniel hadn't found me out by the lake, teardrops frozen on my face, I think my soul would have disappeared before daylight. But he did: Daniel found me. I didn't want to see him—not at first, at least. I didn't want to see anyone, and I think he knew that. But he was there, nonetheless. Back at Mama Bessie's he sat with me late into the night. I didn't want anyone else there.

It was nighttime, or very early morning, when I picked up my writing tool. I should have been sleep, but sleep just wouldn't come, not then. I felt broken. Fate had pointed its long finger at my name. So I sat by candlelight and pulled out a small journal Mrs. Rosa had given me.

One more year. One more year, I'd say, if yesterday was today. One more year I'd hold this hope, so sure, this love, still pure. I'd ask my mind, "How long do memories stay?" And I'd ask my heart, "Can you hold on just one more day?" But today, I sit silently. Tears won't even come. I sit and I wait and I listen. If he is dead, his spirit will come. It must come!

But alas! I heard nothing, I saw nothing, I felt nothing. A tear finally did come, followed by a symphony of rain down my cheeks.

Why can't I feel his death? And why does hate come so easily? I hate them for drowning my soul and taking a life needed here in the world. But Mama's words burn like hellfire in my ears. "Love beats it every time. Love kills hate every single time. Love lives on till the end."

Well, I ask, Mother, is this the end?

CHAPTER

❧ 47 ❧

AFTER HEARING OF JOHN'S DEATH, I WANTED TO GIVE UP ON all I did, all I had. John was gone, and in his memory lived a part of me that was now gone too.

But I realized I had to go on, for Daniel, for Florence, for the children who now depended so much on me and my words of encouragement. I had to move on for the part of myself that was still present, conscious, and alive. The part still proclaiming, this is not the end.

December rolled by, and I found myself in the year 1824: another year in this freedom land. January and February flew past me without my recognition. I made it my purpose to come closer to God and to myself. I had always gone to church, every single week, but this was different. I sank far down into myself, listening closely to what was inside. Beyond the sadness, beyond the fear of what lay ahead of me, I sought out a place within where God sat. I prayed blindly to God and to that peace I knew was in my spirit. I devoted my time to teaching, finding joy in the students' smiles and determined faces. And somewhere in all of this, I found a small hope, hovering somewhere in me. What was it that I was hoping for? I didn't know.

I tried in every manner at first, after John died, to avoid Mrs. Rosa. Something about sharing pity didn't strike me well, and I felt it would be best if I kept my distance. But soon enough, I couldn't escape the pull of Mrs. Rosa. She was like a mother to me, and I found myself eventually scurrying back to her house, back into the world I felt so comfortable in. When I went back the first time, after many months, she welcomed me with open arms and dried my tears even before they fell.

Mrs. Rosa helped me, more than anyone, with my growth. I was able to set a piece of my heart in her hands for healing.

"These books have been sitting, waiting for you, Anna." I nodded. "I can see your heart crying riverbeds of tears, but things will be all right. Sometimes, I've got to remind myself of that, but deep down, I know it to be the truth."

"How'd you know what happened, Mrs. Rosa?" I looked at her tired eyes and thought she had gained some years in just the few months since Mr. Caldwell's death. She still had the same patient, dignified composure, however, and I was easily enfolded into her wings.

"Your friend—Florence, I believe—she stopped by to speak with me. She figured you hadn't been by in a while and wanted to explain things to me."

"I'm sorry, Mrs. Rosa. I just haven't felt quite like myself."

She drew her arms around me and held me close for a long while. My tears spilled on her shoulder and she wiped them away.

"Anna, they are seasons, that's all," she said. "Life is littered with them. The springs and summers—they're so hot, so safe, so beautiful. But then . . ." She stopped as Little Sue, who had been sleeping on a pillow in the corner, clutching her bean baby doll, lifted her sleepy head to her mother and blinked twice.

"See daddy?" the little girl asked, lifting her arms, so Mrs. Rosa could pick her up. Mrs. Rosa walked over and lifted her up, then sat back down with the child on her lap.

"Daddy?" the child asked again, but it seemed more habit than a real question, as if her dreams were filled with images of a person who had been stolen from her reality. Little Sue laid her head on Mrs. Rosa's shoulder with a whimper and closed her eyes again as her mother stroked her hair.

"Shh, Little Sue," Mrs. Rosa said softly. Then she turned back to me. "But then the falls with their chills, and the winters with their bareness and freezing condemnations must come and go as well. But it's all meant to cycle onward. That's what life's about, Anna."

In the days that followed, I let Mrs. Rosa's words sit in my mind so I could consider them.

Florence's reaction differed from Mrs. Rosa's. She worried about me the most. At first, she just couldn't understand, despite my painful attempts to explain. She felt it was her duty to bring me back across the separation I had created. But her attempts only frustrated her, pushing me farther into my corner. She confronted Daniel about me when she thought I wasn't paying attention, and labored over the "right words to say."

"Give her a little bit of time," I'd hear my brother say. "Anna will find her way back. You'll see."

Daniel was right. After I swam in my grief for a while, I finally chose to come up for air, for good. Then, Florence settled back down.

"You seem different, Anna," she said to me one day in early March. "It's almost like you left for a long time an' came back as someone new, or just . . . just a little different from before."

I shrugged and smiled. "What's so different? I still look like me, I still act like me," I said calmly, knowing that all those physical things made no difference. I knew that my feelings had changed me.

Florence looked at me closely. "You're, well, I don't have no words for it," she said, throwing her hands up.

But I wasn't the only aspect of her life that had changed. She and Daniel were growing very close. She'd taken well to Daniel's proposal that she accompany him to the Hadson community meetings, even though she'd always swear it was a waste of time. She'd try to persuade me to accompany them every week, but I preferred my solitude and went with them to the meetings only once in a while. Later on, I'd look up and see Florence strolling back through Mama Bessie's door, exhausted, exclaiming that she would never go to one of the Hadson meetings again. But she did go, and I found out that her complaints about the meetings really were only an act.

"Florence? Don't mind what she say to you, Anna, she loves them meetins! She found herself a voice she ain't neva

434

had befo', an' oh what a loud, strong voice she got. Don't let her fool you," Daniel told me.

I laughed. "You're not fooling anybody either, Daniel. That glow in your eyes shows me that there are other things running through your mind about that lovely friend of mine."

Daniel shrugged but smiled warmly. "Life gonna bring what's it's got to bring. Guess at some time, you gotta learn to accept that good that do come round."

I heard him well and wondered why he hadn't already put his words to use and asked for her hand.

CHAPTER

❧ 48 ❧

IT WAS MARCH 20, 1824, A BEAUTIFUL SATURDAY AFTERNOON. The trees and flowers were blooming and the birds sang sweet melodies to the cool breeze. But I wasn't outside.

HAPPY BIRTHDAY MIS ANNA

When I awoke that morning, I found these words carved into a wooden food tray in Mama Bessie's kitchen. I smiled to myself and looked up to see small, mischievous faces peeking out from around the walls.

"What is this?" I called out with a laugh. The faces suddenly popped out, and twenty small children gathered around me, excited.

"Sebastian says it's your birthday today."

I looked up in the doorway to see my brother and Florence grinning. "My birthday?"

"You said you was born when the flowers started bloomin'—I figured this was a mighty fine day for that to be," Daniel said with a shrug.

"C'mon with us," the two of them said. I followed them out the door, and twenty pairs of feet followed in my footsteps.

"Hey!" Daniel called out as we neared the church. "Our

schoolteacher's a year older!" It was clear that some of the townsfolk had gathered for some festivities after a church gathering. The people in the churchyard gradually ceased their talking and called out cheers instead. I laughed and thanked the crowd, stepping toward Daniel to whisper how unnecessary I thought all of that was.

"Unnecessary, maybe, but you sho' deserve it," he said as everyone trickled back into their own affairs. The children had spread about among the people, having lost interest in the morning surprise.

"Well, I thank you, anyway. You sure deserve that much," I said, hugging my brother.

"I've already gotten what I deserve," he said, pulling Florence close to him. Florence smiled like a child.

I had planned to spend the day at Mrs. Rosa's, but I found her immersed in the activities here at Hadson's church. I, too, melted into the activities in the churchyard. I talked, wandered about, and watched the children play games. I listened to the music and admired the dancing that had naturally sprung up. I sat down with Mrs. Rosa beneath the canopy of a tree, watching Little Sue play with the other children.

Here I was, learning to live with the part of me I had left. Here I was, consumed in the love this family had to offer me. Here I was watching the two people closest to me: Daniel and Florence. Here I was, confined within my contented solitude.

A tap on my shoulder interrupted my thoughts.

"Anna, hey! Congratulations about this day." Henry addressed me, all smiles.

I hadn't seen Henry for months and hadn't talked to him for perhaps just as long. Florence had told me he was again, spending significant time with another lady. Out of the corner of my eye, I saw Mrs. Rosa inch away from us.

"Also came over to say I'm sorry," Henry continued.

Why is he sorry? Shouldn't I be the one apologizing?

"Heard about your friend, Anna."

"You did?" I asked him, a bit concerned that folks knew I had known a man from a plantation in the South.

"Ya, heard someone you really cared for died—that's what I heard." I nodded up at Henry, glad that he'd heard nothing about John having been a runaway.

"Well, I thank you for that, Henry."

"Are you . . . you doin' all right?" he asked.

"Yes," I said, "I think this part of me is doing real well."

He kneeled by me in silence as I began to pour out what had been on my mind for too long.

"Henry, I know this was a long time ago and all, but I have to apologize to you for responding like I did back at that dance—"

"Naw, Anna, don't apologize. There's no need to. I . . . I guess I can understand now." He sighed, then looked into my eyes. He really did have a genuine spirit. All the uneasiness I felt before was gone.

"I should've done something different, that's all," he said, holding my gaze.

"No, Henry, it wasn't you," I explained, shaking my head.

"Yes, it was me, Anna. I should've . . . I thought . . . if

I had . . ." He stopped and awoke from his reverie. "But, anyway, that was then, and you were right, it was a while ago. Don't want you feelin' bad, Anna. You see Hattie-Mae over there?" I looked over to where he nodded and recognized Hattie-Mae. She stood talking with a drink in her hand and was obviously pregnant.

"That's Hattie-Mae Johnson now. She's my wife."

I smiled at Henry, wondering how I'd missed word of the marriage. I felt a subtle sadness creep up on me, and I had to scold myself for allowing it to.

"That's great, Henry. Seems like you've already started that family you wanted."

He nodded. "One more thing before we leave," he said, standing up and reaching into his back pocket to retrieve a gift. It was a flower—small, simple, and beautiful.

"Here, happy birthday. It was the best I could do when I was tryin' to find something to represent . . . well, to represent the person you are, guess I could say." He lowered his voice a bit and bent forward, looking at his feet first, then into my eyes. "You a good person, Anna, an' always gonna be special in here." He patted his chest. "You a friend, or whateva you wanna call it."

He brushed grass off his pants and remarked with a chuckle, "Look, that flower matches your dress."

I took the flower and placed it in my hair.

"Oh, an' you teachin' is such a big thing in Hadson. Proud you done that for the community. Maybe you can teach our child too."

"Of course, Henry, thank you," I said as he retreated. I

felt relieved, more so than I thought I'd feel after talking to Henry. Both of our burdens seemed to have been lifted.

"I have a gift for you, Anna," Anita said to me as we finished up teaching for the day, a few days after my birthday celebration. She looked at me with her characteristic solemnness.

"From you?" I asked Anita, surprised.

"No, no," she said, shaking her head. "I said that wrong. It's not from me. I wish I could give something this significant, but it's a gift from the old man."

"How is he?"

She shrugged. "He's pretty bad off. I don't think he'll be around much longer."

"What is it that he wanted to give me?" I asked her.

"Don't get too excited—"

"Anita, tell me!" I shouted.

She chuckled without smiling. "He wants to build that school of yours. He said it would be good for the community. What do you think?"

I stared at Anita with wide eyes. "He's building us a school?"

"Sure is," Anita said. "He's hiring out a few young men around Hadson to build it. He wants you to select a good plot of land, and he'll have the school built."

I walked closer to her, not quite believing what I was hearing. She stood with her hand on her hips, waiting for my questions.

"Anita, I've never even met Old Joshua."

She responded, "That's right, but I told you, he's the reason I've been with Mrs. Rosa all these years. He's been stuck on the idea of education the whole time I've known him. When he heard what I told him about you, and how I came out to teach a few days a week, he wanted to give what he could before he dies. He'll take care of the building, the desks, and even the outhouse for the girls and the boys. Whatever else is needed, like books and such, that's something you—or we—have to take care of."

I shook my head in wonder.

"But the money for the supplies is no problem. We get the money from the church, sometimes, and I don't think charging the children who have parents 25 cents a month is a bad idea," Anita said.

"Is he really talking the truth, Anita?" I asked her, excitement traveling up and down my spine.

"Sure," she said simply.

"Please tell him how grateful I am!" I said to her.

Anita nodded. "I'll see you in a couple of days," she said, turning to walk away.

"Oh, Anita!" I said, calling her back after I had shaken away some of the shock.

"What if . . . what if older folks want to start learning?"

"Then we'll figure that out."

"I can't believe this!" I said with a large smile.

She turned back around quickly, but not before I saw the corners of her mouth curl up in a small smile.

CHAPTER

❧ 49 ❧

"Hey, Anna," Mrs. Rosa said, answering the door with a tired smile.

"Hi, Mrs. Rosa. I know it's a bit early, but I—" The door came open wider.

"Don't explain to me, Anna. I'd let you in here even in the early hours of the morning—you know that. I'm up, the baby's awake. We haven't seen you in a while, and Little Sue's been asking about you."

I stepped into the house behind Mrs. Rosa. I had errands Mama Bessie needed me to run, but I had news for Mrs. Rosa and wanted to share it all before I began my day.

Mrs. Rosa returned to her desk and to the plate of food that sat there. I saw Little Sue tumbling around on the floor, amusing herself. I laughed at the spectacle.

"Auntie numba two!" the little girl said, running over to me and throwing her arms around my legs. I twirled her around, then let her continue playing.

"Mrs. Rosa, I wanted to tell you about the school building that's being built, but I'm sure Anita's already shared that."

Mrs. Rosa nodded.

"Have you gone by to see the plot of land? They haven't done much with it, but oh, I feel so good inside, like . . . like I know for sure this is the right thing to do for Hadson!"

Mrs. Rosa returned my smile. "I haven't seen it yet, Anna, but I will. And I can't tell you how proud I am of you—you and Anita. I know if Caldwell were here, he'd feel the same. Actually, speaking of your school, and of Caldwell, I have something for you." She hopped up and left the room. When she came back, she was grasping something.

"He didn't make it to give this to you, but he wanted you to have it." She held out a glass jar filled with coins.

"Mrs. Rosa, I can't take this. You need it!" I said, without moving to take it.

"No. We have what we need, Anna, all we need. Caldwell started saving this for the school. You should have seen the man when I told him of your idea. He talked of what you've done for this community with a pride he hardly even attached to his own work. So use it for the school."

I shook my head.

"Mrs. Rosa, this school has already received so many blessings. I don't need this to keep it moving forward! You keep it, if not for yourself, then as my gift to Little Sue."

Mrs. Rosa smiled at me and shook her head. "You know, you've grown so much in such a short time."

"Well, thank you, Mrs. Rosa."

"It's the truth. But please"—she extended the jar toward me—"accept Caldwell's gift. He left us with money, Anna—he knew he had to." I took it from her, and let it rest in the crook of my arm.

"How did you earn your money before, Mrs. Rosa?"

She sat back down.

"You were paid for tutoring?" I asked, perplexed.

"Of course I was! That was my job."

"But I didn't pay you anything."

Her smile was broad and warm. A sight I hadn't seen in a long time.

"You were different. You paid me with your will to learn and your success. Peggy's folks paid, and the old man took care of Anita. I believe they're related some way, but I've never found out her story. Perhaps if someone hadn't pushed either of those girls to get educated, they would not have."

"What about Peggy?" I asked.

"When I stopped for a while, her mother put her in the school in Dayton—the same one Caldwell told me he first saw you at. After that, she didn't want to come back."

"Well, Mrs. Rosa, I actually came here to ask you something about working. You think, maybe, you'd enjoy teaching? Anita and I spoke about it. We thought, with Mr. Caldwell not being here and all, you might enjoy sitting in a classroom with plenty of students." Mrs. Rosa averted her eyes at the mention of her husband.

"You'd like me to teach?"

I nodded. Her hands, which had been busy, now sat motionless before her.

"But you don't need me, do you?"

"Word has spread about the school, Mrs. Rosa, especially with the building being under way and all. I have almost every child in town coming to learn. Not only that, but the church funds dedicated to this school are split so that Anita and I receive a certain portion of that money. And some parents sacrifice some of their hard-earned money every month to pay me for doing this. But now, see, some of the grown folks in Hadson want to learn, and they offered to pay me, but I can't do all of that on my own, Mrs. Rosa. I wanted to know if you wouldn't mind coming to teach them."

Mrs. Rosa absorbed my request before stepping over to me and throwing her arms around my neck. Little Sue laughed with delight, seeing her mother's sudden excitement.

"Anna, Anna! This is perfect!" She, too, laughed. "My heart has always been in teaching, tutoring. But without Caldwell as my connection to the world, it seemed unlikely that I could continue. I thought I would have to work in a house in the city to provide us with income. Anna, you don't know what this means to me. Thank you!"

I let my thoughts drift into their own patterns. The tension that I had felt locked up in my chest for weeks had been alleviated.

Walking back down the road that morning, I thought about how there seemed to be a place for Mrs. Rosa in my heart right next to Mathee and Mary. I thought of my brother and of Florence, who would lay down their lives for me. That was love: There was a freedom in that.

I let the tears fall as I thought of Mr. Caldwell and John, who died for causes they believed in. That was determination against all odds: There was freedom in that.

I held my hands to the sky, remembering that, a few short years ago, I couldn't even pick up a pen to write the letter *a*. That was education: There was freedom in that.

And my feet, they carried me where I wanted to go, bound to no chains of bondage: There was freedom in that.

I smiled to the skies as I made my way back home, thanking God.

That moment gave me peace inside my soul: In that, too, there was freedom.

CHAPTER

❧ 50 ❧

THE OLD MAN DIED BEFORE HE COULD SEE THE FINISHED PRODUCT of his investment. It took a little longer than expected to actually purchase the land and, then, to actually build the school. But by the middle of July, the stacked wood and cleared land had been transformed into a small but beautiful school building. God was answering my prayers.

One afternoon, walking back to the house from the place in the yard where school had been held, I stopped when I saw a figure sitting on a bench. It was Daniel.

I collapsed next to him, tired from the day's work.

"The school's done," I said to him, wiping away the raindrops that fell on my eyelids.

"Sho' is. Lookin' nice, too."

I turned toward him.

"What's wrong, Daniel? And don't say 'nothing,' brother, I know you better than that."

"It's 'bout time fo' me to get married," he said simply, but I could tell he wanted to hear what I had to say.

"I think that time was a few months ago."

His mouth laughed, but the rest of him didn't. "Ya," he

said, nodding. "Woulda married her a long time ago, but she tell me, 'wait till September.'"

I laughed. "What's so special about September that makes it any different from March or May?"

He shrugged, then grinned. "She's jus' like that. You know her!"

"Sure I do." I smiled back.

"It's a different thing, Anna, likin' somebody like that. Things I used to think an' say, I don't really think an' say no more. Lots a things I wouldn't do fo' no one 'cept you an' Mama, now it's the same wit her. An' it's a different kinda feelin'."

I felt starved for that feeling, too. But this was not my time to talk, it was his.

"Then you gets to thinkin' 'bout a family, an' makin' money to buy Flo things she needs, an' then . . ." He laughed at himself. "*Then* you gets to thinkin' 'bout how a chile gonna come round. You think 'bout him growin' inside, an' bein' born, an' him bein' set in your hands fo' the first time. You look down at a little face, thinkin' you starin' at your own self in a mirror! Changes you, Anna. Cain't think like I used to. Gonna be callin' myself a husband fo' my Flo, an' gonna be a pappy fo' a little boy or girl gonna grow up an' ask, 'Auntie Anna, my daddy, was he a bad chile when he was my age?'"

I laughed with my brother, but then settled into seriousness.

"And then it gots me thinkin' 'bout my pappy, what he was like, how he treat womenfolk, if he felt like I did when he seen Mama. Got me thinkin', what would he be like if he was still livin'? What would he say to my children? What would he say to me? You think he be proud've me, the man I am?" Daniel asked me solemnly.

"Of course he would, Daniel. Of course."

He sighed and stared at the mud running between our feet. After a while, he took his shirt, which lay across his lap, and threw it in my face. I laughed, pulled it away, and hit him with it. We could've been little children again, running around barefoot back on the plantation in Tennessee.

"It's for the rain," he said.

"Well, then, don't throw it in my face like that!" I laughed some more, and held his shirt over my head as he continued.

"Then, Anna, I think about you."

"Me? For what, Daniel?"

He glanced at me quickly, then away again. "Jus' a little worried 'bout you, that's all." I would have laughed at his comment, but his face was stonelike.

"Worried? Daniel—"

"I can hear you, Anna, sayin' 'I'll be fine.' An' I know you will."

"So, what you so worried about?"

"Anna, same's you know me like nobody else do, I know you jus' like that, too. I can tell something's wrong deep down, an' I know what it is too. It's that way you carry yo'self when a male is wit you that makes me understand what it is."

"And so, what is it?" I asked him, interested to know.

"It's John. Don't know if he's still in your thoughts. Think you always keep him in your prayers. But I know, with no doubt, he's still rushin' through your blood." I listened to the rain and knew that what Daniel was saying to me was true. The thoughts of John weren't so painful anymore, but somewhere, there was that longing, still burning, that I never had the heart to let go of. Daniel saw straight past everything else and right to that place inside me.

"Daniel, if it's running through my blood like you say, I don't think I will ever be able to wash it away. But that doesn't mean I can't make a decent life for myself. I have folks who love me and care for me. I have my school, and that's what really holds my heart—that place where my happiness lies. Seeing the joy on the children's faces is what keeps me alive. That's all I need right now. Of course it's been hard knowing that I'll never . . . I'll never see John again. But I think God has given me this path to walk on in order to change things for the better, and I am grateful for that."

Daniel looked at me, and I could see he was convinced. I even felt, for the moment, that I had convinced myself.

"You know, Anna, I wonder sometimes why freedom can't just be real freedom. Why can't we live like white folks, if we just as free as them? I don't understand. They snatch my pride there in the city, and it hurts . . . it hurts bad, Anna. But you know what? It hurts even more to know that I cain't do nothin' about it. I cain't even be a man, sometimes, fo' the people I love. It's like we walked from one kinda bondage, Anna, to another, an' I don't like it at all. But there's little I can do."

I smiled softly, thinking of the different way Mrs. Rosa, taught me to look at freedom.

"Daniel, what is freedom, really? It seems like freedom means having the ability to call yourself master, and to live just as any other person does. But don't you remember? Can't you hear Mary, sometimes, explaining what true freedom is, how true freedom comes about? Our real freedom is in the heart and the mind."

I put my hand on his shoulder. I understood that whether Mary's words were there for our inspiration or not, the restlessness and anger that Daniel felt mirrored what I felt sometimes and what most of us in this black community thought. But we both knew that no matter what was done, the love that existed between us as family and as friends could not be taken away.

After a little while, as we sat back in detached thought, I embraced him, an embrace that seemed to take us back through everything we had shared in our lives, things that made us inseparable.

When at last I stood to walk away, I saw Florence head down to where Daniel sat and seat herself next to him. At that moment, my happiness for the two of them prevailed over the other feelings in my heart.

But later on that night, as I got ready to lie in my pallet, silent streams of tears ran down my face. But I kept hearing the words I had held so close.

I'll see you again, Sarah, I promise.

When, John? When? You're supposed to be dead, but I haven't even felt your spirit! I feel empty. I miss you, and I need you to come to me like Mama does sometimes and even Mary did once! But you, the one I need the most, seem so far away. Do you see the same sun rise that I do? Am I going to be with you on the other side? I cast these thoughts out to the night as I fell onto my pillow and drifted off to sleep.

The luscious scent of the forest fruits filled my nose as my toes tried to keep themselves from being buried within the soil. They had been carefully groomed, as had the rest of my body, for this sacred occasion. As I glanced up, my eyes caught the reflection of a domelike shape that radiated out with a reddish orange glow. The ocean had captured the sun as it sat idly on the horizon.

Am I on the other side?

I felt a tingling sensation as I reached out and touched the sun. I felt bright and happy.

Your ceremony.

The whispered words rang loudly through my ears. I opened my eyes and brushed my hand across my skin. I wasn't myself. I was . . .

"Mijiza!" The name of my mother was written across the covers of books scorched by fire.

I felt my feet moving forward, one step, then another, then another.

"You're late!" A girl my height came running at me with a head cloth she wrapped around me.

"Late for what? The sun's not done setting. I'm on its time."

"But you're late!"

Images spun before me then halted.

The touch of a hand on my own was cold. The sun had disappeared.

"Come on. He's here, living in this place!" the girl screamed.

"Who, Mr. Caldwell? I know, I know!" I screamed back, but she was already skipping away.

Talking drums rang loudly in my ears. They spoke out in unison, repeating our family name in a rhythmic tone.

Ba-ha-tee . . . Ba-ha-tee . . . Ba-ha-teeeee . . .

My heart fluttered. Or was it Mama's heart? She was the bride. I was the bride.

We watched our feet move once more, slowly now, through rich black soil. A figure in white standing before us whispered our name.

Mijiza.

That was the name his lips formed. But that's not what I heard. Instead, I heard him scream, *Ayanna.*

My head jerked around as my feet stopped. They were no longer Mama's smooth, carefully groomed feet. I touched my back and felt the welts that slavery had inflicted upon me. I was no longer Mijiza. But I was not Ayanna, either.

No, my name is Anna.

Sarah, you mean.

No, Anna! I raised my head to stare into those eyes. My lips shut.

He had come to my dreams.

CHAPTER

❧ 51 ❧

I WAS ALMOST EIGHTEEN YEARS OLD. HOW MUCH DIFFERENT would I have been if those eighteen years had been spent in the land where I was supposed to be, the land I was never supposed to have left. Sentwaki, my brother, would not be lost from me. My mother would be alive. And I would never have had to wish that John were still alive. Eighteen years I would have lived in happiness, had they left me where I belonged in my homeland. But that was not my fate.

However, today's occasion was not another birthday celebration for me. It was not quite that time. On this day in late September, 1824, we were celebrating the union of my brother and my best friend.

The ceremony took place at the church, like most other weddings. Florence and Daniel beamed throughout. Uniting them was a man of later years, our preacher. He had performed this ceremony so many times over the years that he knew the vows of marriage by heart. I stood, my fingers grasping my arms, while this man of God walked them through the ceremony.

"Can you believe this?" Daniel asked me afterward as we celebrated behind the church. He had released Florence's hand just long enough to come speak to me.

"Yes, I think I can," I said to him as he grinned at me.

Florence was just as excited and dashed happily between me and her other guests. When I found the chance, however, I separated myself from everyone.

Easing into my own space where my thoughts could flow freely, I enjoyed the solitude by the lake, where the fresh wind washed my face. I would only stay for a few minutes. I had wanted peace on this happy day, but hazy memories haunted me and I felt unsettled.

Why does today have to be one of those hard days? Why is it so difficult for me to accept that John is gone?

I felt my eyes brimming over, and a second later, I was kneeling by the lake, hugging my knees. No one was around: I didn't want anyone to see me so upset on my brother's wedding day. But I heard footsteps behind me, then a sigh much like my brother's. I wiped my eyes without looking back at him.

"Daniel, brother, please don't mind me. I want you to be happy today, not worried about me. I thought I was alone out here."

Silence.

"Really, brother, I'm sure of what I'm saying. You can let me be."

Still not hearing an answer, I looked out over the lake. I really didn't want to complain, but Daniel was here and he wouldn't leave . . .

"Daniel, he promised, he promised! It wasn't right to promise like that, but he did. The pain is easing inside, but he'll never be washed from my blood, never!" I exclaimed, and then lowered my voice and head in sadness and frustration.

It sounded as if Daniel was trying to clear his throat but stopped short. I continued on, welcoming the chance to release what I felt inside.

"I miss him, but I don't long like I used to. It's like my heart knows that no other heart could fit better, and it seems content with that. But sometimes it seems as if we danced just yesterday. In my sleep, I still spin higher and higher in his arms. And his hands . . ." I laughed, remembering.

"But they say he's dead. Dead! I haven't felt it yet, though, and I know I should have. It's been nearly three years since I saw him last. Maybe he had found someone else and shared her dreams instead before he passed on. But no matter, now that he's gone, the piece of my heart made to love anyone like that is gone with him."

But some promises are meant to be kept.

This statement rang through my mind, almost as though someone had spoken them to me. I heard the words, and felt a strong reaction inside to hate them. But suddenly, I felt strong arms, not at all like Daniel's, encircling my body. My will must have been weak, for as my body tensed and my mind refused to recognize that touch, my heart melted into the moment. I felt warm breath on my neck.

I felt the lips, the nose, the pulse of a ghost! I froze, but my heart quickened.

"I bin standin' here, jus' a listenin' to you. That feelin' you felt deep inside, that was me, Sarah. I done promised

I'd come, an' here I am, flesh, bones, heart, an' all—my soul, too, all here fo' you." The words that came tumbling out from those lips engulfed my spirit.

I couldn't move! I couldn't breath! I couldn't see! Everything in me said it was real, but how could it be?

Am I asleep or dreaming? I prayed not, but I had to be. They said he was *dead*!

I shuddered, knowing that the arms encircling me had to be those of a ghost. I was dreaming, surely, but how could those words come so clear, so near, so real? Why would my mind be so cruel to me?

My lips parted before I had time to think further.

"John?" Implausibly, I addressed him. Then I turned, slowly, afraid of what I might see, or not see. What I did see was his face. That face, with the strong, dark, elegant features I had remembered so clearly. Maybe my mind was playing tricks on my soul.

But that can't be.

I didn't understand. I could touch him: his skin, his arms, his chest, his face. I could feel his warm hands cupping my shoulders. I could smell the scent of his skin, of his sweat. I could hear his voice, deep, clear, and comforting. And his eyes! I could stare into those eyes of his, eyes that bore into my own, right through to my heart.

How could spirit be so real?

"John . . . you . . . you're dead!" I told him.

The ghost smiled.

"That's what the paper done said. What's your heart say?"

I shrugged, trying to grasp the memory whole in my mind before the ghost disappeared.

"The paper, ya . . . my heart, maybe . . . Maybe you're an angel! But I thought angels had big old wings!" I said, still searching for answers that would explain what was happening. At that, the spirit threw back his head and let out a deep laugh. The sound began and ended like the rising and falling of the tide and rumbled heavily in his chest.

"An' angel? Look at me!" he said, turning around so I could see his full form. "I haven't died yet, pretty gal! How could I? Hadn't found you befo' now!" He stepped closer to me and gently nudged my gaping mouth closed with his fingers.

I shook my head. "But I saw your name. . . ."

"We had to say I was dead so they'd stop lookin' for me. I hid wit a Quaker man who helped me almost the whole way. They said Finch killed me, but Finch himself is 'gainst slavery, and he the one put it out in the papers and everythin'. But . . ."

He looked at me with sad eyes. I stared back, still not believing, trying to make sense of the words in his story.

"I prayed it didn't reach you wherever you was. How could I die befo' findin' you, Sarah? You my life, my freedom. Even if you had a family an' everything, I'd jus' be happy to say I found you, an' more than glad to see you agin. But God had it so I could find you right here, like this!"

Despite the education I had received, I couldn't think of anything to say. So, instead, I buried my face in his chest and collapsed into him, escaping from everything else but this moment with him. As the moment matured, I began to see that this man I was embracing was no more a ghost than I was. This all was real, and my heart understood this before my mind and body did. We stood embracing for what seemed an eternity, and an eternity was just where I wanted to be. Tears were streaming down my face, but my grip didn't loosen at all.

"John . . . how . . . I can't . . ."

"Shh. Don't gotta think 'bout nothin'. Jus' gotta soar, right here, wit me." John's voice resonated through my mind and awakened within me a feeling that my soul hadn't allowed me to forget.

As we returned to the church setting, John's arm clasped around my shoulder, Daniel approached us. His figure was almost hazy to me.

"Daniel," I said, "it's John . . ."

Daniel laughed, hearing the disbelief still weighing down my words. There was a sad edge to his laughter that I barely noticed in my daze.

"Just doesn't seem real," I said, tightening my grip on John's arm for fear of him disappearing.

"Yeah, he came by this way," Daniel explained as Florence walked up to his side.

"Heard us out here an' stopped to get somethin' to eat. Said he had been travelin' for a while. But then I caught sight of him, or I reckon he saw me first. You shoulda seen him! His face lit up like a candle when he saw me. 'Course, the first words he muttered to me was somethin' like 'Sarah . . . where's Sarah.'" Daniel smiled, but I saw some sadness in him behind his joy. After talking with John for a little while longer, sharing conversation I only caught bits and pieces of, he disappeared back into his celebration. Florence lingered longer, a large grin stretching across her face.

"So this is the John you told me was still livin', but we convinced you he wasn't."

"This is him."

"Well, John," she said, smiling over at him, "I'm Anna's good friend, Flo."

Hearing my new name, he looked down at me, and then back toward Florence.

"Well, it's good to meet you, Flo."

She smiled once more, then turned and followed Daniel back into the crowd.

"Anna? That's what they call you round here?"

"That's what they call me."

"Think I like it."

I smiled.

"You know, *Anna*"—he looked out at the dancers who had gathered—"got somethin' to ask you."

I laughed up at him, and held out my hand, knowing he wanted to dance with me. He took it without pause, and we walked toward the dancers together. Every person around us had disappeared. It was only him and me.

"Can we jus' sail away, you think?" And I flew away on his whisper, in his strong arms.

When we stopped dancing, breathless, we heard shouts of praise from the people around us. But we walked slowly away from the celebration, shoulder to shoulder, just the two of us.

"I was worried, but I think I know now that you're still just plain old John," I said, looking up at him.

He laughed. "Wouldn't be no one else." After a few minutes, he stopped and asked me another question.

"Sarah—*Anna*—can I look at you good? Ain't bin able to do that so well yet."

I stopped in front of him, and he backed away and crossed his arms, attempting to examine me while I giggled. But his eyes locked with mine, and he seemed to have lost the key. I laughed and leaned back onto him, and we fell back into step.

"Don't have to look at me so hard, John. I'm here!"

"Ya, you here, Sarah. Anna. You here."

As we walked farther and farther away from the wedding, we drifted in and out of conversation. We shared memories, ones that just appeared out of the hidden places in our hearts, and we tried to speak of John's escape and my school and the kind of life John wanted in Ohio. But disbelief stalled those conversations. They would need to wait for another time.

"Looka here, Miss Anna, if that's what I'm s'pose to call you. I don't wanna hear nothin' else 'bout nothin'! Jus' sing or laugh or don't do nothin' but lean 'gainst me like you doin' now. That's good 'nough fo' me. Got the whole world an' my whole life to talk 'bout all that important stuff. Right now, jus' wanna be wit you. That's all that mattas."

So we walked on down the path toward the school building. I found myself lost in John's frequent smiles down at me, every glance proof that he really walked by my side. When silence descended upon us for long moments at a time, it spoke louder than our words. I observed that John had new lash marks around his neck that disappeared down his shirt and that his hands were calloused like before.

"Anna, these three years done made you different. You a grown woman, taller than befo', tho' still pretty an' all. You sound different, too, like bein' free done made you handle life as if you know you really own yourself."

I smiled softly. "I do, John. I do."

He nodded and continued, "Speak like you done bin educated yo' whole life, too. Got a lot to teach me."

I laughed at that, sipping in his talk like I was quenching my thirst.

"But even wit all that, you still ain't changed. Your soul is still the same, an' that makes me happy."

I looked in his eyes and sighed, shaking my head.

"What?" he asked, innocently. "That's good, ain't it?"

I laughed. "Sure it is. It's just . . . John, I thought you were dead! I thought I'd have to wait until I died to see you again."

John stopped and turned to me, seriousness covering his smile.

"Sarah, I didn't know three years could be so long—

three years away from you. I'm . . . I'm sorry, Sarah. Three years waitin' sho' ain't the same as two years runnin'. Didn't know where you were. Gotta say, there was times I didn't think I could keep lookin' my whole life. I figured jus' wat you say, that when I die, an' when you die, then I see you agin. So, well, I thought 'bout bein' wit someone else. But there ain't no harm in that, right?" he asked, looking at me uncertainly.

I shrugged the thoughts away, my eyes on the ground ahead of me. "John, how can I say there's harm in that when you're here?" I asked him, softly, my eyes returning to his face.

"Well, anyway, it seems I could neva think that too long, anyhow," he said, walking once more. "Jus' couldn't. Made up my mind I'd search round an' round this country fo' you, long as you still had to be found."

"How'd you find me?" I asked him.

He looked at me strangely and laughed.

"Sorry, Miss Anna, but that's one question I jus' don't have no good answer for 'cause I jus' don't rightly know."

We reached the school. John stood in front of it, his hands on his hips, and inspected it from the edge of the clearing.

"So, this is what you bin up to. Havin' schools built an' all. All this, fo' you?" he asked, amused.

I laughed. "I'm a teacher, John. It's for the children."

He nodded. "Teachin'. Well, you sho' is my Sarah."

We lay down, him on his stomach, and me with my head on his back. The sunset looked on, brightening the sky, expressing how happy it was to see my joy. John hopped up and lifted me again in his arms. We danced to our own music. We ran through the schoolhouse. We laughed until it hurt our bellies. We fell, exhausted, to the grass when the sun had completely set, and looked at the stars.

I drifted off to sleep lying in John's arms, guarded by his watchful gaze. He touched his lips with mine. He wiped my tear away. He picked up my finger and ran it down his cheek, under his chin, and up the other side. I knew what God had brought back into my life: John was my angel whether he knew it or not.

If I had two wings, I would take those wings and cover you, completely, until not an inch was visible, so you'd be protected . . . from everything.

CHAPTER
❧ 52 ❧

IT WAS DANIEL, THAT NIGHT, WHO BROKE DOWN CRYING.

John had been around for two days, and it was the second night that the four of us decided to come together, eat, and share stories of escape.

There were living quarters on the second level of the schoolhouse. In the weeks after it had been finished, I had fixed it so that I could live there until I could build my own house. It had two small rooms. The bedroom had a round table that was pushed into the corner and a single broken-down night table next to the pallet I had set on the floor. The cooking area was actually in a room below.

But I wouldn't be alone here now. I had John. He would be living with some of Daniel's friends until it was appropriate for him to move into the schoolhouse.

"One day real soon, after I find me a job, I'm gonna make you one of them nice beds, Sarah," John told me. I grinned with delight.

Each of the rooms upstairs had a single window, while the large schoolroom downstairs had three. In addition, there was plenty of room outside to start a garden if need be and for the schoolchildren to play.

It was in my room that I intended the four of us to sit that evening. When Daniel and Florence arrived, I was setting two biscuits and some bacon on the four plates. I greeted them, sat them in my room with John, who was busy fixing my night table, and went back to preparing the food. Daniel poked his head through the doorway.

"Anna," he said softly, walking into the room.

"Hey, Daniel, what is it?" He had hardly sat down in the chair near me before the tears came to his eyes.

"I know . . . I know you may have it in your head that Mama jus' didn't run."

I stopped what I was doing, staring hard at the food in front of me before turning toward him.

"Well, I figured since John came by himself, she . . ."

He hung his head. "He didn't come by himself, Anna. Talked to John about it. Mama, she ran with him, Anna."

My knees buckled and I sank to the floor.

"Where is she?"

"She went wit him, Sarah, but she didn't make it."

"They didn't catch her, did they?" I asked Daniel in a horrified whisper.

"Naw," he said, shaking his head. I felt relieved, but overwhelmed with sadness. A memory suddenly came to mind.

"I had a dream about Mary," I began, afraid to look up, afraid I would see accusation of me not sharing this with him leap from Daniel's eyes. "She was flying in the sky with my real mother, and they both had wings, like angels. I think Mary . . . I think she wanted to tell us that she . . .

466

she's content where she is. That she's happy, and even freer than we are."

Daniel's tears flowed as he ran his nails across the floor boards.

"They was split up, like me an' you. John found her. He found her lyin' there. He said—he said there wa'an't a line of struggle 'cross her face. Seem like God jus' come an' stop her heart so quick, she ain't feel a thing."

I pulled lightly at my earlobe and looked up at my brother. "You're not feeling that you're to blame, are you Daniel?" I asked him softly. He put his thumb to his lip in thought.

"Thought I would. Thought I—" Florence pushed the door open, cutting him off, and got ready to open her mouth as if to ask what was taking so long. But seeing Daniel seated like he was, and his wet cheeks, and me seated on the ground, she changed her mind. She walked over and stood behind Daniel, placing her soft hands on his shoulders.

"Thought I would feel that way, Anna," Daniel continued, "but it's almost like I hear her sayin' that's what was for her—that's what was to be. Wa'an't nothin' I could do about it." He then stood up. Florence leaped at the chance to embrace him in a hug, which he fell into weakly. I found my breath and told them to grab their plates of food. We headed on into my room and listened as John recounted his escape.

"We ran round Thanksgiving, the year afta you and Daniel left, Anna," John explained.

"Jus' a few weeks lata, Mary and I was separated. I had

to keep runnin' an' when, I reached Kentucky, I met up wit a Quaker man, Lorenzo. He say somethin' needed to be done to get them slave catchers away from me. It was easia than I thought. He tole a friend've his, Finch, 'bout how he wanted to call me dead in the papers. Didn't see it fo' myself, but I was tole that's what happened. Afta that, I didn't have to run no more. I traveled as Quaker Lorenzo's servant till I got to freedom." John described the intensity of his escape and how, even after he was proclaimed dead, he had to be very careful.

He addressed Daniel but watched me carefully, trying to figure out how much I knew. "I didn't say, but I saw Mary fo' she closed her eyes for good. She tole me, she say . . ."—he paused and looked over at my brother—"she say she'll always be wit you in your hearts. She said death don't take away a person's spirit, it jus' lets that spirit get closer to you. Then she jus' . . . she jus' closed her eyes an' was gone."

Daniel squeezed his eyes shut and pursed his lips.

"It was her time to go, Daniel. That was all. She's in a better place," Florence whispered.

He nodded. "I know."

Time swallowed the space and slipped into the crevasses of intense sorrow and immense joy. That night, after Florence and Daniel had left, I walked out into the fields, alone, my eyes skimming the stars.

A breeze brushed by my face, and I closed my eyes, feeling the tears streaming as the spirits about me sang loud and flowed through my own soul with a love that was untouchable in the physical world. I dared not whisper the words "thank you" for fear of disrupting the unspoken gratitude.

I heard Mary laughing in my ear. She was telling me that things would indeed be all right.

Mama Mijiza stood by watching, saying nothing. She was content and knew that I knew this.

I stared at the schoolhouse, my thoughts carrying me back to etching crooked letters in the soil and on discarded newspapers back on the plantation. I closed my eyes and imagined each and every child in my school holding books, writing books, influencing the law, speaking in front of crowds of blacks, whites, and Indians, too. I had found my passion, and my heart was full.

And then there was John. It seemed like I had stepped back into something timeless that we shared, something that brought him out of the depths of the impossible, right to my side. Was this the usual life of a slave girl who ran to freedom? Was there any such thing? I had decided to carve out no explanation of how and why John had reappeared in my life. Instead, I melted into every desire, every longing, that shone on his face. I saw the satisfaction of freedom shining in his eyes, and it was like staring into a mirror.

I went back inside with my burdens carried away, for the moment, by the night. Sinking down into the warmth and security of John's presence, I allowed him to embrace me while he let me deliver all the love and desire that I had forgotten existed.

We lay absorbed in the peace and satisfaction of the moment.

"You know, Anna, I don't know where all your fortune comes from, but it's a beautiful thing," John said.

"Comes from my name," I said simply.

"You mean, Bahati?" John asked.

"Yes. It means 'our fortune is good.'"

John looked at me, amused. "How you rememba that?"

I shrugged. "I've always known it."

John stared at the ceiling in silence for a little while, then turned back to me and said, "I think, Anna, that the last name Bahati, would do me jus' fine."

In that moment, my life flashed before my eyes: living with Mama in Africa, being transported to America, enduring the life of a slave, and taking ownership of my life in what I called freedom.

"Well," I said, looking into the eyes of my soul in masculine form, the man lying calmly next to me, "I've certainly lived up to that name, for my fortune is, without a doubt, good."

AUTHOR'S NOTE

To all of my readers:

The insightfulness that the topic of slavery offers was introduced to me at a young age. From the age of ten, I felt the inspiration arise in me to create this story, not even dreaming that it would manifest as it has done. I can gladly see the dispersion of this knowledge as *Good Fortune* passes from hand to hand. For this and the many other blessings that have come with this book, I thank all who have placed a helping hand in this process: my sisters for their love and criticism, my parents for their support and guidance, every ancestor of mine that walked upon the gloomy road of slavery, and ultimately, Mother/Father God.

I had several motivations for writing this novel, the first of these being the genuine love for and greater desire to learn about my history, a passion instilled within me at a very young age by my parents. At some point during the writing process, I felt driven to teach what I had learned through my writings. What is more, my memory races back to a true story, retold to me by my aunt of Rose Caldwell, my great-great-great-grandmother. This story was my final and most influential motivation for completing the book.

Imagine:

A small body, a child, thin arms dangling next to hips that have seen merely twelve years. She absentmindedly swings her left leg slowly

back and forth, her bare feet playing with a small rock on the bank of the
Mississippi River.

"Rose . . ."

*The memory of that whisper encourages the young girl to bring a
stubby finger to her eye, quickly brushing away a tear that had escaped
from her saddened soul onto her dark cheek. She can't help fooling with the
sides of the rags draped over her small body, the only clothes she has ever
known. Rose purses her lips as she replays the last moments she had with
her mother through her mind. . . .*

*"Rose, chile." Her mother kneeled down in front of the girl, a frown
creasing her weary face.*

"Yes, Mama?" Rose responded as she turned to face her mother.

*"You listen close. See dis 'kerchief here?" Rose nodded slowly, trying
her best to memorize every line and shape that formed her mother's face.*

*"When you can't see this here red 'kerchief wavin' in the wind any-
more as that ship there take me away, then you know, you ain't eva gonna
see your mama again. . . ."*

*Rose feels tears spilling methodically from her eyes as she recalls her
mother grasping her shoulders as they embraced for the last time in a hug.
She whimpers quietly as she remembers her mother turning away, just
another sold slave, gone forever as the last of that red cloth disappeared
over the horizon.*

The image of that little twelve-year-old girl staring out over
the Mississippi River at her mother's red handkerchief until it
slipped from her sight, has stayed with me as I have mused over it,
trying to intertwine her spirit into this story, *Good Fortune*. Anna's
story is not that of Rose Caldwell, but rather a representation of
the journey that our ancestors endured from Africa as they were
bound in slavery. In order to create this ambitious and fictitious

character of mine, I listened to stories, read accounts, researched, and placed my heart into an existence that seems as real to me as any true narrative from the past would be. I have done my best to weave together a tale that will bring to light what many young adults do not know. Events such as the Middle Passage and the selling of human beings, all defined in this system of slavery, echo upon the steps of history itself. They were as real as you and I. I hope the story has the power to remind today's youth and those young at heart of a past that should not be forgotten while simultaneously releasing invisible chains: by-products of the past that undoubtedly still exist today.

Oftentimes, as I stare at Anna's soul, I find myself hankering for changes that could possibly alter the past for the better. This is impossible: We can merely take what was and walk forward, understanding the lessons, forgiving, and doing our best to change situations that mirror what our ancestors had to go through. It is true that even today, in countless areas of the world, slavery still does exist. Perhaps our eyes should remain open for the sake of these people, and for the justification of our ancestors. They are begging for peace, screaming in our faces. Are we taking the time out to listen, leading lives that we can be proud of?

I ask you, my readers, to listen and to become that light the world needs in whatever manner suits you best. It is my wish and my prayer that whoever may crease the pages of this book, encasing him- or herself within Anna's life, will walk away with a new sense of understanding and a greater appreciation for the difficulties endured as well as the unshakable strength our ancestors held on to so that we as a people, every single one of us, could exist as we do today. It is your responsibility, as the reader, to take with you the image of these people as well as those of other cultures who also experienced such atrocities. We all should help keep their stories, their lives, and their struggles alive within our hearts so that all people in this world can move on, sailing beyond the bondage that seems to prevail today: that of materialism, hate, manipulation, anger, and unnecessary warfare.

I leave you with that challenge, and hope that you embrace an appreciation for humanity and its countless dimensions. I challenge you to become one of the many benefactors of the beautiful idea of change, and to be the very best that you can be.

So, as the reader, open your minds to this painful excursion into the past, and prepare your hearts for the joys and pains *Good Fortune* has to offer, for you will be taken on a journey rich in history, culture, and excitement. I give you the story from my soul: the story of Sarah, of Anna, and of Ayanna Bahati.

Love to all,
Noni Denise

FACTS AND FICTION

FICTION

The story of Ayanna Bahati does not depict the life of any factual person in history. None of the characters represent specific people that existed.

FACT

Anna's story delineates the spirits of the African-American peoples in the early 1800s. The system that held her in bondage, chattel slavery—where African people and those of African descent were made the property of others and forced into physical labor—was very much in effect during the early 1800s, and existed in America for over 250 years.

FICTION

The nightmares that Anna have throughout *Good Fortune* reveal a "story behind a story," in which she is captured from her homeland on the African continent, taken across the ocean, and finally separated from her brother on the auction block. These, in keeping with the fictitious character, are fictional interventions.

FACT

However, the transatlantic slave trade that Anna's "story behind the story" refers to was real. For nearly three centuries, African people were bought, sold, traded, carried across the Atlantic, and tossed into the system of slavery. With a close look at the dates during which *Good Fortune* takes place, Anna would have been taken from her homeland around 1811—three years after Congress passed the law that prohibited the importation of slaves into the United States after January 1, 1808. Illegal importation existed quite a few years after this law had been passed: Over a million African people were illegally imported into the Americas after 1808. Congress then passed the Act of 1820 to prevent such illegal trade, or "piracy" as they termed it, from occurring.

The Middle Passage is also subtly alluded to in Anna's nightmares. This passage from Africa to the lands in the West took weeks, and often months. The "cargo," as the African prisoners were regarded, was situated in the bellies of the ships in such inhumane ways of confinement that many did not live through the voyage. Packed between bodies; surrounded by loathsome smells of defecation, decay, and disease; lying still without any means of mobility, these individuals underwent a wretched and horrendous journey that carried many into the hands of bondage, while leaving millions of African bodies lying, chains still intact, at the bottom of the Atlantic.

FICTION

The plantation in Tennessee on which the story takes place, and the characters that are built around the plantation life are also fictional pieces.

FACT

Plantation Life

The setting in which the characters of the plantation were placed is based on slaveholding plantations that existed in Tennessee. There were not many large plantations in this state in the early 1800s, and those that existed specialized in the growing of tobacco, cotton, and corn; livestock tending; and the cultivation of other products or, in most cases, some combination of these. Plantations during this time period varied in the way slaves worked, how they lived, and the extent of their suffering based on the status, wealth, and power of the plantation owners.

The raping of servant women was not uncommon on slave plantations throughout Tennessee and other slaveholding states. Especially after the importation law of 1808, owners felt it "necessary" to breed their own slaves, from which new generations of mixed children arose.

Religion on the Plantation

The Christian religion was a large component of slavery in the South and it served more than one purpose on a plantation. The plantation owners would often use Christianity to make slaves believe that obeying them and working for them was the only way to freedom. At the same time, religion was a large part of the slave community. It was a means of escape to many, one that could not be found in the physical world. Oftentimes, slave owners would bring in religious speakers for the slaves, or would even have a slavehand schooled in the ways of "preaching."

African-American Vernacular

The dialect used in the text is a very loose representation of the speaking patterns adopted by the African people who were tossed in a world they knew nothing of, and by the generations that came after them. The purpose of writing the story in such a manner was to pick the reader up and drop them in this time and space, allowing them to maneuver in Anna's world, getting a true sense of how it would have been had Anna's story been real.

FICTION

The slave song Aunt Mary sings to Anna in the first section of *Good Fortune* is a fictitious creation, as is the tale Uncle Bobby tells of Liza.

FACT

These creations were intended to represent the wide plethora of slave songs and spirituals that came out of the system of slavery. These African-American art forms helped create a strong black tradition, shaped by the necessity to escape, in some manner, the dehumanizing institution by which these individuals were bound. Religion, stories, and even secret codes that aided runaways in escaping were all echoed through these traditions of black communication and art. Today, they are essential tools in helping to define the slave experience during this time period.

FICTION

The black communities in the final section of *Good Fortune*— Gibson, Hadson, and Riverside—did not exist in Ohio in the

1820s. Also, while Dayton was (and is) an actual city in Ohio, all of the people and places I describe as being part of this city are fiction.

FACT

Ohio

Ohio became a free state and entered the United States in 1803, the year the newly formed Ohio Constitution outlawed slavery. However, discrimination and racism still existed. As was stated by Dr. Billingsworth in the book, any African American who entered Ohio with the intention of settling had to post a bond of five hundred dollars, in order to ensure good behavior. They had to register with the county clerk and produce and carry free passes that stated that the African-American individual was truly free. These requirements were outlined in Ohio's Black Laws of 1804 and 1807.

Black Communities and Concerns

During this time, African Americans in Ohio established black communities. From Ohio's establishment until 1829, the year many of the black population left Ohio for Canada or other free states, Ohio's black population grew. Free blacks did not necessarily feel the entirety of a free life, for there was still segregation, and the laws between blacks and whites were not balanced. Freedom was not what many had imagined. Although free passes were a necessity, they meant little in many circumstances where blacks could easily have been taken back into slavery. In fact, the Fugitive Slave Act of 1793 stated that runaway slaves could be returned to their rightful "owners." There were laws that were constructed in the North between 1793 and 1850 (with the passing of the Fugitive Slave Act of 1850) that attempted to ensure the personal liberty of blacks. Therefore, while it did inspire caution in the fugitives that ran north, the Fugitive Slave Act of 1793 was not as great of a threat as the subsequent Act in 1850.

FICTION

The runaway ad in the book for John is almost completely rooted in fiction and simply adds to the plot and storyline. For one thing, such an ad would not have been posted in the first place describing a runaway found, killed, and a reward paid. Second, rarely, if ever, would such news have been sent from Tennessee to an Ohio paper—the topic would not have been "important" enough.

FACT

Phillis Wheatley and Jupiter Hammon were real figures in history who helped bring to light the capability of the African-American individual to command the art form of writing.

Phillis Wheatley was the first African American, and only the third woman in America, to publish her poetry. She was kidnapped as a small child from West Africa, named after the ship that carried her, and was raised as a slave in America. Here, she was extensively schooled and began to write poetry, at quite a young age. Her first published poem came out in 1767.

Jupiter Hammon was born a slave, but learned how to read and write when he was young. A poem of his printed in 1760 made him the first African-American published writer in America

(Wheatley first had her works published in England). His poem, "An Address to Miss Phillis Wheatley," which is referred to in *Good Fortune*, was an actual work of his that he wrote for the female poet. In 1786, he gave his famous speech "Address to the Negroes in the State of New York."

FICTION

Caldwell's character is fictional. Much of his storyline is based more on fiction than fact. While his marriage to Mrs. Rosa was certainly possible, the ways in which he maneuvers between the black world and the white world were creations of the author. The phenomenon of "passing" as white, as Caldwell does, is really an idea and concept that became prominent in the early twentieth century.

FACT

The Early Existence of Black Schools

Education was easier to access in the North than it was in many areas of the South, but black schools did not start gaining prominence until the latter part of the early 1800s. However, schools for blacks did exist in the North beforehand. In New York in 1787, white elites founded the African Free School for blacks. Even though the school was replicated in other areas, it did not appeal to the majority of Northern blacks, and it was not widely attended.

In Boston, Massachusetts, in the late 1780s, a good number of blacks strongly resisted the injustice that arose when it came to educating their black youth, and in 1798 more than fifty of these black citizens established the African School. This school was officially recognized by the Boston School Committee in 1812 after countless petitions. Also in Boston in the early 1800s, black students attended white schools, though this was rare. In Ohio, however (Ohio being rather young in comparison to other northern states), the first free black school, Harveysburg, was not built until 1831.

Anna, having stepped into a small town that knew nothing of such cases, can only build dreams about gaining an education based on what she sees and hears. Her fear that education is not a possibility for her come from her knowledge of the South and of the small town she finds herself living in.

Anna's Education

Anna's search for an education is not intended to show that there were no opportunities for African Americans to get educated in the North. In her circumstances, in the small town she arrived in, she felt limited by what was around her, and rightfully so. What is more, when Caldwell and Mrs. Rosa warn Anna about the dangers associated with getting educated, they are by no means implying that, in itself, striving to get educated was a dangerous venture. The problematic societal issues lay in getting educated in white schools, and after attaining an education, using it in dangerous ways, as Caldwell did. Such was the case with author David Walker, who in 1829 wrote an appeal that created much controversy throughout the nation, and possibly led to his death, due to the impact it suggested making on the black communities in America. Some even believe that Nat Turner's rebellion came about because of this appeal.

FACT OR FICTION?

In the end, Anna, through a miraculous unfolding of events, is reunited with John. Such a twist of fate this is, and such a difficult ground to tread upon in attempting to shed light on the unromanticized planes of truth. And yet, was it not possible for but one circumstance to wriggle through the desolation slavery and its effects caused and blossom in an optimistic light? Was it totally misheard of for a single heart to beat so richly that in all the abjectness, all the pain, the stripping of pride, the suffering, and the loss, not one beating heart could attract a blessing wished for to the doors of reality? Is it a venture into the unreal or simply a dip into the uncommon? Certainly such an ending speaks to an author's right to play with the boundaries of facts versus fiction.

So, fact or fiction? You choose.

FACT OR FICTION?

"Mama used to always tell me that you could find the greatest freedom in your mind."

Such is the quote that echoes strongly through the pages of *Good Fortune*.

In today's world we are now searching for that place within us, a place our ancestors would perhaps call freedom. Their fight was different in fact but the same in substance. We are running, trying to escape the mentality that has grown like a weed by our side. We are searching for that self, for that peace, for that contentment. Where is it? Where could this freedom be? Is it in the memory of the past, the recovery of our culture, the understanding of one another and of humanity in order to create a better future? Is it in our willingness to move beyond subjective mentalities and to love without condition or reason? Is it in our ability to utilize the gifts we have and the inspiration inside of us to open our hearts and our minds? Is it in the power we have to free ourselves from the bondage of our own fears that keep us from getting up and striving farther when we fall, and giving our best even when there's nothing more to gain? Is it in the time it takes to surpass our own limitations and to set ourselves free? The quote states, "the greatest freedom lies in your mind." Is this fact or is this fiction? It's your journey. You choose.

ACKNOWLEDGMENTS

I'm feeling multitudes of gratitude to all of you who've helped me through this beautiful, wonderful journey. I am so very grateful to the people that have shaped this experience for me, the voices that remained undaunted in their never-changing exclamations that shouted through every in and out of this journey: "Of course you can!" I appreciate you, your support through this journey, and your belief in me.

To my family: I thank you for your love—there is truly nothing more beautiful in this world. To my siblings: Dara, beautiful one, for that brilliance in mind and in Spirit that never ceases, I mean *never ceases*, to inspire; Camara, manager, for watching me plant seeds and helping me cultivate them in growth; and Desmond, my role model, for being more than available, for laughter, for your love, your unwavering support, and your valuing all that I do— thank you! To my parents: I can hand you no amount of gratitude that fits, lest I chase down something that has no beginning, and has no ending. Mom, my soul's reflection, I thank you for your patience, your presence when the muses fail, when the lights grow dim, when the patience quails; thank you for being there, for giving me the sparks to reignite my own power and faculty within with your brilliance, with your beautiful energy. Daddy, my father, thank you for being a strong mirror of me, for listening even when

I'm convinced that you aren't, for the time and energy that you've invested in me and in my life; you ARE this project as much as I am. What more could one ask for? I appreciate all of you.

To my mentor, Kwame Alexander, I'm grateful to you, and appreciate your open, enriching, inspiring personality that makes me want to pick up a pen and get to it! Thank you for your time, for being such an incredible agent of mobility who knows how to get things done. This project would not be where it is if it wasn't for you. To Dr. Bertice Berry, to Tananarive Due, I am astounded by the ways in which you never fail to spread your wings of guidance over me without question, without hesitancy, without fail. Thank you for giving me this sense of knowing, I am immensely grateful.

To my uncles, all of you who have been quite instrumental in this process—Uncle Jake, Uncle Craig, Uncle Reggie—I appreciate you for your unselfish commitment to helping me move in the direction I need to go; to my aunts—Aunt Sharon, Aunt Dee—for receiving those necessary calls, for being there to piggyback off of and share with; to my extended family in your support, your advice, your love; to my Hillside family—Reverend Dr. King, Rev. Sharon, Mrs. Kilgore, and all others—for that spiritual energy you've taught me to cultivate within and spread without, thank you!

I send special thanks to Rubin Pfeffer, your energy is very much alive and present in this project; to my agent, Conrad Rippy, for your friendly and tactful way of maneuvering so professionally through this process.

To my instructors that helped transform mere lessons

into life—Mr. Key, Mrs. Kent, Mrs. Holland, Dr. Pattiz, Mrs. Beatles—thank you for your commitment to perfection, it can only rub off. If only the world had more of YOU! You broadened my agency and truly convinced me that I have what it takes to be me. Thank you.

To each individual who has placed a hand, in any form or manner, in the process: Mrs. Clarke, Nia Damali, Deborah Simmons, my editor Alex Cooper and the entire Simon and Schuster crew, Carol Mackey, Aunt Pauline, Mrs. Oparah, Glenda Carpio, thank you all for your time, your dedication, and your support.

And, of course, to all of you close friends who pushed the inspiration seed: "Is it out yet? I can't wait. I'll be the first. I'll wait in line. I'll spread the word!" To you who support without expecting in return, who promise to be but a smile away, each one of you, amazing people, you know who you are! Thank you.

To my readers, what is this without you? And to my writing influences, the Deepak Chopras, the Dan Browns, the Anthony Browders, the Khaled Hosseinis, the Shakti Gawains, the Pauline Hopkinses, and the Tananarive Dues of the world, and of course to our President Barack Obama and First Lady Michelle Obama, I see you, I hear you, I am listening . . .

And finally, to the Spirit within me, the God all around me, to the Universal Intelligence that moves about and commands this life, giving me instruction to let go and enjoy the ride, it is to this perfection that I give the ultimate thanks.

You all have shared so much with me through this process, and now here I am to give it right on back to the world.

Much peace, and many many blessings.